SHEA SWAIN

CHAINED
to the
DEVIL'S
SON

Chained to the Devil's Son

Copyright © 2016 Shea Swain

Chained to the Devil's' Son is intended for 18+ older, and for mature audiences only.

Editing and Interior design by: Masque of the Red Pen
Cover Design by: Blue Sky Designs Boston

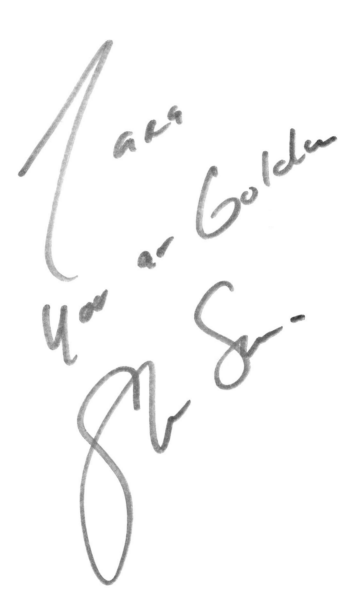

Chained to the Devil's Son

Abuse is something that can affect anyone of any age, gender, the rich or the poor no matter your race or beliefs. It can take many forms, physical, emotional, sexual, and neglect. We all deserve to live a full and happy life. If you are anyone you know is suffering, get help now. There is help available.

OTHER BOOKS WRITTEN BY

SHEA SWAIN

Lascivious

An Erotic Novella

INVIDIOUS Betrayal

A Full-Length Paranormal-Sci Romance

ABSOLVE

A Short Romantic New Adult Drama

Winter's Icy Heart

A Contemporary Romance Novella

NO MORE WERE THEY A FAMILY.
THEY WERE BURIED, BROKEN, AND LOST.

PROLOGUE

SUMMER OF 1976

The sound of the gunshot was deafening as it shattered the calm night.

They were driving to Alabama. Had been driving for a long time when Evelyn's mother, Pearl, asked her father, Harland, to stop at a motel they were approaching. Only her father didn't stop. He continued driving so long after her mother's request that even the signs to direct them to food and fuel grew scarce. With nothing to occupy her mind, Eve fell asleep.

When Eve woke, her mother was urging her father not to pull onto a dirt road that looked deserted but for the beat-up mailbox that stood out like a beacon off the main road. They were just going to ask for directions or maybe use the phone; at least that was what her father said.

Eve listened quietly as her parents' debated what to do. Whether to knock on the rundown farmhouse door or to chance driving further because they were clearly lost. Her mother spoke of her unease. Having been raised in the South, she warned them that they needed to be ever cautious.

Harland was of a different breed. He had been raised among gentler white folk who seemed more apt to spear you with words rather than a sharp knife. He believed in the power of words, wholeheartedly. Harland Jones also believed that most people were well-meaning organisms who when given the facts were reprogrammable, at least that's what he often said.

Eve's father ended up winning the debate on whether to knock on the old farmhouse door or not. Eve fought a grin when she saw the handsome smile he always flashed when he won an argument. It was rare for her father to win one against her mother, who was a thinker by trade. He even offered Eve a wink as he gracefully slid from their vehicle and climbed the cracked stairs. He walked with that same grace before knocking on the tattered screen door.

Eve could barely see the girl who opened the door, and for a moment, it seemed as if the girl was going to allow her father to use their phone. Then, Eve heard someone yelling from inside the house. She tensed when a fuming man with stringy dark hair shoved the girl out of the way and pushed the screen door open wider. The man began yelling at Eve's father, who held up his hands in defense and seemed to speak calmly, which was his way.

Eve couldn't make out what was being said, so she rolled down the car window. The word 'nigger' was said a number of times by the man. She heard that word before, but it didn't have the sting it had on this man's lips. Eve's father must have felt the same because instead of arguing with the crazy-eyed man, he just shook his head and turned around.

Eve didn't even hear when her mother got out of the car, but she did and was ushering her husband down the porch stairs and toward the car. Her parents' slow trek back to the car didn't hold Eve's attention. Instead, she looked back to the door of the house, only to find that the angry man had disappeared back inside.

Shea Swain

Eve settled back in her seat but kept her eyes on the dark house. She wanted her parents' to move faster. She had a bad feeling in the pit of her stomach and wanted to get away from this house as fast as they could. Her heart sped up as she silently willed them to move faster, to run if possible. The walkway wasn't paved, and her mother was wearing heels. So while they tried to maneuver over the pebbles, neither her father nor her mother saw the angry man stepping back into the doorway with the long gun in his hands.

Eve did, and she screamed for her parents' to turn around. She screamed for them to run, but there was no time for either of them to react before the man took aim. Eve watched in horror as her father's chest exploded outward. She held her breath as her father slowly dropped to his knees. She saw the shock on his face and the sorrow in his gaze as he locked eyes with her briefly before falling to his back.

Mommy! Eve's panicked gaze immediately sought out her mother as she prayed that what she was witnessing from her family's car was just a nightmare.

Eve's ears rang from the loud blast, but she heard her mother scream as she frantically tried to stop the bleeding from her husband's chest wound. Wide-eyed with terror, Eve's young mind tried to process why this was happening. Shaking with fear, Eve watched through teary eyes as the girl from the house came to the doorway again. The girl was screaming and pointing when a boy rushed out of the darkened doorway and ran toward the man who now towered over her mother with the gun still in his hands.

"Mommy!" Eve shouted to her mother. Her mother didn't answer as she cried out for him, her father. Eve watched helplessly as the man raised the gun and slammed the handle down on her mother's head.

JUNIOR

Jason Ray Shaw, aka Junior, tried to ignore being shaken awake, but it was useless because Sadie Shaw was determined. He groaned then rolled over and opened his eyes to see his sister's beautiful but worried face looking down at him. Though she was five years older at seventeen, she relied on him for a good deal of support. Clearly, his sister needed him right now. She was crying, her brows were pinched, she looked freaked, and she was shaking him as if he was still asleep.

"Wake up, Junior. Dad…doing bad, bad," she said as she continued to shake him.

With a curse that would make a saint's ears bleed, Junior moved Sadie aside, slid out of bed, and pulled on his worn jeans then his socks as best he could. Sadie said a bunch of words but she wasn't making any sense, her crying jumbled everything. *God, my life is shit.* Not because of Sadie. She was his special girl. The doctors said retarded, but to him, she was just plain special, and he loved her just the way she was.

No, Sadie wasn't the problem.

As Junior followed Sadie out of his room, he heard the tell-tale signs that his father was drunk again. The sounds of shotgun blasts were a constant here at home sweet home. The neighbor's dog was probably on their property again, and his sauced father was trying to shoot the damned thing…again. Seeing no reason to rush but wide awake now, Junior ranked Sadie's frantic pulls and urging low as he made his way through the hallway and down the stairs to the first floor of the house. It was only when he heard screams that he stopped dead in his tracks.

"Help them," Sadie cried as she pulled at his arm.

A second later, Junior was shoving Sadie behind him and running for the front door with no idea what awaited him. He pushed through the open doorway and stopped to take in the scene before him.

He saw… Junior blinked then blinked again. "What have you done?" Junior yelled. Cefus Shaw swung around with the gun aimed at him. Junior held up his hands and took a step back. "Pop?" Junior murmured.

Cefus' eyes were absent of any recognition or humanity. Junior saw this side of his father before. He endured many beatings that followed his father's drinking and this, what he saw, was that look. Junior gazed pleadingly into those hard, unsympathetic eyes enough in his short life to know that there would be no compassion. Would this be the night the old man ended it all for him? As he did often in times like this, Junior thought of his sweet, innocent sister.

Sadie was the only person in this world who Junior cared about. If he took anything his father ever said to heart it was, 'Blood boy'; the old coot would say 'it's all you got in this world.'

"Pop," Junior said again, cautiously.

As if jarred awake, Cefus lowered the shotgun a few inches, now aiming at Junior's chest instead of his head. Recognition flashed in Cefus' light glazed-over eyes before he blinked. "What the hell you doing sneaking up on me, boy," Cefus hissed before turning back around. With his father's focus away from him, Junior took a calming breath then looked past his father.

A woman was lying beside a man who had a huge hole in his chest. Junior immediately felt sick as pain and empathy slammed into him for the strangers. *Cefus done did it now*, he thought as he took a measured step closer. Junior was turning his gaze on Cefus when he saw *her* out of the corner of his eye.

In a station wagon that had one of those wheeled storage moving containers attached to it was a girl. Her face was streaked with tears. Her eyes were pinned on the man and woman lying unmoving on the ground. Her mouth was wide as her screams filled the night. He hadn't heard her until now.

How did I not hear her?

Cefus heard her, and he was about to shut her up, permanently.

Junior moved; later he would wonder what propelled him to do it, but there was no time to dissect his actions now. He ran down the gravel walk as fast as he could, blocking Cefus' view and the barrel of the shotgun that he aimed at the car window where the girl was howling.

"Get the fuck out of the way, boy, for I fill you with holes." Cefus' words were slow but not slurred. That bastard wasn't as drunk as Junior originally thought. His father was a hell of a shot which explained why he actually was able to hit that man dead center in the first place. Cefus being sober…

"You need to think right now, Pop," Junior said. He shook his head when he noticed Sadie coming out of the front door. Sadie understood and quickly went back inside. "If you shoot that shotgun one more time, the Wilsons will have the law out here again. How you gone explain this," Junior motioned to the dead man. He only heard one shot so he assumed the woman may still be alive. "These aren't dogs, Pop."

"The hell they ain't," Cefus said, motioning with the barrel for Junior to move out of the way. "Niggers and dogs are one in the same. Now move your ass, boy."

"Sheriff Gifford won't be able to sweep this under his hat if you harm the girl. She's not a man, Pop. They won't see her as a threat like they might her parents'." Junior realized the girl had gone silent, but he couldn't check on her just yet. He was trying to reason with a man of many faces, and both their lives were on the line. The drunk, the punisher, the racist, on rare occasions the apologetic father, and now the murderer was staring at Junior as if he were a stranger.

Junior heard the gun cock. *Will he really shoot me?* The thought to appeal to the father in Cefus, the father he had never been, popped in Junior's head. "I'm your son, your blood." Cefus actually grinned, and that grin said none of that mattered. "You say that's all we got is each other, Pop."

That got Cefus to slowly lower the shotgun with a sigh. He stood there with his eyes on the girl in the car then he looked down at the woman lying at his feet. Cefus seemed to think for a moment then his eyes lit up. Junior's stomach churned because that look was one of his father's scariest, and by the way, Cefus was peering down at the woman's thighs, exposed by the rising hem of the dress she wore...

Junior could almost see the cogs in Cefus' depraved head turning. It was then that Junior realized that he should have let Cefus kill the woman and the terrified girl. That would have been more humane because now he and Sadie weren't the only prisoners of Cefus Shaw.

Junior glanced over at the woman. Her head stopped bleeding, but she still didn't move. She was balled up in the corner of their cellar. Beside her was the little girl. The girl was silent as tears ran from eyes that stared outward, seeing nothing he guessed. She hadn't made a sound since he'd brought her inside.

I have to get them help.

Junior climbed the stairs two at a time, emerging from the cellar with a purpose. He didn't make it out of the kitchen before he heard what often made him cringe. When his father shifted in his old recliner, the sound of the weathered springs always gave a warning. Most times Cefus was getting up to grab another beer but every so often it was to have one of their special talks.

"Where you think you off to, boy?" Cefus called out.

He must still be in the chair. *Damn,* his father's voice sounded clearer than it did just ten minutes ago when they carried the girl and the woman inside. Junior froze just outside of the kitchen. A wall blocked his view of the recliner Cefus sat in. He needed to think of something and fast.

"That man can't stay out there like that." The image of the man lying on the porch flashed in Junior's mind. He pushed aside any visual signs of disgust as the sound of footsteps hitting the wood flooring reached him. Those heavy footfalls always made him tense. Mostly because Cefus wanted to have one of his special talks and Junior always walked away from their talks with a bruise or two.

Being as Cefus was a little soberer tonight, Junior may well walk away with a broken bone. When sober, Cefus was more father than fighter but still was an abusive prick, and the sober beatings had more impact. Him being sober had its benefits too. It also meant there was a chance Cefus could be convinced to do the right thing. Junior just had to persuade him.

"You think to go against me and help 'em?" Cefus stepped into the hallway. He moved forward, backing Junior up into the kitchen until he was against a wall. Cefus placed his hand on the dingy wall beside Junior's head and leaned in so their noses were inches apart. "You'd see me in jail for killin' that uppity nigger who tried to get into my house…" Cefus seemed to be searching for something to add then said, "Was I to just let him touch Sadie?"

Junior tried not to flinch as his father yelled his question. Showing weakness would add fuel to the already blazing fire. He could do nothing about the droplets of moisture that flew at him or how his father's hot breath threatened to singe his skin as it trailed over his face. Junior just stood straighter and stared into his father's eyes, clenching his fist.

Don't flinch, don't flinch.

Speaking now would only get Junior busted up; it usually did, but he had to try. What he needed to do was calm Cefus down so he could get help. Junior waited and watched in silence as his father's breathing slowed and his eyes went from wild and angry to calculating.

"You just like your whore mother. Probably got some of my bitch of a mother's ways running through your dumb ass too." Cefus shook his head. "Or maybe that school got you thinkin' you smarter than me, boy, but you not. What you think gone happen to Sadie if you go and tell about what happened here tonight. You think they gone let you stay together? Allow a fourteen-year-old boy," he sneered, "to take care of a dummy like her?"

"I'm twelve," Junior mumbled. Before he knew what was going on, Junior was pressed against the wall, and Cefus' hand was around his neck. Dull nails cut into his skin, effectively cutting off Junior's airway. He knew better than to fight back or buck. He would be beaten to a pulp. All he could do was pat at his father's arm.

"You what I say you are, boy." Cefus increased the pressure as he stared into Junior's watery eyes. "Some of those free thinkers will see me fry for killin' that animal," Cefus spat, looking and pointing in the direction of the barn with his other hand. He turned his reddened and narrowed eyes back on Junior and smiled. "As I see it, you're an accessory to murder, boy. I figure they will see it my way too." Cefus tightened his hold then released Junior before walking away.

Junior choked for air as he fell to his knees.

ONE

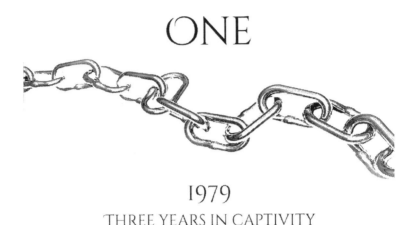

1979
THREE YEARS IN CAPTIVITY

Eve dozed in and out of sleep in the backseat of her parents' station wagon. There wasn't a street or directional sign for some time but that didn't deter her father. He rubbed his eyes for the third time in ten minutes. He was tired, but he was also driven by excitement. They all were.

Life in Maryland was great, but the new job in Montgomery was going to make their lives so much better. At least that's what her parents' told their family. But that was only if they got there. Eve stuck her lips out and sighed. To her, it felt like they were never going to get to their new home. They'd been driving for days.

Well, maybe not days, but it felt like it.

"Harland, dear," her mother blew out a tired breath. "We're lost. You're tired, I'm tired, and Eve is asleep. Let's just find a motel."

Looking out of the window under heavy lids, Eve took in what seemed like endless darkness. Her father yawned causing both her and her mother to follow with a yawn of their own. Eve was a little on edge, and that's what kept her eyes mostly open. Driving with a tired person was always scary.

Her father glanced over his shoulder at her then to her mother and smiled. Eve often heard him tell her mother that she was the most beautiful woman he'd ever laid eyes on. So when he said it now, her mother shyly grinned like she always did then looked down. Usually, he said, 'How in the world could such a beautiful woman still be shy after thirteen years of marriage is beyond me,' but he didn't say it tonight.

"We'll stop at the next gas station," he promised then looked ahead into the darkness.

"I love you," her mother, Pearl, said.

"I love you too," Eve heard her father say. *Everything was perfect*, she smiled as she drifted off to sleep again.

A horrible sound ricocheted through her mind, pulling Eve from sleep. She sat up on the grimy mattress in the corner of the dark room and tried to breathe in and out slowly. It was rare for Eve to dream, but when she did it was never some magical manifestation of a fairy tale. Whenever her mind relaxed enough to allow dreams, her dreams were usually dark and always the same. It was always a nightmare.

Reflecting back on her nightmare, Eve thought that day was one of the best in her life. That night…that night three years ago was the worst. Her father's life ended, and hers and her mother's life drastically changed. No more were they the Jones family from Baltimore heading to their new wonderful beginning.

They were buried, broken, and lost.

Eve rubbed her eyes with the palms of her hands to clear the fog of sleep. She pushed the thin covering down her body, exposing more of herself than she liked. Reaching for the bottom of the mattress, she grabbed the oversized dress that was given to her years ago. It was tattered and torn, but it still hid her shape from his greedy eyes, and that's what was important.

She covered her hair with a piece of torn cloth she made from an old black t-shirt, tucking the shoulder-length braids she wore on each side of her head up under the fabric. Her stomach rumbled from hunger, but she easily ignored it.

After three years of being fed scraps, Eve was accustomed to going without even though her body still complained. Basic needs like sleeping, bathing, or using the toilet was no longer done at her will. Even now her bladder threatened to overflow, but that too was a muscle she tamed.

Eve scooted off the mattress and stood. The metal around her ankle was like a second skin so there was no thought associated with lifting the coiled length to carry with her. Throwing the loops over her shoulder was common as well.

Eve glanced over at Sadie, who lay in her bed a few feet away. Sadie slept soundly, but she always did. It was said that Sadie was mentally slow, but Eve relished the simplicity of thought Sadie often showed. It was as if her mind had a restart button. She seemed to forget all the bad.

After watching Sadie for a couple of minutes, Eve stepped into the hallway. With her rope chain secured, she moved as silently as she could to the kitchen. She hung her chain on one of the large nails that were hammered into the walls throughout the house to keep it off the floor. Eve learned early on that *he* wasn't too coordinated when drinking. The day he'd tripped over her chain resulted in a beating that would have been much worse if it weren't for her mother.

Eve tried not to think of him. She hung the remaining loops of her chain on a kitchen drawer handle, making sure there was enough give to move around the kitchen with ease. She washed her hands then began preparing breakfast. After setting the table for three, Eve toasted the bread and put the eggs and bacon on the stove. She poured orange juice into three glasses and placed them on the weathered table then turned back to finish up the eggs and bacon. Her stomach growled, but she knew better than to eat what she was cooking. Again Eve ignored her hunger.

Eventually, she plated the cooked food. She was turning around to place two of the plates on the table when Eve saw a shadow out the corner of her eye. Her heart stopped, and her hands tilted when she jumped back. It took a bit of juggling to prevent the plates from falling from her clenched hands.

A sigh of relief almost escaped her when she realized the shadow was Junior. He was sitting at the table. Though his presence did nothing to settle her nerves, he was much better than the alternative.

Their eyes met. The intensity of his attention alone jumbled Eve's nerves anew. She once again fumbled with the food. When Junior jumped up, reaching for her or the plates, Eve jumped back. She lost hold of one of the plates she just gained control of. There was nothing Eve could do as she watched the plate wobble in her hand then tip over. The plate and food seemed to drop to the floor in slow motion, only to speed up just before hitting the floor with a loud clatter.

Eve felt every bone in her body ache as she stared at the mess. How long she stood there, stock still as the runny eggs coated the floor, she didn't know. She jolted into action when she heard a noise from upstairs. Eve stabilized the other plate she still held then placed it on the counter before falling to her knees to pick up the food that landed at her feet.

She flinched when she saw Junior's hand come into view. Eve scooted back and instinctively brought her knees to her chest and wrapped her head in her arms for cover. "I'm sorry. I'm so sorry." She apologized over and over again while bracing for the blow that was sure to come. Eve silently prayed that her mother wouldn't hear the beating she was about to receive.

JUNIOR

Junior pulled himself out of bed and threw on some denim jeans and a long sleeve shirt. He hurried to the bathroom, took care of his needs then washed his face and brushed his teeth. When he heard the sounds from the kitchen below his room, he knew it was Eve. She was getting up early the past week to cook. It was something Pearl usually did, but since she wasn't feeling well, Eve took up her chores.

He hurried down the stairs, his bare feet making little to no sounds as he entered the kitchen. Junior halted in the oversized arch entryway when he saw her. Immediately, he felt the urge to help out and actually took a step toward Eve to do just that, but he caught himself. Helping came with consequences that Eve would pay for in the end if his father found out. So he stood in the entryway watching her go about the chore.

The oversized dress Eve wore was one of Sadie's from when his sister was younger. It was a few sizes too big for Sadie then, and it dwarfed Eve's small frame, but she didn't seem to care. Junior wondered what size Eve really was now. She'd grown so much in three years.

Junior found himself wondering what her favorite color was but shook the thought out of his head. His father never allowed Eve or her mother to have anything other than old clothes and enough food to keep them alive.

Junior entered the kitchen, sat at the table, and watched quietly as Eve continued to cook with her back to him. She moved around with a confidence that said she knew her way around and knew what she was doing even though her mother rarely let her in the kitchen. Clearly, Pearl was teaching Eve to cook when he and Cefus weren't around.

Seeing her move around with confidence and ease was a side of Eve Junior had never seen before, and it intrigued him enough that he didn't announce his presence. He realized too late that his silence was a mistake. He watched Eve turn around, her eyes widened, and a low hiss came from her mouth as she jumped back. She was able to regain control of the plates she held, but when he got to his feet and reached out to help, Eve jumped back.

Junior didn't so much as see, but he heard the plate hit the floor.

Eve placed the other plate down and immediately got to her knees and began picking up the mess. Junior's pulse raced as he squatted down to help. They needed to clean the mess up, and they needed to do it fast.

That was his second mistake.

When Eve noticed him helping, she balled up and began pleading with him. Eve's reaction set off a throbbing ache in his chest. He knew the brutality his father was capable of but that wasn't him, and it hurt that she would react to him in the way she was. Frowning, Junior couldn't think of any time he intentionally harmed Eve or her mother. If anything he tried to make things easier for them.

"Eve, please," Junior whispered, "You have to be quiet. You'll draw him."

Eve closed her hand over her mouth but continued to keep herself tucked in the little ball she wrapped herself in.

Junior shook his head but turned his attention to the mess. He used pieces of the broken plate to gather the ruined food. He then rushed over to the sink and swept the food into the garbage disposal. Junior grabbed a handful of napkins and wiped up the stains the food left on the floor. He barely had time to grab the broken plate from the sink and throw it in the trash before Cefus stalked into the kitchen. Junior couldn't help his initial reaction as his body went rigid, but he relaxed before Cefus noticed.

"What the hell was that ruckus?" Cefus yelled. He balled his fist and pinned a shivering Eve with a death stare.

It was Thursday morning, and Cefus wasn't intoxicated, yet. He drank during the week, but he saved 'ass over feet' drunk for the weekends. The weekends brought out the violent, insulting, nasty, man who operated on autopilot. Cefus could be reasoned with in this state.

"Rushing, dropped my plate," Junior said with a confidence he didn't have. When he noticed Cefus' eyes on him, he added, "Coach wants me there early to run drills. He says some men are coming to watch me and Rafael on Friday." Rafael was a really good quarterback, and with Junior's speed, they were practically unbeatable.

Junior could hold onto a football through punishing hits, and he was a fast runner too. He avoided getting tackled. Time and again Coach told him that he was a natural; that he could get a free ride to college then get a pro gig if he put in the time and effort.

Cefus grunted, but he didn't say anything else about the broken plate. Junior knew that bringing up football was the perfect distraction, but lately, Cefus' reactions to the sport were altogether different. Cefus was a legend in high school football and still basked in that glory. He even forced Junior to play, in an attempt to hold on to that glory. Though, instead of gloating about how good his son was, Junior noticed that Cefus showed little interest nowadays.

When Cefus took a seat at the table, Junior let out the breath he was holding.

"You'll never be as good as I was," Cefus announced with a sneer. His shoulders were back, and his chest pushed out. "Davy can have you run drills your whole damn life, but you ain't me, boy. You know it, and he knows it too." Cefus looked angry, seeming to have worked himself up with just a few words. He stared at the spot his plate was supposed to be, his jaw clenching and releasing repeatedly. "None of them scouts gonna waste a single second with you. They comin' to see that spic friend of yours, Guzman, not you."

A lump formed in Junior's throat. He forced it down as he let it sink in that the one thing that he and his father had in common just vanished. It was better not to respond so Junior turned around, picked up one of the full plates of food off the countertop, and placed it in front of his father. Still on his feet, he glanced over at Eve, who was still on the floor, attempting to clean it.

Junior turned back to his father who was now staring down at Eve. "Go wake Sadie," Junior ordered Eve without looking at her. She didn't need to be around with Cefus brewing. "Yeah, maybe, Pop. You coming to the game on Friday anyway?"

Try harder… Junior thought as he realized he couldn't keep Eve off Cefus' radar.

A rumbling sound worked its way up Cefus' throat as an answer to Junior's question, but his father continued to regard Eve as she unhooked her chain and left the kitchen. "Damn girl has the body of a boy." Cefus shook his head before shoveling more food into his mouth. He lifted another fork full of eggs and meat into his mouth a few times before fixing his gaze back on Junior. "The toilet needs plungin'." Cefus got to his feet as he drank the orange juice down. "See to it that the pup takes care of it."

Cefus left his empty plate on the table as he moved past Junior, making his way toward the front door. Junior followed. It was then that he realized Cefus was dressed for work; he usually worked mid-shift. "You going to work?" Junior asked.

"That asshole Brett Hammonds went and got his thumb cut off." Cefus took hold of the door handle but turned his head around to face Junior. His eyes were narrowed and one corner of his mouth twisted. Junior knew the look and what it meant. Cefus didn't have to put the orders into words. After three botched missions to get help and living in constant fear for those around him, Junior knew to keep his mouth shut.

Junior lowered his head in response. Satisfied with Junior's submission, Cefus left the house without saying another word.

A minute or so after the front door closed, Junior heard his father's truck start up. Junior didn't move a muscle as the unmistakable sound of tires rolling over the gravel driveway reached him. When the sound faded, he ran upstairs and quickly took care of the mess Cefus left in the bathroom before returning to his bedroom. Junior opened up his closet and grabbed the bottle of fever/pain pills he hid in some old shoes. He got them from the clinic for what he reported was a football injury a couple of months ago.

Junior ran down the stairs to the kitchen, navigating the familiar obstacles in his way. He opened the basement door and flicked on the light before grabbing the glass of orange juice and the only plate of food that was still on the countertop. Moving quickly down the stairs while trying to be mindful of the food and drink he carried, Junior made his way to the small room that sat directly in front of the stairs.

Inside the room was dark, so Junior left the door open so some light could filter in. He placed the plate of food and drink on a makeshift table, an overturned crate that had a piece of wood on top of it. Pearl was lying on her mattress, her head on the end beside the makeshift table. The mattress was much thicker than the thin foam mat she had last year. It took a little acting on his part and a few complaints to coach Davy about his back before his father was encouraged to get a new mattress for him.

Cefus didn't like his old high school classmate, Davy, who was the football coach. But more importantly, Cefus refused to let anyone, let alone his rival, think he couldn't manage his own household. Cefus also hated handouts. So a week and a few punches to Junior's gut later, his old mattress was replaced with a better quality, gently used mattress from the thrift store.

The end reward was worth the punishment, and his plan worked. Junior was able to give his old but perfectly fine mattress to Pearl. Now she wasn't virtually sleeping on the floor.

A thick blanket he'd also given Pearl, covered her completely, leaving only the hair on the top of her head visible. She didn't move when he entered, but that could be because she stopped jumping in fear when hearing people enter her space a long time ago.

He hoped that was the reason why she didn't move.

Junior kneeled beside Pearl's bed and pulled the sheet from over her face. With her asleep, relaxed, Junior could think of no other who could match her beauty inside and out. Unlike his father, Junior loved the even cocoa color of her skin. He hardly saw many fancy women in person, but he knew instantly that Pearl was rare. She walked, talked, and carried herself in a way that he imagined royalty would.

What she endured daily was unspeakable, yet she remained sweet and gentle to Eve, Sadie, and him. He remembered the day after his father threw Pearl and Eve in the cellar. With all she was going through, Pearl pulled herself together for her daughter and subsequently for him and his sister.

Pearl was the best thing that happened to him.

Junior smoothed his hand over her hair then moved down to her forehead. He sighed. The stress that rode him for the past few days evaporated. Pearl's fever was gone. Junior slid his hand under her head and gave her a slight shake to wake her. "I have some pain reducer and food," he told her.

Pearl gently stroked his hand then tried to push him away. "Give the food to Eve," she said so low he hardly heard her.

Junior squeezed his eyes closed and swore to himself. To see her suffering day after day under his father's hands tore at him. She had little strength in her frail body. "You need to eat, Pearl. Sadie makes sure Eve eats, so your care falls to me. Come on." It was helpful that Sadie took to Eve instantly. His sister treated Eve like a doll, cleaning, feeding, and caring for her.

He gave her a gentle tug. Pearl grunted in protest then pushed herself into a sitting position. He noticed her swaying to one side so he reached out to stabilize her. Once she was sitting up on her own, he pulled the bottle from his pocket. "Open up," he ordered.

Pearl trustingly allowed Junior to place the pills in her mouth. He hoped the pills would at least help with her other aches. But he could rest easy now that her fever was gone. Junior placed the cup of juice in her hand, but they both held on to it as she took several sips. Pearl coughed then began to choke, so he pulled the juice away and rubbed her back gently.

"I need to get you and Eve out of here."

"No!" Wide eyes stared at Junior. "Promise me you won't do anything to anger him, Junior," Pearl wheezed. When Junior didn't answer, she took hold of his chin.

He noted how weak her grasp was. Junior clenched his teeth in anger but said nothing. He didn't want Pearl to waste the little strength she had arguing with him.

"He nearly killed you the last time you attempted to free us. Cefus is a vicious, evil man that you shouldn't provoke again."

"I know."

When Pearl's hand slid from his face, Junior lowered his head to hide his glossed-over eyes. Crying was for the weak. That's what Cefus always told him and repeatedly beat into him. Eventually, Junior learned to hold in his tears and take every beating as a man should. He still grunted, sometimes a scream would escape due to the pain, but he never let a single tear fall and he never would.

Junior learned to just shut out every sound, close his eyes, and let himself drift to a special place whenever his father wanted to teach him a lesson. A place where his mother would hold him and tell him things would be alright. Of course, he knew things were shit. That life would never be okay. Hell, he even accepted that his mother never wanted to hold him in the first place.

Rubbing his hands on his jeans, Junior asked, "Why don't you fight him anymore?"

"He threatened Eve. I have nothing left other than my Evelyn and you kids. Sometimes we must sacrifice to protect the ones we love, Junior. You sacrifice every day that you leave this house and return. You come back because you refuse to leave Sadie behind."

Junior felt Pearl's hand on his head. She stroked his long blond hair from root to end, stopping just above his shoulders. He leaned into the motherly touch absently as he looked at her.

She offered him a slow smile. "You'll be a man one day, big and strong."

"What will that matter? Cefus will always be bigger. He will always be stronger than me."

"Don't you believe that, Junior. Don't you ever believe that," Pearl said. She gave him a bigger smile that chased away his helplessness at that moment. "Now—" Pearl took a deep breath then continued, "I will eat the food, but you have to promise me some things."

Junior nodded, eager to please her. He'd promise Pearl the world if she asked.

"Promise me you'll work hard in everything you do. Don't listen to your father's hateful words. He's a miserable evil thing, and you are not him. You're just a fifteen-year-old boy, and you're more man than he'll ever be."

"I promise." Junior tried to spread his mouth into a smile even though he didn't share Pearl's faith in himself.

"Work hard and be the man he isn't."

Junior tried to fight the tears that rolled down his cheek but he failed. *I always fail*, he thought as Pearl's cold hand touched the side of his face. She wiped his tears away.

"What happened to my husband is my fault, and I will never forgive myself. I let him come to this door. Maybe this is my punishment. But my faith won't allow me to believe that what I endure is in vain. You and Sadie needed someone to show you kindness. It just so happens that I got that task."

Pearl couldn't believe that, but she was right. He and Sadie didn't have many nice people in their life. At one time, Junior thought that Sheriff Gifford was a fair man. That was before Junior tried to help Pearl, after the first time Cefus raped her.

Three days passed since the night Cefus murdered Pearl's husband. Cefus was drinking the entire time. Junior woke to her screams that night.

When Junior finally got the basement door open, he discovered why Cefus decided not to kill Pearl. That night Junior tried to stop his father. Physically, there was no way for him to harm a man Cefus' size at twelve years of age, and he didn't. Cefus ended up breaking Junior's arm, cracked three of his ribs, and fractured his jaw that night. Junior lay in his own blood in a corner of the basement for hours while Pearl was repeatedly raped and beaten.

Even when Cefus was done, he didn't give Junior a second glance as he climbed the stairs to get a beer and sit in his favorite chair. It was Pearl who tried to help him, even in her battered state. She wet a cloth and cleaned him up even though he wasn't able to help her. Finally, the next afternoon, Cefus took him to the local clinic, refusing to take him to the closest hospital in Anniston.

Four days after the Jones' were abducted, after the brutal rape and beating, Junior tried to tell Sheriff Gifford who was called by the suspicious clinic staff. Suffering through every painful breath it took to form each word, Junior slowly told the Sheriff the tale that landed him in the clinic this time.

"Keep it to yourself, boy," Sheriff Gifford told him. Wrapped in bandages and virtually immobile in that clinic bed, Junior had no choice but to listen to the man he once respected. "There's people out here worse than your pa, and if he ain't around to care for Sadie, then she gets taken away. A feeble-minded beauty like your sister won't do well in one of them crazy homes. They'll use a sweet little gal like Sadie, and there won't be nothing you can do. Now you listen to me, boy. You keep your mouth shut about what happened and what still goes on in your house. Do that and you keep your precious sister safe...understand?"

Junior had no choice but to nod his head. He did understand, and that understanding was like a noose around his neck. With pain slicing through his beaten body and fear chilling his bones, Junior realized that he, his sister, and the new captives in his house, were on their own.

Sheriff Gifford's gaze was focused on Junior, then after several pained heartbeats, Gifford gave a slight nod, turned then left the clinic room. Later, Junior found out his injuries were blamed on a group of mystery trouble making teens.

Things became clearer to Junior that day but still, some things remained a mystery. Like why most of the town hated yet feared Cefus. Yeah, his father was meaner than a rattlesnake and as strong as an ox, but he was just one man.

Branson wasn't a large town. The people numbered just under a thousand, with a few dozen occupants living on the outskirts. Some of the people were still caught in the antebellum era frame of mind, but most were nice people. People who were open-minded and fair. Still, Cefus managed to intimidate most of them too. The ones he didn't intimidate were raised to mind their own.

Pearl reached for the juice, tugging Junior from his thoughts. He helped her lift the glass to her mouth again. She promised to eat, so that was one less thing for him to worry about. Sadie and Eve were safe from his old man's anger for now, so that was another relief. Junior took on the task of trying to keep them all safe.

Cefus drank less due to his reemployment at the plant, but the drink didn't make him an abusive prick. He didn't need to drink to be, well, Cefus.

Pearl grunted as she tried to push the worn but clean blanket away. Junior leaned forward and pushed the blanket down enough for her to kick it away with her feet. She moved to stand, so Junior got to his feet to help her up.

"I want to get cleaned up before I eat." Pearl moaned as she stood.

Junior noticed that she held one of her arms close to her abdomen. "He beat you last night," he snarled. *Where was I?* Pearl often tried to take the pain without making a sound so they didn't hear her, but he still should have heard Cefus' yelling. "Is that blood?"

Pearl shook her head as she looked down at her thin nightdress focusing on the juncture between her thighs where a red stain spread. "He didn't beat me. I'm having another miscarriage."

Junior gave a curt nod. He knew some of what to expect from the last miscarriage Pearl had. She would need to have more pain medication, food, and rest.

"Sadie knows what to do, and Eve has been helping me with the housework."

Pearl nodded that she was ready, so Junior looped the long chain rope that was secured around her ankle around his arm. It was slow going as he helped Pearl to the bathroom located on the other side of the basement. She had to stop every so often, her grimace the only indication she was in pain, but eventually they made it to the crudely-built bathroom.

The sink was stained and cracked, the toilet small, and a step-in shower was just a shower head on the wall and drain on the floor with no door for privacy. Junior turned on the shower, adjusted the temperature until it was warm then pulled the curtain that posed as a shower door closed, leaving Pearl alone.

He winced at the thought of Eve knowing that her mother was being regularly brutalized, let alone was impregnated by his father again. The girl had little shelter from the wrong that was being done to her mother. Pearl fought hard in the beginning, but she seldom screamed anymore for fear of alarming them, especially Eve. He often saw Eve crying whenever the commotion coming from the basement was loud enough for them to hear, but oddly, Eve never tried to go to her mother.

Junior suspected that Pearl made Eve promise to stay in Sadie's room no matter what she heard. Under the harsh conditions, Eve had no choice but to grow up fast. The good thing was that Junior sensed that she was strong like her mother. In fact, Eve didn't shed a single tear in the kitchen when the plate fell. Eve was a survivor.

"I'll send down the girls to help you." As Junior walked away, he heard Pearl whisper her thanks.

Junior climbed the rickety stairs, taking two at a time. He headed straight for Sadie's room as thoughts of what his life was like before Pearl and Eve came, flipped through his mind. Pearl was somewhat of a mother figure in his life. His own mother ran off when he was seven-years-old. He hated her for leaving Sadie, for leaving him.

What kind of mother leaves you with a man like Cefus, even if it is your father? He asked himself that question often. He didn't have much of an example of what a mother was supposed to be, yet he knew that Pearl was it.

The cement floor in the basement was cold, but Junior barely noticed the chill on his bare feet. But he did notice the wetness of the kitchen floor when he stepped on it. Eve must have mopped up the floor. He jumped over the section that had been spot cleaned then went looking for the girls.

Over the years, Junior learned to survive in a house with an abusive father. Going shoeless and learning every loose floorboard was a way to go unnoticed. His stealth movements were ingrained, second nature, and that was most likely the reason Eve didn't hear him approaching for the second time today.

She sat on the edge of the mat she used as a bed, with her profile to him. Junior froze in the doorway, unable to look away. He never saw Eve without one of her worn oversized dresses and head covering. Her fingers stretched out the velvety black waves of hair that fell to her bare back, exposing her delicate shoulder as she untangled them. Her skin had always reminded him of the Toffees his English teacher brought to school on Mondays. Junior never liked toffees but seeing how closely the candy matched Eve's skin, it made him want to give toffees another try.

Standing in silence, Junior watched Eve's fluid movements with fascination. He saw ballet dancers perform at his school once. Eve moved just like them as if she were performing. He knew that Pearl was graceful but Eve; he really never paid her any mind. What amazed him most was that her youthful, perfectly proportioned face showed no signs of the hard life that were shoved on her.

Junior's thoughts stalled as Eve swept her hair over one shoulder, giving him a clear view of her naked chest. He'd never seen a naked girl before.

"Morning, Junior," Sadie said, drawing his attention. Her voice was drowsy but held its usual sweetness.

Junior quickly spun around giving his back to both girls. With whatever spell he'd been under broken, he fought through his embarrassment and said what he had to say, "Pearl needs help." His words came out more like an order than a request.

Junior took a step forward to leave but before he did he glanced over his shoulder at Eve. She had her dress in one hand, covering her developing breasts, and her other hand was busy trying to fit the scarf thing over her hair. Their eyes met for a brief moment. Eve's expression was blank, and Junior couldn't help but wonder what she was thinking. It wasn't as if he could ask her; she almost never spoke to him.

Does she hate me like she must hate Cefus? Is she scared of me?

The incident in the kitchen proved that she was scared of him. Only, he didn't want her to be.

Understanding that he wasn't going to convince Eve of anything right now or anytime soon, Junior sighed as he headed back to his room to finish dressing for school. He would still make it there early, so if Cefus decided to check up on him, Coach wouldn't have to lie.

After dressing, Junior went to his closet and pulled out the old shoe he used to hide his sock filled with money he earned from odd jobs around town. He pulled a twenty bill free and pocketed it before placing the sock and shoe back in its hiding place.

Junior grabbed his sneakers out of the closet, pulled them on, then jogged downstairs. He called out his goodbye because he was uncomfortable with facing the girls right now. He left out the front door, locking everyone inside just like Cefus demanded whenever they left the house.

Junior strolled down the long drive to the main road. Usually, the bus would pick him up for school, but because he was going in early, he would have to walk the five miles.

Just a short time into his long walk, he heard the rumbling of a truck. Junior moved out of the road and onto the grass but continued walking. The familiar truck passed but pulled off a few feet ahead of him. Junior jogged the short distance. He smiled as he peered at his neighbor and Digger, who barked and wagged his tail.

"Hey there, Junior, you want a ride?"

"Hi, Mr. Wilson," Junior looked down the road he was headed then back the way he'd come, "if I don't take you out of your way." Mr. Wilson shook his head so Junior climbed inside the truck, pushing Digger out of the way then closed the door.

"Here you go." Mr. Wilson pulled a twenty from his pocket and handed it to Junior. "Mabel told me you help Ellis mend the fence a few days back."

"Yes, sir," Junior said, taking the bill. "Thank you." He slid the money into his pocket.

The Wilsons were their closest neighbors. They had two children, but they were young, still in primary school, so Junior often helped the Wilsons out with odd jobs around their farm. The Wilsons paid him for assisting Ellis, their field hand.

Junior often thought his helping out benefited him way more than it did the Wilsons. He got to drive their truck and farm equipment, learn to fix stuff—because he watched more often than he worked—and he made money. Plus, he really liked being around the Wilsons. Watching them around one another, simply enjoying each other, was comforting to him. Junior got to see how a real family lived and loved.

"Mabel mentioned that she misses Sadie. Is she all right?"

Junior allowed Digger to lick his hand as he relaxed in the seat. "Everything's fine."

Mr. Wilson pressed the gas and the truck moved forward. "Well, let her know Mabel and the kids miss her company."

"I will," Junior said with a smile. Mrs. Wilson was teaching Sadie to cook, clean house, and sew but because Pearl was at the house now, Sadie didn't venture far—seeing as she liked caring and spending her time with Eve.

For the rest of the ride, Mr. Wilson and Junior talked about football and the farm. Focusing on the conversation was increasingly hard because all Junior could think about was Eve with her long, wavy hair.

He never really considered if she was pretty or not. She was real pretty. He knew that now, but he knew he could never think of her like that. Yet, he found that when the conversation lulled, he kept going back to thinking how pretty she was, and that had to stop.

TWO

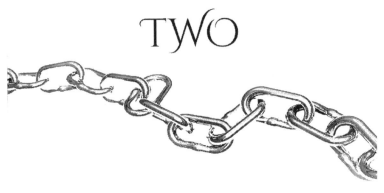

OCTOBER 1980
JUNIOR

Although Junior smiled and laughed when someone looked his way, he had no desire to celebrate. Parties just weren't his thing. So he found a quiet corner to escape but was sought out and surrounded after just a few minutes' privacy. Clutching his cup of untouched alcohol, Junior counted down the minutes until he could leave without offending his teammates.

"Coach is coming!" someone yelled out over the loud music.

Sam Tate jumped up from the sofa. He and a few guys on their football team started hiding the alcohol and Mary-Jane while others held Coach off, with stupid conversation no doubt. Coach was obviously on to them because he walked around the interfering group and motioned to the radio. Someone turned down the radio so the coach's voice could be heard throughout the first floor.

"Tate, I know that's not marijuana I smell." Coach Davy spied the drinks and drugs that some of the party goers didn't have time to hide, but he ignored them as he made his way through the house.

Sam froze then ran to the kitchen and attempted to sweep all the contents off the album cover that read Rick James/Stone City Band, in a plastic baggy.

"Shit, Tate," George Kent said in a hushed but not so quiet tone. Junior covered his smile with his cup as George followed Sam into the kitchen. "I just separated all the seeds." The two fought over the cover and plastic bag for a few seconds before Sam got fed up.

Junior actually laughed when Sam smacked George on the head. He leaned forward and slid his cup under the folding chair he sat on then relaxed back. He didn't need a lecture when he wasn't doing anything, but he could see that Coach had him in his sites.

When Coach stopped in front of Junior and raised his brow, Junior shrugged. Coach pointed toward the back door, so Junior quickly untangled himself from Patsy Dobbs' hold and followed Coach Davy outside.

"I thought you stayed clear of scenes like this, Junior." Coach stopped beside a tree so Junior stopped too. "But here I find you and Guzman, who by the way is passed out on the front lawn."

Junior looked down as he rubbed the back of his neck. "I just came because the guys wouldn't take no for an answer, Coach."

"You can't fall for this peer pressure shit, Junior. When you go off to college, you're gonna wanna have fun. Drink, smoke a little pot, play with girls like Patsy, but I promise you all of those things lead to trouble."

"You know I don't drink or smoke, Coach," Junior reminded him.

Coach Davy placed a hand on Junior's shoulder. "I know, but just because you aren't doing it doesn't mean you won't suffer from the fallout of being around people who do." Coach Davy gave him a knowing look then sighed. "Look, Junior, you remember those friends I called to look at you and Guzman last season. Well, they've been keeping an eye on you both. And with you about to break your father's season rushing record, they're very interested in you coming to Texas to play. You don't want to mess that up."

Junior nodded but wasn't sold on Texas or any other place if he couldn't bring Sadie along. Thinking of going anywhere right now wasn't an option. Football was originally a way to make Cefus happy. Then it was a reason not to go home. If football could get him and Sadie away, he would do it. But playing for any reason other than a way out—Junior wasn't interested enough in the sport.

"I'll play my game, Coach, but I can't think about what ifs."

The noise in the house hushed for a brief moment then seemed to amplify as a chorus of cheers rang out. All of a sudden Junior was thankful that Coach pulled him outside. He hated parties.

"Playing pro ball is your future, and the right school will get you there," Coach told him. Obviously, Coach thought differently.

Junior shifted from one foot to the other as Coach put pressure on his shoulder and held his gaze. He hated to disappoint one of the few men that cared enough to help him. He wished he loved the sport. The fact that he was said to be a natural made him feel as if he was being ungrateful.

"I appreciate what you're doing for us Coach. I won't disappoint you."

"You never do, son. Another Shaw in the record books, hot damn." Coach Davy smiled, giving Junior's shoulder another shake before letting him go. "Well, I'll get out of here before someone thinks it might be funny to take the coach's car for a joyride again." Coach Davy gave Junior a nod then walked back toward the house, disappearing into the crowd.

"You lonely out here all by yourself." Terry Kershaw's sexy southern twang wrapped around every syllable of each word like melted, sticky sweet caramel.

Junior didn't care for caramel. It wasn't the taste so much as the consistency. It's like you chew and chew until you have to give up and just swallow.

"I was just heading back inside," he said. He tried not to look at her huge tits that were squeezed into her low buttoned tight top or her round ass that was peeking beneath the high-cut shorts she wore as he moved around her. He noticed and had his fill earlier. He wasn't dead, and he was far from a saint.

It wasn't as if Junior didn't like Terry. He didn't know her well enough. Not liking someone was energy he didn't care to waste on people he didn't know well. It was that he knew her type. There were girls, women, vipers, and leeches his friends would often say.

His friends failed to classify the ones like Terry. The heartless—the kind of female who cared for nothing other than a good time was more his speed. You didn't have to coddle them like a girl. You didn't need to care about their wants, make them happy, or treat them like a lady like you should. Being a bitch was often a symptom of being heartless, but their bite wasn't debilitating like that of a viper's. Vipers could poison you and everything you loved.

The heartless good-time girl had a story but rarely shared it. They never stuck with anyone or anything other than their own agenda. Usually, that meant moving on to the next best thing. Maybe he was an ass for not caring what drove them to sleep with whichever guy that could hold their attention—apparently he was that guy more often than not.

Maybe Junior should have felt some kind of way for being viewed as that "guy", but he didn't care. Everyone had a need to fill. He had the ability to fill that need plus regret-free sex was a rite of passage that Junior enjoyed. It was one of the few things in life he could enjoy.

But something about Terry was off. He saw the heartless in her, witnessed it a few times, but he also sensed that she was a "latch on and never let go" type *if* she found the right guy. Junior wasn't interested in being that guy. So he left her and didn't make eye contact as he walked away.

Inside, Junior was unable to find a quiet corner like he had before he left, so he chose the least crowded spot which was a wall beside the stairs. He planned to stick around for a little longer. That should keep the guys off his back for a few weeks.

"Shaw! My brother from another mother," Rafael Guzman yelled from across the room.

The quarterback with the golden arm pushed through the crowd as he made his way over to Junior with a girl attached to his side. She was of average height, nicely stacked, and had the look of a girl that played little games. Her grin widened when their eyes locked. She apparently liked that he openly ogled her.

"Have you met Crystal?" Guzman asked. "She's a little older than us but is very eager to meet you."

"Hi," Crystal greeted and smiled. "I've heard a lot about you."

"That so," Junior raised a brow at her accent then shrugged, "and you still wanted to meet me." She definitely wasn't from Branson or anywhere nearby.

Crystal looked him up and down then twirled her hair and tilted her head. "Sweetie," she leaned forward and whispered in his ear, "not just meet you. I want to do so much more."

"And...that's my queue. Check on y'all later," Guzman said, but he gave Junior a look that asked if it was cool to leave her.

"Later," Junior said with a partial wave. At the same time, Crystal took his words and gesture as acceptance and sidled closer to him. He could sense that there was no need for a show or false pretenses. Junior pushed off the wall, wrapped his arm around her waist, and pulled Crystal against him so she could not only hear his interest but feel it too. "You staying or going?"

Crystal's eyes darkened with desire and anticipation. Her chest rose with a sigh. "I'm going with you, stud."

Her comment confirmed that she had heard about him. Junior was happy to confirm the rumors. He was known for three things in their little town. He was fast, took no shit, and was hung like a horse. It also helped that he took pride in whatever skills he had so he didn't half-ass anything. He might be young in age to some, but he knew women.

Other than hard work and sports, there was nothing else to keep a guy busy in the south. Why not try to perfect your technique? He gave, took, and gave some more until the female he was with passed out from a mixture of pleasure and exhaustion. The problem was, though he reached completion, each of his partners was forgettable.

Junior led Crystal outside, proud that she could hold up against the scolding looks from the girls he didn't choose tonight. It was clear that Crystal wasn't timid either because she stared back at every set of eyes that stared at her. He chuckled. Junior liked a girl that didn't wilt under pressure.

They barely made it inside his truck before Crystal had her hands in his pants and gripping the throbbing part of him that was as eager as she was. There would be no small talk, and after he was done, she would be too tired to talk. He liked it that way. No one needed to know his fucked up story and to be honest, he wasn't interested in theirs.

He stripped Crystal easily and managed to just get his pants down to his thighs before she had him in her mouth. Tipping his head back, Junior groaned. Moments like this, he forgot about his responsibilities. He forgot about keeping everyone he cared about alive. He forgot about the last beating or the ones to come. Sex was an escape; his drug. He liked to get high as much as possible because it enabled him to forget his father—the monster that fed off his fear—and the monster he feared he'd one day become.

It was a little after three in the morning when Junior turned the key in his front door. He knew the old man was home because his truck was parked on the front lawn, or what would have been a lawn if the grass would grow. Where the truck was parked was also a tell that Cefus was drunk. Cefus went a couple of weeks without getting ass-over-foot drunk, after beating Junior bloody for the truck he drove.

Even with all the money from his odd jobs, Junior couldn't afford the truck his neighbor, Mr. Wilson, was selling. But Mr. Wilson refused to sell it to anyone else and took what Junior saved, eating the difference. He said that since Junior was the only other person to drive the six-year-old but still like new vehicle, that it would be a shame to allow anyone else to have it.

The gift—and that's what it was really—didn't sit well with Cefus, and after Mr. Wilson refused to take it back and Junior refused to sign it over to his father, the beaten that followed ended up being one for the record books. The only reason the truck wasn't beaten to shit along with him was because Cefus realized how handy another driver in the house would benefit him. The old man didn't have to take Sadie to the doctor or market shopping anymore. Plus, Cefus decided he liked having a backup if his truck ever broke down.

Worry and regret coated Junior's mind as he pushed the door open and walked inside the house. He shouldn't have stayed out, leaving the girls to Cefus' whim.

It was dark inside, save from the moonlight that filtered in through the open door. Cefus sat in his chair; the low light and shadows gave him an ethereal look that caused Junior to take a step back. A warning chill went through his body. Cefus was in a mood. If it wasn't for his fear that the women in the house would suffer, he'd book it out of there.

"Did you put your hands on them?" Junior's voice shook, but he didn't know if it was from fear or anger because he was drowning in both.

"Always the fuckin' savior," Cefus spat out. Each word dragged but could be understood. He tilted a bottle of beer to his lips and took a long drink. "Must be something you got from your whore mother."

It was common for Cefus to bring up his mother. He never held back the insults, even when Junior was younger; Cefus used the vilest words to describe his mother. The woman who showed him and his sister love and cared for them, for a time anyway. Though she'd abandoned them, the insults still hurt him to hear. Even though Cindy Anne Shaw never really loved them, Junior still felt the urge to protect her name.

He didn't say a word, though. He just clenched his jaw and looked down.

Cefus chuckled, "You never did like me callin' the whore a whore, did you? You want to shut me up don't-cha, boy? Think you somethin' now. Gonna best my record and be the big shit in town." Cefus got to his feet and gulped the rest of his beer down.

Junior took shallow breaths as an attempt to prepare himself. A person could prepare for a fight, but there was no way to prepare for a beat down. Cefus wanted to thrash on something tonight, and Junior was his favorite punching bag.

Better it be me anyway, he told himself.

Something moved in the corner near the hallway that caught Junior's attention. It was Pearl. She sat on the floor beside the wall. *How long has she been there*, he wondered? She seemed unharmed, but he still wondered if she was the opening act for the rage that was about to be unleashed on him. He hoped not.

Pearl's eyes reflected the fear Junior begged her time and time again not to voice. It was like that with them. He spoke up for her and did his best to protect her from Cefus' anger, and she tried to do the same for him. The problem was that shit didn't sit right with Junior. Neither one of them were built to endure these damn beatings. They were both slender of frame, but Junior was lean muscle, fast, and trained to take a beating. Pearl was a woman who was frail, delicate, and beautiful. Way too precious for Cefus' anger.

Pearl's teary eyes pleaded with him. She wanted him to run, but he wouldn't. He never did even though he wanted to. *Can't risk you guys*; he'd always remind her afterward.

It was the shift of her chain links that had Cefus' attention turning to Pearl. He dropped the empty beer bottle to the floor then stalked toward her with narrowed eyes. Damned if Pearl didn't get to her feet, ready to take on the beast. Unlike Junior, she almost always fought back. Junior knew the sick bastard liked it when she did.

"Coach Davy thinks I'll break your record. He has every confidence that I will blow it to smithereens." Junior didn't have to force the smile that pulled at his lips. He knew he would demolish his father's season rushing record, could have last year if he was determined to do so.

"Junior, no!" Pearl's voice sounded small, full of regret.

His words had done what he wanted them to. Cefus growled then spun around and charged him. There was just enough time for Junior to brace himself for the impact. Cefus plowed into him, catapulting both of them out the door, over the porch stairs, and to the ground.

Pain exploded through Junior's body when he landed hard on his back, dirt and rocks dug into him, with the weight of Cefus making it worse. His head hit the ground then bounced up only to hit again. His teeth rattled, but he somehow avoided biting his tongue off.

Intoxication had no effect on the old man's motor skills, never had. In fact, it sometimes seemed that alcohol for Cefus was like spinach to Popeye. The fall didn't slow him in the least. Cefus got to his feet then pulled Junior to his. Cefus liked to pretend they were a match and was facing off as equals. Sixteen, abused, and made to fear the very man that should have protected him; Junior was no match.

They both knew it.

After the second solid punch to his face, Junior's vision blurred, but Cefus wouldn't allow him to fall. He held Junior up and punched him so hard in the side that a rib or two had to have broken. Junior tried to push away, but the blows kept coming. His head, torso, face; nothing was off limits. Dazed and confused, he tried to cover his face and head as much as he could.

The sound of rattling metal and frantic screaming centered his dizziness long enough for Junior to focus on what was going on. The attack stopped. Junior realized he was lying in the front yard on his back. It hurt to breathe. His eyes were puffed up and blood was streaming into them. His head felt as if his skull was cracked open.

Junior pried his eyes open to see Pearl clinging to Cefus' back while Sadie was trying to push their father back. Even the girl was outside, and she had a hold of Cefus' arm. They couldn't be near his beast of a father in the rage he was it.

Junior tried to get to his feet, but his body denied him. He couldn't help them. The pain that hollowed him had nothing to do with his injuries as he saw Cefus slap Sadie so hard that she cried out and fell to the ground. The bastard threw his head back, hitting Pearl in the face. She dropped to the ground, but she instantly grabbed hold of Cefus' leg. But it was when Cefus' closed his fist and punched Eve on the side of her head, and the girl dropped lifelessly to the dirt that Junior roared.

There was only one way to distract Cefus.

"You sorry sack of shit," Junior yelled. He'd never been so brazen in the past. Never called Cefus' anything other than Pop or by his given name.

Cefus was bent over Pearl. He dropped the hand that was wrapped around Pearl's neck and looked over his shoulder at Junior. A smile teased at his lips as he stood straight.

"That's right. You know you're shit." Junior tried desperately to get to his feet, but his body wasn't cooperating. He glanced at Pearl, who took the opportunity to crawl over to Eve. Cefus stood over him now, glaring at him with hate burning in his eyes. Junior spit a mouthful of blood that gathered on his father's boots. "I'm going to shatter your measly fucking record, take Sadie and leave you just like Cindy did."

Junior laughed then. It sounded maniacal and eerily familiar, but he didn't care. First, he was getting Pearl and Eve to safety. He didn't know exactly how yet, but he was. Then he was going to prove he was the best running back in the country. He was going to take the first offer from whatever school showed interest in him, with one stipulation. He needed to bring his sister. He had to make football his life, their way out.

It was a hoarse gut-wrenching cry that filled the night and ripped Junior from his thoughts. It took almost a minute for Junior to realize that it was him crying out. The pain was like nothing he'd ever felt before. His hands clawed at the ground around his leg that was twisted at an unnatural angle. Junior's vision flickered in and out. His voice abandoned him. He could only gasp and sputter spit as he tried to make sense of what happened. He saw the stunned shock on the only face he was able to focus on.

He smiled, forgetting the pain in that brief moment as he and Eve gazed at each other. She wasn't dead. *Eve.*

"Shatter my record now, you little shit."

Pain erupted through his lower body as light exploded behind his eyes then Junior saw Cindy Shaw, his mother. She wore a bright smile on her beautiful young face as she waved for him to come to her. Somewhere nearby, something loud shook the earth then everything went black.

Eve

No, no, no, he's not moving. Eve crawled over to Junior; her hand hovered over his leg that didn't look like a leg anymore. She could hear Sadie behind her, yelling at her father, threatening him. No doubt they were going to pay for their choice to get involved, but she didn't care right now. Her hand went to her mouth to silence the cry that wanted to escape. He looked…he didn't look…

"Is he breathing," her mother whispered. Pearl's voice was thick with emotion as she inspected Junior's leg.

Eve looked over her shoulder to make sure that Sadie still had the shotgun pointed at Cefus. *Shoot him*, Eve thought as Cefus slowly inched closer to Sadie. The words echoed in her head. It wasn't Christian; she knew her mother would chastise her for the thought, but Eve didn't care. She wanted him dead.

"You hurt Junior, Daddy," Sadie sobbed.

"You stupid bitch. You think you can shoot my gun then point it at me," Cefus demanded as he inched closer to the porch where Sadie stood.

"I'm not stupid," Sadie screamed, and then cocked the shotgun again.

Eve actually prayed that Sadie shot the gun, but that didn't happen because Cefus stopped in his tracks. A faint light suddenly slinked across the front of the house. It lasted only a second, and that was all the time Cefus needed to rush up the stairs and grab the gun from Sadie. He slapped her face so hard that Sadie fell a second time.

Cefus pointed the gun at his daughter.

"Don't," Pearl screamed. "Someone's coming." She pointed to the light that was a good distance away but closing in. "Think about what you're about to do."

Almost immediately, Cefus swung around and pointed the gun at Eve. "Get in the damn house, all of you—" the wicked gleam in his eyes seemed at odds with his demand, "—or I will put a hole in your daughter's chest."

Without hesitating, Pearl took hold of her chain and climbed to her feet. She used her body as a shield between the gun and Eve as she eased her daughter to her feet. They clung to one another as they inched past Cefus and up the porch stairs, their chains and their heavy breathing were the only things that centered Eve. Pearl reached for Sadie then pulled them both into the house.

Eve didn't wait to see her mother close the front door, but she heard it slam as she gathered her chain and ran down the hall to the room she shared with Sadie. She kneeled at the window, taking her usual position when she wanted to see outside without being seen. She watched Cefus bend over Junior and say something she couldn't hear. Eve also saw the light that they noticed earlier was coming from a truck that barreled up the drive and onto the yard a few feet from the Junior and Cefus.

It was the neighbor, Mr. Wilson. He jumped out of the truck and a large dog she saw a number of times, followed him. Mr. Wilson rushed to Junior's side while the dog barked at Cefus.

"I heard a gunshot. Since Digger was in the house, I figured something was wrong. What happened here, Cefus?" the man asked.

Cefus didn't seem like he was going to answer. Instead, he stared at the barking dog with contempt until Mr. Wilson stopped looking at Junior and stared at him.

"I heard noise. Came out to see what it was, found him out here like this," Cefus lied. "Fired a warning shot case they weren't done." Cefus focused on the dog again. "Why'd you bring the damn fleabag? You know I don't like him on my property."

"Who would do this," Mr. Wilson asked, ignoring Cefus. "Quiet, Digger," the man simply said. The dog shook his head a few times but sat then lay beside Junior. Eve watched as Mr. Wilson stood then jogged to his truck and pulled out something that looked like a blanket and placed it over Junior. His hands moved a lot, but Eve couldn't really see what he was doing.

Look at the blood on his hands.

Eve wanted this over. She wanted Mr. Wilson to look at Cefus' hands. She wanted that dog to rip out Cefus' throat. Eve wanted to run from the house, scream to the world about what he did to them, to her father who laid buried somewhere on the property.

Eve grabbed hold of the curtain, clutching it tightly in her fist, ready to rip it free and expose herself. She didn't want this life anymore.

A moan from somewhere in the dark stilled Eve's hand. She looked over her shoulder at her mother who cradled a sobbing Sadie in her arms. One glimpse at the woman who gave birth to her had Eve second guessing herself. She turned back around and gazed out of the window into the dark night and saw Cefus with his shotgun still in his hand. Eve had no doubts that he would kill them without batting an eye. He would kill them all, even Mr. Wilson, who had a wife and children.

Do I tempt the Devil?

Understanding slammed into her like a fist to her chest. It was fear that kept her mother chained and not the metal that was wrapped around her ankle. Eve gathered that it was the fear of losing her that kept her mother somewhat docile.

Was she her mother's only chain? Eve let the curtain fall from her hand then turned around and slid down to sit on the floor. Her mother was rocking Sadie in her arms a few feet away. Tears fell from both of their eyes as her mother hummed some old church hymn Eve could not quite remember the words to.

She felt warm tears leak from her own eyes too because she just realized that the metal link around her ankle was useless as well. Her heart was tethered to this place as long as her mother was here. Eve would do anything to keep her safe. But that wasn't all. Eve cared for Sadie; she had always been nice, loving, and motherly to her. She would even admit that she loved the woman who was always so gentle and sweet.

Eve didn't like it when Sadie hurt, and whenever Cefus hurt Junior, Sadie felt it.

It dawned on Eve that she didn't want anyone to get hurt. She didn't trust Junior. He would be a man soon, and Cefus' blood flowed in his veins. But she didn't want to see him hurting as he was.

When he cried out, she ran to help him. Her mother and Sadie did too, without even thinking about the consequences. They mostly stayed out of Cefus' way when he beat Junior. Well, she and Sadie did. Her mom always intervened when the beatings were bad. Yet they all tried to help tonight...because they were all in this together.

Will he live through this beating? Did Cefus finally kill him?

Eve dropped her head in her hands. A shiver ran through her body, and she could no longer hold back the flood of tears that fell from her eyes. What happened to Junior mattered to her, and that scared Eve more than Cefus did.

She wasn't just chained to her mother and Sadie. She was chained to the Devil's son.

THREE

Eve

The book sailed across the room in a high arch, bounced off the wall, then hit the floor. Eve followed the path of the book as it slid across the floor and under the bed. It was the third time Junior threw the book and the third time she went and retrieve it.

"I don't want to read the damn book, and I don't need you to read it to me," Junior snapped. He lay on his bed with his upper body propped up on a couple of pillows, staring at the ceiling.

With Junior's help and the use of his library card, her mother taught her well. She was working out of college textbooks and reading adult novels. Her mother also helped Junior, who apparently wasn't a good student before their arrival. Even Sadie learned to read better.

Eve didn't try to convince him. So instead, she gave him a once-over. His leg was also propped up on pillows, a cast covering his upper thigh, down his leg, and most of his foot. Only his toes were visible.

"And before you ask, I don't want a shower either."

Eve narrowed her eyes and just stared at him. It had been a few weeks since the night she thought his father finally killed him. Junior survived but from what she overheard, his leg would never be the same. She understood his sour mood, but no one should sulk in misery or their own funk for too long.

"If you prefer me to wash you here, then so be it?" Eve stood up from where she sat at the edge of the bed and picked the book up off the floor.

"I don't need your help, and you don't want to help me anyway, so why pretend," Junior sneered. "I'll tell the asshole you did your job; just leave me alone." Junior let his head fall to the side and faced the wall.

Most of his outward bruises, the black eye, and a few gashes, were healed, but she suspected the mental ones were still raw. At just twelve, Eve was pretty knowledgeable concerning mental abuse.

Heavy footsteps sounded on the stairs, so Eve quickly tucked the book under the bedspread and went to sort some clothes Junior threw in the corner. "Stop acting as if we have a choice in the matter," she mumbled.

Eve felt the familiar hate mixed with fear as the monster of her nightmares stomped his way toward Junior's room. Cefus took her chain off because they didn't reach all the rooms on the third floor, and she couldn't care for Junior. Her diminutive freedom had a price, though. She was Junior's full-time caregiver.

Eve knew better than to look like she wasn't busy, so she tossed around some dirty clothing in a hamper, hopeful that Cefus wouldn't take notice of her. He usually didn't.

"Not off your ass yet, boy," Cefus grunted from the doorway.

Eve glimpsed Junior over her shoulder. Instead of staring at the wall, his attention was fixed on his father. His eyes were slit, and his lips were spread into thin lines as if he were about to snarl like a dog. His body actually shook with restrained anger. She was sure this was the first time Junior saw his father since the night his leg was broken. A Mr. Davy came by a couple times during Junior's stay at the hospital to get Cefus to visit.

Cefus never had as far as Eve knew.

"Get out," Junior hissed.

Eve couldn't believe her ears. *Did he have a death wish?* She couldn't take another night like the one that put Junior in the spot he was in again. *What is he thinking?* No one poked a bear and lived to tell the tale? She tried to look busy but peeked over at Cefus.

"Still sore about that ass whoopin', boy? Well, get over it. Football ain't for everyone. Your good for nothin' ass would have tanked anyway. Better you deal now than later, so get your ass up and back on your feet. Mr. Bride says he can use you at the mill. You don't need no more schoolin', and I need the money. Your sorry ass ain't gonna live here for free."

Hmmm, Eve thought, *it was clear Cefus' didn't have much schoolin'.*

Cefus stalked over to the bed. "Since they ain't found the 'ones responsible for your injuries,'" Cefus grinned, but it died away quickly. "Those state folk gonna be stoppin' to check on you now. I got warnin' today but next time they just gonna come over without. Spendin' all that money on gettin' you right makes them think it's okay to poke their big ass noses in my damn business.

"You done right by keepin' your mouth shut while you were at that hospital, but if you let shit slip out that ungrateful fuckin' trap of your'n when those people are here, what happens to Sadie will be on your head. Why just the other day, Jessie Hertz asked if our sweet lil' Sadie was any good at cookin'. We both know he ain't interested in her cookin'."

Eve tried to melt into the background, to stay as still as possible, but she couldn't help herself. She spun around to look away from Cefus. Biting down on her lip, she managed to suppress the gasp that almost spilled out of her mouth. Eve stared down at the twisted flannel shirt in her clenched hands.

No one could be that cruel.

When Eve turned around, she saw that Junior's entire body was coiled tight as tears streaked down his face. His breathing was heavy, and one of his hands was clenched. The other, he wasn't able to fist completely because of the splint holding three of his fingers still.

"Keep your sick friends away from my sister," Junior spoke each word slowly as if he were speaking to a child.

Cefus chuckled as he stepped closer to the end of the bed. "Old Jessie had a thing for your whore mother for as long as I can remember. When she first run off and left you worthless lot with me, I thought maybe he went with her, but—" Cefus shrugged, "—I guess he chose to stay with Lucy and the kids. Now Jessie has eyes for Sadie. I can see why. You both got more of your mother's looks than mine 'cept Sadie's a bit curvier than Cindy was."

Junior pushed up with his one good arm as if he was going to get up out of the bed. "I'll kill him if he ever touches my sister."

Eve kept her head down but continued to volley her attention between the two. She knew the moment she saw the wicked grin appeared on Cefus' face that he was going to do something. She just knew better than to react. Junior, on the other hand, was totally taken by surprise when Cefus struck.

Junior could do nothing to prepare as Cefus raised his foot and brought it down on Junior's cast leg. The pained cry that came from Junior caught Eve off guard even though she watched as it happened. She was unable to stop herself from whimpering as Junior fell back on his pillows, clutching the upper part of his cast leg and howled.

Her own outburst drew Cefus' attention. He quickly crossed the room with her in his sights. Eve backed away, but Cefus was on her in a blink of an eye. He grabbed hold of her neck, and all Eve could think of was a line from one of the romance novels she just read. *His eyes were filled with wicked interest.* She didn't understand what that meant when she read it, but she knew now.

"Lookie what we have here," Cefus sang as he tilted her head from one side to the other.

Instinctively, Eve wrapped her hands around Cefus' wrist and arm, pulling away from him. It probably wasn't a good idea to dig her nails into his skin, but Eve was just reacting. Clear thinking had nothing to do with it. Eve soon realized that though Cefus could break her neck if he wanted, he didn't tighten his hold. He was playing with her.

Cefus smiled while he inspected her. Every part of Eve's body that his eyes focused on—her covered hair, her lips, and her neck—heated under his gaze. With guarded eyes, she stared back at Cefus. Would he hit her? Or worse, touch her in places her mother feared he would?

"You have your mother's looks, but that's all," Cefus said dismissively as his gaze dropped to Eve's chest. His brows creased with what seemed to be curiosity as he lifted his free hand toward the oversized shirt she wore. "Unless there's something hiding under these big clothes you wear." He grabbed the bottom of her shirt and pulled at it.

Eve let go of Cefus' wrist and did her best to keep him from pulling up the shirt to expose her chest and the material her mother made her use to tie her breast down. His grip on her throat tightened as the tug of war on the old shirt continued. She was fighting for air and so much more.

Cefus' smile broadened as he let go of her shirt and raised his hand in a high arch. Eve braced herself for impact.

"I have to use the bathroom!" Junior yelled. When Cefus froze, his hand hovering over Eve, Junior added, "Those folk won't be happy if they find me lying in my own piss."

Cefus looked around Eve, who was balancing on her tip-toes, to regard Junior. "What the hell are you yelling for, boy?" Cefus released Eve, and she scrambled back as far as she could while gasping for air. He gave her a look that told her that his examination of her wasn't over. "Clean him up, pup, then you best disappear before those people get here." He turned toward the door to leave but looked over his shoulder. "I don't have to remind you of what will happen if you attempt to run or try to get those people to help you, do I?"

"No," Eve answered. Her head hung low as her fingers stroked her neck.

Cefus explained to her in great detail what would happen if she indeed managed to escape. His words, 'If some sympathizers decide to arrest me for treatin' "animals" like animals,' my friends will hunt you and your mother down and do such horrible things to you both that you will wish you were both dead.' As bad as her life was, Eve had no desire to know what it could be if she defied Cefus.

"That's a good dog." Cefus exited the room. His footfalls led away from the room and down the stairs.

Eve stared at the empty doorway Cefus passed through. He never touched her like that before. He hit her of course, but he never touched her that way. What if he didn't stop?

God, she couldn't stop the fear that took root in the pit of her soul. She felt its vines as they grew and spiraled around her heart and up into her mind. Each vine, a new terrorizing thought for her to dwell on.

"Eve."

Is this how my mother feels every time he touches her? Dirty, ashamed, angry.

"Eve?"

It was the urgency in Junior's tone that brought Eve back. She turned around to see him desperately trying to get out of his bed. Eve ran over to help him. She carefully moved his legs over the edge of the bed so he could balance on the uninjured one while she pulled him up to a sitting position. Eve felt Junior wrap his arms around her neck for support, but even after she managed to get him upright, he continued to cling to her.

At first, she thought he was scared. The fear of reinjuring a healing broken bone had to be…well it had to be scary. And his father may have damaged his leg more with that kick. But when he pulled Eve closer, to a point where their bodies almost touched, she knew it was for her that he clung on.

"I'm sorry…"

Eve quickly pulled away, separating them and cutting off whatever it was Junior was about to say. A strand of her hair got caught in his hand splint, but she quickly worked it free and as a result, she jostled him. Eve watched him with a mixture of curiosity and anger as he lost his balance and rocked forward. He had to catch and right himself before he fell, and that meant putting pressure on his broken leg. He groaned.

Though she felt bad for causing him more pain, Eve didn't need or want his concern.

"I didn't mean the hug the way you think I did." Junior's unbending cast leg lay straight out in front of him. It appeared awkward, but she assumed it was a way that allowed him to sit on the edge of the bed without pain. "You aren't my type." When Eve gave him a confused look, he added, "That's not what I meant. I mean to say that I would never…" Junior shook his head.

For a moment, Eve was relieved, but Junior continued to make his point. *Type*; was he referring to her skin color? His father had no problem touching her mother, in private anyway. And there were some that were alright with mixing the races. There was even a television show that her parents' used to watch called the Jefferson's. The neighbors Helen and Tom Willis, an interracial couple, were married.

"You're just a kid. Plus, I'm with Terry," Junior finally added.

Oh, he thinks I'm just a kid.

Eve thought herself smarter, and she dealt with more things than most adults have in their entire life. She would be thirteen next month, and he was only sixteen, which meant that after his birthday in February they would only have about two years separating them.

...then there's Terry. Well...good.

After several seconds of embarrassing silence on her part, Junior asked, "Are we solid?"

Once again Junior's concerned tone pulled Eve from her thoughts. She was sure she was frowning, so she quickly relaxed her muscles with the hope that she might be able to pull off a look of indifference. Though the question confused her so…

"Solid, it means are we alright. My friend Guzman says it all the time." Junior adjusted his position and reached for his crutches.

Eve got to the crutches first and placed them in his grasp. "I didn't know you had friends other than *Terry*," she said plainly.

Junior frowned this time as if offended, but he seemed to think over her comment.

Eve didn't mean it as an insult. She really didn't think he had any friends. While he mulled over his response, Eve took that time to look at Junior—really look at him. He changed so much since her, and her family came upon Hell's doorsteps. The tall, gangly boy with the dead gray eyes and platinum blond hair was gone.

In his place was a lean muscled teen. Junior's shoulder length fair-colored hair darkened some but retained its light hue along his hairline and sprinkled throughout. His face was tan from being outside a lot and it was smooth, aside from a faded scar that slashed through his left brow and another that appeared on the left side of his chiseled jaw that curved under his chin. Surprisingly, his nose was straight, with no signs that it was ever broken before.

His eyes, they weren't dead anymore either. They reflected determination and… Eve saw something else in his eyes that he lacked a couple of years ago. She saw the same darkness that Cefus' eyes held, but in Junior, it seemed to lay in wait.

"Yeah," Junior muttered as if speaking to himself, "I guess I have a few friends." Then he did something Eve never saw him do. Junior looked up at her and smiled.

As if a light flashed on in her head, Eve realized that Junior was handsome. Actually, he was very handsome. Her mother once said that Junior was a nice blend of movie star pretty-boy and a ruggedly handsome cowboy. Eve never really had the opportunity to get caught up in any movie stars, let alone swoon over one. So she didn't really know what the "movie pretty-boy" look was, or the "rugged cowboy" for that matter.

Eve knew that her father was handsome and read all about what folk considered it to be. Most of those books only featured white men so based on those ideals, Junior was above standard. But she didn't really have a solid idea of her own preference.

Eve's heart never sped up nor did her face and neck ever feel hot because of something as silly as a boy smiling at her. *Until now.* She actually had to fight against the frantic rhythm that pulsed in her ears and the heat that crept up and warmed her back.

"What's wrong," Junior asked. He used the crutches to pull up and then balanced his weight. "Did Cefus hurt you?"

"No," she bristled. "Don't you have to use the bathroom?"

"I just said that to…" He dismissed what he wanted to say with a scoff of breath. "Are you hurt?"

For the first time since he'd returned home, Junior was using the crutches. All because he was concerned for her, and he'd lied too.

Well, he shouldn't have.

"No. Nothing's wrong," Eve grunted as she moved back a step, out of his reach. They stared at one another for a few seconds before she quickly crossed the room to put more space between them. Eve looked over her shoulder. "We should get you cleaned up."

"You're not going in the bathroom with me." Junior followed her with short choppy steps that was evidence he didn't use the crutches much. "If you help me cover the cast with a plastic bag and take off the hand splint, I can do everything else."

"And let you fall and hurt yourself worse. I'm going in with you." Eve stood aside so he could enter the bathroom. "I'll keep my eyes closed tight and help you when you need me. When you shower, the curtain will hide most of you. I don't want to look more than you don't want me to see, but I need to be close. In case you need my help."

"Fine," Junior groaned as he went inside.

JUNIOR

Eve stood with her back to him. *Hopefully, her eyes are shut.* Junior sat on the closed toilet seat and worked his dirty clothing off. The deed was exhausting and took a lot longer than he thought. So much so that he found himself wishing for one of those hospital gowns that barely covered his ass.

When Junior was finished undressing— which took a lot of acrobatics— he wrapped his lower half in a towel and told Eve he was ready to get in the shower. He held his leg out and watched Eve wrap the cast in a trash bag she must have brought up earlier. After checking for gaps in the cover-up she made, Eve turned the water on and checked the temperature. Junior allowed her to help him get his uninjured leg over the high rim of the tub, placing a good amount of weight on her shoulders. She held up under the pressure.

His cast leg remained on the outside of the shower as Eve undid his hand splint and placed it on the edge of the sink. Cleared to wash, Junior closed the curtain as much as he could, then removed the towel from around his waist and tossed it to the floor. The whole ordeal took a lot out of him, and after he was done washing, Junior wanted nothing more than to get back in bed. He could probably sleep for a year straight.

But who will watch my back?

Eve handed him a clean towel through a space in the curtain. He used it to dry himself as much as he could before he wrapped it around his waist. They managed to move, pull, and twist his clothing on while keeping his privates covered but had to skip the underwear altogether. He was back in his room before they heard a knock at the front door.

Junior whispered his thanks in Eve's ear as she helped him lie back on his pillows the hospital gave him. Eve moved fast but still managed to be gentle as she placed one of the extra pillows under his leg before she scampered out of his room and down the stairs. Junior heard a door shut, presumably the one to the basement, before the sound of the front door opened.

He heard when the social worker introduced himself. He didn't hear Cefus greet the man with his name, though. Cefus said Coach Davy's name then began speaking in a clipped tone. It wasn't long before the rumble of footsteps climbing to the second floor reached him. His father was such a dick to everyone.

Does Eve see me as a guy, like in a boy/girl way?

The thought was random and so out of place, but Junior just remembered her expression. She looked hurt when he called her a kid. *Well, she is.* Eve wasn't like other girls her age. She didn't try to sneak a peek at him like some of the girls he knew would have if given the chance.

The knock on his door was so light, or his two guests didn't knock at all before they entered his room. Or maybe he just didn't hear the knock because Eve was on his mind. Junior tried to focus on the men who were standing over him with a concerned look on their faces. But all he could think of was Eve and how she was helping him. How she stood quietly in the bathroom and waited without a hint of anger or resentment. How she read to him even when he repeatedly tossed the books aside. Why didn't she ever try to retaliate against him for his father's deeds?

It also dawned on him that during the entire time she was with him since coming home, he didn't hear the constant chorus of her chain.

DECEMBER 18, 1980

Guzman turned Junior's truck onto the dirt driveway at a faster rate of speed than what was necessary. The container Junior held in his lap shifted with the turn, but he managed to hold onto it.

"Jesus, if I want to die I don't need your help." Junior eyed his friend from the passenger seat.

"Yeah, I'm pretty sure Terry will want that honor." Guzman let out a howl of a laugh that brought a grin to Junior's face. The laughter subsided just as Guzman pulled up in front of the house. "You know she's not going to let this slide, right?"

Shrugging, Junior pushed open his passenger side door. "She can do whatever she wants. This isn't negotiable, Guzman, unless you don't want to."

"I told you already that I don't mind. Hell, you're my bro. Besides, I like driving your Blazer. It's roomier than my hatchback. I just think that Terry and your dad would rather she drive your truck and chauffer you around." Guzman tapped the steering wheel nervously as he watched the front door. He shook his head then looked over at Junior, who managed to get out of the truck without assistance.

Resting his weight on his good leg, Junior reached for his crutch that sat between them. Guzman helped, handing it to him then said, "It's just that I don't want to cause trouble for you."

Junior placed the container he carried on the seat as he worked the crutch under his arm. At Guzman's words, he looked over at his friend and frowned. Concern was plastered all over Guzman's face. Junior knew that it wasn't Terry Kershaw that worried his friend because he just started dating her a few weeks ago.

No, it was what Cefus' response would be when he found out that Junior was giving Guzman his truck until he could drive it again. His racist father's reaction was what caused his friend's unease. The story Junior would tell Cefus, if asked, was that he needed a chauffeur, but the truth was that Junior didn't trust his father. To him, Cefus hated it when he accomplished anything. Hell, if Cefus had his truck, he'd probably sabotage it in some way.

"He can't do no more than he already has. Besides, I doubt he'll volunteer to drive me around." Junior lied easily to assure his friend everything was fine. He picked up the container, tested his weight on his leg with his crutch under his arm, then closed the truck door. He tapped on the roof a couple of times. "Thanks, man, I appreciate it."

"Solid." Guzman nodded his head several times, as if mentally pumping himself up, then he gave Junior a smile that didn't quite reach his eyes. "We're gonna get you back on the field in no time, Junior." He continued to nod as if convincing himself that he spoke the truth. "Just keep working out, stretching. I'll be throwing you the ball again in no time. Then it's you and me, man, riding horses in fucking Texas."

Junior forced a smile because the sparkle in Guzman's eyes told him that his friend needed to be reassured, even if it was another lie. "Texas," Junior said with conviction as he slammed his hand on the roof. Then he backed away from the truck.

"Texas," Guzman yelled out as he pulled off.

Junior watched as his friend drove his truck down the drive until it disappeared from view. He turned and slowly climbed the porch steps while he held the Styrofoam container in his hand. He heard the neighbor's dogs bark at his departing truck. He hoped they stayed in their own yard from now on; Cefus made it clear that he had no problem killing who he felt were trespassers. Luckily, the Wilsons realized how dangerous his father was and erected a fence.

At the door, he transferred the container to his other hand and pulled his keys out then opened the door. The house was quiet. It usually was so it didn't raise any red flags. Junior made his way through the foyer and toward the kitchen. There were a few hours before his father got home, but he didn't want to drag things out. He had a feeling that what he did might not go over well, so he just wanted to get it over with.

Nervous energy ran through Junior's veins as he sat the container down on the table. He opened the lid then frowned and closed it. He opened and closed it a few more times before he closed it and pushed it across the table.

Junior took a deep breath then slowly let it out. He rubbed his hands on his sweatpants, ignoring that one leg was cut high to accommodate his cast. He planned this for a little over two weeks but was so fucking nervous...

If Pearl...

Pearl told him that it would go better if he did this alone. Plus, she wasn't the same since he got out of the hospital. God only knows what happened to them when he was lying in that hospital bed. No one would say. The only thing he knew was that Pearl was confined to the basement now, her chain drastically shortened.

Sighing, Junior called out, "Eve."

There was movement in the basement below then the sound of footsteps as Eve climbed the stairs. Pearl would keep Sadie downstairs because they planned it that way. This was his thank you for Eve alone. It would be his disappointment if Eve threw it back in his face. He let out a nervous chuckle.

When Eve reached the top of the stairs, she lowered her head and waited. *Waited.* She waited for his orders like he was her fucking overseer as if he was an active participant in her and her mother's torture. Offended, Junior just stood there in silence. Didn't she know *he* did whatever his father ordered him to tell her to do, himself, whenever he could get away with it? He had to be careful because if he ever was caught, he was certain they would both suffer.

Didn't he treat her with patience and kindness, ignoring her altogether when his father was around so he didn't bring unnecessary attention to her? He never yelled at her and never hit her. He pretty much avoided touching her until these past few weeks since his injuries. Yet she treated him as if he was his father.

It was unlike Junior to care about how someone saw him. No one but Sadie ever meant enough to him to care, but it seemed that changed when the Jones' came knocking.

Get it over with. "I…," he started, but just reached across the table. Eve's eyes followed his actions and rested on the container that held the three thick slices of chocolate on chocolate cake. A single candle stuck out of the center slice. "Happy thirteenth, Evelyn."

The hesitant smile that lit her pretty face was amazing. Seeing that smile was so worth a beating if he was caught, and it guaranteed that he was going to buy her cake next year and the year after.

FOUR

DECEMBER 29, 1982
JUNIOR

A quiet calm set in over the Shaw home during the past few months. It was something Junior hadn't felt since his mother left, but even so, he couldn't relax. He couldn't let his guard down, had to be prepared. Turning his attention from the house he would never call a home, he tried to focus on what he was doing.

"Why is she always talking to herself?"

Junior looked up at Terry Kershaw. Her long blonde hair, bright blue eyes, and model physique made her a stone-cold fox. She had every warm-blooded male in Branson County and the surrounding area dropping to their knees for her attention, but for Junior, she never held his interest for more than a roll in the hay. Maybe guilt was why he kept her around so long. Lord only knew why she kept coming around.

"Why are you here, Terry?" Junior ducked from under the hood of his truck, wiping his hands on a cloth that dangled from the waistband of his jeans. He glanced over at Sadie, who was sitting on the wraparound porch beside her bedroom window. She placed a chair there so she could talk to Evelyn through the window years ago.

Junior strolled around to the opened driver's side door and reached inside. The engine turned over with a twist of the key. He listened to it hum for a few seconds before he turned it off.

Before he knew what she was doing, Terry sidled up to him, placed her palm on his chest, then trailed her hand downward over his abdomen. Junior shook his head as he grabbed hold of her wrist before she could reach his jeans.

Terry pushed her lips out in a pout but didn't pull out of his hold. "I thought we could talk," she said stepping closer him. She brushed her red lips across his jaw.

Junior leaned back before her lips found his. "Done talking, Terry"— he looked into her eyes, wondering why the pretty blues never stirred anything in him— "done with you touching me too."

Pulling out of Junior's hold, Terry stomped her foot on the dusty ground before taking several steps away from him. "What the heck is your problem, Junior?" Terry whirled around, pinning him with wide eyes and a weak smile. "We're good together. Don't you see that? I made a mistake, but I'm not sorry for it. You belong with me."

Junior rubbed his head, relishing the freedom the haircut he got a month ago gave him. He needed a change, some kind of sign that he wasn't stuck in stasis. That he was making progress, so he got a haircut.

He sighed, thinking of how physically and mentally tired he was. The need to free himself of one of the nooses around his neck was presenting itself, and he would be a fool not to take it.

"We"— Junior motioned to Terry then to himself— "don't exist anymore."

"I did it for us. Don't you understand? You and I are meant for each other, Junior. Even your pa says so." The comment earned her a scowl and an angry grunt. Terry shook her head realizing her mistake of mentioning Cefus. "I just meant that he thought the idea of me having your baby was good. Even my folks loved the idea."

Junior slammed the truck door shut then walked around to the front of the truck, reached up and slammed down the hood. "You lied to me. If there was one thing I thought we had in common, it was truth. From the very beginning, you knew I wanted out of this place." He tried to remain composed, but he felt his anger stir. Terry made him so damn mad it took effort to push the anger down. "You knew we were just enjoying each other's company. You told me you could be with me without the promise of more. Then you try to tie me to you, to this town"—he swung his arm out, motioning to his house— "to this place…"

Junior cursed then started for the porch where Sadie now stood, watching him. He took a few steps forward before Terry grabbed his arm. Junior turned around to face her in hopes that she would say her peace then leave.

"I'm sorry," Terry cried out. "I really thought I was pregnant."

Tears streamed from Terry's eyes, but they did nothing to change Junior's resolve. He witnessed her attention/pity-seeking antics enough over the years. Though, there was something…more in her eyes now; it didn't matter. Terry wasn't what he wanted, and he never led her to believe that she was or would ever be.

"We're done." Junior turned away from her again. He had to explain to Sadie why he was so angry.

"I thought you loved me?"

Junior spun around so fast that Terry had to take a few steps back. He promised himself long ago that he would never allow a female to witness or be the recipient of his anger, but Terry just crossed the line he so explicitly drew for her from the start of their relationship. It was a relationship, an agreement based on his need to feel something and to quench her desire to have him.

At a time when his life took a nose-dive from the ledge, it was precariously balanced, he accepted, even encouraged her attention. And even though he'd been as clear as bold print about what he wanted and didn't want, he had no one to blame but himself.

"LIES," Junior yelled. Terry gasped. Her wide, wet eyes stared back at him with shock as her body trembled with fear. "I have never said those words to you or any woman other than Sadie. You were on the pill, and I never touched you without protection." His voice picked up volume with every word. "Tell me, Terry. How the fuck does a woman get pregnant on birth control while the man uses condoms?" He stalked toward her.

Terry's eyes grew wider when he grinned.

Junior knew full well that his face, which was often compared to his mother's, transformed when he was angry. It was the part of himself that he couldn't change and hated the most. Yet, right now—at this moment—he relished the small similarities that connected him to his father.

Cefus terrorized the small town, and to this day, he maintained that fear through intimidation, secrets, and brute strength. For the first time in his life, Junior embraced his darker side. "Do you think because I live in this Podunk town that I'm some illiterate hick who can't string together a complete thought? Or is it that you think I'm desperate because I lost out on a life of playing professional football?" He stopped mere inches from her, satisfied that she was biting on her lower lip. It was what Terry did when she was nervous.

She opened her mouth to say something then closed it.

"You thought I wouldn't find out. You think that all those girls that hold onto your every word are loyal to you. Could you not see that they were waiting to get something on you just to tell me, thinking I would drop you just to give them a chance? I know how you sabotaged my condoms and stopped taking your pills. I'm only eighteen; I live in Hell. Why would I want to be anyone's father?"

A soft moan that grew into a high-pitched sob escaped Terry's mouth. Her full breast heaved with every dramatic breath she took. She wrapped her arms around her flat abdomen that he once believed carried his child, then bent forward and shook her head. "It doesn't have to be a lie"— she sobbed— "I want your baby, Junior. We can be happy; you, me, and our baby. Your dad said he would even give us some land to build a house. Our very own house, can you imagine." She reached for him.

Junior moved back to avoid her extended hand. He chuckled, not believing his ears. All the pieces finally fell into place. Still, he wondered if it was Terry's or Cefus' idea to poke holes in his condoms. Honestly, it didn't matter. Terry wasn't pregnant so he'd dodged a shotgun blast to his already fucked life this time around.

"Goodbye, Terry," he said calmer than he thought he was capable.

Terry silently pleaded with him with her reddened eyes, but eventually she realized he wasn't going to change his mind. She slowly walked to her father's truck, looking over her shoulder at Junior when she opened the door and climbed inside. Their eyes met, but he narrowed his, cutting off whatever she thought to say.

When she started the engine, Junior turned and stomped his way to the rickety porch. He forgot that Sadie was watching and as he reached the steps, she came forward. Her face was pinched with worry, and she was rubbing her hands together like she often did when Cefus yelled.

"Okay?" Sadie asked him.

Junior rubbed his head. If he could wipe what Sadie witnessed from her mind, he would. She saw much worse, but the fact that his anger was on display for her made him even angrier.

71

"You are mad," she said when he didn't respond.

He worked hard to sound calm. "Not at you, Sadie."

"At Terry then," she asked.

Shaking his head, Junior said, "No, Sadie. I'm mad at myself." He touched her cheek that was blushed pink from the chill in the air. It was the end of December, and the weather was mild. "Go on inside, Sadie. We'll come back out later." As usual, Sadie did as she was told. Junior moved to follow but stopped and glanced at Sadie's bedroom window. He silently cursed then entered the house.

J unior fumed as he paced from one side of his room to the other. It took almost thirty minutes for him to cool down after seeing Terry ride off. He fell to his bed face up, placed his hand behind his head, and thought about the turn his life was taking. Over two years ago he was on a path that would take him away from the hell he was living day to day. He should have known Cefus would never allow him to win in any way.

One surgery fixed his broken leg, another fixed his arm. Physical therapy and weight training at the school gym and at Coach Davy's house helped him, but it wasn't enough to get him back on the field. He was lucky that he could even walk with just a slight limp.

That night, two years ago, when Cefus broke Junior's leg, he stole the future Junior stupidly entertained. But it was Sheriff Gifford who brought Junior to heel. When he brought Sadie to the hospital to visit under the guise of questioning him about what happened to him that night, Junior got the message loud and clear. The fear on his sister's face as she looked at him sealed his mouth shut. He wouldn't risk her.

He wanted to save them all. A thought occurred to him. What did Pearl and Eve really think about him? Did they think him a coward?

Dark brown eyes with lighter brown specks manifested in his head. He realized he knew exactly what Eve thought of him. Reflected in her eyes whenever he managed to look into them, was pure hate.

Junior sighed. The peeling paint on his ceiling started to take the shape of certain patterns to him, and for years he was usually able to lose himself in them, thinking that they were places and things far from here. But for some reason, all he could do was see those damn brown eyes.

He shifted on his mattress, adjusting his aching leg in a more comfortable position.

When Eve and Pearl first arrived, Junior didn't care if Eve liked him or not. He still took on the job of protecting her regardless. Her feelings about him didn't mean anything. But recently, all that changed. But not the way she looked at him.

It was the way he looked at her that was different.

Eve was tasked with caring for him after he was released from the hospital. His father even removed her chain so she could come up the stairs and tend to him because the cast on his leg and the one on his arm prevented him from doing it himself. She helped wash him, fed him when he refused to eat, she even entertained him when he sulked about the shit-hand he'd been dealt. She didn't allow him to sink into the pit of despair; a place he would have surely come out of angry and blameful at the world and everyone in it.

He would have become Cefus if not for Eve.

To say that he didn't understand her was an understatement. Eve hated him but cared enough to help him with gentle hands. Of course, Cefus was the motivating factor that made her care for him. Hell if his old man was going to hire a nurse like the folk at the hospital suggested when he had free labor from Pearl and Eve. With Coach Davy and a state representative checking in on him from time to time, Cefus had little choice but to make Eve do it.

But Cefus didn't make her treat me gently or read to me daily.

Sure, Pearl most likely told Eve to be nice to him even when he was an ass but sometimes…sometimes it seemed that Eve wanted to be nice to him. And what did he do to repay her? He thought about her in ways he shouldn't, that's what.

God, I'm a sick fuck just like my father, lusting after someone who hates me.

Junior rolled over and threw his arm over his eyes. His muscles slowly relaxed and his mind erased any trace of Terry or the argument they just had.

Eve's eyes flashed before his closed eyelids before Junior dozed off.

Eve

Eve saw the truck when it pulled onto the property through Sadie's bedroom window. For reasons she couldn't put into words, the sight of Terry annoyed her. Ever since the pretty blonde started coming around the year before last, after Junior got hurt, Eve disliked her. Maybe it was because Terry was the only living thing that Cefus didn't run away from the house with a shotgun. Or maybe it was that Terry had the freedom that was so viciously taken from her. Whatever the case, Terry was not someone Eve wanted around.

Sighing, Eve decided that she didn't want to see any interactions between Junior and his girlfriend. The last time curiosity got the better of her, she saw things she was sure no one should witness. Things that whenever Eve looked at Junior without his shirt, images from that day invaded her thoughts. And lately, his clothing or lack of, had nothing to do with the thoughts she was having about him. For some reason, Eve couldn't stop thinking about Junior.

Just like now.

Frustrated with herself, Eve pushed up off the mat she used as a bed. She instinctively reached for the chain that was secured around her ankle, but there was nothing there. It was removed two years ago and was never replaced. Eve often looked for her chain, as if it were a phantom limb.

"I'll be back," Eve said to Sadie, who sat outside on the other side of the open bedroom window. A glance in Junior's direction showed Terry leaning on his truck. Ignoring the odd sense of discomfort from the missing chain that used to encase her ankle, Eve left the room and the fresh spring air she was enjoying through the open window.

Eve tapped on the basement door to announce her presence before she opened it and descended the stairs. The basement was no more than a storage room that really wasn't fit for living. The large space was filled mostly with broken furniture and junk, except for a utility room directly across from the stairs and a bathroom.

The door was ajar so Eve stopped just outside the room. A large electrical panel with a metal door sat on one wall, two wide floor-to-ceiling shelves that held her mother's few possessions sat along another wall, and a small crate that was used as a side table sat beside the mattress. On the bed was where her mother sat, reading a book.

"I thought you were getting some fresh air?" Pearl asked.

Eve leaned on the frame of the door and shrugged. "Terry's here."

Pearl gave her a twisted-lipped smile and a look that Eve didn't quite understand, but she wasn't about to question what it meant. Eve reached for her missing chain but quickly abandoned the action then entered the room. She sat on the bed.

"I didn't like the ending." Eve frowned as she looked at the paperback her mother held.

The novel told a story of Richard, a rich and powerful man who wanted for nothing but the affection of a woman who had no love for him. The heroine, Rebecca, who did love him, never won his affections. In the end, Rebecca married another to secure her future and the future of her bastard child she conceived with Richard.

"Would you have preferred that Rebecca had won the love of the man that held her heart?"

The response didn't need much thought for Eve, so she answered immediately. "I would rather Rebecca accept that Richard was unworthy of her affection and raised their child alone. A woman doesn't need the love of a man. She especially doesn't need to marry someone she doesn't love to feel whole."

"No?" Her mother frowned.

"No," Eve answered, looking her mother head-on to convey her point.

Pearl dog-eared the page she left off on before setting the book on her lap. Eve immediately knew that she unconsciously set herself up for one of her mother's 'life lesson' speeches. Having a mother who was a teacher had both its advantages and disadvantages.

Pearl had a way of analyzing everything. It wasn't a bad trait to have, but for Eve the sky was just blue, and the earth was just round. Yes, there were reasons for this and that, but those components didn't need to be broken down. Eve felt her comment didn't need to be analyzed either.

"I know you're young, but do you believe in love, Eve?"

Taking the book from her mother's lap, Eve flipped it over so she could see the cover. The design pictured a love letter that was torn in several pieces with a long-stemmed rose beside it. Eve traced the raised thorns on the rose.

"I just don't see the point of it. Why fall in love when it doesn't last? Rebecca loved Richard, Richard loved Janet, Janet loved herself, and Mitchell loved Rebecca, but neither of them loved each other." Eve shrugged then motioned to the other books on the shelves. "I've read all of those books. Most of them have an unrealistic happy ending. The rest are so sad and too depressing. I don't think real love is like that."

"What do you believe love is like?" Pearl asked.

"It's nothing like in these books." Eve placed the book back on her mother's lap. "Those men are sweet, giving, and gallant...they are perfect and treat women like they are treasures. Real men are selfish, hurtful, and make stupid decisions."

"Eve," Pearl placed her hand over Eve's, "your father was just like those men in those books." Pearl motioned to the books the same way Eve did. "He was all of those things and more, sweetheart. Yes, there are bad men in this world, but don't let their actions determine the worth of all men." Pearl leaned forward and placed her palm on Eve's cheek. The chain around her ankle shifted when she moved, causing Eve to focus on the metal links. Pearl placed her finger under Eve's chin and firmly lifted it so that they were eye to eye again. "All men aren't like him. One day you'll be free of this place. When that happens, I want you to find happiness."

Shocked, Eve grabbed Pearl's hand that stroked her cheek. Her mother never spoke of leaving this place. Eve was warned to never speak of leaving, because if Cefus ever got wind of it, he would kill them or worse. Eve knew her mother feared that Cefus would eventually want her in his bed too.

"What are you..." Eve's words were cut off by thunderous yelling. Both she and Pearl got to their feet. Eve climbed the stairs and hurried to Sadie's bedroom, but Pearl couldn't follow, resigned to only listen from her cell.

Once inside the room, Eve immediately fell to her knees and peeked through the curtains of the open window but was mindful to stay hidden. Outside, only yards away, Junior was full-out yelling at Terry. Sadie was still on the porch, but she stood closer, witnessing the confrontation.

"Sadie," Eve whispered, "do not move any closer." Just those words had Sadie wrapping her arms around one of the porch posts, no longer inching toward her brother.

Eve never saw Junior so angry. His eyes were narrow, and his chest heaved up and down as he spoke. She also noticed how the veins in his neck bulged with every word and for some reason she couldn't look away. His anger was explosive and in so many ways he reminded her of Cefus, but what surprised Eve was how Junior restrained himself. If it were Cefus Terry was facing, Eve was certain she would have been bloody by now.

"No," Eve whispered. *Junior is going to hit her.* She watched helplessly as Terry stood frozen in fear while Junior stomped toward her. Eve didn't know what Junior's breaking point was, but she was pretty certain he was close to it. She shook her head, praying that Terry didn't say another word; that she would turn around and just leave. Just because Eve didn't like Terry didn't mean she wanted to see her get hurt.

It was clear by the frightened look on Terry's face that she sensed the danger, but it seemed she was determined to plead her case. Eve gasped, realizing that though Junior looked livid, he allowed Terry to speak her peace. Terry said a few barely audible words as she cried, but they didn't have any impact on Junior. He just quietly told her goodbye when she was finished.

Eve couldn't take her eyes off of Junior. He breathed through his anger as he watched Terry leave. When the truck disappeared down the drive, Eve watched him walk up the porch steps, still frightened by the anger she saw vibrating through him and fascinated by the way he restrained it. She vaguely heard Sadie ask Junior a question, and he offered a response, but because her focus was on how he didn't react the way she thought he would, Eve didn't hear what the question was.

Junior held back. *Why did he?*

Junior was his father's son. Usually, Eve avoided him, though she did accept the books he often brought from the library. She also never complained when her mother tutored him alongside her and Sadie. There were several occasions when he tried to protect them, taking a beating from Cefus for his efforts each time. But even so, Eve never warmed up to him. Maybe it wasn't right to judge Junior for his father's deeds, but it was likely he would follow in his father's footsteps.

Yet, he walked away instead of hitting Terry.

As Junior opened the screen door to the house, he looked her way. Their gazes met briefly before Eve turned from the window and leaned against the wall. She exhaled, realizing she was holding her breath. Eve quickly crossed the room, heading for the basement.

Her mother waited at the bottom of the stairs. She was pacing and mumbling to herself. "What's going on?"

"I don't know. Junior is angry with Terry." Why he was angry, Eve didn't know.

Pearl nodded as if she knew something Eve didn't. She moved around Eve and opened her mouth to…

"What are you doing?" Eve grabbed hold of her mother's arm. "You can't call him to you. He's angry. He'll lash out, and you need to be careful," Eve said, pointedly glancing at her mother's rounding stomach.

Pearl squeezed Eve's hand then pushed it away. "Junior is nothing like his father, Eve. You know that," Pearl said. She studied Eve, her brows crinkling with confusion. "Don't you?"

Eve shifted under her mother's gaze, unsure of what she knew. Junior showed that he had more control than Cefus today, but how long would that last. Plus, Junior made her feel things. Things that excited and scared her, and she didn't want to feel this way.

She didn't want to feel anything at all.

Chained to the Devil's Son

FIVE

JUNIOR

Junior cursed then glanced at his alarm clock that sat on his nightstand. He had a few hours before he had to meet Coach Davy and some of his old friends he went to high school with for dinner. He couldn't wait to see Guzman, who came home from Texas to visit his parents' for the holidays. Junior knew that it was useless to dwell on his hard luck when he was genuinely happy that Guzman was playing college football.

"Get up and get ready," he urged, talking to himself.

A loud noise had Junior up, on his feet, and running toward the stairs. He descended the steps quickly, jumping down the last five. Junior's landing was less than stellar, and he was pretty sure he reinjured his bad leg, but he ignored the irritating ache as he pushed himself to move faster.

Cefus' raised voice blasted through the house, and Junior prayed Sadie and Eve didn't get to the basement before him. The relief Junior felt when he ran into them in the hallway almost knocked him on his ass. Sadie, the bigger of the two, rubbed her eyes to rid herself of sleep, successfully blocking Eve's exit.

"Stay here," Junior yelled as he moved past them as fast as he could. He glanced over his shoulder and saw that Sadie looked aware now. "Don't let Eve out of that room, Sadie." His sister would follow his instruction so that he only had to worry about Pearl…and his own skin, of course.

Cefus' voice carried through the basement door only to amplify as Junior pulled it open. "You nigger whore," his father yelled. A pained grunt followed.

It took everything Junior had to stay upright and push away the pain in his leg as he took two steps at a time. Pearl cowered against the wall beside her door, balled in the fetal position. Cefus stood over her, kicking Pearl with his booted foot. To prevent the next blow to Pearl's midsection, Junior pushed Cefus hard enough for his father to hit the far wall.

"Boy, I'm gonna fuckin' kill you," Cefus said after righting himself.

Junior saw Cefus' fist coming. The blow connected with Junior's jaw causing his head to snap back. The punch hurt like hell, but the very man he faced now and the years of beatings conditioned him. Junior shook off the sting, balled his fists at his sides, and spit out the blood collecting in his mouth. He angled his head so that his face was partially hidden but his eyes were visible.

"You can try," Junior said, licking blood from his bottom lip.

Junior rolled his shoulders and flexed his muscles. Coach made him work out until he was sure he'd pass out; didn't get him back on the football field but it did pay off. Junior discovered his love of the gym, to use fitness to relieve stress and tension.

Junior was taller, able to stand eye to eye with Cefus. Bigger, his body was always lean, but now he was more defined with more power behind every punch.

Cefus chuckled; his body coiled, ready to strike. "You think you can take me, boy?"

Junior stared at Cefus, taking a step back. He wasn't that weak kid anymore…physically anyway. He fought all comers and won, but he was still fighting the mental hold and his fear of his father.

Hold your ground, asshole. Junior took a step forward.

"No," Pearl climbed to her feet from behind Junior. "No, it's over... It's done." She was doubled over, unable to stand up fully. "See, I'm bleeding. It's done." She waved her bloodied hand in the air.

Junior watched as Cefus glanced at the blood on Pearl's hand. *Damn.* Junior took another step forward, but Pearl angled in his way.

Cefus grinned then focused back on Junior. "I'm gettin' tired of you steppin' in between me and my bone, boy. Families all you got, and that bitch ain't it." Junior didn't back down and actually tried to move Pearl out of the way. Cefus spit at his feet. "Then let's see what you got."

"Somebody's coming," Sadie called from the top of the stairs.

No one moved. Junior saw the tick of Cefus' jaw and wondered if his own jaw was ticking too. It wasn't until they heard the knock on the door that Cefus tilted his head toward the stairs but kept his hate-filled steel eyes on Junior. The smile that spread across his face was full of menace.

"Another time then," Cefus promised Junior with a wink. He then glared at Pearl. "I ain't done with you, you temptress bitch. Not by a long shot." Confident as ever, Cefus turned his back on Junior and stomped up the stairs.

Junior watched Cefus until he disappeared from view then wrapped his arms around Pearl just as she groaned. She was bleeding, but he wasn't able to tell where from. What if he wasn't home? He bit back the realization that he could have lost Pearl tonight.

Where is the blood coming from? "Where's the bleeding, Pearl?"

Junior frantically moved his hands over her face and head, tangling his hands in her thick tresses. He continued his search, moving to her neck then arms, but she grabbed hold of his face.

"Junior," she whispered loudly, "Junior." She struggled to get him to meet her gaze by holding his face in her hands. "Have you lost your mind?" Pearl gave his head a good shake. "He's going to kill you for this."

Junior blinked several times before he was able to focus on Pearl's face. He wanted to go after Cefus and rip out his father's spine and dance it into the dirt. He wanted him, Pearl, and the girls to walk out the door and never look back. He wanted to be free so badly that it was blinding.

Where can I take them? Will he come for us?

The walls seemed to be closing in on him. He needed to fix this. Junior moved to leave, but Pearl grabbed his arm. At that moment, a series of knocks hit the front door upstairs.

"You can't keep doing this," Pearl pleaded. "He's going to kill you." Pearl tugged at his arm when he tried to pull away. "Why don't you understand that your father is dangerous?"

"I can't sit back while he keeps hurting you," he shouted. "We can't keep living like this."

Pearl grabbed his face again. "Please, Junior," she begged. "I'm stronger than you think. I'm fine, I swear it." She dropped her hands and stood up to her full height. "The blood is from my monthly. I'm fine."

Junior could hear Cefus' voice from above. "Are you still trying to make that no-good kid of mine upstanding, Davy?"

Coach Davy responded, but what he said was low and unclear for Junior to hear down in the basement. Not thirty seconds passed before Junior heard the front door slam shut then soon after the engine of Cefus' truck roared to life. Coach was most likely still outside, waiting for him.

Torn, Junior stared at Pearl. The need to run after his bastard father was overwhelming. Winning wasn't an issue. He wouldn't win, and he didn't care. *You'll leave them unprotected*. Without his interference, the girls would be at the mercy of that asshole.

They couldn't take much more of this. They all needed out of this situation. "I can't keep…"

Pearl held his head steady and looked him directly in the eyes. "He will kill Eve and possibly Sadie if you keep this up. They've been off his radar, but if you keep pushing him… I won't be able to take it if something happens to her, Junior. I just can't," she sobbed.

Junior needed to think. In an effort to calm down, he closed his eyes and shut out the world around him and tried to remember something good. She invaded his thoughts instantly. He gasped, shocked that his mind had brought her forth when he hadn't thought about her in so long.

Cindy's bright blue eyes were so clear. The smile she always wore in these visions was beautiful and welcoming. Her long corn-silk blonde hair that flowed down her back and over her shoulder was the same color as his. He remembered that it used to tickle his face and neck whenever she held him close. Her skin was soft and always smelled like…she always smelled like fresh cotton. Junior used to love that about her.

"Junior," Pearl whispered and shook his head again.

Opening his eyes, Junior focused on Pearl's face and the pleading look she wore.

"Your friends are getting impatient," she said then grimaced. The knocking on the front door had become frantic.

Junior wanted it all to be over, brought to light. At that moment, he didn't care what Cefus would do to him. He was tired and wanted it done. But he had to think of the end result too.

"Junior?" Guzman's muffled call reached Junior in the basement.

"Go," Eve whispered, "I'll take care of my mom."

Junior didn't even notice that Eve came down into the basement. It was what she always did when someone came to the house, but Junior wasn't thinking straight right now. He focused on her for a moment, and some foreign feeling took hold and tightened in his chest. The feeling was gone just as fast as it appeared.

Junior nodded but avoided looking at Pearl or Eve. He climbed the stairs, passing Sadie as he hurried through the first floor to get to the door. He pulled the front door open just before Guzman could knock again.

"Shit, man." Guzman had his arm raised in the air, prepared to knock at the door again. "I thought that asshole had done something to you." Guzman visually examined Junior then smiled. "He's fine, Coach," he called out then pulled Junior into a hug. "I missed the shit out of you, man."

Junior hugged Guzman back but looked to Coach Davy as he came from around the side of the house. Coach appeared relieved. "I fell asleep. Sorry," Junior mumbled. Junior saw how Coach and Guzman eyed one another. "We're gonna be late, we should get going." He led the way to the car. Both men silently followed.

The conversation during the drive to meet the rest of the guys was light. They talked about the weather, Texas, how Guzman liked the football program, and college girls. Guzman frowned when Junior didn't show much interest in talking about Texan babes, but he knew enough not to dwell.

After dinner with a few fellas from the old team, they drove to their old high school and played a light game of football for fun and old time sake. Being on the field again felt good, but Junior wasn't able to focus much so he sat out the last half of the game. His mind kept returning to Pearl, her bloody hand, and Eve.

"Woman trouble," Coach asked?

Junior hung his head. "It's that obvious?"

"Well," Coach said as he sat beside him, "I heard about you and Terry." Junior just nodded. "Plus your best friend is in town and you haven't smiled once tonight. Not that you smile a lot but…I thought if anyone could put a smile on your face it would be Guzman."

"Never had much to smile about, Coach," Junior said, "but I can assure you that Terry is the furthest thing from my mind."

"Anything I can do?"

At that moment the football whizzed toward them, causing Coach to duck out of the way. Junior easily caught the ball and hurled it back at Guzman, who flashed them a grin as he caught the return throw.

"Nope," Junior said, popping the p as he turned back to Coach.

Coach was always there for all of the guys on the team, but he put in extra time and effort with Junior. Junior appreciated it because in all honesty. Coach Davy was his only male role model.

Coach nodded as if he understood Junior was remiss to discuss his problem, but then he said, "I want you boys to succeed. Not just in football but in life. Football didn't happen for you, Junior, but that doesn't mean you won't succeed in life. I didn't see myself as a coach for my old high school, but I love what I do. I've got a good wife, two awesome children, and you boys." He placed his hand on Junior's shoulder. "What I'm trying to say is that if you find something you love, if it's a job, a woman, or a hobby, you may find the peace you *need*. You have a gentle spirit like your mother."

Junior tensed at the mention of his mother. "I don't remember much about her. She left when I was so young."

"I know, son. It confused me and Patricia at the time and still when my wife brings up her old friend, we can't understand why Cindy up and left you both. My Patricia and your mom were very close, so she often struggles with not hearing from Cindy. I imagine you and Sadie struggle with her absence too, and living under Cefus' brand of parenting can't be easy. What I can tell you is that Cindy was decent and fair. You have that part of her inside you, Junior, and if you find what makes you happy, that dark side you got from your father won't be fed."

Junior didn't respond at first. He just sat there quietly as he absorbed what Coach told him. Then he sighed and said, "I'm solid, Coach."

Coach dropped his hand off of Junior's shoulder and cleared his throat. "Good. So, about this woman trouble... If it's not Terry, then which of our girls has caught your eye?"

Without pause, an image of Eve formed in Junior's mind. A memory soon followed.

It was a few months ago when she and Sadie were seated on his bedroom floor as they played in each other's hair. He was on his bed reading an old car magazine when Eve's laughter caught his attention. It was a quiet infectious giggle. Rare, of course, but it had the power that could make the surliest person happy. Junior looked over at her and for some unexplained reason, Eve seemed different to him.

Junior realized at that moment just how adorable the mole on her neck just under her jaw was. Her cute nose slightly turned up at the end, and her soft, big brown, soulful eyes that were shadowed by impossibly long lashes was so clear to him at that moment. He took in her smooth, unblemished cocoa skin, the thick coils of her long raven hair she often kept covered, and her perfectly-shaped pouty lips.

For the first, Junior saw a young woman and not just the kid he needed to protect. That didn't make him smile then. It confused him if anything. But he smiled at the memory now.

A husky roll of laughter came from Coach Davy. "Looks like you've already found what's going to make you happy."

Junior shook his head. "I don't think so."

"Don't give up just yet, son. The way I hear it, you have a way with the ladies."

"Not this one." With that said, Junior rose, deciding to rejoin the game.

CEFUS

Cefus took a long drink from his beer then lowered it, never fully resting the bottle on the bar. The Tow Hole Gentleman's Club was located in the middle of nowhere and was almost two hours from his home. The music was so loud that you had to get up close and personal to hear another person talk. The building was filled with the smell of cigarettes, cologne, and sweat. And the place sold flat, expensive beer and greasy, tasteless food but the women were a strong draw.

Pure American ass and tits were why Cefus drove the distance. Plus, he liked the Tow Hole. Cefus felt at home at any place that sold him booze. It wasn't his usual watering hole; hell he passed three bars on the way, but he needed to get his head on straight, and that meant some distance and relief.

That black bitch is gonna push me too damn far, he thought as he finished his beer and slammed the bottle on the bar. She successfully turned his goddamn son against him. Junior always tried to protect the whore when he was younger, but Cefus hoped to beat the care out of him. He hoped Junior would be more like him than Cindy.

I'm gone need to do something about that boy and soon.

Cefus ignored the irritated look the bartender gave when he slammed the bottle down. He pushed his stool back and moved to take a seat near the stage. He chose a seat that had no one on either side then called over the waitress.

Mallory, a waitress he occasionally spent private time with, sauntered over and took his order. She had a nice ass and a pretty enough face. Not an elegant beauty like Pearl, or even a county-fair beauty like Cindy, but she had her uses.

Cefus grunted as he thought of the two whores who complicated his life.

Mallory placed his beer in front of him, and Cefus tipped her. She gave him a sweet smile and arched her back a bit so her ass stuck out of her little black ruffled skirt as she walked away. His cock twitched as thoughts of what he planned to do to her tonight went through his mind. Paying for pussy wasn't something he liked doing, but sometimes a man needed his cock in a mouth that wouldn't go all Jaws on him.

Their agreement was an unspoken one. If he showed up at the club and Mallory was there, they left together at the end of her shift. It didn't matter what her other plans were because Mallory always put him first whenever he was there. Women always wanted more.

Until they get to know me, he chuckled.

With his plans for tonight solidified, Cefus relaxed and watched the show. It wasn't until he'd been sitting for thirty minutes without a refill that he realized Mallory didn't check in. A quick glance around told him that the place wasn't too busy. After another ten minutes, Cefus got up and made his way to the bar.

"Another beer," Cefus demanded. "Mallory still around," he asked as he waited for his beer.

The bartender, a bald, bearded guy with watchful eyes, gave him what could be a 'fuck off' look but then nodded to the area of the club where the owner and VIPs hung out. Cefus looked over his shoulder at the closed-off area.

Usually, that section of the club was empty, mostly unused, but tonight it was bustling with a buffet of scantily-clad women and high-cost liquor, all focused on one man.

Cefus grabbed his beer and made his way back to his table by the stage where he could get a better look at the man of the hour. It surprised him that the 'man' looked more like a 'boy' of the hour. The kid didn't look much older than Junior.

Cefus knew how good looking he was. Looking at this kid, though, Cefus refused to admit to himself he was a little jealous. This kid and his son shared the same shade of corn-silk blond hair any white American would be proud of. Cefus had black hair. It was one of the things about himself he couldn't help.

Cefus noted more things about the stranger when the kid turned around and stared right at him. The boy had a proud straight nose, a chiseled jaw, dimpled chin, and a set of determined brows. He also had the oddest green-blue eyes Cefus ever saw. And what was even odder was the fact that the eye color was clearly visible under the dim lighting.

A bad ass in his own right, Cefus held the kid's gaze. He felt his anger stir when the kid smirked as he whispered something to Mallory, who happened to be seated on his lap. The kid continued to stare at Cefus then gently pushed Mallory to her feet. He tapped Mallory on the ass as she walked away; all the while he continued to stare at Cefus.

Irritated and always ready for a brawl, Cefus slammed his unfinished beer down on the table and got to his feet. Everyone else in the shithole of a club knew Mallory was his when he was there. He would just have to teach this snot-nosed kid the same lesson he taught the others that thought to challenge him.

And he fucking felt challenged.

As Cefus made his way toward the VIP area, he noticed how all the girls laughed, smiled, and catered to the brat. He was probably some rich man's son that had more than enough money to spend. And that was okay with Cefus. It was better to see money in the white man's hands than the lesser races, but the little shit had purposely goaded him and needed to be taught a lesson.

It was a flash of black, seen from the corner of his eye that had Cefus focusing in another direction. Mallory was shuffling away from the asshole that owned the place and moving toward the rear of the club where the offices and dressing rooms were located.

Cefus stopped in his tracks. *Where the hell is she goin'?* Cefus looked at his watch. It was only 12:30 a.m. Mallory had a little more than an hour to go before they headed out. Cefus changed direction and headed for Mallory.

"You know the rules, Cowboy," the owner said as he placed a hand on Cefus' chest.

Cefus stopped a few feet from his destination. He swatted away the hand that dared to touch him. "Don't touch me unless you want a broken hand." His threat got the attention of two of the big men that policed the place. The two men walked up and took positions behind him. Cefus ignored them as he and the owner faced off.

After a few seconds of them eyeing one another, neither wanting to give in, Mallory stepped out from the back. She looked nervous when she noticed Cefus. "Uh...I uh," she stumbled over her words. Then she looked past Cefus to the VIP section. That seemed to give her confidence. Mallory straightened and said with conviction, "Something came up. I can't meet with you after my shift tonight." She moved past the small gathering and walked toward the exit, ignoring Cefus.

Cefus followed Mallory, also ignoring the men that followed him. "What the fuck do you mean you can't meet with me? And where the hell are you goin'?" Cefus grabbed her arm when she reached to open the door. He swung her around to face him.

"Now, buddy, you know it's hands off the girls unless they want you to touch them," one of the muscle head's said.

Cefus dropped Mallory's arm and turned to face the pair. He usually only had to straighten out a customer or two with no interference while hanging out here, but he wasn't averse to putting these two in their place. One of them looked to be some kind of mutt mixed-breed while the other seemed to be white, though you can't be sure these days. What Cefus was sure of was that the white guy had chosen the wrong side when he paired up with the mutt to go against him.

Feeling a little tipsy but sure, Cefus swung a fist at the mutt, connecting with his jaw. Taken off guard, the mutt fell into a passing customer. The white guy didn't move quick enough, and Cefus managed to hit him solid in the gut. With a chuckle and a pointed glare at the owner who was watching, Cefus grinned then left the club to find Mallory.

The parking lot was big, but it didn't take Cefus long to locate her. The kid was leaning on some fancy sports car only a city boy would drive, with Mallory situated between his legs. They were too far away to make what he was saying, but the kid was talking to her, and her dumb ass was eating up his every word.

Angry, Cefus closed the distance.

He never had to hit Mallory before. She listened like a woman should, but the bitch was gonna be punished for this. Before Cefus reached them, the kid opened the passenger side door, and Mallory ducked inside. That pissed Cefus off more.

"She's leavin' with me, boy," Cefus said as he reached for the door handle. He didn't even get hold of the car handle before he was on his ass with a blood spurting from his nose.

What the hell just happened?

"The name is Caleb Scott, Shaw, not boy. You should remember that."

A little disorientated but much more pissed off, Cefus jumped to his feet. His gaze fell on Mallory first. She sat in the car facing forward, her face expressionless. Cefus thought it odd that she wasn't watching them, but he figured that she'd seen him bust a few heads before and wasn't anxious to see it again.

She'd see enough blood when he got her ass to the motel. Cefus found his target when he shifted his view. Eager to get this fight over with, punish, then bury himself inside Mallory's mouth, Cefus faced the punk kid, Caleb, with his signature grin. Cefus had to admit that the kid had balls. The fact that he managed to get in a lucky punch was odd but to top that off, the little fuck actually laughed when presented with the look that made most people piss their pants.

Cefus struck out, but the kid easily dodged the punch. He threw two more but none of them hit their mark. There was a pain in his right side, then Cefus found himself on his ass again. Pain exploded from his side as he moved to get up, but Cefus only let out a curse. The pain sobered him right up and amplified by ten when Caleb yanked him to his feet. Cefus dangled like a cat being held by the neck, the tips of his toes barely touching the ground.

As he looked at the kid, Caleb, whose name he would probably never forget, Cefus realized he pegged this guy all wrong. The pretty-boy rich brat was a rouse because the eyes Cefus stared into were those of a seasoned killer.

"What to do? What to do," Caleb asked, actually seeming to contemplate his options. "I thought that the taint of your bloodline would diminish with breeding. Clearly, in your case, I was wrong."

Cefus' attempts to free himself were useless. Never one to back down, Cefus ordered, "Let me go, you asshole." The strength Caleb had to hold him up like he was a rag doll was unnatural, and Cefus had to wonder if he was drunker than he thought.

Caleb frowned then shook Cefus like a troublesome pet. "Just being around you for under an hour has tested my patience. Oh, how I would love to end you right now. But life, even one as worthless as yours, has value – a penny perhaps. I suppose there is hope; that son of yours has promise." Cefus watched as Caleb cocked his head to the side as if listening to something. "I bet without your influence for a time he may just free himself from your miserable clutches."

With more care than Cefus expected, Caleb lowered him to his feet. It was then that the sound of sirens filled the night. Clutching his side, Cefus cursed again. No one ever called cops to the Tow Hole. The meatheads usually dealt with any problems on their own.

What happened tonight that got the cops called?

A banging noise behind him had Cefus turning his head around to the Tow Hole's door. The loud, annoying music from inside the club filtered out through the opened door. The bartender stood in the doorway, scanning the parking lot. When his gaze fell on Cefus, he pushed his shoulders back and hollered, "Don't you fucking move."

In pain, angry, and a bit confused, Cefus looked around the parking lot until his gaze fell on a new scene. Mallory was out of the car and leaning over Caleb, who was spread out on the ground beside his car. The guy's shirt was torn, and his face was battered and bruised.

What the hell was goin' on?

The next thing Cefus knew, he was being lowered into the back of a police cruiser. Apparently, the bouncers weren't going to press charges but that freak of nature, Caleb Scott planned to.

Cefus stared at Caleb as he sat on the ground accepting medical attention from the emergency workers. All the while looking like an innocent kid. Yet, when that sadistic grin and those eerie green-blue eyes met his, Cefus saw more demon than do-gooder.

Cefus had been bested. "Fuck!" he yelled.

SIX

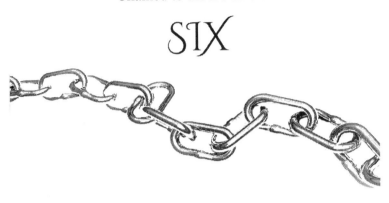

JUNIOR

Junior was mentally exhausted when he got out of Coach's car. He missed Guzman, and if it were any other time, he would have enjoyed seeing his best friend, but his mind was with Pearl and the girls. All night he worried that Cefus returned home before he could. That his murderous father probably finished the job he started about six years ago. That Pearl and Eve were now buried in the yard by the old, dead tree he used to climb as a kid.

By the time he said his goodbyes, Junior was wired and ready to explode. He didn't wait for Coach to pull off before he ran up the porch steps. With his keys, the ones he'd fiddled with the entire night, Junior pushed open the front door. He was immediately taken back by the silence that met him. He closed and secured the front door then took measured steps toward the basement.

A terrible scream sliced through the silence.

Junior hurried through the house and down the basement stairs, skidding over the last few. He made up his mind while out. Tonight they were leaving and if he had to kill Cefus... Well, he would if he had to.

The door to the room Pearl occupied was wide open and what Junior saw on the other side of it stopped him in his tracks. Pearl lay flat on her back with her legs bent, her dress was hiked to her stomach, and a pillow in her hands that she had pressed against her chest. She was sweaty, looked tired, and she continuously gasped for air. Eve sat beside Pearl's head, wiping her face with a cloth while Sadie was positioned between…between Pearl's legs.

A look of pain crossed Pearl's face then another scream charged the air, this one louder than the one before. Even with Pearl planting her face into the pillow. Junior made a strangled sound that was loud enough to get everyone's attention. But Pearl's face was the only one he focused on. Her pained expression disappeared, replaced with a look of fear then relief.

Junior opened his mouth to say something, anything, but he swallowed his words as the sound of a baby's first cry stunned him into silence.

Eve

Eve watched in awe as her mother nestled the newborn to her breast. She never saw something as amazing or alarming as childbirth before. The books she read on the subject, to help out when needed, could have never prepared her for the reality of it all. She'd never seen her mother in so much pain before. The entire experience was frightening, and if it wasn't for Sadie's help, things might have gone horribly wrong.

Sadie sat on the edge of the bed with a look of pure love and admiration on her face as she peered at the baby. Her mother, exhausted and half asleep, didn't immediately grab for the small boy. He cried for a short while, and their mother vacantly looked at him. Eve was too scared to move. It took Sadie to place the baby in his mother's arms and offer him her mother's nipple for him to quiet.

For months, Eve and her mother feared Cefus would harm the unborn child, but they managed to keep him in the dark. Well, until today. By all accounts, the baby was a miracle. Cefus discovered the others, each time beating them out of her mother. But the tiny little guy who was latched onto her mother's breast survived.

Eve didn't really know how she felt about the baby yet. All she knew was that when Cefus found out, he was going to be very upset. Her mother was usually his target and in her condition, weak and recovering from childbirth, she wouldn't be able to take his punishment.

Maybe Junior could take it somewhere before Cefus returned. Leave it on some nice folk's doorsteps or something.

Eve hardly prayed. Her mother being the religious one, giving thanks and offering her praise even though help never came. But Eve couldn't help asking for divine intervention when she realized her mother was in labor and in pain. She prayed that her mother would survive the birth. So when Sadie stepped forward taking control of the situation, for the first time in Eve's life she thought that maybe there was hope.

"Sadie was amazing," Eve said. She looked up at Junior, who still looked a little pale, then to Sadie. "She knew exactly what she was doing."

"Yeah," Junior offered as he looked to his sister then to the baby. "Because the hospital is so far, my mom and a few other women trained to be midwives. Sadie would often tag along and eventually she was helping them deliver babies."

Eve watched as Sadie scooted closer to the babe and began caressing his tiny head. The baby was small. His skin was light and creamy but wrinkled. He had a full head of silky, straight black hair that curled at the ends. Eve couldn't quite decide if she thought he was a cute baby or not.

"What are we going to do?" Junior asked. He scrubbed his hand over his face then looked at the baby again.

The thought of leaving the baby on someone's porch lit up in Eve's head like a spotlight. She was about to pull Junior aside and offer the solution, but Junior didn't wait for a response. He spun around and ran up the stairs.

Junior's sudden burst into action brought Eve's thoughts to a halt. Where was he going? Eve glanced at her mother who was asleep while the baby nursed. She could see the bond Sadie had with the baby as clear as day. Her mother, on the other hand, she wasn't so sure a connection was there, considering who its father was. Her mother protected it when she carried him. But now that the result of her abuse was actually here, Eve wasn't sure how her mother felt.

What Eve knew was that the babe would be fine in Sadie's care. So she hurried after Junior, again happy to have no chains to hinder her movements. She found Junior in his bedroom. He had a pillowcase in his hand and was stuffing it with his belongings. A duffle bag filled with clothing and his extra pair of sneakers sat open on his bed.

Junior didn't look at her when he said, "Gather whatever you don't want to leave behind."

Eve couldn't believe her ears. Excitement and fear flowed through her as the thought of her and her mother being free of this place. "Where are we going?" As soon as the question came out, she wanted to take it back. She didn't care where they went as long as it was away from Cefus.

Junior looked utterly lost as he avoided her eyes. The worried expression that crossed his face told her that he didn't know nor had a plan. Either way, Eve didn't care. And she wouldn't let him care either. She was about to tell him so when a hard knock sounded at the door. They locked eyes, both pairs wide with fear.

JUNIOR

Something dark and cold crept up Junior's spine as he descended the stairs, and it wasn't from the cool draft that always seemed to reside in the house. The door shook with the force of the fist that pounded on it, but that didn't coax him to move any faster. He wanted to stall because he needed a plan, but making Cefus wait would not go over well.

Scared, angry, unsure; nothing came close to describing Junior's internal struggle as he took each step toward the inevitable confrontation that stood behind the front door. It was time to finish this, and there was no turning back.

If only we had more time, time to leave before he came back.

The banging grew in force and urgency as Junior approached. Cefus lost his keys only a few times in the past that he could remember. The first was when Grandpa Shaw, Cefus' father, passed on. Junior didn't remember that one, but the two other times were both on the anniversary of Cindy's escape of him, of them.

If Cefus was drunk enough…

Junior shook the hurt from his mind and readied himself as he stood in front of the door. Each time Cefus lost his keys, he was too drunk to move let alone think. Sheriff Gifford drove him home, and it was Sheriff Gifford who knocked at the door now. Junior knew it, and that meant Cefus would soon know about the baby.

I need more time.

"Junior," Sheriff Gifford yelled, "I will break this damn door down if I have to."

A creak that sounded behind him had Junior whipping his head around. Eve crept down the stairs and was moving toward the kitchen. He waved at her to move faster then called out, "I'm coming."

When Junior opened the door, he didn't expect to see just Sheriff Gifford standing on the porch. The sheriff's car sat on the drive, running with headlights on, but it was too dark for him to see inside. Sighing, Junior moved past Sheriff Gifford to help his father inside but was pulled back by his arm. Junior quickly yanked free of the sheriff's hold. The touch wasn't painful but at the same time, Junior didn't want the sheriff to touch him—ever.

"Your Pa ain't in the car," Sheriff Gifford said as he adjusted his hat. "I came to tell you he's decided to go away for a spell."

Another vacation?

The last "vacation" Cefus Shaw took was a few months before the Jones' arrived. Junior and Sadie continued their normal routine, having no place else to go. He went to school, and she helped out the neighbors during the day. At night, Sadie cooked, and he cleaned. It was the most peaceful and stress-free time in their lives. Sheriff Gifford checked on them often. He and his sister knew better to ask for anything or about Cefus.

Cefus stayed gone almost an entire month then.

Sighing, as if he was annoyed and wasn't beaming inside, Junior moved back to the front door and pushed it open then tapped it to close. He may just get a little time to plan their escape.

"Junior," Gifford called. Junior stopped the door from closing and turned around. "New rules, since you've grown a bit. Cross into another county with or without your sister without my knowing or talk about your guest to anyone, we will hunt you all down and drag your asses back here." Sheriff Gifford regarded Junior's bawled fist with a smirk but settled his hand around his gun. "Sadie will be tortured and used before we kill her, then you'll be locked in a hole and charged with her murder."

Junior saw red, and his eyes must have reflected his anger because he moved an inch toward his target and was staring at the barrel of a police-issued pistol.

Cursing, Sheriff Gifford grinned. "It amazes me that you still got fight in you, boy. I thought for sure Cefus beat that buck out of you. Think on this," Sheriff Gifford said with a calmness that spoke arrogance. "When you're dead, what's gonna happen to your sister...and your pa's pets? I have no taste for either, but I promise you that finding volunteers won't be too hard. I'm sure you've heard that Sadie already has an admirer."

Junior forced himself to relax his hands and took a step back.

"Glad we understand each other." Sheriff Gifford studied him for a while, with the gun still pointed at his head. Something sparked in the lawman's eyes that Junior swore was interest, but then the sheriff shook his head. "Next time you even look like you want to oppose me, I will shoot you. Don't for one second think that I don't know how to make a body disappear. Now get the hell inside." As Junior backed through the doorway, Sheriff Gifford kept the gun trained on him. "Remember, someone will always be watching, boy." Sheriff Gifford winked as Junior closed the door.

Eve didn't know what to do as she walked down the basement stairs. Above her, Junior was on the porch talking to someone. Below, Sadie was posted in front of her mother's room. The door was closed and Sadie held a rusted pipe in her hands and a look of determination on her face. Eve was certain Sadie was prepared to defend the baby and his mother with her life.

The sight of gentle Sadie with a potentially deadly weapon, the birth, and fear of what Cefus would do, had Eve drained. She didn't know how drained and exhausted she was until the front door slammed upstairs. Drained or not, none of that mattered because Cefus was home and she was prepared to fight or die.

We're leaving tonight.

Eve allowed that knowledge to sink in and infuse her with strength and determination. So when she heard the commotion upstairs, she glanced up knowing it was time to fight back. Eve turned her attention to Sadie and then the closed door her mother was behind. She debated with herself about staying and protecting her mother, the baby, and Sadie or to go help Junior. Eve lowered her head then lifted her gaze back to Sadie, who looked just as conflicted. It wasn't until they heard a gut-wrenching howl that both of them came to a silent decision.

Sadie moved first. Eve followed, determined that she was going to help Junior and Sadie protect her mother and the baby with her dying breath if she had to. Both of them darted through the kitchen. Eve was on Sadie's heels so when Sadie stopped short, Eve ran into her. They stumbled forward but managed to stay on their feet.

It only took a second for Eve to right herself, and when she did, she looked around the living room, stunned. It looked as if a tornado was let loose. The tables were broken, furniture turned over, photos and magazines were scattered. The only thing left untouched was the small television and the stand it sat on.

A hollow ache pulsed through Eve's chest as she surveyed the mess. If this was the state of the house...what would Junior look like?

"Junior," Sadie breathed.

That was when Eve saw him. Junior stood with his back to them. His shoulders rose and sank with every deep breath he took. His head was lowered, but his profile was visible, his fists were balled up, and his body rigid. He looked lethal, and it was a look she was all too familiar with.

Eve forced her gaze away from Junior to search for Cefus. It wasn't long before she realized Cefus wasn't in the room...or in the house for that matter. Then it dawned on Eve. The disarray in the room was caused by Junior and him alone.

"Where's Pa?" Sadie's tone was low, careful.

Junior tilted his head in their direction but didn't look at them. "Both of you go back downstairs."

Without waiting for Junior to repeat himself, Eve pulled a reluctant Sadie with her as she backed away. Quietly, they walked through the kitchen and down the basement stairs. All the while Eve's mind raced with questions. What happened? Why did Junior freak out? What would Cefus do when he returned? And what would he do when he saw that he fathered a baby with the nigger he loved to hate?

JUNIOR

Junior took the gathered wood from the broken side tables and went out to the unused barn that sat on their property. It took some time to unlock the thick chains used to secure the barn doors, but he unlatched the lock.

With his anger still on the surface after the sheriff left, Junior went to his father's bedroom and kicked in the closet door. He quickly found the lockbox that sat on a high shelf, which held the keys to every lock his father claimed as his property and pried it open.

Now, he peered up at the barn with a weary heart. The last time Junior was in the old structure was years ago. That night he hid evidence of a murder. He was the one who drove the wagon and the small cargo trailer that was hitched to it inside this barn.

Junior took a step forward, then another, and soon he was inside the barn. It was dark, with only the light from the moon spilling in through the open double doors. The way the light illuminated the space was creepy and a feeling of nausea surfaced along with painful memories. Junior took a shaky, deep breath then quickly buried the horrors that the space brought forth and glanced around. It appeared that no one had been inside since that night.

Walking over the threshold, Junior moved past the trailer that leaned to one side, most likely due to a flat tire. It was dusty, untouched for years, and when he made it to the driver's side window, a bloody handprint on the door was still visible even in the moonlight.

His print, Mr. Jones' blood.

Junior jumped back, dropping the broken pieces of table to the dirt floor. He vigorously rubbed his hands on his jeans as if blood still covered them. *Lingering inside here is ridiculous,* he told himself as he briefly closed his eyes. Junior turned and stomped back to the entrance and started hauling the rest of the broken pieces of furniture into the barn. It took a few trips, but when he was done, he locked the barn doors up again and made his way back to the house.

"What happened?"

Junior didn't look at Sadie. She was standing between the living room and kitchen, waiting for him. She wanted answers, Eve did too, but he couldn't give them anything. Not when he didn't have any to give.

"Not now, Sadie," Junior said as he moved around her without meeting her pleading gaze. "Tomorrow,"—he continued toward the stairs— "I'll tell you tomorrow."

"Okay."

His sister's soft voice echoed in his head as he made his way to his room. He had small cuts on his hands that needed cleaning, he needed to come up with a plan, and there was a baby in the mix. Right now, all he wanted…needed, was to sleep. So when his body hit the mattress, and his head fell to the pillow, which had no casing, his eyes closed and his brain shut down almost immediately. Yet, in his sleepy haze, Junior felt a gentle, comforting warmth that brushed over his cheek, warmth that he nestled into.

Eve

Why on earth she followed him to his room, Eve couldn't say. Even more perplexing was why she sat on the edge of his bed and touched him, caressing his face. That was a bigger mystery.

Had she lost her mind? That was the question Eve kept asking herself as she prepared breakfast the next morning.

Cefus didn't return last night, but it wasn't unusual for him to stay out all night or all week for that matter. Junior was still in his room, asleep. She and Sadie slept in the basement. Well, Eve didn't sleep. She kept watch until about fifteen minutes ago then decided to cook. Her mother needed to eat.

As the thick slices of bacon sizzled in the frying pan, Eve looked out of the small kitchen window that gave her a view of the side and some of the rear of the property. A large old bare tree stood apart, alone. The frost of the winter's breath left chilled dew over everything outside, but the tree seemed...unaffected. Its thick, naked branches pointed in every direction, and even without leaves the tree looked strong and full of life. It looked peaceful and chaotic.

"We need to talk."

The deep sound of Junior's voice had Eve jumping around and raising the fork above her head in defense. Her heart thumped as if it were a caged rabbit fighting to get free. It wasn't until she looked at Junior's expressive eyes that she lowered the fork but didn't fully relax.

Junior looked hurt then offended. His wounded gaze changed as he looked at her face. When she found his eyes again, it was anger Eve saw in them. She took an apprehensive step back. Her movement seemed to provoke Junior more, and he grunted before looking away.

Eve stared at his back as he walked to the kitchen table and took a seat. She stood stock still as she watched him place his elbows on the table then dropped his head in his hands. Junior rubbed his head a few times before returning his attention to her. Eve quickly turned around and busied herself with finishing breakfast.

Occasionally, she felt his eyes on her, but she didn't turn around. When the food was done, she separated it into four portions. She placed one in front of Junior without looking at him. She left one healthy serving on the counter for Cefus, then took the two others and quickly headed to the basement. Before she put her foot on the step to go downstairs, Junior spoke.

"We need to talk so…"

"I'm just giving this to Mom and Sadie," she whispered then hurried downstairs.

JUNIOR

Junior didn't know what he expected when he entered the kitchen this morning, but what he got almost sent him into a rage. He found Eve in the kitchen cooking as usual, but this morning her hair was uncovered. Frizzy, loose waves hung to her mid-back. She was wearing one of the more fitted dresses that Sadie had given her, revealing her feminine curves that he had no clue was even there. Eve was slender but had filled out in all the places that mattered to a man. Her waist was small, her hips wider and her round…

She shouldn't be dressed like that.

"We need to talk," he told her. And what did she do…? She damn near came out of her skin with fright. Every time she looked at him with those brown fear-laced eyes of hers, he wanted to scream. He wanted to cry out that he would never hurt her. That he would die protecting her and the others. He almost did a few times, yet she still feared him.

When she shrank away earlier, he wanted to hit something. Instead, he sat down at the table and tried to rub some calm in his head as he counted to twenty. He tried not to look at her when she put a plate of food in front of him, but he did watch her hips sway as she walked away.

Did she even know she was doing it? Or what a walk like that did to a man? What men like Cefus would do to her?

Irritated even more, Junior pushed his plate aside and repeated one thru twenty again. Calmer, he could only imagine what Eve was trying to say to convince Pearl to eat today. It was common for Eve to make a hearty plate of food for Pearl when Cefus stayed out all night. Usually, the two ate starches and beans but only given meat whenever he or Sadie snuck it to them.

When Eve appeared in the basement doorway a few minutes later, her head hung, and her hands were busy twisting a strand of her hair near her breast. She looked so innocent that he mentally kicked himself for thinking of her in the way he was lately. She was seventeen, but her knowledge of the world was much less than her actual age.

"Sit," Junior told her. It came out more like an order and not like a request so when Eve sat on the floor he cursed. He really had to get his shit together when around her. "Not on the floor, Eve. In the chair." He pointed at the space across from him.

Eve's big, doe eyes looked at him with curiosity, but she stood up, slowly. She moved silently to the table, watching him as she did. Junior forced himself not to look at her body as she approached. It was a hard fight, but he won and felt relieved when Eve made it to the chair and sat after a brief hesitation.

Her eyes were cast down at the table.

"Cef-," Junior stopped when he heard Eve's stomach grumble. "For goodness sakes," he said as he pushed out of his seat. He went to the counter, grabbed the plate that was usually meant for Cefus, then went back to the table and sat down placing the hefty portion in front of her. "Eat," he said, meaning it to sound like an order this time.

Eve raised her gaze to his, hers confused.

"Eat," he said again. Junior picked up his fork and began to eat. It was an effort on his part to make her feel more comfortable because he definitely didn't have an appetite at the moment.

She didn't pick up the fork right away. For a few minutes, all she did was watch him eat, but he figured that her hunger got the best of her because she eventually lifted the fork and dug in.

"Cefus is going to be away for a few days and..." He started but couldn't find the words he wanted to say next.

Eve stopped eating and looked at him. The hope in her eyes burst outward like the sun but with his continued silence that glow dulled then died. "But we can't leave."

"No," Junior admitted, "he has Sheriff Gifford and who knows who else watching us." He sighed then said, "That's who was at the door last night. He warned me to stay put, or he will kill Sadie and say I did it. He said he would then take you and Pearl, do what he wanted with you."

Her eyes watered. "What are you going to do?"

"I don't know yet. Last time he left it was for a little over three weeks. It was just me and Sadie then. Your mom isn't well."

"What of the baby," she whispered.

He had no answers for her. "I don't know..."

Eve sat up straighter; her watery eyes looking more focused and sure. "We should take the baby away. Give him to a family that can take care of him." She lowered her head and added, "Before he comes back and..."

Stunned, Junior just stared at her for several seconds. "No," Junior said, frowning, "the babe stays with us. He's our blood. He leaves when we leave."

"Okay."

Okay... What did that mean? Junior shook his head. Did she not trust that he wanted out of this hell hole? He needed Eve to know that he was going to get them to freedom; he just had to come up with a plan. "We are getting out of here, together, I promise. It's just...we have to wait a little while longer."

"Okay," she said again before looking back at her food. Eve nodded then started to eat again.

For several minutes, Junior watched Eve eat. At first, he stared because she threw him for a loop with her comment then with her acceptance. But after a moment of watching her, he realized he took pleasure in seeing her eat, filling her belly. He found himself lost in her movements. For someone who was raised in captivity, she carried herself with grace and poise. Her shoulders back, her head up but her eyes were on her food, her elbows off the table.

Eve's dark hair was free, a wavy mass of dark length that she pushed back and behind her ears a few times. He wanted desperately to touch it, understanding now why Pearl demanded that she covered it up. The dress she wore was red and blue, the colors long faded from wear and wash. It was loose but still fit in ways that it shouldn't.

"Why are you wearing that? Why is your hair not covered?" His words must have startled her because Eve looked up at him with wide eyes filled with fear. Again, her fear angered him.

"We needed all we could find for the birth, blood." Eve looked down, and when she lifted her head, she never met his eyes. Anytime their eyes ever met it was always brief, never lasting longer than a moment. "My hair,"—she took hold of a thick piece and stroked it— "I...I just forgot to tie it up."

"You can't-" Junior started to speak but stopped because he noticed Sadie entered the room. She stood at the top of the stairs with a bundle tightly wrapped in her arms.

"He needs milk," Sadie said, looking sad and worried. "Pearl too weak to feed good."

Junior jumped to his feet. He was in the basement and kneeling over Pearl within seconds. Her skin seemed paler, not its usual smooth, beautiful glow, when not bruised. She was asleep or too tired to open her eyes, and she was shivering. Without another thought, Junior pulled the keys from his pocket and unlocked the chain then lifted Pearl and the blankets that covered her in his arms.

"What are you doing?" Pearl's voice was weak and low.

"I'm moving you upstairs. It's too cold down here, and I want you to be more comfortable." Junior held her close as he slowly carried her up the basement stairs. His leg definitely wasn't going to reward him for the extra weight, but Junior did what he always did. He dismissed the pain and focused on his task.

"Where are you taking her?"

"To my room," Junior said. Only Eve blocked his way.

"You can't walk up another flight of stairs. Your leg," she said, reaching for her mom.

"My room, my bed," Sadie offered then led the way.

They were both right and though Junior didn't want to accept defeat. He knew he may not be able to make it up to his room. So he nodded and followed Sadie to her room where he lay Pearl down on the bed. She looked so frail that Junior found himself doing something he'd never done before. He leaned down and put his forehead to hers for several seconds. When he lifted, he kissed Pearl on the head.

Junior stood, moved toward the door, and out of the room. "I'm going to the store so make a list of everything you all need." When he approached the stairs that led to his room, he hesitated for a moment before shaking his head then climbing them, two at a time. He made a decision. No more would he fear reinjuring his leg. That fear was stifling him and hindering his full recovery. Football wasn't going to provide the means, but he needed to start protecting and caring for his family.

SEVEN

MARCH
Eve

Winter was gone but the chill of the season hadn't vanished yet. Eve read about the idea of a fresh new start with the onset of Spring. That the cleansing of the cold months paved the way for a new beginning, a rebirth of sorts. A new and wondrous beginning that should be embraced and celebrated. There would be no one celebrating on the Shaw farm.

This day, with the light of dawn taking the lead, she found her mother's lifeless body lying in Sadie's bed, the baby sleeping soundly in her arms. Her face looked so serene. Eve knew something was wrong. After unsuccessfully trying to raise her mother from her perceived sleep, Eve broke down for the first time since her captivity. She screamed her pain then just fell to her knees and sobbed.

Sadie found her first. She kneeled on the floor, holding Pearl's ice cold hand, crying. Sadie cried quietly, then started pacing the room in some kind of trance-like state, repeating the word, "Again" over and over. But it was Junior's response that worried and scared Eve.

Of course, he heard her tortured scream. He ran to her at full speed, his chest rose and fell with exhaustion as his shadow fell over her. When she looked up into his face, concerned eyes posed an unspoken question while his parted lips opened to take in deep breaths.

It didn't take long for him to figure what was wrong. Junior moved so fast to her mother's side, with his face twisted in anger that Eve grabbed for the baby in an effort to keep him safe. She still didn't know why Junior listened at her mother's mouth then covered it with his. She watched, her eyes wide, body leaning forward, her heart beating frantically as he moved from covering her mother's mouth with his to pushing down on her chest.

After several minutes, Eve knew that Junior's efforts were moot. His movements became clipped, rougher. His eyes were as big as saucers, his breathing raspy as he frantically switched from covering her mother's mouth then pushing on her chest. Unable to bear it any longer, Eve handed Sadie the baby and wrapped her arms around him.

"She's gone, has been for likely most of the night," she whispered. Her words seemed to snap him out of whatever crazed state he was in. A blubbering, tearful mess, Junior shook her hand off his shoulder then started punching several holes in Sadie's bedroom wall before he stormed out of the room.

Why did you leave me?

Eve closed her eyes and let out a deep sigh. She held her sleeping brother close, knowing that he was too young to know what significance this day held. How this one day would affect the rest of his life. At three-months-old, he was too young to understand that they were both forsaken.

"Did you want to say something?"

Eve lifted her head to look at Junior. She never liked looking him directly in the eyes, but she needed him to see her pain because she had no words in her.

No words were going to make this right.

A grief-stricken moan came from below so Eve lowered her gaze to Sadie. The sun was slowly creeping away, but even in the faded light of day Eve could clearly see her tear-streaked red face. Sadie sat on the patch of fresh dirt with a tattered brown teddy bear clutched to her chest.

The more Sadie's sobs grew, the more Eve felt her chest constrict, and the more she wanted to just run. She just wanted to run.

Buzzing in the distance caught Eve's attention. It was a bug of some sort. It wasn't important, but it gave her something to focus on, to take her from this moment. She focused on the flying bug as she rubbed her brother's back to keep him calm, asleep.

Her gaze tracked the flying bug as it did a series of acrobatic circles in the air before flying off too far for her to see. She lost it. *I'll lose everything.*

"I'm not much for words, and I don't know if there is a God. But if there is then I know that Pearl is," Junior whispered, "in his care now."

Eve didn't look at Junior, but she did look as he lifted the dirt on the shovel and threw it over the blanket that covered her mother's body. She watched as the dirt covered and spread around her still form.

Sadie broke then. She tossed the bear in the grave and spread out flat beside it, speaking words that Eve couldn't make out. She dropped her hand in the grave, grasping the lifeless covered hand in hers as Junior continued to fill in the hole he dug that afternoon.

"I said a prayer," Sadie said as she sucked in a few gulps of air.

"That's good, Sadie, but you have to move your hand." Junior softly spoke but slowly continued to fill the hole. Sadie moved her hand like Junior said.

Eve kissed the baby's head. He started to stir but settled back down when she snuggled him closer. *Would her brother listen to her? Or would he listen to Junior?* It was such an odd thought, Eve knew, but nothing in her life was remotely normal. Why would her thoughts be?

The past three months proved to be the most taxing. They had been the hardest months of her life, physically and psychologically. After having the baby, her mother never fully recovered. Her body was abused by Cefus for so many years that all she really had left in her was to give her child life.

Eve used her finger to pinch and dry the tears that threatened to fall. She wanted to let go. To cry, to blame, to scream, but it wouldn't help. Nothing would help so she would not cry. After swiping the pesky tears away, Eve opened her eyes. Junior was watching her, his expression blank.

"I'm sorry," he whispered.

Eve couldn't stop the aching blow Junior's words forced her to feel. He looked so sad and so lost; all she wanted to do was hold him. To tell him it wasn't his fault. No one seemed to understand how ill her mother was and most of the time she seemed fine. They were just laughing at something yesterday evening, together, the four of them, as they watched television together.

We watched television together, like normal people.

Who knew it would be the last time she would hear her mother's laugh?

"Me too," Eve sighed. It was all she could say. Turning, she walked the distance between the large tree that was now her mother's grave marker to the house and her prison.

TWO WEEKS LATER

JUNIOR

Inside the old house was never his favorite place but since Cefus' absence the past three months, Junior grew to stomach the place more. It almost felt like a real home when he had Pearl, Sadie, Eve, and the babe. Even with the threat of Sheriff Gifford over their heads, they found a way to exist with some semblance of peace.

With Pearl gone...not so much.

Junior worked more in order to afford the new cost of having an infant. Arriving home used to be the highlight of his day and there was always a good, hot meal waiting. A meal Junior was grateful for and honestly felt he earned. After dinner, he helped with the babe any way he could which meant him and Pearl played with the little guy while the girls cleaned.

They had a bit of a routine down. Eat, clean, then a bit of television. Watching television was never one of Junior's favorite things, but he did like seeing the girls watch. Cefus didn't allow anyone to use the little tube. With the old man away, Sadie began turning it on.

Junior smiled at the memory of the first time Eve sat in front of the television and watched a show. He couldn't remember what show played on the tube, but he did remember her face as she watched. Junior was seated on the very end of the sofa, leaving the center cushion free for the babe to sleep while Pearl sat at the other end. From his vantage point, he saw Sadie and Eve clearly, but it was Eve who he focused on.

The tube seemed to hypnotize Eve; her big expressive eyes were glued to the screen. Her excitement clear by the way she kept moving her hands from her lap to cover her mouth whenever something a little funny happened. Junior was sure it was to smother a laugh or cover her smile. When she couldn't hold her laughter back a second longer…a quiet giggle escaped. Junior was certain her laughter was the same musical tune angels made when singing their praises.

Junior was regularly shocked by the pleasure he felt from just seeing Eve in high spirits and regularly found himself smiling when she did. There was nothing in either of their lives to really smile about, yet they each found some reasons. Eve found joy in something that wasn't available to her in years, and Junior was happy because she was.

The recognition of his happiness being linked to Eve's unsettled Junior at the time. He quickly let his smile fall away and absently looked around the room, wondering to himself if anyone noticed. Pearl did. Her knowing eyes met his. Embarrassed, Junior looked away but not before he saw Pearl's mouth form a wide smile of her own.

Junior never witnessed such a beautiful sight from Pearl. Her smile was light and hopeful. It was the sun shining on a cloudy day. Junior promised himself that it wouldn't be the last smile he'd get from Pearl.

But it was.

"It was," Junior muttered as he placed his chilled hands on the cold ground. He sat under the old oak so many times in the past couple of weeks that the ground molded to his body. Junior never liked the tree much; it gave him a sense sadness, but it was where he often found himself lately. With Pearl buried beneath it, the tree gave him some sort of comfort now.

Junior pushed off the ground and stood over the large rock he laid over Pearl's final resting place. The rock wasn't big enough to be recognized as a headstone; its only use was to mark her grave for those who knew what lay beneath.

He regarded the rock through tear-filled eyes which gave a kaleidoscope effect to everything he gazed upon. Junior had trouble focusing as his mind floated from one issue to the next. The loss of another mother; constant scenes of Pearl were pressing down on him. He was also worried for the safety of the girls, his brother's care, getting them all away from Cefus before his return, and then there were the crazy feelings he had for Eve.

Am I cursed to lose everyone I love?

"Damn!" Junior cried out into the darkness. He never admitted to loving anyone but Sadie, not even to himself. It seemed silly to try and hold on to the lie now. He loved his mother, and with the loss of Pearl, he was too wounded not to admit that he did. He still loved her, even though she left him and Sadie for a better life. Considering his life with Cefus, he couldn't blame her. He hated his mother too. *She should have at least taken Sadie with her.*

Heartbroken and unsure of what he should do, Junior gave the grave of the woman he loved like a mother one last look before aimlessly walking away.

The pitch black night nearly shrouded the figure that sat against the tree, allowing Eve to only see his outline. It was Junior's nightly routine, sitting under that ominous, towering oak. Eve hadn't been back under the tree since her mother's sudden death and impromptu burial. There was no need to return in her opinion. Eve didn't "believe" like her mother had. What Eve knew for a certainty was that Pearl Jones' soul was no longer here, and she'd be damned if she was going to cry over an empty body, a rock, and a patch of dirt on the murderer's property.

It was bad enough that she couldn't forget the image of her mother's lifeless body the morning she found her.

In an effort to purge the image from her mind, for the moment, Eve tried to focus on Junior again. She gripped the sink's edge and leaned forward, her face almost flush with the streaked kitchen window. No, she was unable to find even his outline anymore.

Why she even concerned herself with where he was, was laughable. They weren't friends and any nice treatment he bestowed her was likely done to soothe her mother. He hadn't even spoken directly to her since her mother passed.

Eve wasn't sure how to feel about his silence. On one hand, Junior terrified her. She saw so much of Cefus in him when he was angry, and she often wondered when he would accept his birthright and become his father's son in all ways. On the other…he never hurt her, her mother or Sadie. So far, Junior was even nice to the baby, caring for him, playing toe-eating games, and blowing raspberries in the baby's tummy. He didn't even seem to mind the baby's crying, reacting only with concern and comfort.

It was so confusing, Junior's temperament.

She was also very confused about her own feelings concerning him. Eve found these *feelings*, that began months ago quite annoying. Even more so when he was around. Her heart would speed up when he entered a room she was in; her body felt both hot and cold. Before, she didn't look at him because she had no desire to; now she found it hard to look at him because she wanted to.

Eve's reaction to Junior made no sense at all, but it was clear what it all meant. She read endless romance novels over the years. Eve knew the signs of infatuation— the flipping of one's stomach, the come-hither glances, the anxiousness one felt when the object of their affection entered the room. She knew what it all meant, but that was the confusing part. She didn't want to want Junior, and she needed it all to stop.

Looking down, Eve realized her thoughts were distracting her from finishing the dishes. She washed and rinsed as fast as she could, trying to be hidden away before

Junior came inside. Once done, she hurried to the room she shared with Sadie.

"He's sick, Evie."

Eve stopped cold just inside of the doorway. She looked to the baby bundled in Sadie's protective hold. His cheeks were red as his tiny body lay limp. No, no, no, this couldn't be happening.

JUNIOR

Why he chose the barn as his escape, Junior didn't know. It was cold and…and it didn't matter because it was better than going inside the house. Inside the house the weight of all his problems felt heavier, suffocating. He didn't want to go inside just yet.

Junior eyed the keys dangling from his fingertips. The keys he never returned to Cefus' room after he took them. Ever since taking command of the keys, Junior wondered what locks each opened. It didn't dawn on him in all the time he carried them that one might belong to the abandoned trailer attached to the wagon— the Jones' wagon— until now.

It took a few tries with a few different keys, and even when he found the right key it took a bit of force and a lot of wiggling to get the lock open. With care, Junior pulled open the door to reveal floating dust inside moonbeams of light and the odor of musty air. Undisturbed labeled boxes, pieces of furniture, and toys were stacked neatly inside the small trailer.

A treasure trove of the Jones' personal items that his father never cared to go through or destroy lay before him. Junior felt compelled to open one of the boxes that were labeled EVE, but resisted the nagging urge and opened the one labeled 'photos and small things'. The first item he saw was a framed family portrait.

Junior stared at the photo for a while, his thoughts silent. Pearl sat on a high-back wooden chair that looked regal. She sat with her back straight, her chin was up, and her hands were together in her lap. Pearl's long hair was pinned up in the front but fell loose in the back. The one time Junior saw Mr. Jones, the day was filled with such turmoil that seeing, actually seeing Mr. Jones, was impossible. As he looked at the image of the man now, he was impressed. Mr. Jones was tall, had perfect posture, and strong shoulders. He was a handsome man. Just looking at the image, you could see the pride in the Jones'.

A pride Junior realized he had never felt. His frame seemed to shrivel, his shoulders slumped, and he sighed as he continued to inspect the photo. He focused on the young version of Eve. She looked so happy in her Sunday's best with her long little pigtails. Her smile must have lit the entire studio that day. She had the kind of smile that made others want to smile. The photo couldn't have been taken too long before they happened upon the Shaw farm.

The screen door slamming shut and the shuffle of fast approaching footsteps had Junior putting the photo down. He didn't bother shutting the trailer or locking the doors as he rushed out of the barn. He saw his sister running toward him. He met her halfway, ignoring the ache in his leg. "What's wrong?"

"Junior, help! Junior, please!" Sadie was winded, frantic. "It's the baby. He's real bad off," she said. With every other word, she sucked in a much-needed breath.

Junior beat on Dr. Steuben's front door for over three minutes before he heard movement inside. He breathed a sigh of relief when the lights inside came on.

"Shit," he mumbled. At exactly the same time headlights from what looked to be Sheriff's Gifford's cruiser illuminated the front porch. "Shit!"

He knew that Gifford's deputies were watching him, often feeling eyes on him or actually seeing them. Tonight, Junior didn't care what happened to him. He was getting help.

"What the hell are you doing here, boy?" Sheriff Gifford yelled as he slammed the cruiser's door. The sheriff's eyes narrowed. "Why the hell are you here, and what the hell is that?"

The disgust on Gifford's face angered Junior. He pivoted away, taking a few steps back until he was against the door. "He's sick," Junior barked, covering his brother who was nestled in his arms. "He needs a doctor."

"Whose baby is that?" Sheriff Gifford tried to look over Junior's shoulder, staring at the bundle for several heartbeats. "Good Lord," Sheriff Gifford hissed as he reached for the baby. "Boy, is that what I think it is?"

Junior turned out of Gifford's reach, using his shoulder to prevent him from touching his brother. He lost too many people he cared about. He couldn't save Pearl, but he wasn't going to allow her babe to die. He wouldn't let anyone else he cared about die.

"Put it out of its misery; do it back on your farm then bury it with the rest of the fucking garbage."

Seething with anger, Junior couldn't stop the words that came out next. "He's not garbage so fuck you, asshole!"

"You just signed your death certificate, you little shit." Gifford grabbed Junior's shirt, fisting it.

"You're not Cefus, you backwater fuck," Junior spat as he pushed Sheriff Gifford hard. Gifford's face went from inflamed crimson to parchment white as he lost his footing and stumbled backward down the porch steps. Junior was surprised that the man was able to right himself instead of falling to the ground. "You better kill me." Junior bent to place the baby on the lone rocker that sat on the porch.

As if on cue, the baby started to cry.

Gifford started back up the stairs just as the door was pulled open. Junior could see Dr. Steuben in his peripheral. Feeling safer, he took his eyes off of the sheriff long enough to pull the baby back to his arms.

Junior fixed his gaze back on Sheriff Gifford as he spoke through gritted teeth. "The baby is sick." The sheriff cursed, but Junior ignored him. "Please, Dr. Steuben." Junior exposed his brother's face. Dr. Steuben's curious gaze went from the babe then back up to him. "Can you help him?"

Dr. Steuben extended his arm, opening the screen door wider as he stuttered, "Well don't just stand out there. This chilly night air isn't going to help."

A puff of warm breath escaped Junior's dry lips, clouded as his shoulders slumped forward. Dr. Steuben would never know how his agreeing to help restored some of his trust in the people in the small town.

With a new sense of urgency, Junior stepped inside. As soon as he moved through the doorway, he was shoved aside by Sheriff Gifford. No, Junior wasn't at all surprised. It was less than ideal to have the man hovering over his shoulders, but it was better than the sheriff driving out to the farm and following through with one or all of his threats.

The door creaked as Dr. Steuben eased it shut, his attention rapt on whatever Junior's and Sheriff Gifford's combined presence seemed to suggest. As if he was pinched into action, Dr. Steuben shook his head and pushed the door closed then motioned for Junior to follow him as he moved past both men.

"Good thing I heard the baby crying," Dr. Steuben mumbled as he continued to the living room and down a narrow hallway.

"You say one wrong word..." Gifford whispered. The stench of the canned sardines he was often seen eating, rose and encircled Junior, causing his eyes to burn.

"Yeah, I'll wish I was dead, I got it." Junior didn't give the sheriff a backward glance as he caught up with the doctor.

Dr. Steuben used his hip to push another door open, letting them inside. Junior heard a low click right before bright light illuminated the space, making even the dullest of white and colorful items in the exam room look new. He blinked a few times then focused on the room again. The worn furniture and floor appeared new; it wasn't. Junior was in this room a hundred times before but never gave its appearance a second thought until now.

"Come on; lay the lad down so I can take a look."

Junior glanced over at the sheriff then down at the babe. He held his brother closer, peering into wide gray eyes like his own, silently promising that everything would be okay before gently placing the babe on the exam table. The babe's high-pitched wail and thrashing told them all that he wasn't happy with being put down.

Junior hovered, tapping his hand on his leg as he watched the doctor's every move. He glanced over at Gifford, wondering what the man was planning to do. What Junior did know was that Gifford, hell even Cefus, held a healthy dose of respect for Dr. Steuben. Maybe it was the Doc's German ancestry or the fact that this was the only doctor office for miles and miles. Or it could have been that the Steuben family owned a good deal of property in the small town. Whatever the case, Gifford seemed hesitant to act.

"When was his last diaper change?" Dr. Steuben asked. When Junior didn't have a ready answer, the doctor kept his head lowered, but his brows and eyes rose up over his spectacles to pin Junior. "Okay?" Dr. Steuben fastened the diaper back. "When did he last eat?"

Again, Junior was at a loss. "I don't know."

"What's his name?" The doctor continued his examination, but when Junior didn't respond he asked, "Do you know at least that much?" Dr. Steuben rose to glare at Junior but used his palm to make small circular motions on the babe's belly. "Hell, Junior, whose baby is this?"

"It's his baby," Sheriff Gifford quickly sputtered.

Dr. Steuben cursed. "Does Cefus know?"

Junior didn't think of Dr. Steuben questioning his brother's appearance or how it related to him. Looking at his brother now, as if for the first time, Junior could see the babe's ethnicity clearly. The babe's warm toffee skin was much darker than Junior's ivory tone. His hair was virtually black, silky curls, and his face was round. A button nose that was so cute and little, Junior often found himself kissing it. Everything about the child was the exact opposite of Junior, except for the babe's huge eyes. Eyes that were classic Shaw silver, bright and clear.

What could he possibly tell the doctor that wouldn't get him, the doc, and the babe killed?

"No," Sheriff Gifford answered quickly.

Junior was stunned into silence. He started to answer the question meant for him, but the sheriff answered before he could. As he flipped the answer over in his head, he realized that it was best that everyone thought that the babe was his. Cefus wasn't going to ever claim him, but Junior would be proud to.

"Well, you better break it to Cefus." Dr. Steuben stared down at the babe, his brows pinched together. "I've never directly reported any of my suspicions about what goes in that household. I've always felt a man's home is his business, but I won't look the other way with this one." Dr. Steuben met Junior's gaze. His expression changed from ashamed as if remembering all the times Junior was treated for his own 'clumsiness', to a look of understanding, then determination. "Where was the child born?"

"He's never seen a doctor; he was born at home," Junior offered before Sheriff Asshole said something stupid.

Dr. Steuben opened his mouth, and it hung open for a few seconds, then he exhaled and cursed under his breath. "It never ceases to amaze me, the closed minds in this town. Modern medicine isn't evil, Junior." Dr. Steuben shook his graying head, mumbling curses under his breath. "Right off I can tell you the baby is dehydrated. I strongly suggest that you take him to the hospital for a full examination and blood work."

Sheriff Gifford crossed his arms over his chest and widened his stance. "Doc, you gonna have to fix 'em up here."

The doctor pulled out a small clear bag of fluid, a small needle, some gauze, tape, and a tiny board of some sort. He washed his hands then went to work. Sure hands had the baby fashioned with an IV within minutes.

"Todd Gifford," Dr. Steuben's voice was stern and unyielding as he spoke, "Do I question your policing skills?" The doctor wrapped the IV with more gauze. "No, I don't, because I am not an officer. So, I'd kindly appreciate you to not questioning my doctoring skills." Dr. Steuben set his attention on Junior. "Give me a few to get dressed. I'll accompany you, and here hold this up." He handed Junior the clear plastic bag of fluid and positioned Junior's arm in the air.

"There's no need for you to leave the comfort of your home, Doc. I'll take 'em." Sheriff Gifford focused on Junior.

If the stare down the sheriff was giving Junior was meant to be cold and hard, it lacked the steel Cefus' stare held. Junior wanted to laugh at the man and his false sense of power. Gifford was no Cefus. The man was a phony, a lapdog for the town bully, whose only power was the ability to observe then report back to Cefus.

I should just kick his ass. Yet, Junior knew Gifford held some authority, and he couldn't afford to be put behind bars, so he just shook his head and looked down at his brother.

"I have some supplies to pick up at Anniston General anyway. I may as well go now rather than later." Before Dr. Steuben left them in the room, he swaddled the babe up in a fresh white blanket he pulled out of a cabinet then placed him in the cradle of Junior's arms. Dr. Steuben had Junior sit, reminding him to keep his arm raised before he left the room.

"While you're in the big city, I'll be at your house. Remember, my cousin is an officer in Anniston, and we have a lot of friends. If I so much as hear a whiff of anything, I will make your sister suffer."

That was it. Junior moved to get to his feet, but Sheriff Gifford pushed him back then stepped on his foot. The sheriff pressed hard enough to rent a painful gasp from Junior. "No need you getting all worked up there. Just do what you've been doing. Keep your mouth shut."

EIGHT

JUNIOR

The doctor drove them to the city of Anniston; inside the vehicle was virtually silent, and Junior was fine with that. He knew that Dr. Steuben had questions, and he wasn't prepared to answer. Each time the doctor glanced his way, Junior attempted to look busy. When the babe started to cry, Junior's relief was probably reflected on his face. Only his reprieve didn't last long. The little guy was easily cooed with a little formula Dr. Steuben provided them with and a bit of baby talk. All that worked until his brother fell asleep.

"Why doesn't he have a name yet?"

Junior felt the doctor's eyes boring into the side of his skull. He couldn't tell the man that after the baby was born, Pearl didn't name him. That the babe's mother fed and cared for him as if she were doing it on instinct, but he feared that she didn't feel a motherly connection to him. Junior couldn't blame her really. A babe from such origins was probably hard to accept even if they were faultless.

After Pearl's passing, Sadie mentioned that they should name him, but Junior felt that maybe it wasn't his right. That right belonged to Eve. She didn't give the baby a name that he knew of, and he wasn't going to pester her about it.

"I guess just haven't found one that we liked enough," Junior offered as an excuse.

Dr. Steuben pulled his car into a parking space and shut it off. "Well,"—he looked at Junior— "better think of one now. The fact that he was born at home and had no medical attention is one thing; these folk are akin to caveman mentality and they are going to squawk, but to not have a name for the lad most will find unacceptable. These people are not going to swallow the stuff I'm fed by my neighbors on a regular basis back home."

Junior tried to think of names he would like to name his son but came up empty. He never considered having kids until Terry tried to screw him over, literally. He gave a silent sigh to acknowledge his dodging that bullet. Back to the babe, he tried to consider what Eve might like. Lately, she watched a lot of television. He thought of the shows she liked, and there was one in particular that she loved to watch: Kojak.

"Theodore Shaw."

It was a name he hoped Eve and Sadie liked because as soon as the woman at the reception counter asked, that was the name he gave. When the receptionist asked Junior his wife's name, his head could have separated from his body and floated away. He didn't answer right away, and the older woman looked up from her paperwork to glare at him with pursed lips. The receptionist didn't ask for the mother's name; she assumed he was married to the mother of his supposed son.

"Evelyn."

An hour later, as he sat beside the little crib *Theo* slept in; Junior reminded himself he had no choice in the matter. He had to give Evelyn's name as his wife and Theo's mother. Of course, his lie would open up another can of worms. Sheriff Gifford and the rest of the town were sure to hear that he just claimed a black woman and child as his. But he couldn't risk his brother being taken from them and placed in the care of the state.

He'd easily lie again to prevent that.

What Junior needed was a plan. Cefus had been gone for three months already. Who knew how much longer they had. He trailed his finger over his brother's clenched fist, his devotion and protective instincts overflowing for the babe. "Claiming you is the right thing to do," Junior said, knowing he made the right decision.

"It sure was."

Junior looked over his shoulder to find a tall, attractive woman with a big smile on her face, staring down at Theo. He didn't hear her enter the nursery over all the noise going on in the room from the staff dealing with babies, and he was a bit surprised that she heard his words.

He heard a bit of an accent and she was dark enough to speak of some Hispanic heritage. Her fitted suit jacket and skirt said she probably didn't work for the hospital.

"Good Morning!" Aside from her accent, her voice was somewhat a nasally whisper and it really didn't fit the "prissy" look of her. "My name if Teresa Hall. I am the case worker who works in the office with Mr. Hopkins. You recall Mr. Hopkins, right?"

Junior nodded. Mr. Hopkins was the social worker who checked in on him after his father beat him and broken his leg. Junior always suspected that Dr. Steuben's wife reported his father then…and he believed it even more now.

"I was assigned to little Theo here." She glanced down at his brother again, her smile growing. "He is so cute."

"Thank you." Junior's voice cracked. Yawning, he rubbed the back of his neck as he looked away from the woman. The doctors at the hospital wanted to keep Theo overnight, and he was told that someone would want to talk with him about Theo, but he was hoping he missed this little visit. Junior didn't want to leave Theo, but he had to. He had to get his story straight and to do that he needed to think.

Junior was hoping to be gone, but Dr. Steuben was taking longer to pick up the supplies he came for so Junior had no choice but to wait and now…

"Do you mind stepping out in the hall so we can talk?"

Junior gave her a tight nod then followed the woman out of the nursery. She sat on a long bench that was against the wall across from the nursery. He sat down beside her as she placed a folder she pulled out of a case on her lap and opened it. Mrs. Hall asked him questions about Theo's care; a good deal of them he was unable to accurately answer. It didn't take long to figure out that Mrs. Hall was going to want to talk to Eve and eventually she said as much.

Dr. Steuben arrived just as Mrs. Hall stood to leave. Junior suspected the doctor's timing was no coincidence. He appreciated Dr. Steuben wanting to ensure his brother's safety, but Junior didn't need this shit right now.

What he needed was him and Eve on the same page and on the same team. Considering what she'd been through, he wasn't sure if she would be a team player. Hell, this was the perfect time for her to get the hell away from the Shaw hell house.

Eve scooted the heavy drapes aside and peeked out of the living room window for the hundredth time. The police car pulled in front of the house about three hours after Junior left with the baby and was parked in front of the house the entire night and all morning. She swallowed, ignoring the vile, sickening taste in her mouth as her nerves settled in the pit of her stomach.

Something bad happened; she was certain of it.

Dropping her hand, Eve watched the curtain fall back in place. She worried her lip and tapped her fingers on the outside of her thigh as she followed the worn path she no doubt set from pacing back and forth from the kitchen to the window.

Sadie was planted at the table eating toasted bread and jam. Every so often she would look up with her beautiful, soft gray eyes and smile as if she didn't have a care in the world. Eve sat across from her, forcing a smile when sweet Sadie glanced her way.

"He will keep our brother safe," Sadie grinned wide, exposing jellied teeth.

It didn't take long for Eve to understand that Sadie was not only special but unique. She was smart and mature in some ways but innocent and childlike in others. Her ability to learn was greatly hindered by some difficulties that were clearly mental, but what worried Eve more was that Sadie seemed to trust people in general, and that wasn't so good.

Of course, Sadie understood when bad things happened, but she seemed to forget those acts easily. As if she actually forgot that the person did wrong. Eve's mother would say that was a wonderful trait, but in truth, it was one that could get Sadie hurt if no one watched out for her. It was why every decision Junior seemed to make was based on Sadie's well-being.

So when Sadie's facial features scrunched for the third time since her sitting, Eve said, "That man outside is fine, Sadie. Stop your worrying."

"But he might not be."

Eve explained that the officer parked in front of the house had already eaten three times that morning. Of course, Eve didn't know for sure if the guy had eaten but she didn't care. Plus, Eve didn't want Sadie catching the officer's attention. The only thing Eve knew about men for certain was that some took what wasn't offered. Sadie was beautiful and had that innocent quality that evil men preyed upon. Cefus taught her that.

"Okay," Sadie mumbled. She looked dejected, but her expression only lasted a few seconds before a hopeful look replaced it. "You think our baby will be back soon?"

Eve sighed, long and loud. She was trying to cover her worry so Sadie wouldn't feed off of it, but Eve was tired of waiting, tired of worrying, and tired of not being able to express it all. The police sitting outside didn't settle her either. The presence of the lawman only alarmed her more.

"You think the officer is thirsty?"

Eve took several breaths to stave off the urge to scream. It was even harder to form words to speak without yelling every word. Eve never lost her temper in this place. Her mother repeatedly expressed to her that doing so would end badly for them. That in this place, neither of them had the luxury of expressing themselves in any way. Eve managed, no matter how difficult, to keep her feelings, her opinions, and her wants locked away. She did for so many years, and with her mother, her rock, gone...

Don't I get something for myself? I can't sit here anymore, she thought.

"Sadie,"—Eve rubbed her forehead, "I..."

The familiar sound of the door screeching open staved Eve's words. Both she and Sadie looked at one another before they jumped to their feet. Sadie moved toward the front door while Eve moved toward the basement.

It was the familiar sound of Junior's voice that halted Eve's steps. She turned without thinking and rushed to the living room, surprised by her own excitement to see the baby again. The realization that the baby became so important to her in such a short time had her stopping cold, delaying her reunion just beyond the dividing wall.

Her eyes fell to the floor. *I don't just care for him because he's a helpless baby, do I?* Eve didn't want to think of what loving another person would do to her mental state.

Eve's next steps were slow, heavy with the weight of understanding as she moved around the wall. Her hands itched with anticipation as she took in Junior. The first thing Eve noticed was that Junior's arms were empty. *Empty?*

Her eyes followed his empty hands, up his arms, then focused on his face. Junior's eyes were rimmed red—like he was crying. *What happened?* Junior rarely cried.

Eve didn't even notice when she bent her index finger of her right hand to pick at the skin on her thumb. "Where's the baby?" she heard herself whisper. Junior's bloodshot eyes fell on her. *Something went wrong.* Eve took a step toward him. She no longer saw Sadie even though she stood right beside Junior or the room that encircled them. All she saw was Junior at that moment.

Junior promised her that everything would be alright when he left with their brother, but here he stood, without him. The fear of what may have happened hit Eve like a punch to the stomach. She had to grab the wall to stay on her feet as her mind fought to shut down all the bad possibilities that could have happened to the baby. Her hand shook, her eyes blinked involuntarily to hold back her tears, and her throat dried.

Keeping the baby safe wasn't just an empty promise to her mother. Maybe this was her punishment for not allowing herself to acknowledge her love for the boy until today. Maybe it was because she avoided holding him as much, or caring for him the way Sadie did. Okay, and maybe she didn't name him but she… she needed her mother's son to love, to care for, to live because if she didn't have him, she had nothing.

"Where is he," Eve demanded. Her voice was strong, her shoulders back. Eve formed fists with her hands as she took another determined step toward Junior. She was prepared to fight for him.

Junior's shoulders sagged as he held up his hand. "Wait," he sighed, "Theo's fine."

"Theo?" Both Sadie and Eve questioned at the same time.

Junior looked away and shrugged.

At least he had the decency to look ashamed from taking that right to name the baby from her. They should have agreed on a name together. Though Eve was a bit surprised that Junior named their brother, she actually liked the name, but she didn't want to discuss it now. She wanted to know where —Theo—was and why Junior wasn't with him.

"Go get him," Sadie spoke up. Her cheeks were a bit rosier, and a slight smile lit her beautiful face. "He's probably hungry and—"

"What happened? Did your father's friends do anything to harm him?" Eve interrupted as she inspected Junior for obvious bruising. When she found none, she continued, "Is he... Did you get him help?" Junior didn't answer right away, and Eve couldn't contain her anxiety any longer. "What happened, Junior?" she implored.

"Doc questioned me on whose baby he was; I froze. Sheriff Gifford answered before me. He said Theo was mine."

"Yours?" Eve frowned.

Junior nodded. "Theo is safe but in the hospital. They said he has a virus and is dehydrated. It will pass." Junior lowered his gaze, shifting from one foot to the other. "I had to lie to keep him." He rubbed one of his hands over his thigh then slid his gaze to Sadie. "We can go to the hospital later to see him. He's going to be fine, they say."

He pinned Eve with determined eyes, making her want to look away. Walking toward her, Junior took hold of her hand and pulled her over to the sofa. Eve didn't resist, sitting down to face him like he prompted. He glanced over his shoulder at Sadie. "I smell breakfast. You mind making me some coffee and heating me up some food." Sadie nodded and bounced off singing Rock-a-bye Baby.

"Look," he said, facing Eve again and speaking low so that he couldn't be heard by Sadie. "We, *you* need the proper documents for Theo. Saying he is mine is the smartest thing we can do for now. When you get out of here, you'll need that piece of paper."

Eve didn't respond. She was trying to go over what Junior meant by 'when she got out of here'. Her freedom wasn't enough. Once she knew that Sadie and Junior were alright, she would make certain Cefus didn't just walk away with all he did. "He must pay."

"He will pay, but so will I."

What has he done? "What, why?"

Junior shook his head. "Look, I don't know what will happen to me when all that happened here comes out, and it's not important. I just figure that saying that Theo is ours will cut Cefus' claim on him forever."

Did he say ours? Eve thought she heard him say 'ours' but that couldn't be right. "Ours? You said that he was ours." She was certain that she heard him wrong. When she felt his warm thumbs rubbing the back of her hand that still sat in his, Eve frowned then yanked her hand away.

"Yes, ours," Junior sighed, "yours and mine. Before we leave this place for good, I have to make certain Sadie is in good hands, that she will be alright when everything comes to light."

A few things occurred to Eve at that moment. The first: there may be a possibility that Junior could be faulted for what had occurred in this house. Secondly: he really was planning to get them away from Cefus. He thought it was okay to publically lay claim to her— a black girl— and a bi-racial baby. Lastly, when he touched her hand, rubbing it in the way that he did, it felt like an internal blaze lit in her, traveling up her hands and scorching through her entire body.

It was a blaze she could never show that she actually liked.

Eve turned away in an attempt to hide her shameful thoughts. "You did nothing wrong here," she mumbled.

"The authorities might not see it that way." Junior got to his feet. "Besides, it doesn't matter." He started for the front door as he said, "I have some things for you, then I need to eat and get some coffee in me before I get back to Theo."

JUNIOR

As Junior rinsed his plate in the sink, he couldn't help wondering exactly what Eve was doing at that exact moment. He knew he should be thinking of what his next move would be, of what he needed to do to get them all to safety. If only Eve's image wouldn't slip inside his thoughts, pushing aside everything else.

He turned off the tap and thought of how he took her hands in his yesterday afternoon, cradling them in his as he brushed her soft skin with his thumbs. She didn't notice at first and allowed him precious seconds to caress her soft skin. Touching her, it sent such an intense jolt of need while offering him a sense of peace. The disgusted look on her face hurt him. Junior tried not to flinch when she ripped her hand from his grasp. He tried not to take the disgusted look on her beautiful face personal, but it was hard.

*She's still scared of me...*and she clearly doesn't like me.

Either was painful to accept because he couldn't turn what he was feeling off. He tried. God, he tried so damn hard.

It wasn't necessary for her to fall for him. Junior just wanted Eve to like him. His only care was keeping her, Pearl, and Sadie as safe as he could. He hardly had time to care what she felt.

Why did things have to be different? Junior welcomed different but did it have to be his emotions that were affected? Of all the girls he knew it had to be the one girl who hated him. Sighing, Junior had no choice other than to accept that things were different for him. He was damned. The fact that Eve was upstairs showering and changing into her mother's clothing that he found in the barn, and all Junior could do was think of how she went about the task was proof.

Junior used a towel to wipe the water from his hands as he remembered their talk earlier; he couldn't help noticing how different she looked to him. She was always beautiful, but since she started going outside during the day, of course remaining out of site on the property, her skin had a glow that he didn't notice was missing before. Her eyes gained a bit of wonder in them, most likely from all the things she was able to experience now. Even her temperament, though restrained, seemed brighter somehow.

Junior wanted Eve to feel better too. Trying to make her life as normal as possible, considering their situation was vital to her emotional health. He figured a good start would be to give her some of her parents' belongings. When he presented her with a small pile of clothing, undergarments, shoes she may or may not fit, and some toiletries he found in the barn, she just gave him a confused look. It was only when he dangled the necklace and a picture in her face that she realized what those things were. Eve reached for the picture and necklace so fast that he fumbled with the rest of the items to keep from dropping them.

Without looking at him, she had grabbed the rest of the things from him and disappeared with a whisper of thanks. The truth was, Junior would always treasure that moment. No, he couldn't tell how she felt about having a small piece of her parents' again. He didn't know if his offering saddened her or made her happy. Eve didn't wear her emotions…neither of them did so he could understand that. What he did know was that she recognized that locket and looked at it and the photo for a moment as if the memory of seeing her family, all of them together, had meaning. He knew it did, and he'd given her that.

Happy or sad, Junior was sure he made her feel something, and he liked making her feel. If only he could coax her to smile like Sadie and Theo could. She smiled at television shows occasionally; she even smiled at words she read in the books he borrowed for her but never at him. All she gave him were frowns, looks of confusion, but mostly plain indifference. Junior enjoyed seeing her smile, but he would like to be the one to be the cause, just once.

A light knock on the door and a shake of his head shut down the direction Junior's thoughts took. He needed to get himself on track. That meant dealing with folk he didn't want to deal with. Folk like Sheriff Gifford. Junior knew that he would have to deal with the man sooner or later, but he was hoping on later. The sound of a car's engine outside said he had to deal now.

Now isn't a good time. Hell, never was too soon.

Junior felt that they, like him and Cefus, was coming to a standoff. He and the people holding him from his goal were going to knock heads real soon. He just needed to bottle his anger a little longer.

Stay calm, stay calm, he whispered to himself as he made his way to the front door. Calm gave way to shock when Junior opened the door. He eased his opened mouth closed, hiding his surprise beneath a practiced, cool expression.

"Hello, Junior," Teresa Hall said with a smile.

"How have you been, Junior?" Mr. Hopkins asked as he walked up the porch stairs.

Junior looked from Mrs. Hall to Mr. Hopkins with a confusion that was apparently expressed on his face because Mrs. Hall dismissively waved at Mr. Hopkins.

"Mr. Hopkins and I thought it better if he accompanied me," Mrs. Hall said as she glanced around Junior to look inside the house.

Instinctively, Junior blocked her view with his body. "Why are you here?" He couldn't help how blunt the question sounded. "What's wrong with my...son?" He hoped that neither of the social workers thought too much of his pause. Claiming Theo was going to take some getting used to.

"No, heavens no,"—Mrs. Hall answered with a wave of her hand. "Your little guy is perfect. In fact, I checked on him right before we drove here. That is why I've, we've come. Theodore's nurse says he'll be released to you today so I thought that before he is, I would visit."

"Let us inside, Junior," Mr. Hopkins said. The man was big and his voice deep. Much deeper than Cefus'. Hopkins' hair was cut military style, and Junior had a feeling that Hopkins got those muscles in actual active duty. The one thing Junior liked and loathed about Mr. Hopkins was that he was a no-nonsense kind of guy.

Reluctantly, Junior stepped back giving them room to enter. Just as both of his unwelcomed guests moved forward, Junior heard the groaning engine of Sheriff Gifford's cruiser before he looked up and saw the car traveling up the drive. Of course, the sheriff's lackeys would have reported that Junior had company.

"You in some kind of trouble, Junior?"

Junior didn't realize that Mr. Hopkins hadn't moved away from the entrance like Mrs. Hall did. Instead, he stood right behind Junior, looking out the door as well. "No, sir," Junior said, glancing over his shoulder.

"Okay." That was all Mr. Hopkins said.

Junior watched as Mr. Hopkins led Mrs. Hall to the living room. Having visited several times during the past, Mr. Hopkins knew the layout. It wasn't until Junior heard the creak of the porch steps did he look back out of the door he still held open.

"What the hell is going on here, boy?" Sheriff Gifford asked low enough that Junior was sure no one else heard the question.

"They're to make sure that Theo is safe here," Junior whispered back. "Guess they don't trust me...or they don't trust Cefus." Junior closed the door after Gifford moved past him and into the house. Sheriff Gifford tried to reach for Junior's arm, but Junior jerked out of his reach as he moved toward the living room. "Save your threats. I know the routine."

When Junior and Gifford entered the living room, Mr. Hopkins and Mrs. Hall greeted the sheriff, but each gave Junior a questioning look. Neither said anything about it so Junior decided to get on with the show.

"So..." Junior said as he stood in the entryway of the living room. Mrs. Hall and Mr. Hopkins took it upon themselves to sit.

"Well," Mrs. Hall said as she reached into her case that sat beside her foot, "I was hoping to speak with," she glanced at an open folder she sat on her lap. "Eve, your son's mother."

Sheriff Gifford's reaction was immediate. He stiffened, stepped in front of Junior, and said, "The girl isn't here."

Junior knew that Mrs. Hall would want to 'see' Eve. What he didn't know was how it would play out. He could lie and agree with Gifford because of course, he didn't want to cause Eve any more unease. But now, at this moment, he saw the benefit of this gathering. Junior saw a way to gain some needed freedom, but not for him. Also, he didn't care for Gifford's nerve.

Mrs. Hall looked at him, her expression disappointed. "She's not here?"

"No," Junior stepped out from behind Gifford, "she's here."

"I'd like to see her," Mrs. Hall pressed her lips together and sighed as she looked from Junior to Sheriff Gifford.

Sheriff Gifford grabbed Junior's arm and spun him around, stepping in front of him. "I need to talk to you," he gritted out, "now."

Junior ignored the nails digging in his forearm as he grinned at Gifford, but his words were meant for Mrs. Hall. "I'll just go get her."

Sheriff Gifford's wide eyes took Junior in as his mouth formed a large O. Junior pulled free of Gifford's grasp then left the room.

"What the hell are you playing at, boy?" Gifford demanded in a hushed tone dripped with restrained anger as he pinned Junior to the wall in the hallway, fisting his shirt. The sheriff glanced over his shoulder to make sure they were hidden from view.

Junior grabbed hold of Gifford's arm, reminding himself that he had a plan and to not attempt to break Gifford's wrist. He was tempted, though. "You saw them. Do you think that they are just going to leave and be done with this? I'm pretty sure they aren't going to look the other way, Sheriff." Junior shrugged.

Gifford kept hold of Junior's shirt as he lowered his head. Junior didn't move as the sheriff's brows wrinkled. It was clear the man's tiny brain was trying to figure out what to do.

Knowing he needed to say something else to convince Gifford, Junior added, "If they don't see her they will probably start poking their noses into Cefus' business." Junior slowly turned his head and looked around the hallway dramatically. "Next, it will be you they'll be investigating and your happy little town."

Junior saw the exact moment he had Gifford.

Sheriff Gifford grunted then pushed Junior toward the stairs. "She talks, you'll wish she hadn't."

Junior stumbled forward a few steps but easily got his footing before he started up the stairs. He eyed Gifford over his shoulder as he climbed, pinning the man with a hated look. Putting up with the sheriff's bullshit was becoming harder and harder, and accepting that he could do little to the scuzzy bastard grated on his nerves.

It was becoming harder to control his anger. Junior would only admit to himself that he sometimes provoked his father to suffer a beating just to find some calm. But Cefus wasn't here now, and the ache in his leg became all but a mild irritation, leaving him no outlet for his smoldering anger. Working out with Coach at the school gym helped, but with Theo and all the bills falling to him, he had to work more.

Sighing as he reached the top of the stairs, Junior hustled down the hallway to the bathroom and knocked on the door. He needed a release. A fight would do, but he couldn't afford to get in trouble. Or maybe a romp in the sack with one of his admirers would do the trick. That was Junior's thoughts as the bathroom door swung open. Fights and girls faded as he peered down at Eve. He had to take a few steps back and fist his hands in order to keep them off her.

She's stunning, he thought as he unashamedly took her in. Stunning was a word he rarely, if ever, used yet it was the first word that came to mind. Eve was absolutely stunning. She wore a light blue dress with quarter length sleeves; the fabric hugged her breasts and waistline but flared out over her hips. Her hair, usually all tied braids was slightly parted in the center then twisted up, falling into shiny coils that cascaded to the middle of her back.

The dress length went a little past her knee. Her legs were smooth and long and on display. The shoes she'd chosen were flat and by the way her toes bunched in the front, they were too small. Junior made a mental note to remedy that as soon as possible.

"Don't she look pretty?" Sadie's satisfied grin blazed as she swayed from side to side. "I like her hair the best and the pretty dress. Can I have a pretty dress, Junior?"

"Sure, Sadie," Junior answered absently as his gaze traveled back up to Eve's eyes. He heard his sister, knew what she asked, but he wasn't capable of focusing on what she wanted right now. He was trapped by the beauty of the small woman in front of him. "I need you..." Junior began to say but stopped. He watched as Eve's eyes widened, but to his relief, she didn't retreat. He would have kept it at that, telling her he needed her. It wasn't the time if ever there would be. "Uh, I need you to meet some people."

Eve immediately shook her head. Her surprise turned into fear right before him. She backed into the bathroom, bumping into Sadie. "I can't...I don't," she stuttered as she tried to move behind Sadie. "I can't."

Junior reached for her arm and pulled her to him. His grip was firm, but he was sure that he wasn't hurting her. He tried to ignore the feel of her soft flesh beneath his touch, but it was hard.

"This is for Theo, Eve. We want him back, right?" She nodded at same time Sadie said yes. "Then you have to talk to them. They're from Anniston; the same people that used to visit me when I was hurt to make sure I was okay here. They just want to talk to you to make sure you are fine, and that Theo is safe here. We need to convince them that he is ours," Junior tried to stress the word. "And that he is...safe with us. We could lose him if they find out the truth right now, Eve."

"No," Eve breathed.

Junior let go of her arm but fought the urge to touch her cheek. He knew the gesture may not be comforting to her like it would any other woman, but he wanted so badly to touch her. "No," he agreed, instead.

Eve stood up straight and gave him a nod. Junior didn't smile though he wanted to. She was beautiful, smart, and most of all, Eve was strong. He knew that from the very first night he saw her, and it was one of the qualities he admired most about her.

He led the way, knowing without looking that Eve followed.

NINE

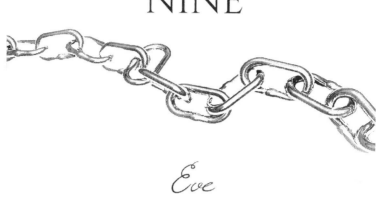

Eve

It felt as if she was walking to the gallows, like in one of her historical romance novels. Eve willed herself to relax, for her heart to stop pounding, for her hands to stop shaking, but her body wouldn't listen. Why she thought it would now, she couldn't fathom. Her body never listened to her when she berated it for responding the way it did to Junior.

So why would it take heed now?

She was still reeling from when she pulled the bathroom door open and found Junior staring back at her. His attention was slow and methodical as if he were committing every detail of her body to memory.

Her immediate response was to cower but then another sensation took hold. A pulse of sorts vibrated through her core. It was the only way she could explain it. Eve felt tingles when reading her romance novels, and if she had to admit it, she felt a tingle or two whenever she thought of Junior without his shirt. But never did she feel what she felt just minutes ago when he looked at her. Usually, she felt angry that she had any feelings toward him.

That wasn't the case today. Eve felt bold as she stared back, intrigued and somewhat flattered by his attention. If

147

she were completely honest, after she dressed and combed through her hair, Eve wanted Junior to see her. She wanted to see his reaction to her transformation. But all that, his response and hers, was forgotten or rather pushed away as she quietly followed him. Eve glanced over her shoulder to see Sadie closing herself inside the bathroom just before descending the stairs.

Eve's heart raced now, and it was for an entirely different reason.

There were people who wanted to see her; people who would determine if she would see her brother again. *What are they going to ask me?* More importantly, what would she say? As Eve took her time stepping off the bottom stair, her mind raced with more questions, ones that she had no answers to.

As Junior led the way through the short hallway to the living room, he glanced back at her. His brows furrowed as if he was concerned. Was he just as worried about what she would say? It was the first time she was able to talk with someone outside of the Shaw farm. She could expose all the horrid treatment that she and her family endured.

She considered revealing herself to the social worker who visited Junior on several occasions after he broke his leg, but she didn't. Eve kept her mouth shut and stayed hidden because of fear. Her mother often told her that they could only trust one another, and she needed to be wary of the few people who Cefus let in his home.

Eve feared that at some point her mother became used to being a prisoner, that life here was…well, it was life. But Eve never assimilated. She didn't lose hope or her will to be free.

Those books she lost herself in spoke to Eve. She wanted just a morsel of what the characters in those books had. Her mother told her that those stories weren't at all accurate when it came to men, but life could be exciting and whimsical if you made it so. The heroes with their daring rescues, strength, and unyielding devotion and love. It was easy to fall for them.

Eve envied the heroines, with their beauty, grace, and determination. But what she loved the most about those books were the locations. She often imagined all the places her books spoke of. The description of scents and vivid scenery sounded amazing. Yet, all Eve wanted was 'normal'—whatever normal was—and her freedom.

I can have it, Eve thought, as her gaze fell on the attractive Hispanic woman and the muscled man who stood when she entered the room. All she had to do was tell these people her story.

"Hello, I am Mrs. Hall, and this is Mr. Hopkins," the woman said as she extended her hand. "Do you prefer Eve or Mrs. Shaw?"

Eve strained to keep her face neutral as she moved closer to Junior. She wasn't certain if it was the woman's gesture to take her hand or that she referred to Eve as Mrs. Shaw that had her shrinking behind Junior. Or maybe it was the unyielding hard look of the man, Mr. Hopkins, who looked as if he could crush a skull with his bare hands. But if Eve had to pinpoint the source of her anxiety, she would have to say it was Sheriff Gifford and the threatening stare he fixed on her.

Her mother's words, the ones she used to say during the first year of their captivity, rang in her ears like a specter's warning. "Cefus has eyes and ears everywhere, Evelyn. People who are just as depraved as he is, baby."

Eve knew it to be true. She often saw the sheriff from Sadie's window; he'd even been inside the house, but she was never in his presence. He appeared to be the oily type of man she saw on television. His hair was slicked to his head with chunks falling free. His shirt and pants were pressed, and she assumed clean but looked well worn, with his law badge weighing his shirt down on one side. His lowered brows and twisted, thin lips gave him an intimidating look.

When Eve noticed the gun belt with the firearm in the holster, her breath caught in her throat. She froze. Her eyes saw nothing but the gun; her ears heard nothing but the screams from the night that changed her life. The scent of her father's blood actually swirled around her. It was as if she had been propelled back in time and placed at the moment that still haunted her nights.

"Eve…"

Junior whispering her name did nothing to pull her frightened gaze from the gun inside the officer's hip holster. Terror took hold. Eve knew that she was failing her brother. She needed to get it together, but all she could focus on was that gun and her memories.

"Eve."

The warmth that Eve suddenly felt on her face was what broke the trance she was in. She shut her eyes, and when she opened them, she was no longer focused on the gun. Junior stood in front of her, his concerned gaze was spellbinding as he stared down at her. The only long piece of his cropped dirty blond hair flopped to one side as he tilted his head, to get a better angle to look deeper into her eyes. Junior's grip was firm, but it was his anguished look that held her steady.

"I won't let anyone hurt you, Evie." Junior stared into her eyes for several seconds before he leaned forward and gently kissed her. His lips, surprisingly soft, pressed against her skin for just a brief moment, but it was enough to pull her from her traumatic thoughts.

Feeling overwhelmed by Junior's peculiar action toward her, Eve took a deep, shaky breath. She didn't resist when Junior pulled her head to rest on his chest then wrapped her in his arms.

"What do you say we step outside?" Eve heard Mr. Hopkins say, but she wasn't sure who he was talking to. Soon after she heard movement and footsteps.

Eve continued to take deep breaths but didn't make any attempts to move out of Junior's hold. His chest was firm and his arms wrapped around her so protectively that she didn't want to move. In fact, all she really wanted to do at that moment was to stay in his arms, and that surprised her.

Eve was lulled by Junior's attention: the way he rocked from side to side; the way he softly smoothed her hair down with his hand had her so relaxed that she could have fallen asleep. So much so that she almost forgot where she was, who Junior was, and that they weren't alone. If it hadn't been for the sound of the woman in the room clearing her throat, Eve just might have fallen asleep. Junior forgot about their guest as well because he sighed and gave Eve a regretful look as he pulled away.

"I actually hate guns myself," Mrs. Hall spoke up.

Eve looked over at Mrs. Hall, who was still seated on the sofa, noticing that the woman's expression was one of understanding. That eased Eve's nerves a bit more.

No one said anything for a few seconds. Eve cautiously watched the woman who surveyed them quietly and when Mrs. Hall's eyes focused on an area just below Eve's waist, Eve looked down to see what the woman was looking at.

Mrs. Hall gaze was fixed on Eve's and Junior's entwined hands.

Eve felt a blast of heat hit her as she stared at their connected hands. Her eyes moved with the motion of Junior's thumb as it stroked the back of her hand. It was something she would not normally accept but at this moment, she needed it.

"Eve, if you would sit for a few and answer some questions for me, I will be out of your hair in no time. Junior, would you excuse us?" Mrs. Hall patted the seat beside her.

Eve looked at the seat offered to her then to Junior for direction. If he was worried, concerned, or whatever, his facial expression didn't show it.

"I'll be close," he said as he peered down at Eve. Junior kept hold of her hand as he escorted Eve to the sofa. He continued to hold it as she took a seat. He gave her a firm squeeze before he let her hand go and left the room. Eve was still watching the archway he'd left out of when Mrs. Hall cleared her throat again.

"I just have a few questions for you, Mrs. Shaw."

"Eve," she whispered.

"Excuse me?"

Eve thought of her mother and how elegant she was. She used to love just watching her mother so she decided it was her mother she would pretend to be. Eve straightened her back, raised her chin, and spoke clear. "Eve. Please call me, Eve."

Mrs. Hall nodded. "Eve it is." The woman gave her a smile.

Eve remembered her mother's smile and did her best to mimic it. The smile must have worked because Mrs. Hall's smile widened and the woman visibly relaxed. Then the questions began.

JUNIOR

Junior tried not to look nervous in front of Mr. Hopkins or Sheriff Gifford. He didn't want to bring any more attention to his situation than what he already had, but he was busting at the seams, thinking of what was being asked and said inside the house. He crossed the porch and plopped down on the chair that sat in front of Sadie's bedroom window. He pushed the chair on its back two legs; his feet flat on the ground for balance, he let his head fall back with his eyes closed in an attempt to seem relaxed.

"If I could ask," Mr. Hopkins said, sounding nonchalant, "what is the reason for your visit today?"

Junior peaked from under one eye to view the two men that stood on his porch. Mr. Hopkins was leaning against the house while Sheriff Gifford was facing the road. Gifford's back was to Mr. Hopkins, but Junior could see his expression clearly, and the sheriff looked at a loss. That lost look lasted only a second before it morphed into anger.

"That's my business…sir," Sheriff Gifford grunted. "Junior—" Gifford stomped down the porch steps. His car was parked half on the grass and half on the stone walk. When he opened the cruiser's door, Gifford stared at him in an attempt to force his thoughts into Junior's head.

Junior tipped the chair forward so that it was back on all four legs and peered back at his father's watchdog with narrowed eyes. He understood and heard the silent threat loud and damn clear. Only Gifford felt it necessary to continue the staring contest for several seconds before looking past Junior toward the house.

Gifford's lips stretched into a sly grin. "Hey there, Sadie, you're looking quite sweet today."

"Hi, Sheriff," Sadie said in her usual up-tempo happy tone.

Junior's hackles rose, but he fought down his annoyance. He hated that the bastard felt he could threaten him with his sister. His father, Sheriff Gifford, any man that would threaten an innocent person as leverage wasn't a man at all.

Gifford's grin grew as he opened his car door. He looked over at Junior again, winked, and then slid in behind the wheel. Junior watched with disgust as the cruiser backed up and drove down the path toward the road.

"Hello, Sadie," Mr. Hopkins said. Junior saw the man give Sadie an easy smile. "You think I could have some of that delicious lemonade of yours?"

Junior felt his anger dim. He watched his sister shriek with excitement as she backed into the house, letting the screen slam shut. "Thanks." Junior gave Mr. Hopkins a nod.

During the time when Mr. Hopkins used to visit, Junior kept the man at arm's length. Theirs was a relationship that was based solely on their jobs. Junior's—to hide what was going on in his horrid house. Mr. Hopkins—to find out what was going on in the home Junior lived in because of suspicion of abuse.

In the end, Mr. Hopkins found out nothing during his weekly visits during those two months, except maybe that Sadie meant the world to him. But apparently, everyone knew what Sadie meant to him.

"No favor to you really; I love Sadie's lemonade." Mr. Hopkins tilted his head in the direction of where Sheriff Gifford just rode off. "So, he's a barrel of fun."

"He's a tool." Junior shrugged.

"Want to talk about it?"

"Nope, not really," Junior told Mr. Hopkins.

Sadie soon came out with two large glasses of lemonade. She handed Mr. Hopkins one and then gave Junior the other before hopping off the porch. Sadie glided over the pebbled drive to the field of high grass that desperately needed mowing.

"So," Mr. Hopkins spoke up after a long silence, "when did you meet your wife?"

Junior peered at his guest for a moment before he answered, "I've known her for a few years." Hopkins watched Junior as if waiting for more, but Junior wasn't the type to offer information. "How long you plan on coming out here this go round?" Junior asked eventually.

Mr. Hopkins lifted the glass to his lips and took a long drink while looking over at Sadie who was spinning in a circle. When he pulled the glass away, Mr. Hopkins sighed. "This is Teresa's rodeo. I'm just along to see that it goes smoothly."

"Because I'm the big bad wolf," Junior sighed.

"We both know who the big bad wolf is, Junior. I didn't ask before, but you're an adult and a father now; why do you stay here…with him."

Junior didn't say anything right away. He knew he had to be careful of his answer, or he may raise more red flags. Obviously, Junior never confirmed with anyone what living with his father was really like and though he felt that this man could help him, he needed to be careful of what he said right now. He needed time for his claim to Theo to become official and a safe place for Sadie, Eve, and the babe before he told whoever would listen about Cefus' crimes. Though he felt that Mr. Hopkins was on the up and up, the people he cared for weren't safe just yet.

"Family is all we have in this world."

Eve

Mrs. Hall gave the impression that she was different. The way the woman spoke softly, the sincerity in her eyes, the easy, genuine smiles she offered. She seemed to be 'one of the good ones'. That was a phrase Eve recalled her mother would often say.

The image of Eve with her mother and father filtered through her mind. The memory was one of her favorite holidays. Easter was always fun for Eve. It meant that she got to wear a pretty brightly colored dress the entire day opposed to having to take it off as soon as she returned home from school. Eating lots of chocolate and candy was alright, and even though her mom fussed about her consuming too much, her dad's decision to allow it always won out. Her father hid eggs for her, and cousins, and friends to find. Even sitting through church was bearable on Easter Sunday.

"Eve," Mrs. Hall lightly touched her thigh. "Did you hear me?"

Eve blinked a few times and forced herself to focus on the woman in front of her. She often got lost in her thoughts when a pleasant memory of her life before their 'wrong turn into Hell' came to mind. As she looked at Mrs. Hall, Eve suddenly realized that she hardly thought of her father anymore. Not as much as she thought of her mother. That saddened her.

"Mrs. Shaw—"

"I prefer Eve," she reminded the social worker, snapping back to the conversation, "please."

Mrs. Hall nodded with a sympathetic smile that Eve couldn't quite understand. "Eve, I thank you for answering all my questions, but I have to say that I don't feel comfortable closing your son's case just yet. My colleague and I feel that it would be best to keep a close eye on you and your son for a few months." Eve could do nothing but stare at the woman, so Mrs. Hall continued. "Though I have concerns for how you and your husband will care for Theo, being that you're both so young, I believe you two will rise to the challenge. But…your living situation,"—she glanced around the clean but bare living room— "it worries me. I am sure that you know that your father-in-law has a reputation, and we suspect that he is…well," Mrs. Hall struggled with finding the right word.

Eve did something she hardly believed she was capable. She smiled and lied through her teeth. "I promise you that Theo and I are safe. I will never allow harm to come to my…son. Everything is fine."

"I hope so." Mrs. Hall's smile didn't quite reach her eyes. She maintained eye contact with Eve for a few moments before sighing and handing Eve a folder.

According to the state, Junior didn't make enough money to care for her and Theo so the state offered to give them a little help with medical bills and food. Mrs. Hall was going to file the paperwork on her behalf. Eve needed to get this right and not make any mistakes.

"I suppose we are done for now." Mrs. Hall placed her binder and folders in her briefcase and stood. "I need those forms as soon as possible. I spoke with Theo's doctor this morning, and he told me that he may be able to go home today. If you and Junior could fill out the forms for me and drop them off at my office today, that would be ideal."

Eve pushed to her feet and nodded. She shuffled the folder in one hand when Mrs. Hall reached out, handing Eve an envelope.

"These are vouchers that can be used for goods such as baby clothes and furniture, and things *you* may need. We sometimes give them out to help until the paperwork for assistance is processed. I've spoken with the stores in town, only a few will honor them but most in Anniston will.

Eve was shocked by the kindness of Mrs. Hall. She was never on the receiving end of such thoughtfulness, and it brought up an array of emotions to the surface. She had to fight the burning sensation behind her eyes.

"Thank you," she whispered.

Mrs. Hall looked at her, smiled, then pulled Eve into a loose hug. Surprisingly, Eve allowed herself to enjoy the embrace. It was brief and somewhat odd in its angle, but to feel this contact from another who wanted nothing from her was soothing.

Eve knew that her mother loved her, but Pearl mostly wanted Eve's cooperation. Granted it was to keep her safe, but Eve felt the request for submission in every embrace. Every touch from Sadie was a plea to stay with her. Then there was Junior. He was a man. Eve shivered at the thought of what else he could want other than her collaboration to free themselves from the Devil himself.

In the end, would he want Theo? Or would he want something wholly different?

Mrs. Hall rubbed Eve's shoulder. "Make sure to get yourself a few sweaters."

Yeah, Mrs. Hall is one of the nice ones.

Eve nodded as she gave the woman a genuine smile. She wasn't sure what to do next, so she followed Mrs. Hall to the front door that was open with the screen door being the barrier between inside and out.

Mr. Hopkins pulled the screen door open for Mrs. Hall. Eve stayed just inside the doorway, staring past their visitors to Sadie, who was out in the high grass chasing a butterfly. She vaguely remembered that she loved to chase anything with wings. Never did she ever catch any of the insects or birds, but she enjoyed the wind on her face and the carefree feeling when she thought of flying. She knew now that it wasn't necessarily the flying than the freedom.

Movement to Eve's left caught her attention. She looked over and locked eyes with Junior. His expression was schooled to fool the folks from the state, but she knew that he was nervous. Junior stood and as he did, he gave her a partial smile. Eve focused on the change it gave his overall look; though it was minimal, it was impactful. Junior was handsome, but with his smile, he was devilishly so.

The sudden thought of Junior in that way caused Eve to immediately break eye contact. She focused her attention on Mrs. Hall and Mr. Hopkins. He offered Eve a smile as he held open the screen door. Eve felt no fear, like she always felt when Cefus smiled at her. There were no butterflies like when Junior smiled at her. All she felt was the surprising need to answer his friendly expression with a small smile of her own.

"If you need anything at all…" Mrs. Hall smiled, "…call me. My number is on my card in the folder."

Eve nodded then watched as Mrs. Hall, and Mr. Hopkins got inside the car and drove away. When they were a good distance away, Eve turned her attention to Junior. The keys he loosely held on to chimed as they dangled from his fingers.

"Sadie," he called out before turning to Eve. "That little visit may have worked out in our favor. Get inside and lock up. Don't answer the door for anyone. I'm going to get Theo."

TEN

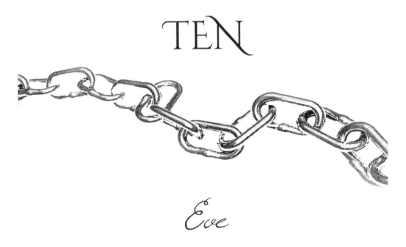

Eve

"Come on," Junior prompted as he pulled the passenger door of his truck open. He reached for her arm but Eve shook her head before he could touch her. "We've discussed this," he whispered as he moved closer. "We need people to see you and Theo. We need people to see that you both are mine."

Eve stared straight ahead—out of the windshield and at the house in front of her—until she heard Junior's claim. A pulse of pain echoed through her chest as she leveled her confused, hurt-filled eyes on him. Yes, they discussed her showing herself in public since the social workers visit a week ago but...

At no point did they discuss her...being his. Like she was property he owned. Like Cefus thought he owned her and her mother.

Junior picked up on what had her so upset because he took a step back. "Eve, I didn't mean it that way. I just meant that we need to be seen together, like a couple. I promised you I was going to get you away from here, and I meant that. We just gotta be smart about it."

"Can I have some ice cream? I always get ice cream when I visit." Sadie clapped her hands. Eve looked over at

Sadie, who was cuddling Theo in her arms. "Boy wants some too."

A slight smile tugged at Eve's lips. Sadie seemed to always know the right time to distract everyone from tense situations. Though it did distract Eve, it did nothing to relax her.

Being free of that aging house that was her prison consumed her thoughts most of the time. To be outside, around other people, to do something as simple as to visit a neighbor, was all she ever wished for. Now that she was able, with Junior as a tether, of course, she was a ball of nerves.

Freedom used to consume my every thought, she told herself as she admired Junior's slate gray eyes. After several seconds, Eve realized that he was staring back at her. Blushing, she quickly looked over Junior's shoulder and focused on the big, yellow beautiful house again. She felt overwhelmed—because of Junior's attention, and trapped— because she had to do the very thing she wanted to, interact with people.

What if these people hate her as much as Cefus did? What if they hate Theo? The list of reservations grew with every passing second. Eve's heart felt as if it was going to burst through her chest, and her vision blurred as she sucked in every breath as if she lacked oxygen.

"Evie," Junior spoke quietly. "Baby, I need you to breathe."

Eve heard Junior say her name in such a gentle manner, and she did her best to focus on the warmth of the large hands that cupped her face. She fought to get back from where ever it was her mind went.

When she was once again able to concentrate on Junior's handsome face, his eyes were wide with panic. His full lips were stretched thin, and his body was so tense she wondered how he wasn't crushing her skull. His tender touch was in total contrast with his body language.

"Sorry," Eve whispered, trying to look down and away from Junior's penetrating gaze.

"Heavens, girl," he said as he placed his forehead on hers. "You just about scared the piss out of me."

Eve held her breath, assaulted by the intense but conflicting feelings that blasted her. Junior's touch, his closeness had her wanting to both rip away and to pull him closer.

"I want ice cream," Sadie whined this time. She shifted beside Eve, on the single row seat they shared. "Can we have some ice cream *please*?"

Junior rolled his eyes but couldn't seem to hold back a grin as he glanced at his sister. "Sure thing, Sadie, let's just get some things out of the way first, okay."

Eve's initial fear dampened just a bit as she heard an exaggerated pout leave, Sadie.

"Hey there, Junior, everything okay?" A feminine voice called out.

Eve peered over Junior's shoulder at a woman standing on the porch. The woman angled her body as if she were trying to see around Junior's large form.

"Everything is fine, Mrs. W," Junior said. His hands fell away, and he moved back a few steps then turned just his head to look at the woman.

Junior turned his attention back on Eve, holding her captive for a long moment. She wanted to shrink under his scrutiny, but she stared back. The intimate way he touched her had Eve feeling jittery again.

Allowing her nerves to get the better of her, Eve was the first to look away because she saw the heated admiration that reflected in his eyes before. It was the look he wore that day he kissed her, and Eve wasn't certain if she wanted him to kiss her again, let alone with onlookers.

Without meeting Junior's eyes, Eve scooted out of the truck. When her feet hit the paved street, she turned and reached for Theo, so Sadie could get out of the vehicle. With

Theo in her arms and Sadie out of the truck, Eve finally looked at Junior. He gave her an assessing, lingering once-over then seemingly satisfied with his findings, Junior turned and led the way.

Eve cuddled Theo closer. Feeling out of sorts from the panic attack and Junior's attention, she used her brother's presence to give her the strength she needed. When Sadie slammed the truck door shut, the noise startled Theo. He jerked awake, let out a tiny whimper, then stretched and contorted his little body. Eve almost sighed, relieved that she had the distraction. She gently bounced him a few times as she rubbed his back. The baby settled almost immediately, once again leaving Eve with nothing to filter the experience of her surroundings.

"Sorry," Sadie winced as she walked up to Eve. "You want me to hold him."

"No, I have him," Eve assured Sadie, holding the baby closer. Theo became her security blanket in a way.

"Okay," Sadie said with a forced smile, "you think we'll get some ice cream?"

Eve tried to hold in a giggle knowing that when Sadie decided on something it was hard to sidetrack her. Eve could attest to that, giving into Sadie on most issues.

After all, it was Sadie that decided all those years ago that I was hers... Not Junior's.

"Later, I think." Eve turned to see that Junior was standing beside the woman who called to him. Eve knew from Junior's morning pep talk that the woman's name was Mrs. Mabel Wilson. Her husband was Mr. Tom Wilson, and they lived on this land for about ten years. They had two grade school age kids, Paul and Lucy, and a field hand named Ellis Kent who Junior helped out with chores from time to time.

As Eve climbed the stairs to meet the woman who cautiously smiled at them, she realized that Mrs. Mabel

Wilson was lovely. Her skin was like fine smooth porcelain, her hair was as black as tar, and her eyes were the prettiest brown she'd ever seen. As Eve moved closer, she noticed that Mrs. Wilson had a sprinkling of freckles on her cheeks and nose. Mrs. Wilson smiled as she extended her hand, and Eve noticed that she had the whitest, straightest teeth she ever saw.

"Hello, Eve," Mrs. Wilson said. Shyly, Eve slowly placed her hand in Mrs. Wilson's, who gave it a gentle squeeze. "I'm happy that you decided to join me for a bit this afternoon."

Eve held Mrs. Wilson's gaze and studied it as best as she could. She had no skill at judging character. She wanted to like the woman that had a welcoming smile, but everything inside her yelled not to trust anyone.

"Hello," Eve mumbled.

There were an awkward few moments of silence then Mrs. Wilson's owlish gaze fell on Theo. "Oh, my." Mrs. Wilson bent forward, closer to Eve. Her head whipped around. "He has eyes just like yours..." she said to Junior but finished with an, "Oh."

"Yeah," Junior agreed as he kissed Theo on the head.

The woman raised an eyebrow as she leaned back and looked at Eve, then to Junior, and finally to Theo again. Clearly, Junior didn't tell the woman his little farce when he told her he was bringing someone to meet her.

"And this little guy is…

"Theo," Junior answered,

Mrs. Wilson reached for Theo. Instinctively, Eve nestled Theo closer to her. Mrs. Wilson seemed to notice Eve's uneasiness so she stepped back and motioned to Theo. To her credit, Mrs. Wilson didn't look put out by Eve's reaction. Her smile faltered just a smidgeon before she turned to Sadie.

She hugged Sadie to her tight and long before releasing her. "I've missed you hanging around, Sadie." Mrs. Wilson glanced at the watch she wore on her tiny wrist. "I think it's time for ice cream…what do you think, dear."

"Yes!" Sadie screeched as she took hold of Mrs. Wilson's hand and pulled the woman over to the front door.

Eve inwardly smiled, thinking how little it took to make Sadie happy. She wondered if she could ever be happy.

"You cool?" Junior was watching her again. His brows were pinched together and his eyes searching. Lately, his eyes were always searching…for what, she didn't know.

"It isn't too hot, but I wouldn't say it's cool out."

"It's slang, just like *solid*; it means 'is everything alright.'"

Eve nodded as she waited for Junior to move. She wasn't *solid* or *alright*, or whatever cool meant. She was always worried, tired, and fearful of the day Cefus would return. Because according to Junior, Cefus would return and that meant that she had to be prepared.

When, was the question?

She knew what Junior told her was sound. That he needed to work out things before they could all be free. It was just that…she had a feeling that she would die by Cefus' hands the same way her parents' did.

A slight movement from Theo had Eve looking down at him in reflection. She didn't want another of her family members to die. She would do whatever she had to do to make sure that he didn't. Without knowing who to trust, Eve had to depend on Junior. He hated Cefus just as much as she did.

Junior continued to watch her, searching.

"I'm fine," Eve assured him. When Junior didn't look away, she looked out over the porch at the property. The lawn was green and cut nicely. The walkway was a straight path and intact, not crumpled and in pieces. The property seemed well cared for. It was so different than that of her prison that Eve found it hard to fathom that this was a neighboring farm to the Shaw's property.

When Eve turned back to Junior, he was finally opening the screen door. He placed his hand on Eve's lower back, startling her but she soon realized that he was trying to ease her inside. Immediately, Eve noticed the house smelled like baked goods. The smell instantly brought forth a foggy image of an older woman with gentle, caring eyes who…often gave her treats.

Did that happen?

Eve held on to only a few memories of her past, so she wondered if the woman she just saw in her mind was one of her grandmothers or just a figment of her imagination. The scent obviously triggered something. But was it a memory or a wish? Eve no longer remembered the faces and names of her family anymore, but she often had faded recollections.

"Please sit." Mrs. Wilson poked her head out of what looked to be the dining room entryway and motioned to the sitting area. "Or you can come inside the kitchen, Eve."

Junior led her with his hand still on the small of her back to the sofa where they both sat. A few seconds later Mrs. Wilson walked in with a tray filled with drinks and some kind of cakes.

"I hope you like coffee cake and sweet tea." Mrs. Wilson placed the tray on the oval table that sat in front of them. She put a small round lacey object down then placed a drink on top of it in front of each of them then served everyone a slice of the delicious smelling cake. Well, everyone except Sadie.

"Where's Sadie?" Eve asked Junior quietly.

Junior leaned into her. He said nothing at first. Except…Eve thought she heard him inhale deeply. Then he said, "She's in the kitchen, eating ice cream."

"Oh," Eve nodded absently as she tried to focus on something, anything other than his proximity. She shifted Theo in her arms and moved her chin gently over his head, loving the softness of his curls, then kissed him.

"Well," Mrs. Wilson said as she sat, "how are things, Junior?"

Eve looked up to see Mrs. Wilson sitting across from them in a high back chair. She sat perfectly straight and held her glass like what Eve imagined a woman of class would. Like the women in the regency romance books she read.

Junior and their host talked while Eve sort of zoned out. She didn't know about farming, the mill, or any of the people they spoke of. Every so often her ears picked up on something she had a mild interest in, or Mrs. Wilson would ask her something but Eve was too nervous to actually say more than one or two words in reply. She didn't want to mess the plan up and apparently this woman was important to Junior's plan. She wondered what his plan was, really.

Eventually, Sadie entered the living room with a pleased smile on her face. She insisted on taking Theo so Eve could eat her cake and drink her tea, and Eve handed the baby over reluctantly. The conversation around her kept going, but she felt no need to join in so she kept busy with her thoughts for a while.

"Eve," Junior said, placing a hand on her thigh.

Startled by the contact, Eve swung her head around to see both Junior and Mrs. Wilson staring at her. She was keeping busy with cataloging all the wondrous things in her line of sight while paying little attention to the people in the room.

"Yes," Eve stuttered.

"I was telling Junior here that I'm a pretty good seamstress, and I would love to teach you...along with Sadie," Mrs. Wilson motioned to Sadie, "if you'd like."

Eve glanced over at Sadie, who was sitting on the nearby loveseat feeding Theo. Sadie nodded with excitement at the offer.

"I can alter your clothing to fit better so you all won't have to buy new things and can spend your money on the things you need more instead." Mrs. Wilson waited patiently with her perfect smile in place. When Eve didn't answer right away, caution etched the woman's face. "I understand if you rather not."

Rubbing her hands over her legs, Eve saw as Sadie's smile faded. When she glanced over at Junior, he was watching her with concern. Why couldn't she be normal or just act as if she were?

"If you'll excuse me," Mrs. Wilson said as she stood, "I have to check on something in the kitchen."

Eve watched as the woman who wasn't rude so far, left the room. She frowned at her apprehension to allow Mrs. Wilson to help her. The woman seemed nice enough, and Sadie adored her. Sadie's approval meant something.

"What's the problem, Eve?" Junior scooted closer and lowered his voice so that only Eve could hear him. "Mrs. Wilson only wants to help us out."

"But why?" was all Eve could manage. Why was this woman going to help her? What would she gain from it? "So far, everyone I know only does what they think is going to benefit them in some way. That includes you and those state workers who are doing their job."

Eve could argue that everything Junior did from the very beginning, even when Eve didn't understand his reasons, were to help Sadie. And now he championed for his blood brother. No, he wasn't a bad person, but Eve knew she was just a loose end in the grand scheme of things. Yes, Junior would entrust her to care for their brother if in fact he was arrested for being Cefus' accomplice, but Eve was sure if he wasn't worried about his freedom, he would take Theo from her.

There was no one left in Eve's life who would sacrifice everything for her. The only people who did were dead. So no, she didn't trust the woman.

How can I trust anyone, including the man who sits beside me?

In regards to Junior, Eve had little choice but to accept his terms. But accepting Mrs. Wilson's help was different. What did she have to gain?

"Everyone isn't like Cefus, Evie." Junior looked in the direction Mrs. Wilson went then focused back her Eve. He continued in a hushed tone, "Mrs. Wilson is nice and giving. She's never treated Sadie, or me foul even though they know Cefus. They treat Sadie kindly knowing she's different. Her husband, Mr. Wilson, is just as nice. And if you worry about how they are with black people, you don't have to worry. They've employed a hand, Ellis, during summer seasons and treat him like a man." Junior sighed. "Just give her a chance. I won't have you wearing rags any longer, and your mother's clothes aren't a good fit. I want you to have things…" Junior glanced down then back to her.

Are his cheeks reddening?

"Things you like, pretty things. You can use the money from the state on other things you and Theo need. Besides, Eve, you have to learn to be around others, to deal with folk in normal terms again."

Eve would berate herself later but in that moment; she couldn't be blamed for staring into Junior's intense eyes. They usually reflected gentleness when they were focused on her. Often she saw the heat of anger in them, but Junior never directed those steel beams on her or Sadie in those instances. Lately, his eyes seemed to duel between gentle concern and what she thought was the kind of heat that she read about in her romance novels. Could…she be reading him wrong?

Looking away from Junior's pleading gaze, Eve gave him a curt nod.

"Cool," Junior said as he stood. He did something then that she rarely saw him do. He looked down at her and smiled. His smile was infectious and the few times she'd witnessed it, Eve felt like smiling herself. She always fought that feeling, and she fought it now, even as she felt her heart skip a beat.

Eve placed her hand on her chest as she watched Junior leave the room using the same path around the furnishings that Mrs. Wilson took. Eve tried to focus on Sadie rubbing Theo's back while she waited for what happened next, instead of her pesky reactions to Junior. When he returned, after a few passing minutes, Mrs. Wilson was with him. Her lips were spread so wide that most of her pearly white teeth were on display. Even Junior seemed as giddy as a school boy.

Eve never saw him so…so pleased.

"Mrs. Wilson has most of what you need here, but there are a few other things you'll need." Junior walked over to where Sadie sat on the loveseat with Theo. Junior reached out, and Sadie handed Theo over to him. "I'll go to store now so you'll be all set tomorrow."

Wait…was he leaving and not taking them?

Eve pushed off of the sofa but didn't move as she watched Junior hold Theo to his chest and place a loving kiss on the baby's head. Junior then handed Theo back to Sadie and gave his sister a quick peck on her cheek.

He's really going to leave us here.

Eve's brows furrowed as she tried communicating with Junior with her eyes as he walked toward her. *Don't leave me alone with this lady,* she thought and tried to convey.

Junior seemed oblivious to her silent pleas as he took one of her hands in his. He brought their interlocked fingers to his mouth and placed a tender kiss on the back of her hand. She tried to fight the shudder that slivered up from her feet and through her body but was unsuccessful. The little frown Junior gave her told Eve that he knew that she didn't react to a chill in the air. Sighing, because she had little control of her reactions when dealing with him, Eve tried to unlock her hand from his.

Leaning into her, Junior whispered in her ear, "Don't be afraid, Evie. No one here is going to hurt you. I'll never allow anyone else to hurt any of us again." He leaned back but kept hold of her. "I promise."

Sighing, because he wasn't aware of how he affected her, Eve saw sincerity in Junior's eyes. She nodded, coming to terms with what needed to be done. One: she had no choice but to trust in Junior's plan, and Mrs. Wilson was a part of that plan. Two: she would have to get used to his touch, no matter how it affected her because playing a couple meant touching was expected.

JUNIOR

Just as he exited the Wilsons house and stepped foot onto their porch, Junior wanted to turn back around. But he forced himself to move forward, one weighted step at a time. Eve being seen was necessary to his plan.

My grand, currently shaky, plan.

Things didn't go exactly the way he wanted so far. He didn't have nearly as much money saved as he liked. Just a couple thousand now, having used most to pay bills in Cefus' absence. The search for Cindy, his mother, didn't go well either. She left little of herself for him to remember her and nothing at all to track her down. There was one more option for him to try, but he wouldn't use it unless he had no other choice.

It seemed he was virtually at that point now.

Junior noticed Mr. Wilson and Ellis walking up with Digger as he stepped down the last porch stair. He waited until they were close to say his greetings, "Mr. Wilson, Ellis." Junior patted Digger on the head before the dog ran off.

"How you doing on this fine day, Junior?" Mr. Wilson pulled his glove off his right hand and extended it out to Junior.

Junior shook Mr. Wilson's hand. "I'm okay," Junior said, and he was at the moment, "a bit skittish about leaving Eve here."

"She'll be fine," Ellis said, shaking Junior's hand next.

"Bringing her here with you was a big step, son." Mr. Wilson told him as he patted Junior on the shoulder. "This is all new to her, let alone having the baby to care for. This new life you two plan to make together, her surroundings, will be tough on you both. Your differences won't matter in the end if you respect, love, and work with one another. That's what marriage is all about."

Junior showed no visual reaction to hearing the lies he told his neighbors of Eve's sudden appearance in his life. A few days ago he visited the Wilsons. He sat them down and spun a tale of how he visited a neighboring town to party with some friends last year. At that party, he met a young but beautiful girl who caught his attention. That night ultimately ended in Theo's conception and Eve having nowhere to go in her condition.

This was the story he and Eve decided on and the same story he told the social workers and Dr. Steuben.

Mr. Wilson pulled his glove back on then patted his gloved hands together, ousting some matted dust. "I got to get back to work. Just wanted to say hello and to let you know that we're giving your young lady some space, like you requested."

"I appreciate it," Junior replied again, meaning it wholeheartedly. Junior watched Mr. Wilson turn toward the direction he came.

Mr. Wilson looked over his shoulder and gave Junior a questioning look. It was clear the man wanted to ask something, but instead he said, "Only fear, lack of communication and sometimes outside influences can poison a new beginning, Junior. Your son deserves a fair beginning." Mr. Wilson tipped his baseball cap then walked off.

The question went unasked, but the statement was clear. Junior knew that Mr. Wilson's advice was more or less a warning regarding Cefus. Junior wanted to tell Mr. Wilson that he was well aware of the threat. That he would die before, he let Cefus' poison touch his family.

"You heading to the general store?"

Junior looked over at Ellis, who was casually leaning against Junior's truck. Ellis took his work gloves off and stuffed them in the back pocket of his jeans while he wiped his brow with a cloth.

"Yup, you tagging along?"

Ellis opened the passenger-side door and climbed his imposing frame in the passenger seat. He was tall; merely inches taller than Junior but thickly muscled, the kind of frame that only hard work could produce. Ellis had dark skin, brown eyes, a strong jaw, his nose was straight though a bit wider than Junior's, and his lips were well defined and thick.

Junior never studied Ellis before today, but as he did, he realized that Ellis was a good looking guy. Though unaware before today, understanding had Junior turning to look back at the house. *Will Eve think Ellis is good looking? Will she even stay with me now, after meeting others?*

Thump. The sound had Junior spinning his head around to investigate.

"The sooner we leave the sooner we're back." Ellis grinned from inside the truck. He slammed his palm on the outside of the passenger-side door again. "Let's get a move on."

Junior sighed as he tried to shake the crazy feelings that almost had him changing his mind about leaving Eve at all. Not that he wanted her in the car with Ellis either. What he felt, jealousy, it was an odd feeling. He never felt jealous before, but he had witnessed and been on the receiving end of it. Though the feeling to stay with Eve was strong at the moment, Junior couldn't ruin the progress that she already made or turn away from the plan.

So with that in mind, he forced himself forward. He got inside his truck, started the engine, did a U-turn, then proceeded along the long drive to the main road.

"She'll be fine."

Junior didn't respond to Ellis with words. Instead, he just nodded.

"If you know that to be true then why are you gripping that stirring wheel like it killed your puppy?"

Junior examined his hands. It was true. He was gripping the steering wheel so tightly that his knuckles were white. Junior forced his hands to relax even though he didn't feel calm.

"I caught a peek at her when you rode in. I suppose if I had a beauty like Eve, I wouldn't much like leaving her either." Ellis stretched out his legs and rolled down his window. When he glanced over at Junior, he chuckled. "Really just a compliment, nothing more."

Junior frowned, wondering what the hell Ellis was smirking about. He noticed Ellis motioning to the steering wheel again. This time, when Junior looked to his hands, he realized his grip was even tighter than before, which didn't seem possible.

"Sorry," Junior apologized. He ignored the slight ache in his knuckles. "I don't know what's wrong with me."

"Women have a way of bringing a man's inner beast to the surface." Ellis sighed, this time, causing Junior to relax a little more.

"Speaking of beasts, where's Dobs?" Dobs and Digger were the Wilsons' dogs. Digger was a thorn in Cefus' side for years, digging up their dry patches of land. Dobs was maybe a couple of years old and related to Digger—either being his son or nephew; Junior wasn't certain. But whatever the relation, Dobs liked dirt diving just as much as Digger. Cefus hated the Wilsons' dogs, and he'd shoot to kill whenever the dogs trespassed on their property.

"Tom tied Dobs up in the barn. He still hasn't learned not to jump up on folks. Damn dog's a menace to all clothing so Mabel thought it better to keep him away from your woman."

Junior found himself smiling at Ellis' words *your woman*. He was crazy, but he liked the way claiming Eve made him feel. Minutes passed in silence as Junior drove. The entire time all he thought about was Eve being his woman.

"You've got it bad," Ellis finally said, breaking the silence. He chuckled as he shook his head when Junior glanced his way, but this time, the laugh wasn't a pleasant one.

Curious, Junior asked, "What?"

Ellis blew out a breath and shook his head again. "You damn well know what, Junior," his tone was accusing and lacked the playful humor Ellis Kent was known for.

Junior sighed as he made a right at the intersection, onto the long road that would take them to town. "I thought you of all people would be cool with Eve and me being together. I guess I was wrong."

"I'm going to pretend you didn't just say that. Don't feed me that slop, Junior."

Knowing and admitting was two entirely different things, and Junior wished he could claim ignorance to both. But he knew what Ellis meant, and he would admit to that. "I'm sorry. I know you, and the Wilsons aren't like some. That's why I introduced you all to her." Junior shook his head, feeling all of his frustrations bubbling to the surface. "And I have a plan."

"I hope so. He always comes back; when that happens, I will bet Mabel's biscuits and gravy that what he finds going on in his house won't sit well with him. What the hell were you thinking getting that innocent young girl all mixed up in your shit life? Was getting her pregnant some stupid attempt at slapping Cefus in the face to you?"

Junior pulled into the parking space so fast he had to hit the brakes hard to stop from riding up on the curb. He put the truck in park, twisted the keys, then yanked them out of the ignition as he turned his angry gaze on Ellis. "It wasn't like that. You know I don't give a fuck about Cefus or enough about what he thinks to piss him off. Eve and I are... We're in this together. It's not important how we got to this point."

"I hope you got a good plan because... Look," Ellis sighed, "Tom and I have kept our noses out of y'alls business to a point. You know some things about our family that Mabel is thankful that you've kept to yourself. Us, Mabel and I, being blood kin due to our daddy's roaming isn't something our families want everyone to know, but I'm going to be straight with you. It was us who called Social Services on Cefus after you got banged up."

Junior said nothing even though Ellis' admission wasn't a shock.

"And it wasn't the first call Mabel's made to report Cefus. It's just that she called Anniston General and reported her fears to them when you were transported there for surgery instead of the local Sheriff's office this time." Ellis paused. Junior assumed it was to allow him to respond, but Junior kept quiet. "Shit, man, I'm telling you this not to make you mad, but to tell you that Tom and I aren't going to sit by while he beats that baby like he does you. I know I'm overstepping here, but I'm just—"

Junior held up his hand to stop Ellis from going any further. He wasn't mad, and he understood where Tom and Ellis were coming from. He was right there with them concerning Cefus. "I will never let him touch Theo or hurt my family," Junior paused, never admitting to anyone that he was Cefus' punching bag until now, "or me ever again."

Ellis smiled. "Okay, but if you ever need—"

"You'll be the first to know," Junior interrupted.

Ellis pushed open the passenger door. "Good," he said with a half grin. Apparently satisfied with the conclusion of the conversation, Ellis got out of the truck. "You need anything from Bert's?" Junior shook his head no. "Then I'll meet you back here."

Junior watched Ellis stroll toward Henley's Hardware store that everyone referred to as Bert's, due to Bert being the original owner back when people rode horses as a means of transportation.

Two loud thumps on the hood of Junior's truck had him quickly spinning his head around. He relaxed some when he saw Sam Tate leaning on his driver's side door.

"Well, look at who decided to come into town and grace us." Sam grinned as he opened the door and extended his hand for Junior to exit as if he were a chauffeur. "How ya doing, your royal highness?"

Junior got out of the truck, shooting Sam an irritated look but eventually smiled. The two embraced one another and laughed. "It's good to see you, Sam. How've you been?" he asked, actually interested in Sam's answer.

It had been two years since Junior last seen Sam Tate, his old football teammate. Sam had gone off to a small college to play ball in hopes that he could make a name for himself and transfer to a larger school with a bigger football program. Last Junior heard was that Sam was doing well.

Sam winked. "Good. Football isn't my future; had to drop out of school, but I met a nice girl and her parents' love me. Her pops runs a car dealership and gave me a job." He patted Junior on the shoulder then playfully punched him in the arm. "It's not what I planned, but it's good money and," Sam wiggled his brows, "I get to sleep with the boss' daughter so I'm coming along well. I hear you've been busy."

177

Junior's eyes rolled skyward. Dr. Steuben told his wife Janice everything, and if Janice knew anything, the entire town knew. With a chuckle, because his plan to have as many people as possible know of Eve's existence was working better than he expected, Junior stepped up on the sidewalk. The more people who knew of her, the less likely Cefus would kill her like he did her parents'. That was Junior's mindset anyway.

Leading the way to his destination, Junior knew Sam would follow. "Yeah, I suppose I have."

Sam walked beside him with a silly grin plastered on his face as he shook his head. "I thought for sure Terry Bradshaw had her claws in you so deep that you'd never escape."

Junior noticed Sam shivered as if someone walked over his grave. Terry had that effect on people he guessed.

"So…" Sam looked at him pointedly, "…are we going to talk around it or can we just get to the meat of the matter?"

Junior side glanced at his friend. They weren't close but Junior wasn't close to anyone really. If he had to label the people he knew, Junior would definitely have to say that the Wilsons and his teammates above all others, were as close to friends as any others in his life. With Sam's role decided, Junior couldn't help the roar of laughter that bellowed from him. He ignored the frowns and curious glances from the people around them as he continued to his destination.

His laughter continued when he glanced over at Sam, who looked confused at first then began to laugh as if he'd finally got the punch line of the joke told minutes ago.

"Wait," Sam asked after their laughter subsided, "what are we laughing at?"

Junior shook his head as they came to the craft and fabric shop. "Your unmatched knack for getting right to the point, Sam. I think I actually like that about you."

Sam's smiled spread wider, and he stood straighter as if he were the proudest of the peacocks.

"She's beautiful, smart, compassionate, and she's also black." Junior pulled the door open, hearing the familiar bell above the door. He held it open for two women who moved toward the exit. "Hopefully, our son will be the best of her." Junior ignored the women's blatant stares as they slowly passed. Apparently, they heard some of what he said and were moving slowly to soak up more. They were friends of Mrs. Steuben or members of the gossip train, he was sure.

"You say they have some special cloth in this store that stretches with the huge erections I get," Sam said as he glared at the women.

Both women gasped as they sped their steps up and moved through the doorway. Junior couldn't help but laugh as they hastened away. "You're an asshole," he told Sam.

"And proud of it." Sam motioned for Junior to go ahead as he extended his arm to hold the door.

Sam kept himself occupied with looking and touching things Junior was certain his friend had no clue to what they were or was used for while Junior spoke with the clerk and gave his order. When the clerk moved off to fill it, Sam approached.

"You buying this stuff for her?" Sam asked, fingering some of the fabric Junior asked for that was on Mrs. Wilson's list.

"Yeah," Junior answered.

"I heard your ole' man is on one of his vacations. Been gone for a while now, right?" Sam smoothed the fabric that sat on the counter out with his hand. "You know Nashville is a great place to start over. I bet I could get you a job at the dealership. You guys can shack up with me and Fran until you find a place of your own. We live in a good size house near her family. She loves babies, and the Parkers are good people. Unlike these closed-minded hicks, they believe everyone deserves fair treatment."

The offer hung in the air for several seconds, unanswered, before Junior was able to respond. When he was capable, because he didn't expect Sam's offer, Junior's response was quiet and thick with emotion. "Thanks, Sam, I'm grateful for the offer, but we need to find our own way."

Sam nodded his understanding, patting Junior on the back a couple of times. "So, you have a plan then?"

"I have a plan," Junior said just as the clerk returned to the counter. She rang him up and bagged the goods, and Junior paid for them.

Seems everyone was concerned about him and Eve, concerning Cefus.

They exited the store, and he and Sam walked back to Junior's truck where Ellis was leaning against the hood. Ellis nodded at Sam as they approached but said nothing. Sam returned the greeting with a wave.

"Well, Junior, if you're ever in my neck of the woods." Sam extended his hand.

Junior took hold of Sam's offered hand and shook it. "You never know," Junior told him. The sentiment was nice, but it was never going to happen. He doubted he'd be free to go anywhere after he took Cefus down.

"Tell Sadie I said hi, will ya," Sam said as he strolled away.

"Sure thing." Junior unlocked the door, and he and Ellis got inside the truck. He placed the bag he carried between them and started the engine. He needed to get back to the Wilson's farm. He wanted to get back to Eve.

ELEVEN

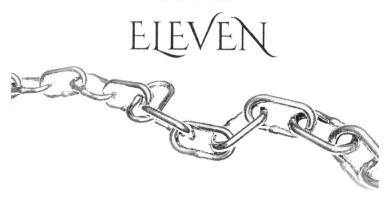

JUNIOR

The house was quiet. Junior was still getting used to that. He always wanted peace and silence, but as of late, he felt the emptiness of it now. It was this way almost every day when he returned from work. Since he introduced Evie to the Wilsons a few months ago, Eve, Sadie, and Theo spent most of their days at the Wilson farm now.

Junior could admit to himself that he missed having them here to greet him when he got home from work, but he'd never tell them. He missed the smile on Sadie's face when he opened the front door, always waiting for sweet treats he brought her. Junior missed his playtime with Theo when he cared for the babe so the girls could finish dinner. Most of all, he missed seeing Evie's beauty when he walked through the door after a hard day's work.

What he didn't miss was the anxious look on her lovely face just after he stepped in from outside. He knew the reason for her fear, and everything in him wanted to abolish, kill and bury it in an empty field. She, like each of them, knew that Cefus wasn't going to stay away for too long. Just like Evie, Junior honestly feared the man's return.

Today Junior fought his loneliness away and trudged to the kitchen. He washed his hands then pulled the seasoned beef loaf that he prepared the night before and placed it in the oven. Then he did what he did four times each day. He lifted the handle of the newly installed phone that the social worker required them to have, and he dialed the Wilson's phone.

When Mrs. Wilson picked up, she greeted him without his having to talk. "Hello, Junior," she said. He could tell she was smiling.

"Hello, Mrs. W. Can I talk with Eve please?"

"She's right here, one moment."

Junior heard the sound of Mrs. Wilson putting the phone receiver down then the sound of her children, Fran, and Paul, playing with Theo. It seemed that both children adored his son…brother. *Theo is my brother*, he reminded himself for the hundredth time.

"Hello."

As always, Junior's heart skipped a beat with such force he usually had to rub his chest. The sound of Evie's voice was something he would always treasure. It was what got him through most days. It was what powered him. It was also what soothed him when he needed to make sure that she didn't leave him. That she realized that she didn't need him and ran for her freedom.

Her voice was his anchor because unbeknownst to Eve, Junior decided that she was his, and he was keeping her.

"Everything alright?" he asked. It was the question he always asked.

"Yes," Eve's voice was lit with excitement. "I've finished the dress! Mrs. Wilson, ah…Mabel and Shirley helped me make my first homemade apple pie today. It smells wonderful," she sang. "Oh, and Sadie is doing so well with her swimming lessons. You should be so proud of her!"

He was. Sadie had a fear of water for as long as he could remember and rarely did she go to the Hole. The Hole was a pond that was located between the Shaw and Wilson land that the town made use of. It was very close, but the hidden path was encased by a densely wooded area.

"That's great, Evie!" Junior couldn't keep her infectious happiness out of his tone. He didn't want to. He wanted Eve happy. He suffered from her absence but did so with no complaints just because she seemed so happy over the past few weeks. "I'll be sure to tell her how proud I am."

After Junior said that, there was a brief, uncomfortable silence between them. Their phone conversations usually consisted of him asking her if she was fine and her saying yes, then they hung up. Today was different, a good different but different altogether. Eve must have realized it too because he could almost hear her mind processing it.

Laughing to himself, he knew he could prolong the awkward silence. "Dinner will be ready soon." Junior decided to end her embarrassment and let her off the line. "I'm going to get cleaned up. Call me when you're ready for me to pick you up."

"Okay," Eve mumbled.

Junior laughed again, this time not able to hide his amusement. "Okay." He hung up the receiver with a smile on his face. Evie hardly spoke to him about anything that involved her day unless it was to tell him something that concerned the house, the baby, or Sadie. Their conversations were very mechanical, of an informative nature and nothing personal.

Climbing the stairs to take a shower, Junior realized that his smile didn't disappeared and was actually growing. Today, Evelyn Jones opened up just a little bit. Today, for a brief moment she treated him like a friend and not the son of the man he heard her call the Devil.

Eve

The sun was still out, but most of the day slipped away. It was a good day. In fact, it was a great day and an amazing few weeks.

At first, when Junior introduced her to the Wilsons, Eve was reserved and frightened. Now, she wouldn't know what to do without the woman who helped keep her days busy and her mind sane.

If not for Mrs. Wilson, Eve feared she would have cracked by now. It was getting more and more difficult for her, the waiting. Waiting for something to happen was so unnerving. She believed that Junior wanted them safe. He showed her that he cared for Theo as much as he cared for Sadie. He would protect their brother, and that was the most important thing, but she was tired of the deadlock they were in.

At least she was almost certain that Junior would not harm her. He hadn't lost his temper at all since the day after the Devil took off. He treated her more than fair, even though she still took care not to say too much or make any mistakes. But she couldn't help but wonder about her and Theo's safety. Junior *was* the Devil's son. Then there was the Devil himself.

When was Cefus returning? Would they be gone before he returned? Was Junior taking the necessary steps for them to leave this place?

Eve glanced at Sadie and Theo as she turned the knob to enter the house she resided. Sadie's smiling face and Theo's curious gaze forced her troubled thoughts away, at least for now. *We will finish out the day with peace*, she smiled, then looked down at her covered homemade pie she held in her hands.

As she led the way into the house, she once again stressed over what Junior would think of her creation. Why she cared what he thought was something she wouldn't question, but now her anxiety because of it was clear. From the gathering of ingredients to the moment her eyes lit with pride at its completion, she worried about his reaction.

Will he enjoy it? Will he be capable of lying to me to save my feelings if he doesn't like it? Do I want him to lie if he hates it?

The questions were endless and so frustrating.

Sadie took Theo to their room to change his diaper while Eve headed for the kitchen. When the scent of dinner hit Eve, a sliver of guilt struck her. For three nights in the past week and a half, she neglected to cook dinner. Junior didn't get angry like Cefus would have. He didn't even complain. What he did was cooked, and he did so often.

Eve stood in the entryway watching Junior as he spooned peas onto a plate that already had meatloaf and potatoes on it. He looked up and smiled when he saw her.

He…smiled?

"I thought you were going to call me when you were ready. But Mr. Wilson rang and said that the Mrs. was bringing you, so I started plating dinner."

Sadie walked up from behind Eve and slid by to take a seat at the table with Theo nestled in her arms. "Ooh I love meatloaf," she said with excitement. "Is it momma's?"

Eve noticed how Junior's entire body went stiff at the mention of his mother. He nodded then placed the pot of peas on the stove. He walked over and took Theo from Sadie then regarded Eve. "Eat, both of you. I'll eat later." When Eve didn't respond, Junior asked, "Is something wrong?"

Everything was wrong. At that moment, watching Junior dish out food, feeling the weight of the pie in her hand, and seeing Sadie and Theo in such a normal family state…she felt as if she belonged. That these…them…they were a family. They were a twisted family but a family nonetheless.

"Evie?" Junior took a step toward her, but Eve held up a hand.

She shook off the unsettling feelings and moved to the counter and placed the pie down. "Nothing, I'm just tired," Eve told him. She quickly washed her hands then took a seat opposite of Sadie. She didn't protest but did mentally note that Junior sat in the chair closest to her when he could have sat in the empty seat beside Sadie.

The first bite of meatloaf was mouthwatering, which made it easy for Eve to focus on her meal instead of her surroundings. She half listened to Sadie as she excitedly shared what her day was like. The sounds of Theo stirring caught Eve's attention more than once, but she forced down any reason to bring attention to herself. Reaching for him would. Instead, she ate quietly. Or she tried to.

"So Evie," Junior said. His tone was careful, light, "how do you like Shirley?"

Eve dismissed the familiarity in which he spoke her name. She also ignored the warm, soft sensation that always followed when she heard him do so. The fact that he insisted on using her name at all should have speared her anger but oddly it never did. She did her best to dislodge her thoughts from her head and focus on the question. Shirley was…

"Shirley is a nice woman." That was all Eve thought to say or wanted to say but…

"She seems nice. She's Ellis' girl then?"

Ms. Shirley was at the farm for a few days, and Junior met her once briefly, so Eve understood why he was inquiring about her. Ms. Shirley was very pretty and would most likely catch many hearts but not Mr. Ellis'.

Laughter from Sadie had Eve on the verge of laughing herself, but she was able to control herself but not completely. A small smile fought its way free. "Oh goodness no," Eve said, fighting her need to laugh. "Ms. Shirley is *no* one's girl, least of all Mr. Ellis'. Besides, if it were possible they could be together, I most certainly doubt she would choose Mr. Ellis. Women do have the right to choose."

Junior used his large hand to rub circles over Theo's back. His cheeks flushed with a little color as words fell from his mouth. "Well, I just, you know. I figured that they…um." He looked at her and together they stared, transfixed by the others sharp gaze. "A woman has the right to choose," his tone was low and thick with emotion.

At that moment Eve saw him so clearly. His brows shaded his beautiful eyes, their color always a quiet mystery that she was reluctant to admit that she wanted to solve. Now as she stared into them, the answer was evident. Winter gray was the color, light, unforgiving; desolate if you found yourself lost in their storm. But she also saw intelligence, strength, and determination when she dared to look.

Reflected in them now were hope, fear, and longing. Eve could ignore what she knew, what she felt, but the truth was crystal clear just like his eyes were. He wanted her to choose him. *Too bad*, she thought as she ran every excuse she could muster silently through her mind.

He was a *man*. Though they had some good qualities, she saw the way Mr. Wilson looked at his wife, read romance novels, and understood that those qualities the author wrote of had to be derived from their own or witnessed experience. Eve observed it firsthand. Her father adored her mother.

Yet his love didn't save her or me from years of abuse.

Thinking of her parents' caused Eve to lose her appetite, but she continued to eat anyway. She heard Sadie explaining that Shirley was Mr. Ellis' cousin so 'God didn't want them to make babies'. It still amazed Eve that as mentally challenged as Sadie was, she was leaps and bounds smarter than most in ways that counted.

"That's a pretty color, Sadie," Junior cleared his throat.

Preening like a peacock, Sadie held up her hand. "It's Pink Lemonade! Shirley painted my nails with her most special color."

Light conversation continued between the siblings, and though Eve enjoyed her interactions with Junior today, she knew that it was a milestone in their situation. She was grateful he let her be. He must have sensed her mood darkened, and it did considerably.

She allowed the hurt and hate she felt for men to power her resistance to Junior. He was one of them. He was nice now, but he would change. He would use her and take what was rightfully hers to give if she let him, eventually. He would breed her and then beat her because of his shame, because he lusted after the spook, the coon, the nigger.

Eve gasped at the unexpected pain when her teeth bit into her tongue. Blood mixed with her food, but she didn't care as she began chewing again. She noticed that Sadie and Junior's conversation paused, and the room fell silent. She hated attention almost as much as she hated being around men.

Using her anxiety to fuel her, Eve got to her feet, lifted her plate and untouched water, and walked them to the sink. She said nothing as she left the kitchen. Usually, she and Sadie cooked, cleaned, and cared for Theo. Tonight, Eve stalked to the room she and Sadie shared and lay on her mattress, wishing she could shut her mind off.

Theo.

Her promise to her mother to care for him was her tether to this world. Apparently to Junior as well, because she feared he would never leave their brother either.

CEFUS

The thing Cefus wanted more than anything in the world was a damn drink. The second thing was to strangle that black bitch of a temptress until she passed out. Then to throw water on the bitch to wake her up so he could do it all over again. She was the reason for all his troubles. The reason he went to the Tow Hole six months ago in the first place.

Then that whore, Mallory, had to go and choose that young asshole instead of him.

Cefus sneered at the thought of that arrogant prick who showed him up. Caleb was his name, and Cefus still wasn't quite sure what it was he saw that night. After all the time he spent behind bars, he still didn't know what happened. He never laid a hand on Caleb, but the kid pressed charges, and he got six months for it.

What he did know was he had some scores to settle and that bitch who started it all was first... Well, she was second on his list. Right after his drink. It was high time she accepted who the master of his house was.

Time for them all to know.

Cefus placed a twenty on the bar. He looked over at Nate, the bartender and owner who was small talking with some guys he didn't recognize. Nate side eyed him but ended up slowly making his way to the end of the bar where Cefus sat.

They never liked each other. Nate was a do-gooder piece of horse shit who didn't know where to place his loyalties. The fact that Nate was also one of the few people in town who didn't flinch when Cefus entered a room was bothersome to say the least.

The need to remedy that was a mild annoyance that pulsed with each tap of Cefus' fingers on the bar. Nate took the twenty, placed it on the register, then placed a filled glass in front of Cefus. No, they never liked each other, but the bastard never turned away his money.

Cefus ignored Patty as she flopped down on the stool beside him. As always, she reeked of cigarettes and dead roses. All women should smell like temptation and taste like sin just like his... He was thinking of his nigger again, had every day for six months.

Loudly cursing, Cefus drew the gazes of the newcomers at the end of the bar and a few locals. He slowly looked around the room with a hard, threatening stare; an invitation. Everyone looked away including the newcomers. Cefus' penetrating gaze landed on Nate, who seemed almost bored. Maybe he needed to show Nate why these fools feared him.

"Where you been?" Patty slurred.

Cefus raised a brow as he turned to Patty. "None of your damn business." He lifted his drink to his mouth and took a long, much-needed guzzle. The alcohol burned as it smoothly slid down his throat. Cefus almost closed his eyes, savoring the golden liquid as if it were the most precious thing in the world. And it was, right now.

When Patty moved her leg closer, Cefus turned and took her appearance in. Her clothing was always too tight, her makeup was always too thick, and her attention was always unwanted. Patty was once a looker; now she was an annoyance, a druggie who slept with anyone for a fix. But those facts didn't stop him from allowing his gaze to dip to her breasts for a peek.

"Just say so and we can get out of here." Her voice would have sounded sexy if she was someone else; someone who didn't smoke two packs a day for over thirty years. "Since you're back from wherever you went, how about having us a reunion back at my place."

He could think of only one woman he desired right now, and that pissed him off. When Cefus gave Patty a dismissive chuckle, she clutched his thigh with a clawed hand and squeezed. Patty gasped when Cefus flung her hand away. "Not with someone else's dick," he smirked.

Patty's expression flickered from hopeful to hurt then angered in a matter of seconds.

"Funny," Patty said loudly as she lifted her drink to her lips, "you'd think you having a baby in your house may have softened you some. But I see you're just as nasty as you wanna be. I feel sorry for that little black girl and her baby."

Before Patty could walk away, Cefus had her by the throat and pinned backward over the bar. Her feet dangled a few inches above the floor as she struggled. Her nails dug into his hand and arm, but Cefus hardly felt it.

"What did you say?" he whispered to her as he took in his surroundings.

A couple of the newcomers came at him, but some of the locals held them back. *Lucky them*, Cefus grinned as he tightened his grip around Patty's neck. He did not just hear what he thought he heard.

The distinct sound of a shotgun being cocked couldn't drag his attention away from the whore who thought to goad him. Never mind that she just said that she knew of his house pets but that there was a baby. *There is a fucking coon baby in my goddamn house.* What the hell happened while he was gone?

"Let her go or by God, Cefus..." Nate growled. The barrel of his shotgun was inches from Cefus' temple. Cefus regarded Nate with a smug smile. "Now!"

You don't have the balls.

Cefus didn't believe Nate would shoot him and would have tested it if he didn't notice Tommy, Nate's brother, on the phone at the other end of the bar. Ten to one that spineless fuck was calling Sheriff Gifford and his lot. It wasn't fear of Nate or his gun that had Cefus dropping a choking, sobbing Patty to the stained floor. It wasn't even the threat of jail, though Cefus was sure that Gifford would never arrest him.

It was the need to get home to find out what his stupid ass son done did.

Damn boy is just like his good for nothing mother.

JUNIOR

At dinner, things were good at first. Things were better than good. She talked; he even saw a slight smile on her tempting face, but then she shut down. It was so sudden, the switch in her. One moment she was there. Eve was actually at the moment as if they were a normal bunch; then the next…nothing.

Absolutely nothing.

Junior turned over in his bed. His attention was drawn to the still night outside his window. No breeze blew. The heat made the air heavy and seemed to drain everyone and everything except the insects and animals. The cricket's song was unending, frogs croaked, and little flying menaces hit his window screen with a sickening sound at times. To a country boy, the heat and sounds were calming, but Junior couldn't get a hold on the peace it offered.

He didn't sleep much over the past months. With the babe's sleep cycle, working, and searching for his mother, sleep was in short supply. What little sleep Junior did manage was fitful, laced with worry and fear. He needed to make a move and soon.

Finding Cindy Anne Shaw and appealing to her to resume care of Sadie wasn't going well at all. The few people who could possibly know where she was, those few relatives Junior managed to locate, hadn't heard from Cindy at all. It was as if she didn't want to be found.

That hurt but Junior had to push his feelings aside. He came to the conclusion that she ran from her life and never wanted to come back. No doubt Cefus made her life a living hell. She found love with another. Junior couldn't hold grudges. She left them, yes, but what he did remember of her was that she seemed to love them when she was there.

Maybe she didn't think Cefus would hurt us.

Whatever the reason she left wasn't the issue now. Junior was man enough to know that your environment shaped you for good or bad. Cindy made her choice, but those choices may not have been as cut and dry as he first assumed. He still hated her for leaving them with Cefus, but living his life, he didn't have to agree, but he could accept Cindy's choices.

Junior had a lead on his mother's sister: his aunt, Judy. He last saw her a year before his mother left them which was over ten years ago. His mother and Judy were close, but maybe that changed in the past years. He heard from one of his mother's cousins who lived a few towns over. She told him that Judy just moved back near Anniston a couple of years ago.

Everything depended on him getting Sadie to safety. Nothing could be done until then. He planned to drive to the address he got for Judy this weekend. Would go sooner but he couldn't take a day off work being as he used all his off days when Theo was hospitalized. Plus, he needed all the money he could get, so he had to wait.

As Junior mulled over what he needed to do, the sound of a strained engine disrupted the outside calm. He shot up from his bed and ran from his room. He knew that engine. Worked on it and knew it like the back of his hand. Fear had him jetting down a few stairs then launching himself over the remaining half dozen steps.

He barreled down the hall and past the kitchen to get to Sadie's bedroom. He vaguely noticed the sound of two vehicles skidding to a stop and car doors slamming shut as he pushed through Sadie's bedroom door, breaking the basic knob lock. He almost paused, realizing that Eve still feared him enough to lock their bedroom door, but he couldn't think of that now.

193

Junior immediately grabbed a wide-eyed Eve up on her feet then as gently and as fast as he could, he lifted Theo from the mattress. "Sadie, roll this mattress and sheets in the corner. Evie, grab as much of yours and Theo's things that you can carry and take them up to my room."

When neither of them moved, he covered Theo's head and ears, gently pressing the babe into his chest and said, "NOW!" Junior felt Theo jump, startled awake, but the babe was easily soothed back to sleep.

Sadie gasped but jumped up and moved to do what he told her. His sister rarely saw him angry. He hated that she did now, but he knew that she would forgive him and act as if nothing happened in a few hours.

Evie, on the other hand, her reaction was hard for Junior to witness. He inwardly cringed as he watched fear spread across her face. The way she took two steps away from him... The hurt look she gave him, but nothing grated more than when her expression flickered and revealed her silent acceptance.

Junior shook the sudden ache her accusing eyes caused in his chest, adjusted Theo in his arm, then grabbed what he could carry. Eve gathered her things as he ordered, but she wasn't moving as fast as he liked. It wasn't until the raised voices— familiar voices—made it through Sadie's closed window, did her mouth drop open and she looked over at him.

Yeah, he thought with shame, *I'm not the only wolf at the door.*

He avoided looking at Eve as she sped up her task. He ushered the girls up the stairs as fast as he could, told them to place the things around the room, and for Eve to lock her and Theo inside. With Sadie behind him, because she refused to let him go alone, Junior made to intercept his father, because yeah...daddy was home.

The bed moved as Eve sat on the very edge. Her eyes were pinned on the bedroom door and stung from her refusal to blink until it was physically necessary. She absently moved her fingers over her outer thigh to feel for the homemade sheath she made from electrical tape and a steak knife she took from the kitchen months ago. She started wearing it after Junior kissed her; fearful of what she often saw in his eyes when she caught him watching her.

It gave her little comfort then and none now.

The Devil was home, and somehow she knew that if she didn't kill him, he would take pleasure in breaking her.

TWELVE

JUNIOR

He's home.

Junior kept repeating those two words in his head as he stood on the porch glaring down at Cefus as Sheriff Gifford tried to talk sense into the old man. Or what Sheriff Gifford assumed was sense, being as he had little himself. The sheriff and Junior weren't exactly friends, so Junior didn't quite understand why the guy and his deputies, Byron, and Colby, were literally holding Cefus back.

And Cefus was plenty mad so Sheriff Gifford and his men weren't faring well at all.

"You claim that nigger as your own; took her and that bastard to town," Cefus yelled at Junior as he continued to try to get around Gifford and his men. "Boy, I'm gonna beat some smarts in you, and when I'm done, I'm gonna kick your damn head in."

Cefus, obviously done with the tango he and Sheriff Gifford were dancing, attacked. He punched the sheriff in the face, head-butted Colby, then elbowed Byron in the neck. "I'm gonna reunite that little bitch with her father then strangle the half-breed." Cefus stalked toward the porch but Byron, who was bent over from the blow to his neck, grabbed Cefus around the waist in an attempt to hold him back.

Junior felt his anger spread through his body as he fisted his hands at his sides. Hearing Cefus threaten Eve and Theo enraged him, but he had to keep a cool head for once in his life. He had to think smart and not rage out like he normally would.

"Sadie, go inside," he said softly but firmly.

Sadie whimpered before backing into the house.

"Dammit, Cefus," Sheriff Gifford said. He spat out a mouthful of blood. "Just listen," he placed himself in front of Cefus again, "If you hurt her or that kid, I can't do a damn thing to help you. The state's involved now."

Junior knew that what Sheriff Gifford said was sinking in for Cefus because the old man slowed some and his brows creased. If Junior weren't simmering with anger, he would have laughed when his father actually pinned him with a look of confusion. As if he betrayed him.

"They come once a week to check on her and the kid. They don't like me much, and I'm pretty sure that if something happens to that girl and her baby, I won't be able to protect you." Sheriff Gifford ran his hand over his head when Cefus stopped advancing. The Sheriff was visibly relieved and honestly, so was Junior.

Colby moaned, still on the dusty pavement while Byron let go of Cefus and dropped to the ground to take a few needed breaths. They both seemed relieved too.

May as well get it all out now, there was no use pussyfooting. Besides, the pacing Cefus was doing wasn't doing much to calm him down as he muttered threats. "Eve is mine," Junior announced. "I'll keep her in check. I'll keep her quiet, but she's mine, and you won't touch her."

Cefus stopped pacing. Byron cursed as he pushed to his feet. Gifford shot Junior a pleading glance of his shoulder.

Cefus' chest rose and fell several times before he spoke. "Boy, are you fuckin' tellin' me...ME," he yelled, "what I can't do in my goddamn house?" He laughed as he narrowed his eyes at Junior. "Just like your fuckin' mother."

On this, Junior had to be clear. He couldn't show any weakness; he couldn't show a single crack. He had to mean it when he spoke his next words. Junior took a step forward. His hands fisted at his side as he pushed his shoulders back.

"Evie *is* mine."

Everyone just stared at him for a few seconds. Byron stared with his mouth open with shock and a hint of fear in his eyes. Colby groaned again as he closed his eyes and cursed. Sheriff Gifford looked as if he wanted to get his hands on Junior and wring his neck.

Cefus looked... Junior could have sworn that what he saw in his father's eyes was pride, before it sputtered out and anger overtook him. A roar or some would say a call of the wild, came out of Cefus that made Junior's entire body tremble. Junior didn't notice before but he was sweaty, and his pulse raced.

It was fear, and he knew it. He wondered if his father could smell it. As he put the thought out of his mind, because Cefus wasn't the big bad wolf, he knew he had to appear determined, unshakable. Even as he swallowed hard, Junior pushed out his chest and stood tall.

Sheriff Gifford and his men had to intercept Cefus again. What Gifford whispered in Cefus' ear as they held him at bay, Junior didn't know. What he did know was that he just ran out of time.

CEFUS

"**Y**ou wanna go back? They are suspicious of you already. If you harm any of them, *any*, they *will* be all over this place. All of what you've done will be brought to light," Gifford whispered close to his ear. "Everything."

Cefus inwardly cringed, hating how close Gifford was to him. He shoved Gifford away but stopped advancing. *He dares to threaten me.* "All of what *we've* done will be brought to light."

Gifford's eyes grew big, and he took a few steps back. Cefus was sure that the man didn't falter from his shove, it was the threat. *Good*, he thought, Gifford needed to know that he was going down too.

"Byron, Colby, wait in the cruiser." Both men stood still, looking from Gifford to Cefus, then to each other, not knowing what to do. It wasn't until Gifford motioned to the car with his head that the young men moved, but did so slowly. "And that's why you need to calm the hell down," Gifford continued when his deputies were out of earshot. "Neither of us needs the attention right now. Let the boy have the girl. He says he'll keep her quiet, has done so up till now. What harm can come from this?"

"My fuckin' son is parading around town with a nigger on his arm. MY SON!" Cefus felt his anger as if he could touch it. His eyes moved to Junior, who stood on the porch. The son of a bitch looked almost formidable, like a fucking Shaw. Junior was always defiant, mouthy, but he never went against him like this. Yeah, the little shit was getting worse over the years, trying to step between him and his bone, but nothing like this.

Cefus shook his head. It took a nigger and her daughter to bring forth that look of fearless determination in his son. It was the look of abandonment, the one that said that you will literally kill to have your way. It was the very look Cefus was trying to beat into the fuck for years.

The nigger…my bone.

The thought of Pearl stirred Cefus' lust. He'd never gone without her body this long and the very thought of sinking into her, having her cry out with obvious pleasure as her mind raged in anger had him so excited that his own rage changed to need.

"It's already done, Cefus." Gifford sighed as he looked over his shoulder at Junior, who didn't say a word since his claim. He was still at the ready, eyes still hard and uncompromising.

Like a Shaw, Cefus thought again.

"Look, I know this isn't what you want but believe me, it can benefit you. With her under the boy's finger, you can rest easy. No threat of getting caught."

Cefus forced his need for Pearl aside and focused on Gifford. The simple fuck actually thought there was a possibility that the bodies would be discovered. If things went as planned all those years ago, Pearl and her daughter would have been buried under the big oak along with the husband and no one other than his household and Gifford would have been the wiser. After he had his fill of Pearl of course, and obviously after he sampled her screaming kid too. The thought of taking the little pup hard and fast had Cefus fighting to stifle a shiver.

He should have mounted that little bitch all those years ago, but Eve didn't have and curves then, spirit, or the fight her mother possessed; she was just as beautiful if not more so. *Fucking temptress niggers*. Why the hell would they be made in such a way? *To tempt, to destroy a white man's sanity, that why*.

Cefus scrubbed his hand over his face and down his mouth. He didn't want anyone to see him drooling. "I would have never been caught. They would have never left this place alive. Now," he pinned Junior with a promise of death and grinned, "Now my actions can be opened to the world."

"She won't betray me," Junior spoke up.

Cefus' hard laughter filled the night. "She won't betray...you? You act as if you have control, boy. Never forget that a dog, no matter how trained, can always bite its master."

Junior sneered, "Evie *is* not a dog, and I trust her with my life."

"Your sister's life too?" Cefus countered.

With a curt nod, Junior said, "Yes."

Cefus simply stated, "It's Sadie who will suffer the most. Are we clear?"

"Crystal," Junior said but didn't relax.

Cefus inwardly smiled. *That's right, boy, never relax around a predator.*

His last stint in jail wasn't a shits and giggles vacation. In fact, Cefus found himself in a battle for survival every damn day during his recent incarceration. He was none too anxious to return. No, it was nothing like town lock-up when the few times Gifford arrested him before they had come to an understanding.

So, I have to act like I accept this…arrangement. Bide my time…or bring down the so-called law on my head.

Cefus never had respect for the law. A bunch of self-righteous rich liberal bastards made them, and they used pussies to enforce them. A man was law in his own home, but those liberal fucks now wanted to invade a white man's space. *And he had to abide.* That was laughable.

Fine—the way he saw it—*I'm damned if I do and damned if I don't.* If I killed the bitch, her daughter, and that damn baby—because the state knows of them—he went to jail and rotted. If he allowed this shit to go on in his house, the bitch daughter tells, he rots. But…if Junior actually can control the little whore, then he could keep his freedom. He'd have to deal with the fucks in town who may want to give him shit over it, but he'd still have Pearl, and he'd eventually have her pup under him too.

Yet, the thought of his fucking son, his blood claiming that nigger and that half-breed…it cut deep. County lock-up was one thing; the penitentiary for murder, a whole new ballgame. It seemed he had no choice, but they didn't have to know he knew it.

"You keep your dog leashed, Junior," Cefus said as he stalked up his porch steps, "or I will put her down and fuck your shit up so bad that you will wish I put you down too." He made sure he gave Junior a hard shoulder check as he passed and went inside *his* house.

When Cefus stepped inside, he saw but didn't study the small differences in his house. Nor did he care. He had one thing on his mind and even though he was angry, even though he couldn't take his anger out on his simple-minded son, he could release some of his stress in the most satisfying way God intended. He would never admit it, but he needed Pearl.

He heard Junior calling to him as he quickly moved through the house and descended the basement stairs, but he didn't slow. He dreamed of her almost every damn night, no doubt it was her devilry that made it so. The way she felt under him, the way she fought and feared him; the ways in which he made her submit. He loved that she still hadn't fully been broken. He would have no use for her when she was.

Cefus came to a sudden stop at the bottom step. The room was empty. *Was she upstairs? That damn boy...he gave her a fucking room.*

"She's gone."

Cefus took a deep breath to gain some kind of control. "You can't be that fuckin' stupid, boy. You can't have let what was mine, loose." He forced himself to stay in place, to stay still, because if he moved, he was going to kill his only son. Cefus never hit Junior to hurt him; well just those few times he lost control. But if Pearl was gone...freedom be damned. He was going to kill his kid.

"I buried her under the oak." That was all Junior said before turning away and walking up the stairs.

Buried her... What?

Shea Swain

JUNIOR

Burying a body was easy, given the right conditions; burying your emotions was damn impossible. Junior knew that Pearl would always be in his thoughts, but he hoped that the devastation he felt when he buried her was gone. But it didn't fade.

Hearing Cefus' reaction to the news of Pearl's death brought Junior's pain back front and center. Junior told his father she was buried under the oak and left him in the basement. After Junior reached the top of the stairs, he heard the beginnings of the rage his father unleashed.

The basement was first. Junior was certain that everything in his father's sight was destroyed. After the basement, Cefus left the house and stormed to the oak tree. Junior didn't try to stop him. He felt disgusted at the thought of Cefus standing over Pearl's grave, but he also knew he had to pick his battles from this point on. So he sat at the top of the second floor stairs where he had a direct view of the front door and was a barrier to the upstairs and waited.

Eventually, Cefus burst back into the house and went to the kitchen. Junior noticed the dirt caked on Cefus' hands and clothing. He winced at the thought of Pearl being unearthed, but he remained quiet.

Still in a rage, Cefus attacked the kitchen. Junior heard cabinet doors slamming, dishes breaking, and things hitting the floor. *Why is he so upset?* It wasn't as if he loved Pearl. Hell, Cefus did all he could to demean and hurt her.

"He managed to get some of her free. He recognized the body I suppose, so he stopped," Sheriff Gifford said as he rubbed his own shoulder. Apparently, the good sheriff tried to stop Cefus from digging up Pearl's body, but it appeared

Cefus wouldn't be swayed. "Take care of it." He rubbed his brow with a handkerchief as he moved to the kitchen.

Junior bit back a curse and his anger. He reminded himself that Pearl was gone…and she wasn't the unmoving flesh that lay under that tree. That Cefus could no longer hurt her would have to be enough. But Cefus could hurt Eve, so Junior stayed put.

"Do you think drinking is the answer?" Junior heard Sheriff Gifford ask.

Yes. Drinking was the answer, Junior thought. He praised himself for not throwing out the old man's liquor.

"Fuck off," Cefus yelled.

"Is Daddy angry or sad?"

Junior looked up to see Sadie standing at the bottom of the stairs. She didn't look scared, but she did look tired. "I really don't know, Sadie. Go on back to bed."

Sadie nodded. Because Cefus was causing more commotion, Junior barely heard her footsteps as she slowly walked back to her bedroom. The next sound Junior thought he heard was the basement door hitting the wall and Cefus stomping down the stairs. Cefus must have slipped at one point because Junior heard the tell-tale sound of a large man slipping down a few stairs and a final thud, followed by loud curses.

A little over an hour later, Junior climbed the basement stairs. His footfalls were as heavy as his heart, but he knew what he had to do. He moved through the house with a little more care. He didn't want to wake the girls or Theo.

Cefus drank himself to sleep and was now passed out on Pearl's old mattress in the basement. That the only reason Junior left the house and got the shovel from the shed. He made quick work of setting Pearl's grave right because he felt uneasy about leaving Eve and Theo in the house with his father.

After he was done, he went back inside, took a quick shower, then easily pushed through his locked bedroom as quietly as he could. He stood silent just inside the room, watching Eve and Theo as they slept. She was in his bed. Junior touched his chest as if he could rub out the odd ache of seeing her asleep in his bed caused. He often questioned how she affected him. Junior wanted nothing more than to slide in behind her and wrap his arms around her. The need to protect her was almost overwhelming, yet it didn't bother him. He felt honored to do so.

He just hoped he didn't fail. He couldn't fail.

With his mind cemented on his goal, Junior locked his bedroom door then crossed to the other side of the room. He slid down the wall, rested his elbows on his raised knees, and let his head fall back. His vigil started now.

Eve

Waking with a gasp, Eve raised her head. Her surroundings weren't all together foreign, but this wasn't Sadie's room. As she focused more on the details: the bed, the sheets that she often washed, the masculine scent—the one that caused an involuntary shudder to run through her body— it was obvious whose bed she was in.

Then like a hammer to the head, it hit her. He was back. Cefus came back last night and tore the house apart. She heard the yelling, the destruction, all behind Junior's bedroom door. She was terrified, wondering when he would come for her, for Theo.

Junior told Cefus that her mother was dead. *Did he care?* Eve had a feeling that it would be like losing a bet for him. It only set him off because he lost his property. She knew that he would want to replace his lost toy, and she was the only option. God, could she lie beneath his hulking form as he took her against her will.

The very thought made tears form in her eyes.

Eve, helpless to her emotions, her watery gaze fell on Theo. He was so sweet, so precious. He looked healthy; he looked loved. Eve came to think of him as hers recently and not as a brother. He *was* hers.

To protect her child, could she do what her mother did.

Yes, she thought. She whimpered and sucked in a breath as she continued to cry.

"I'll die before I allow him to hurt you or Theo."

Eve couldn't help the relief she felt or the sigh that followed. Junior's deep voice slid over her like a warm blanket that she just wanted to snuggle under. Being careful not to disturb Theo, Eve shifted and turned over to locate where Junior was in the room.

He sat against the wall, his features determined but his eyes looked tired. He came to Sadie's room the night before, shirtless and he was still. He often went without a shirt but rarely when they were alone, behind closed doors. The times when she caught him going without a shirt, she always diverted her eyes, finding something else to focus on but today… This moment, she couldn't help looking her fill.

Junior's body was honed and strong from sports and hard work. His skin, tanned and currently glistening from perspiration in the light of the morning sun, was muscled but not so much that he resembled the Hulk. No…she appreciated his form even with the scars that covered him.

Junior's body tensed under her attention. He shook his head as if to clear it, then said, "All I need is a little more time."

She believed him but knew she would do whatever it took until they all could get away from this place. As much as she tried, Eve couldn't deny that she loved Sadie just as she would a sister. Though she feared Junior, always waiting for the moment he would show her he was his father's son, she cared for him as well. They were in this hell together;

they would free themselves of Cefus together. No one should have to suffer him.

JUNIOR

All he needed was a little more time. He told Eve as much but the way she slowly ran her gaze over him, as if caressing him, Junior lost all thought and concern for their situation. Just because of the way Eve looked at him.

Did his desires run the same as Cefus'? Did he see what he wanted to see?

Junior would never, could never be like Cefus. He would never allow it, and that was why he abruptly stood, frightening her. With none of the remorse he felt for scaring her with his tone, Junior said, "Get you and the babe dressed. You can't be here without me, ever." He knew he sounded angry, probably looked it too, but he couldn't help that. "I'm taking you to the Wilsons before I leave for work."

"I have a home visit today." Eve sat up on the edge of his bed as she brushed her hand over her long curly hair.

Would she cover that up again? He didn't want her to. *Shit…focus.*

"Are you going to allow me more time to get us out of here, Evie?"

Eve gazed at him for several seconds, sweeping her eyes over him again before she nodded.

Junior wasn't aware that he was holding his breath until he released it.

If she keeps looking at me like that…

Junior shook his head again as he reached for a clean shirt that hung in his closet. He pulled the shirt over his head and righted it as he made his way for the door. "I'm going downstairs—keep an eye on Cefus while you," he glanced over his shoulder at her, "get ready. I'll send Sadie up to help."

Junior closed the door behind him then jogged down the stairs. In the kitchen he found Sadie making bottles.

She gave him a worried smile then said, "He's still down there." She pointed to the basement then went back to pouring formula into a glass bottle.

"Can you go help Evie with Theo while she gets ready? I'll finish the bottles."

Sadie picked up one of the bottles then turned around to face him. "You won't let him hurt our brother or Eve, will you, Junior?" she asked.

Junior always loved and hated the hopeful look in Sadie's eyes when she looked at him. Even though he was younger than her, Sadie always looked to him for help throughout his life. It was a burden at times, but as he grew he saw it as his privilege.

He pulled Sadie into his arms and gave her a gentle squeeze, holding her longer than he normally would. "I'll do my best to make sure he doesn't hurt any of us more than he already has."

Eve

The shower was the fastest she ever took. Getting back to Theo was her driving force. So when she came out of the bathroom and rushed down the hall to Junior's bedroom, she was hit with a wave of fear when she tried to open the door. It was locked.

Why is it locked?

"Eve?"

"Yes, it's me." A beat later the door creaked open; hidden behind it was Sadie. When she backed away, Eve saw Theo clutched in her arms. Sweet relief…

Eve wanted to take him from Sadie, to feel his heart beat against her chest. To smell his sweet baby scent, but she restrained herself. She saw the protectiveness in Sadie's eyes as well.

Sadie locked the door in an attempt to protect their brother. Eve saw that Sadie would fight to protect him. They all would. They had to work together.

"We should stay here." Not in a hurry to see Cefus, Eve sat on the bed. Sadie joined her with a sigh then sat Theo on her lap, facing her. She cooed and played with him while Eve wondered when things were going to go nuclear.

JUNIOR

Curiosity had Junior descending the basement stairs. His weight caused each wooden plank to bow and strain under his feet, more noticeable now with his slow pace as he focused on each step. He stopped halfway down; peering through the open doorway that led to the room Pearl was housed in. He didn't see Cefus.

Bending forward and using an overhead wooden beam to brace himself, Junior looked over the side rail to see if Cefus was in the back. Nope. Junior continued down the stairs. He would have thought the basement was empty by the assumed silence, but he continued to listen; listened for movement, listened for the faintest of noises. Junior was sure that Cefus didn't leave the basement or the house.

Inside the small room or more like enclosure, beside the rolled up mattress in the corner was Cefus. Just as Junior figured, Cefus was passed out with an empty bottle of liquor still clutched in his grasp. His father's appearance was always deceiving when he was like this, relaxed in sleep. Like this, without the constant scowl, furrowed brow, and cruel twist of his lips, Cefus was a handsome man.

Junior hated to admit that he resembled his father. It was their eyes; Junior heard some refer to them as a haunting ice gray, that clearly relating the two. Their nose, hard jaw, chin, and build were the same. The similarities were obvious, but Junior had enough of his mother's DNA to soften the harshness of his angles. He also had Cindy's corn-silk blond hair, but at times, Junior hated that he did. He realized while looking at his father that the darkness of Cefus' hair added to his threatening look.

"You plan on cuttin' my throat while I sleep, boy?"

The low rattle of Cefus' voice grated on Junior's nerves, but he managed not to sneer. He just held his hands out, palms up as a response.

"Then what the fuck do you want?" Cefus sat up. He rubbed a hand over his face then peered, almost longingly at the bloodied mattress.

Birthing a babe was a messy business, but Junior would bet that a good deal of the blood that stained the mattress was from his beatings.

Why was Cefus staring at the mattress as if... As if he felt remorse when Junior knew with everything inside him that Cefus was a cold-hearted beast that felt nothing.

"Well," Cefus said. He finally looked away from the mattress and pinned Junior with a hard stare, because Junior didn't respond.

"Evie and Theo have a home visit today. Thought you should know." Junior shrugged. He didn't like it down here anymore, so he turned and began climbing the stairs. When he was close to the doorway that led to the kitchen, he heard the distinct sounds of cooking.

He raced the rest of the way up and pushed through the door. Both Eve and Sadie were frightened by the sudden movement, but neither said anything as he stomped into the kitchen. He moved toward Eve but spoke to Sadie. "Take Theo in your room, Sadie."

Sadie moved quickly, gathering Theo in her arms and retreating to her safe haven.

Junior didn't think Eve realized that she was moving away from him, but he let her until she had nowhere to go. When Eve was flat against the fridge, Junior stopped mere inches from her. He gently took hold of her arm and leaned into her. He ignored her delicious scent and the warmth of her skin as he whispered, "Why are you down here...dressed like this," he let his eyes sweep over her, "with your hair out?"

She has no idea how tempting she is, how beautiful.

"He'll expect me to cook and clean like I have been and..."

Junior backed away a few inches to look into her eyes. *Those eyes of hers were always expressive.* "And?" he pressed.

She looked down as she worried her lip with her teeth. She finally spoke without looking up at him. "And, I can't go back to the way it was before. You can't expect me to, not after the past few months," Eve pleaded quietly as she warily trailed her eyes to his.

Of course, he didn't expect things to go back the way they were. Yes, he wanted her large, colorless clothing back; he wanted her soft curls covered. He didn't want Cefus to see how she blossomed into the woman she was.

"My, my, look what we have here."

Junior cursed under his breath. He closed his eyes to calm because he saw the fear that flashed in Eve's eyes. What he didn't expect was how quickly she hid it under what he could only describe as a shield of indifference as she looked past him and turned her attention to Cefus.

Junior still had his hand wrapped around her arm, so he rubbed his thumb over her skin hoping the gesture infused her with strength. Then he started to turn around to face Cefus, making sure Eve was behind him.

"Touch her and—"

Junior didn't get the chance to finish what he was going to say because he couldn't breathe, what with Cefus' hand around his throat, choking him.

"Don't get use to givin' me orders, boy. This is my house," Cefus told Junior but kept his eyes on Eve.

Junior grabbed Cefus' wrist and squeezed. They were in a standoff and Junior couldn't lose. Using all his strength, Junior managed to pry his father's fingers away to breathe but not enough that Cefus would lose face in front of his audience.

"Did anyone hear the door?" Sadie asked as she came into the kitchen with Theo on her hip.

"So this is my little mongrel bastard." Cefus winked at Eve, let go of Junior, and then went toward Sadie.

Sadie instinctively backed away while turning her shoulder so that Cefus couldn't see Theo so well. Her eyes darted between Cefus, who continued to approach. Junior moved fast, making it between them before Cefus could reach her.

"Get the door, Sadie," Junior said while staring at Cefus. The sound of Sadie moving toward the door was comforting. "Eve and I are Theo's parents'. He's ours legally, so you have no claim to him."

Cefus raised a brow.

The sound of Mrs. Hall and Mr. Hopkins coming inside carried into the kitchen. "You may want to clean up," Junior smirked. "We have company."

Eve

Staying focused was hard to do knowing that Cefus was back and somehow creepier than before. Maybe it was the way he looked at her now. It wasn't like the way Junior looked at her. His lustful looks somehow seemed soft, almost sweet even though he scared the heck out of her.

The way Cefus stared at her in the kitchen; it was as if he was undressing her where she stood. There was nothing soft about it either. She hated to admit it but when Sadie interrupted, Eve was relieved. It was embarrassing to admit that she was relieved to have Cefus focused on someone else, though she felt guilty about that now.

"I truly do not understand your decision in this matter," Mrs. Hall stated. "Are you certain?"

Mrs. Hall didn't hide her concern. Nor did her co-worker, Mr. Hopkins, who kept glancing at her from the hallway where he talked with Junior. She knew what their conversation was about. It was the same conversation Eve was having with Mrs. Hall.

"Yes," Eve said with a nod. If she were a seasoned liar, she could ease Mrs. Hall's fears by telling her that Cefus was harmless, that his bark was bigger than his bite. But Evelyn wasn't that skilled. Cefus was dangerous and no one, least of all Mrs. Hall, should see him as anything other than that.

"I'm concerned for yours and Theo's safety." Mrs. Hall placed her hand on Eve's thigh.

The contact would have distressed Eve but since spending time at Mrs. Wilson's home, she was used to social contact now.

"Junior will take care of us." *Truth.* Eve believed this and when she looked over at him, he met her gaze and she felt the truth of her words.

"Well," Mrs. Hall said as she looked from Eve to Junior, "Don't hesitate to contact my office or me if you find yourself in trouble or have changed your mind." Mrs. Hall stood. "Please be careful."

Eve walked Mrs. Hall to the hallway where they met up with Junior and Mr. Hopkins. Eve didn't know Mr. Hopkins well, but she knew an angry look when she saw one. Junior stepped beside her, placing his hand on her lower back. Normally she would question his actions, but today she needed the reassurance, his offered strength. Eve actually leaned into him.

"Before I forget," Mrs. Hall said as she pulled an envelope from her folder. She handed it to Eve.

Opening the envelope, Eve held up Theo's birth certificate. Her heart fluttered when she saw her name down as his mother. She continued reading then paused when she got to the father's name. It didn't say Cefus Shaw, Jr. on the legal document. It read Jason Ray Shaw instead. Never did she hear or see the name before today.

Junior probably sensed her confusion because he took the document from her hands. He glanced over it then folded the document but didn't hand it back to her. Instead, he motioned for the door. "If this visit is over, I must get to work and Eve has to start her day."

Mr. Hopkins grunted something but turned toward the door, and everyone followed his lead. Eve was surprised to see that Cefus was on the porch, sitting in the chair Sadie usually used to talk with her through the window. Eve thought he was gone for the day. When Junior let Mr. Hopkins and Mrs. Hall inside the living room earlier, Cefus couldn't help being himself—rude. He didn't speak but was very expressive just the same. Thank goodness he didn't speak because Eve was sure he would have said something very harsh.

Yet as Eve stood in the doorway, watching her guest descend the porch stairs, she knew Cefus was going to say something. Junior knew too because his entire body tensed.

"It's bad enough they let you people sneak into the country, but now they let women do men's work." Cefus grinned wide when both Mr. Hopkins and Mrs. Hall turned to look at him.

Mr. Hopkins took a step toward Cefus. Junior cursed then moved in front of his father, who climbed to his feet so fast that the chair fell back. Eve was sure Junior was protecting Mr. Hopkins though it looked as though he was preventing Hopkins from reaching Cefus. It was a good thing that Mrs. Hall took Mr. Hopkins by the arm and pulled him the rest of the way to their vehicle.

Mrs. Hall gave Eve an imploring look before the two pulled off. Eve just forced a smile and waved goodbye.

"I need to get to work. Get your stuff together," Junior said as he ushered her further into the house.

THIRTEEN

MID-JUNE
JUNIOR

Junior experienced the longest two weeks of his life. Two weeks of watching over Evie and Theo like a hawk. He made sure that they were never in the house when he wasn't there. That they slept in his room every night, which had its drawbacks. His attraction to Evie increased tenfold. To his disappointment so did Cefus'.

Junior shook with rage whenever he witnessed the way his father looked at Evie. Cefus wore his lust plain as day. Junior often wondered what held Cefus from taking her. Yeah, Junior threatened him, but Cefus wasn't the kind of man to heed threats.

Whatever the reason, Cefus' didn't act on his animal instincts just yet.

With the careful watch Junior kept on Cefus, he wasn't able to follow up on the last lead he had on his mother's whereabouts. He doubted the tense peace would last much longer. Evie's nerves were shot. Any noise had her jumping out of her skin and on the defense.

Sadie's beautiful smile dimmed as she worried about the babe and what Cefus would do to them.

Not only was Junior sick of Cefus' lustful looks and dirty threats, but he was also also tired. Not because he lacked sleep, though sleeping on the hard floor was definitely taking a toll. He was tired of this life and was for a long time now. The fact that he was willing to trade it in for jail was proof enough. So, now was the time. He wanted to finish this no matter the outcome.

He just needed Sadie safe before turning Cefus and himself over to authorities. He even knew how he was going to do it. He planned to contact Mr. Hopkins and Mr. Hall and tell them everything because he knew he could trust them with Evie and Theo and to get Sadie to Cindy. Once he found Cindy.

That was why he went to work this morning and informed his boss that he would drive to Anniston and pick up the parts needed for waiting repairs today. His boss hated making the run and often tried to coax Junior into going instead, so he waved Junior off with a smile.

Leaving town, Junior expected to be stopped. Though Cefus returned, Sheriff Gifford's goons were still keeping tabs on him. Maybe now more than before because Gifford wasn't at all happy with Eve being free to talk to folk. Colby, one of Sheriff Gifford's goons, didn't seem to question his reasons when he pulled Junior over on his way out of town. No one could dispute that mechanics always needed new parts. Colby checked the trunk then sent him on his way.

Before he picked up the part, Junior headed for his mother's first cousin's home located on the outskirts of Anniston. He was told that they were very close growing up and that there was no way they would ever stop communicating. Unable to reach Judy by phone, Junior decided that he would drive there.

Maybe his mother would be there. Maybe he would be able to talk to her.

Junior shook his head in an attempt to wipe the thought from his mind. The chances of finding Cindy Anne there was slim. But he may get lucky and get the information he needed to find her.

With that smidgen of hope, Junior pulled into the drive of 125 Boulder Road, the home of Judy Macomb. The house looked nothing like the farmhouse. It was brick mostly; the windows were clean, and the grounds were neat. The grass was the greenest green and littered with brightly colored toys. It looked like the kind of home Junior wanted Theo to grow up in.

He turned off the engine then nervously pulled the brim of his baseball cap down. *If Cindy is here, can I be nice and ask for what I came for?* What if she turned him away? *Don't put things in your head,* he told himself. Life was hard enough without him psyching himself out.

When the front door opened, and a woman holding a little girl looked out at him, with drawn brows and a frown, Junior sighed then got out of his truck. He strolled up the walk with confidence he didn't have. When he came to the door, he removed his hat. "My name is—"

"Why you're Cindy's boy, Jason." Judy beamed as she adjusted the little girl on her hip. Then her expression soured. "Has something happened to Cindy?" She looked around Junior and peered at his empty truck.

CEFUS

Cefus tossed his keys on the kitchen table. He opened the fridge and grabbed a beer, popped it open, then took a long swig. He held the bottle out in front of him, enjoying the chill it gave his hand and giving it a longing look before finishing it off.

"So damn good to have beer again," he said with a hum of appreciation.

He placed the bottle on the counter and pulled out two more beers from the open fridge, along with some leftover containers. Cefus closed the fridge then turned on the oven. He wasn't sure of the temperature he needed to put the oven on, but that wasn't going to stop him. He piled some chicken, a few carrots, and a biscuit on a plate and put the plate in the oven.

Without care, he placed the covers back on the containers of cold food and placed them back in the fridge then finished off another beer. Cefus moseyed out of the kitchen. It was just after noon; he didn't expect anything to be on the television, but he had shit else to do.

He turned on the television, tuned it to a channel that wasn't playing bullshit, and then plopped down on the sofa. His mind wasn't centered on the program so it didn't matter what was on. Cefus was pissed. Those assholes at the plant actually thought that they could fuck with him.

Did everyone go crazy in the last few months? To think he would be okay with a fucking kid for a supervisor. *A damn kid*, Cefus shook his head.

He shivered as a flash of that freaky ass Caleb guy came to mind. Cefus was ashamed to admit that the kid gave him the willies and for some reason, had him second guessing all the shit he wanted so desperately to do. Not really understanding what happened the night of his arrest, Cefus was unwilling to risk going to the Tow Hole for fear he might meet up with that guy again. That freak-show knew things.

Cefus shivered again. For the first time in his life, he was leashed, and he didn't like it. Didn't like it at all.

The sound of the door knob rattling made Cefus lift his head. He knew that it couldn't be Junior at the door because he didn't hear the boy's truck pull up. That meant that the girls and his mutt were home. He didn't see them much.

It was the temptress, Eve he desired to see. He loved the way she cowered under his glare.

Junior was keeping her close, always watching, but Cefus knew that there was no way his son could keep it up.

The boy was tired and looked it. Cefus planned for Junior's fall to be his rise. After he got between that little bitch's legs, she was his and Junior could fuck off.

I'm tired of playing nice.

The front door eased opened with a *creaking* noise. Soon after, Cefus heard footsteps. He got to his feet, eager with anticipation. He was finally going to have Eve and with no interference. He sighed as the shiver of anticipation poured over him.

JUNIOR

The drive home was nerve wrecking. Aside from stopping twice after his visit—once to get the parts for the garage and the other for something to eat—Junior was stuck in his truck with his thoughts as his only companion for the entire drive. Even music couldn't silence his thoughts.

"No one in the family has heard from Cindy since the summer of '73. We've all tried to see you and Sadie, but your father...he wanted you both to have nothing to do with us. Eventually, we just accepted that we wouldn't be a part of your lives," Judy said.

"Where could she be?"

"As far away from Cefus as she could possibly get, I assume. What I don't understand is why she would leave you both. You two kids were her entire life."

Her life huh, that was laughable. "Cindy had a funny way of showing her love," Junior said to no one in particular as he recalled the conversation.

Junior looked ahead, following the roads to home pretty much on autopilot. When he made it to the lengthy road before he came to his long drive, deciding to take the parts to the garage tomorrow, he continued on without notice of much. The sun was still out; it was early evening, but he wanted to clean up and think about things before getting the girls from the Wilson farm.

It was only when he noticed all the lights from the vehicles in his drive that Junior realized something was seriously wrong. He pressed the gas pedal, speeding the rest of the way to the house. He slammed the brakes before his truck barreled into any of the other vehicles. The screeching of his tires caused several of the people standing around to turn his way. Junior recognized a few of them.

Lights from the ambulance spun as Junior's head grew airy, light. *What the hell happened?*

Mr. Wilson rushed to his truck as Junior was getting out. With his hands extended, Mr. Wilson held Junior back, along with Mr. Hicks from a neighboring farm.

"What the hell happened?" Junior tried to push forward. His senses were overloaded by his surroundings and his own fears relentlessly lashed at him. The vehicles, the people he hardly knew converging on the farm; everything had him spinning. The light feeling, it was now as heavy as an anvil. Junior's eyes burned, and he found it hard to breathe.

"There's been an accident."

"An accident?" Junior swept the crowd, looking for his family. Where was Sadie, Evie, and Theo? "Where's my family?" *Oh God, help me.* "Where are they?" he yelled.

The men used more force to hold Junior back as he twisted and ducked in an attempt to get away from them. It was only when he focused and saw a covered figure on a stretcher in the distance that he stopped struggling.

Four men, including Sheriff Gifford and Dr. Steuben, worked to get the gurney through a high section of grass before coming to the low cut part of the lawn.

Who is that?

The fight in Junior faded with every repeated blink of his eyes as he tried to focus. He pulled back, away from his captures, and placed his hands on his head. He turned in circles, searching the crowd again, looking for his family. Whoever was on that stretcher...well, it wasn't... It didn't have to be...

On a second survey of the area, Junior saw Cefus standing on the porch, watching the men roll the gurney. His expression seemed troubled.

What the hell is going on?

"What's happened?" Junior called out again. Not knowing was killing him.

Mr. Wilson shook his head as he looked at Junior with a pained expression. Junior glanced at Mr. Hicks, but the man avoided making eye contact.

I have to get to that stretcher.

Junior faked right then darted left, storming past Mr. Wilson. He heard Mr. Hicks curse and knew he was being followed, but he kept running, his attention on the stretcher.

His bad leg gave him little trouble lately, so he was able to put a good distance between him and his pursuers. Junior's heart pumped faster, and his breaths came quicker. He was inches from the gurney when someone in front of him took him down hard. Junior struggled to free himself, but more people joined in, holding him down effectively.

Junior didn't know who took him down, but he wanted to gut the bastard. He ignored those who were telling him to calm down and to stop struggling. More hands joined the struggle, but Junior fought to get to the covered figure looming above him just a few inches away. He managed to brush his fingertips to the sheet covering the body. He noted the sheet was wet but gave it no never mind.

He extended his arm, giving the sheet a tug. Junior's eyes widened as they fixed on the ghostly arm that was now uncovered. He followed down the length of the arm until he saw the wrist and hand. Drops of water dripped from the fingernails that were painted...pink lemonade.

God no...

"No!" Junior bellowed as he reached. "Help her. Take the damn sheet off so she can breathe."

"I'm sorry, son, she's gone."

Junior knew it was Dr. Steuben who spoke, knew the man was right, but he continued his struggles, fighting harder. He knew CPR; he could help her. He had to help her. "Why don't you help her!" he shouted, piercing the now silent night. "Help her!" he cried until his throat burned.

"You may have to give him something, Doc," someone whispered.

Junior absently realized that several more people surrounded him as he lay motionless on the grass, staring at pairs of dirty boots.

"No...he won't like that."

Ellis.

"Ellis, Sadie..." Junior moaned. His limbs limp, his heart shattered into a million pieces. He slowly eased over on his back and blindly stared up into the clear sky. He was angry, anxious, and he wanted answers, but finally his pain and hurt won out. Junior opened his mouth but didn't hear the wail he let lose as he curled into himself and let go.

Sadie drowned. What's worse, it happened right under their noses. Through tears and her sobs, Eve watched Junior. He sat on the lowered hatch of the ambulance in front of Sadie's body. He was still inconsolable, but he seemed to be listening to the men around him now, offering a nod here and there.

"This is such a terrible accident, dear," Mrs. Wilson said as she moved her hand along Eve's arm.

An accident that should not have happened.

If Eve knew that Sadie wanted to go swimming, she would have gone with her. The last she saw of Sadie was just after lunch cleanup with Mrs. Wilson. Their usual routine was to eat, clean, then Sadie would often go out to tend the animals with Ellis and Mr. Wilson while Eve and Mrs. Wilson did whatever lesson they had planned. It wasn't until hours later that the two men came inside without Sadie. Neither of the men had seen her since lunch, and that's what they reported to Sheriff Gifford.

A search ensued; the Wilson farm was first. Then Mr. Wilson, Ellis, and Eve went and searched the Shaw house and farm together; Junior forbid her to ever go home alone. When they arrived, the house was empty.

Several attempts were made to contact Junior, but it was reported that he went on a work run.

By late afternoon, several neighbors joined in the search, and the entire town was on the lookout for Sadie Shaw. No one expected that she went to the lake alone. It was known that even with her recent swim lessons, Sadie was deathly afraid of bodies of water.

"Damn shame," a man standing nearby said. Several others agreed with nods or somber words.

"That boy must have a demon riding his back, with his luck and all," another person muttered. Again a round of agreements were expressed.

Theo whimpered in Eve's arms so she kissed his forehead and whispered to him to quiet. He was restless as if he understood their loss or picked up on her emotions. He whined, wriggled, and pushed at her, and even after repositioning him a few times, Theo refused to settle. Theo's discomfort must have broken through to Junior because he looked up and focused on her and the babe.

To Eve, Junior looked broken when her mother died, but what she saw in Junior's eyes now… *He looks dead inside.*

Mrs. Wilson placed her hands on Eve's shoulders. "Maybe you should come home with me and Tom tonight, Eve."

Eve could hear Mrs. Wilson speaking, but she tuned everything else that was being said out. Her attention was locked on Junior, and his attention seemed to be on her. Eve saw his grief, felt it in her very soul. She also saw the guilt in his gaze. Junior was always Sadie's caretaker.

"Eve," Mrs. Wilson was insistent as she gave Eve's shoulders a squeeze, "I think it would be best if you came home with us."

Half listening to Mrs. Wilson, Eve continued to stare at Junior. Everything in her screamed for her to go to him, to comfort him, but she couldn't get her feet to move in his direction. Yet, she couldn't leave him either. As much as Eve wished that she didn't have to stay in that prison of a house another day, she couldn't leave Junior alone. She definitely couldn't leave him alone with Cefus.

Speaking of...

Eve forced herself to break eye contact with Junior and allowed the eerie pull of Cefus to draw her in. On the porch, hidden from the glow of headlights, Cefus stood against a porch beam. His attention was fixed on her, ignoring everything else that was going on around them. His expression revealed nothing, but she could imagine what he was thinking. The sense that he probably thought that he wished it was her who drowned instead of Sadie swept over Eve.

Unable to hold his gaze for a minute more, Eve turned to face the open field that led to the pond. In a way, she wished the same thing. Sadie was innocent, loving, and tried her hardest to protect and make Eve's life as enjoyable as it could possibly be under the circumstances. Sadie was her only playmate and taught her lots of things. Most importantly, Sadie showed Eve how to love and care for Theo. Sadie loved the brother they shared just as much as she loved Junior.

She was all that was bright and untarnished in my world.

227

Eve wiped away the warm tears that slid from her eyes. She hated tears, hated the weakness they displayed.

"Eve, sweetheart," Mrs. Wilson moved in front of her, "come home with us, just until things settle."

Again, Eve looked over at Junior. He was talking with Dr. Steuben. Or rather, Dr. Steuben was talking to him. Junior looked crazed, a bit unfocused. Eve would have thought that he wasn't paying attention but for the slight nod of his head every so often.

"I can't leave him."

"I understand, dear, but he won't be too..." Mrs. Wilson's words broke off. Eve turned her head around to see Mrs. Wilson looking over her shoulder to where Cefus stood on the porch, then to her husband who looked a bit worse for wear. Mrs. Wilson regarded Eve again. "We worry that Junior won't be in his right mind and that you and Theo may be better off with us. Just for a few days," she hastily added.

"Junior would never hurt Theo," Eve spoke with conviction, "or me." Her last words were spoken softly, less than sure.

"Oh no," Mrs. Wilson gathered Eve's face in her hands as she stared into her eyes, "Junior would never."

"Junior isn't the one we're worried about," Mr. Wilson added.

Oh...oh. What did they know?

Mrs. Wilson gave her husband a warning look before turning her concerned eyes back to Eve. "There's been some talk; some odd signs of..." Mrs. Wilson shook her head. "I pride myself on not basing my opinion of others on gossip but even without the gossip, Cefus has always worried me. He is a rigid man."

Eve looked past Mrs. Wilson, her eyes landing on Cefus and the wicked grin he brandished.

Why is he grinning?

Someone started up the engine of a vehicle. Eve frowned as she dragged her gaze from Cefus to see what was going on. Junior and Dr. Steuben were finished, and Junior was as still as a statue as he watched the ambulance with Sadie inside, drive away. He looked strong. He always looked so strong, but she knew he was ripped apart inside.

"I have to stay," Eve admitted. Even if she didn't want to, she had to...for Sadie. That was how she tried to explain it to herself even if she knew better.

"Alright," Mrs. Wilson nodded, "alright, but if you need us..."

The rest was left unsaid.

As the vehicle with Sadie slowly drove away, Junior walked behind it. The driver sped up and for a moment, Junior kept pace. Then he suddenly stopped, turned, and began walking toward her. When Junior was in front of Eve, he reached for Theo.

Eve hesitated for only a second, then she placed Theo in Junior's arms. Junior adjusted Theo so that he cradled him on his chest using one arm. He used his other hand to wrap around Eve's upper arm. She winced but didn't fight him. She managed to look over her shoulder and nod a goodbye to the Wilsons before being dragged back into Hell.

FOURTEEN

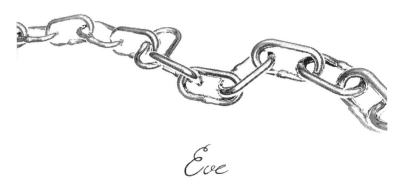

Eve

The days following Sadie's death were rough, but the day after seemed the hardest for both Junior and Eve. That morning, Junior prepared for the day like any other. If Eve didn't watch Junior throughout the night prior, she would have assumed he wasn't deeply affected by the loss.

Seeing Junior suffer that first night wasn't easy for Eve to witness. His stony expression and blank stare were haunting enough, but the moonlight that streamed through his open window illuminated his face in such a way that Eve was able to see every tear he shed.

She wanted to comfort him, to slide down on his makeshift bed in the corner and hold him. But she didn't. It didn't feel right to do so at the time, with the unpredictable thoughts about him that often plagued her. Plus, she was a knotted ball of despair.

Though she felt Junior's pain echo through her, Eve's own pain was much more potent albeit misdirected. She should have been thinking of Sadie; her innocent smile, her gentle spirit, the kindness she always showed, but Eve's fears overshadowed her best memories.

Eve's life was fear. But for a brief moment, for a tiny fraction of time, life was somewhat...nice. Now that small respite was gone; just like her father, her mother, and now Sadie. And what little ground she made with Junior these past months, she feared died with Sadie.

Junior sunk into himself. Now, just days later, Eve never felt so alone. Even in a room full of people.

"Would you like something to drink, dear?" Mrs. Wilson touched Eve's shoulder and gave it a tender squeeze.

Eve forced her attention from the window she was staring out of. Junior's truck disappeared down the drive a long time ago, but she returned to the window to stare after him.

Sighing, Eve regarded Mrs. Wilson. There was no telling how many times someone offered her a drink, but somehow Eve knew that it was more than once. The confused and concerned look on Mrs. Wilson's face was a tell.

"No thank you." Eve forced a smile.

Junior arranged most of the preparations for this gathering, Eve suspected. Whenever they were in the house, he was on the telephone speaking in hushed tones. No one ever used the phone; it was still somewhat foreign to Eve, but Junior was forever on the thing…pinned against the wall like permanent fixture sometimes.

There was no church gathering or singing like it was when Eve's great grandmother passed years ago. Eve remembered all the people in dark clothing, the women wearing veiled hats, and the men dressed in dark suits. Sadie didn't have that kind of service, but a few words were spoken at the burial site by a pastor.

The funeral service seemed more hallow than her Grams' did. Though, she was just a child then.

Voices inside the room had Eve lifting her head. She glanced over her shoulder to take in the room. Mr. and Mrs. Wilson was gracious enough to offer their home for the after burial service. People *had* come. Some came to pay their respects to Junior but left directly after speaking with him.

Others came to signify, to see if Cefus would act up. But Cefus stayed in the background, quiet and looking morose. He pillaged the assortment of food that was prepared then disappeared. Eve hadn't seen him since, and by no means was she complaining.

Those who were still present in the Wilsons home was either here to fill up on the remaining food, the gossip, or were offering assistance with the cleanup. If Eve had to guess, she'd say the bulk of the stragglers were here to listen or to participate in the gossip.

Mr. Wilson tried to prepare Eve, but she still felt the sting with every whispered word about Sadie or Junior. What Eve heard was mostly harmless talk, but sometimes the whispers were hurtful and cruel.

When one of the older women, one with a screwed up face mentioned that Sadie's death may have been a blessing, Eve had to leave the kitchen before she said something that would embarrass her host. Eve avoided the kitchen and the food ever since.

Hours later, the topic of conversation was mainly focused on Cefus. He only made an appearance at the burial, distancing himself. From what Eve deduced, it was typical Cefus behavior. However, the women and some of the men who came to show their respect still seemed appalled as they spoke of him with narrowed eyes and not so quiet whispers.

Eve didn't feel the urge to defend him at any time. She wasn't sure what it felt like to lose a child, but she knew how it felt to lose both parents. Cefus saw to that. So she didn't have any sympathy for the man or care of his feelings.

She did notice his behavior. Cefus seemed somewhat distant since Sadie's death. His attention seemed inconsistent at best, his eyes staring off at nothing in particular when she chanced a look at him. His lack of interest was a bit refreshing since he wasn't gawking at her or evil eyeing Theo?

"Won't you sit down, Eve, rest ya feet a little," Shirley said as she patted the seat next to her.

Eve turned to face Ms. Shirley, who sat on the sofa with Theo nestled in her arms. Theo always seemed pleased to be in Ms. Shirley's arms. Eve suspected it was because she was full figured, plumper in places Eve was physically lacking.

With a nod, Eve joined her friend.

"He'll be alright, ya know. All everyone says is how strong yer Junior is." Ms. Shirley's voice cracked when she said his name, but she coughed it off as she wiped away a tear from her eye. "Y'all be alright," she said again as if willing it to be so.

Eve decided right then that she didn't like these types of gatherings, and she didn't want to be included in any more of them. As she fought her own tears, because promising yourself that you wouldn't cry was plain ridiculous, Mrs. Wilson approached with a plate of food. She wasn't hungry.

As if reading Eve's mind, Mrs. Wilson said, "It's just a little bit of everything." She handed the plate to Eve.

For the next twenty minutes or so, Eve picked around her plate as she half listened to the remaining guests share their happy memories of Sadie while they packed the food away and cleaned. No one would allow her to lift a finger and honestly, Eve didn't feel like she had the energy to. She was mentally drained and stressed. Just breathing felt like a chore at present. So Eve sat quietly, trying to be as inconspicuous as possible.

"If you're ready, I'll take you home."

Eve peered up at Mr. Wilson. She must have zoned out again because she didn't feel his presence or hear him, and he was standing directly in front of her. Eve pushed off the sofa to her feet. She glanced around the room. All the guests were gone, and she didn't even notice.

Flustered and a bit embarrassed, Eve reached for Theo who was asleep in Mrs. Wilson's arms. "I'm sorry. I just..." she started but couldn't voice what she wanted to say. "I'm sorry," she repeated.

"No apologies necessary." Mrs. Wilson gave Eve an understanding smile. It lacked the light the woman's beaming smile usually offered. Before Eve could respond, Mrs. Wilson sped off to the kitchen.

"Here's your bag." Paul handed Eve the bag that held Theo's supplies while Fran waited patiently to give her his tiny shoes. It was easy to forget the Wilsons had two children. Paul and Fran, just ten and nine, often played outdoors. They were great kids and very helpful. Eve couldn't remember ever hearing a bad word about them, and they had such wonderful manners.

Paul helped slide the bag up on Eve's free arm to her shoulder, then she took Theo's shoes from Fran. She then hugged Ms. Shirley, who stood to see her off.

"I know you may want to take your time getting back to your normal going-ons, but it's best to get back into the routine," Shirley said this as she gave Eve a firm squeeze.

"We should meet the day after tomorrow," Mrs. Wilson called as she entered the room with a large bag. She handed the bag to Mr. Wilson. "Just a few things, so you don't have to worry about cooking."

Eve knew it was useless to refuse so she just gave Mrs. Wilson an awkward hug then followed Mr. Wilson out of the house. Once they were settled in the truck and set off, all the thoughts that kept Eve's mind distracted were screaming at her all at once.

What will Junior do now? Will he leave now that he didn't have Sadie to care for? She doubted he would leave her and Theo with Cefus, but...if he did, what would she do?

"You alright, Eve?" Mr. Wilson was standing outside of the truck with the passenger door held ajar. He held the bag of food his wife gave him and had an apprehensive expression on his face. "If you'd rather—"

They were home. "No," she replied with haste as she pulled Theo close and got out of the truck. "We're fine; I'm fine."

Eve hurried up the walk to the Shaw house. Once inside, she placed a still sleeping Theo on the armchair in the living room. After she made sure the baby was secured, Eve rushed back to the foyer to get the food from Mr. Wilson, but he already placed the bag on the table and was making his way out of the kitchen before she got there.

"You going to be alright?" He shrugged as he glanced around the dimly lit house. "Looks like everyone's asleep or gone."

Eve looked out of the open front door. Junior's truck was parked outside, but Cefus' truck was nowhere to be seen. She sighed with relief. She didn't want to run into him tonight.

"I'll be fine. Thank you." Eve moved with Mr. Wilson to the door. He turned toward her and reached out as if he was going to hug her but wasn't certain with his movements. He eventually pulled her into an uncomfortable hug then turned and jogged down the porch stairs.

Eve didn't watch him ride off. Instead, she returned to Theo. She lifted his balled-up mass into her arms then made for the stairs. Theo struggled in her grasp as she climbed the stairs but settled with a few pats to his bottom.

The room Eve and Theo shared with Junior was dark. Eve flipped the switch on the wall that illuminated the room. Again, Theo stirred, but after she settled him on his side of the bed and placed pillows around him as barriers, he fell sound asleep.

Junior wasn't in his corner of the room, and the folded blankets told her that he didn't try to get some sleep either.

Eve wanted nothing more than to lie down and rest her mind and body, but she had to put away the food that Mrs. Wilson gave her.

Tired, Eve glanced at Theo one more time, making certain he was secured, then she left the room, cracking the door behind her. Her mind was set on getting the food in the refrigerator and getting back to the room before Cefus returned from wherever it was he'd slithered off to.

In the kitchen, Eve pulled the items from the bag as fast as she could and proceeded to put them away. She was so focused on making room for all the food in the icebox that she didn't notice she wasn't alone in the room.

"At last," Cefus spoke slowly, using each word as a dull weapon.

The porcelain dish Eve held wobbled in her grasp then fell to the floor, shattering into pieces. Cefus didn't spare her a moment to even turn around. He rushed forward, wrapping his arm around her waist and lifted her off her feet. Eve fought, kicking and scratching at his arm to get free, but all she managed was to lose a shoe.

Cefus grabbed a fist full of her hair and yanked her head back and to the side so that his heated breath caressed her lower jaw. Eve's hands no longer tore at his skin because the urgency to pry his fist from her hair was overwhelming. As much as she tried, Eve was unable to pry his fist open.

Crying, begging, bargaining, they were all useless and Eve knew it. Her time finally came. But she wasn't going to lie down and accept it. Eve kept up her fight to get free of his hold. She knew she wasn't gaining ground, but she did everything aside from screaming.

"Fight me; go right ahead." Cefus chuckled, then pulled her head back a few inches more, licking her exposed neck. "But you scream; you alert that dumb fucker I was cursed with for a son. I will kill him then get that mutt you got sleeping upstairs and take him to the lake and drown him like I did my retard daughter.

Eve froze. All the fight drained from her with Cefus' admission. She was aware of everything in that instant as her hands dropped and rested against Cefus. She could smell the garlic in the pasta that covered the floor, the chill of his cool hands through her thin garment—no doubt from the beers he drank; even the low hum of the aging refrigerator blared.

Her body limply hung, her ass pressed against his hardening cock that he ground into her. Cefus moaned, turned, then took the few steps that brought them to the counter.

Eve didn't fight as he roughly dropped her to her feet and pushed her face down on the countertop. Keeping her pinned with one hand on her head; Cefus lifted her skirt over her ass. She felt the sting of her underwear as it was stretched over her skin and heard the sound of fabric tearing as they finally gave and ripped from her.

Eve felt disconnected as his fingers dug into her ass cheeks. She felt robbed, gutted; Eve felt so horrible that whatever he did to her body was nothing compared to what he already did to her soul.

He took so much, so, so much. Cefus Shaw finally eviscerated her with his confession. He took her father, her mother, and now he admitted to taking her Sadie. The one bright light in the hell she endured for so long.

Why fight it, him? Why? He was always going to win. He will kill Theo next, then her when she was useless to him. The only one who stood a chance of getting away was Junior.

But Junior wouldn't get away if she screamed. He never won when going up against his father. Besides, wasn't that just what Cefus wanted? He wanted a reason to kill Junior, a reason to cause more harm, to destroy everything around him.

He can't win.

As he squeezed her ass with his dry rough hands, Eve decided that she wouldn't give him what he wanted. She wasn't going to cry out. She wasn't going to alert Junior. But she wasn't going to let him have her either. She would kill him first.

"Not going to fight me, little pup?" He smacked her ass so hard the sound and pain pulled Eve from her shock and thoughts. "I loved it when your mother fought me. Made fucking her so much more interesting."

Eve did her best to ignore him as she looked for a weapon. It wasn't easy to do with her head pinned. A knife would be ideal, but anything would do. *Just get him off.* She could find the butcher's knife once she was free.

Just like that, Eve decided that Cefus would not see morning. Even if she was unable to get free and he raped her, she was going to kill Cefus Shaw this very night. Whatever prison she ended up in was going to be a hell of a lot better than the one she lived in now.

JUNIOR

Frozen, staring at the vision before him, Junior took two unsteady steps back. He couldn't believe his eyes. He rubbed them to clear his vision then looked back down at what lay before him. Maybe he shouldn't look at what he found as an offering, but he did. It was a much-needed offering that he planned to take advantage of.

Dropping to his knees, Junior gently brushed his fingers over the scattered cash that littered the dirt floor of the barn. He gathered handfuls of bills of various denominations and stuffed them into a box he took a large vase out of. He sorely misjudged the weight of the dusty old vase and dropped it to the dirt floor. The glass shattered and the long hidden contents now covered the floor.

Junior hurried, picking up the bills with no desire to count it at this particular moment. Whatever the amount, it was a change of luck for them. He came to the decision that he was taking Eve and Theo away tonight. There was no need to stay a moment longer. That was why he left her at the Wilsons earlier.

When he wasn't taking care of preparations for Sadie's burial, he spent the past few days cleaning out the trailer her parents' hitched to the wagon, sifting through the things he thought Eve would want. He wasn't sure she would want to return after they left.

He came up with the plan on the night Sadie passed. His mind was a dark ocean storm, but the same thought kept surfacing amongst the hurt. Get Eve and Theo away from this place. It was as if Sadie was speaking to him from the beyond.

Tonight was the night.

Junior spent most of his free time in the barn. At first, it was to get away, to be somewhere other than in the tomb that he lived in. He lay in the dark, on the hood of the old wagon to just think. He thought of Pearl living the life she was meant to. Her husband was always there with her. They were alive and happy. It was the life they would have had if they didn't stop at his farmhouse.

When he wasn't daydreaming of the Jones' happily ever after, he was looking through their things. With care, Junior unpacked boxes, inspecting the contents before packing them back up. He often came across things he thought Eve would want, like her mother's clothing. There were other things as well. He found picture albums, important documents, and even jewelry. All of which he decided Eve would have.

Sadie was gone. There was nothing left for him to stay. So he started tinkering with the wagon. It didn't need a whole lot of work. Yesterday it started for the first time, and tonight they were leaving. He had a mind to go through a few more things when he found the vase and dropped it.

Junior just discovered the money when the sound of a vehicle riding over the gravel road reached him. He assumed it was probably Mr. Wilson with Eve; based on the sound of the truck he was certain it wasn't Cefus, but he still placed what money was in his hand in the box before running to the barn door to check.

When he confirmed it was who he thought, he ran back to the scattered pile and began to hasten his pace. Though he repacked most of the items he planned to take, he needed to gather his most important treasures from the house.

Junior decided that he was leaving his truck. Sheriff Gifford and his oafs would run him down in it. But with the old station wagon, they wouldn't recognize it and may not pay too much attention, assuming that the occupants were just passing through.

Junior just wanted to be long gone before Cefus returned from wherever he was. The fact that he wasn't home when Junior arrived a few hours ago was another stroke of good fortune.

Junior placed the last of the bills in the box, closed it, and placed it behind the driver's seat. He found a small blanket with pink flowers and threw it over the box. He would find another place for it later.

With that done, Junior started loading the hatch of the station wagon with his, Eve's, and Theo's things that he snuck out earlier. They didn't have much but…well, he would get Evie and Theo all they needed later.

No, you won't, he told himself. He needed to stick to the plan. Which was:

Go to Maryland.

Find Evie's family.

Take Evie to them.

Then go to the authorities, turning himself and Cefus in.

That was the plan…so he shouldn't be worried about the future. Eve's family would no doubt take care of her and Theo's needs until she's capable of doing it herself.

Before he began loading their things into the back of the wagon, Junior took the address book he found in the glove compartment out. He looked over it and found his main target. Reginald Jones was Evie's uncle on her father's side. He seemed like a good start. Junior even called the number from a payphone and asked for the man. Of course, he hung up when Reginald came to the phone. If the man seemed suitable, he would be perfect to care for Eve and Theo.

Junior signed. Theo would never know him.

It was a huge price to pay, being locked out of his brother's life, but it was a price he would gladly pay to keep the little guy safe.

Pushing his feelings aside, Junior got to work. He didn't know when Cefus would return so time was of the essence.

FIFTEEN

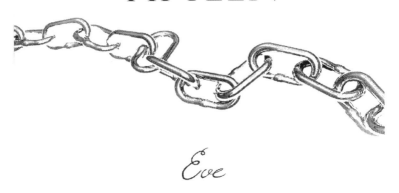

Eve

He was so strong. It came down to that, his strength. It seemed that Cefus had more strength in his finger than Eve had in her entire body. If she could just reach the fork that was just inches from her stretched fingers.

"Think to skew me with that?" Cefus taunted. He still had her pinned to the counter, rubbing his covered erection on her bare ass.

He didn't unzip his pants yet, and she was thankful for that. Each second he wasted was a second closer to Junior coming in. She didn't want that, though. If Junior caught Cefus with her in this position, she was sure he would never survive. Junior would fight to the death, and he couldn't win this one.

So she would get free on her own or...or she would be raped.

Twisting and turning, Eve did all she could to get away. Her eyes burned with her tears and her throat stung with her anger as his clammy fingers slowly slid down to part her untouched flesh. A scream bubbled up, but Eve held it back as she struggled with renewed strength.

"And to think, I parked in the back so I could avoid those nosey bitches who kept dropping off that nasty food."

Cefus tried to push his finger inside her, but Eve was moving too much. "That's it, pup, fight me," he taunted, smacking Eve hard on the ass again.

The pain was so jarring that Eve jumped and must have caught Cefus off guard because the large hand holding her head down loosened. Eve pushed her head back and threw Cefus off a bit. It was enough to get him to lose his balance. She pushed again with all her might but instead of falling like she hoped, Cefus' fingers found purchase in her hair again, and he took hold with a punishing grip.

Next thing Eve knew was she was on the floor, face down with Cefus bearing down on her. She gasped as he yanked her head back but found it hard to take in another breath with her neck craned back.

"I underestimated you, pup, from your luscious curves to your spunk. It's going to be so fun breaking you, just like I broke your uppity nigger mother." Cefus sat up, straddling Eve. He undid his tie, the only one he owned, and tied Eve's hands behind her back.

"You never broke my mother," Eve hissed as she twisted her head to look over her shoulder at Cefus. "She made a deal, one to ensure my safety. You never broke her. You can take my body, but you will never break me."

"I love a challe—"

Eve didn't hear the rest of what Cefus planned to say because his words were cut off by the foot that Junior used to kick him in the face. Eve managed to scurry away just as Junior transformed into what she always feared he would.

JUNIOR

"I fucking warned you." Junior kicked Cefus in the face again, knocking him to his back before he could recover from the first blow. "I told you she is mine." He stood over Cefus, smacking Cefus' hands away as he snatched up his shirt, then commenced to punching his father in the face. "I told you not to touch her. I warned you, you piece of shit. I warned you," he yelled.

He didn't know how much time passed or how long she called his name through the angered haze that had him. Only, he couldn't stop. He had to teach the bastard. He had to make it clear that touching his Evie...

Evie?

Junior stopped mid-punch; he took in the sight of his bloody fist that was inches away from Cefus' face. His father's eyes were glazed, unfocused, and his face was a mess, yet Junior easily dismissed it. He did a quick sweep of the area, his eyes landing on Eve.

She was standing in the doorway with a knife in her hands.

The sight of her, the way her dress hung—torn from her shoulder... Junior once again rained down blow after blow on his father. Cefus moaned as he tried to swat Junior's fist away, but the fury Junior felt was uncompromising. He kept hitting Cefus until his father's head swayed from side to side, like a bobble toy.

Junior let Cefus drop to the hard linoleum floor. He looked at the piece of shit, examining his work without a shred of compassion or feelings of regret. This moment was a long time coming. *Too damn long*, Junior thought as he again glanced over his bruised and bloody knuckles.

"I can't stay here anymore."

He almost didn't hear Eve's whispered words over his heavy breathing and the drumming of his own heart. When he turned to face her, he didn't miss the way she flinched, backed away, and raised the knife she held higher...toward him. He hated her fear of him, but there was no time to discuss it now.

"You don't have to. Go get Theo." Junior went to the sink to wash his hands, glancing down at Cefus as he did. He didn't have to look up as he soaped his hands to know that Eve didn't move. "We're leaving this place tonight. Now unless you want to stay, I suggest you get Theo and whatever you can carry."

Eve

With Theo in one arm and a bag of her things in her hand, Eve descended the stairs as quickly as her feet and balance would allow. When she got to the bottom, in the small foyer, she saw Junior just outside the kitchen. He had Cefus' gun, and she had no doubts that he had it pointed at the man himself, but she couldn't see.

When he realized she was standing there, he hurried toward her. Lowering the gun, Junior reached for her bag. She couldn't prevent her initial backward step. The look he gave her was sympathetic, though she braced herself for his anger just in case. It never came. Slowly, Eve handed him the bag.

"Come on." Junior ushered her out the front door that was already open.

Eve stopped in her tracks when she saw what was waiting. "No!" She shook her head. "You can't expect—"

"I do and you will." He placed the rifle in his hand that held the bag and grabbed her upper arm. Eve pulled away, but he tightened his hold on her. "I know…but it's our only option." He glanced over her shoulder to the house. "That bastard can report my truck missing, but he won't dare report your wagon."

"It's not my wagon," Eve disputed. She looked at Theo then at the wagon. Sighing, she knew she would do whatever she could so that he wouldn't endure any of what she had to. So Eve pulled her arm from Junior's grasp and walked down the few porch stairs to the station wagon. Junior was there to open the passenger door for her and Theo.

Junior waited for her to settle then tried to hand her the gun. She gave him a puzzled look. "I need to get some things. If he should come out that door, shoot him dead, then go to the Wilsons."

I don't think I can shoot anyone, even scum like Cefus. But I can tell Junior what Cefus so boastfully told me. Junior will kill him, and we all will be free of him. The world will be free of Cefus Shaw.

"Junior," Eve looked up at him, "I have to tell you something."

Junior peered down at her. His gray eyes widened then narrowed. His fist came down on the hood so hard the noise frightened her nearly out of her skin. Theo woke with a jolt and started bellowing.

"Shit," Junior apologized as he dropped to his knees between her and the open passenger door. He reached for Theo but Eve held her brother closer. Junior lowered his head to her arm. The contact was startling, but Eve was too scared to move. "I was too late," his head rose, and their eyes met, "I was too late, wasn't I?"

Eve blinked several times before his words filtered through her fear. He thought Cefus raped her. He looked frantic, angry, and on the verge of losing his mind. When she finally was able to speak, she mumbled, "No... No, I was going to tell you that...I don't think I can talk to anyone tonight. About what Cefus has done over the years."

The relief in his eyes was instant. The brush of his lips over her arm was surprising. If he kissed her or if his lips just touched her skin by mistake was unknown. Regardless, her body's reaction was immediate yet unwanted. It heated and hungered for more contact to wipe away the taint of Cefus.

"I'll be back in two shakes." He slid the rifle beside her, closed the passenger door, then ran back inside the house.

He must never know what happened to Sadie. And I can't take much more of his touch, were the overpowering thoughts in Eve's mind. Those thoughts overpowered her questions of where they were going and her fear of everything else to come.

JUNIOR

The silence inside the car was killing him. Eve kept silent after she told him that she didn't want to deal with any police officers tonight. If he was completely honest with himself, and he had to be, he didn't plan on taking her to the authorities tonight or any other night. Well, not until he researched some things first and made sure she and Theo would be alright without him.

He failed to make sure Sadie was safe. He even encouraged her new found love of the water. He told her that he wanted to see her swim so she should practice. Now she was gone.

Junior coughed to disguise the sob that left him.

"Are you getting tired?"

Junior turned his head away from Eve so she wasn't able to see his glistening eyes while keeping his attention on the deserted road ahead of them.

"No. I'm fine." He rubbed his eyes then faced forward again. "Won't you get some sleep?" Her concerned look prompted him to offer a deal. "I promise to stop when I get tired."

"I'm not tired," she spoke with determination.

About thirty minutes later, Eve was asleep. Junior saw a sign for a motel so he took the exit. As he drove, following the directions for the motel, he couldn't help wondering if Cefus came to yet. If he reported them gone?

His plan worked without a hitch. He didn't see a single car he recognized as they made their getaway. The next step was more complicated, but he would worry about that later. Right now he needed to get Eve and Theo more comfortable.

The tall sign ahead of him was like a welcomed beacon in the early morning sky. They made it to Marion, NC. in about seven hours. Junior drove through the green light, and a few hundred feet then made the left turn. He parked out of sight of the motel lobby, rolled up his window, and gave Eve and Theo a quick glance before getting out and locking his door.

The person at the counter didn't ask any questions, and that was good because Junior didn't plan on giving any answers. There was some kind of sign in form, but the guy barely looked at it to notice he gave a fake name. He handed over the fee and had the red key chain in his hands in less than ten minutes.

Evie and Theo were still asleep when he returned to the vehicle. Junior opened the passenger door. "Evie," he whispered, giving her a nudge. When she opened her eyes, he said, "I've stopped to rest." She blinked a few times before she cuddled Theo closer then nodded. "Here," he said as he reached for the babe, "I'll carry him."

Eve allowed Junior to take Theo from her. He backed up to give her space but stayed close in case he had to catch her. She was still under the fog of sleep so he helped her along. There weren't many people milling about, he saw just a few, but he didn't want to bring any attention to them.

Inside the room, he helped Eve to the bed. She lay down without his assistance so he placed Theo beside her and used a pillow to prevent the babe from rolling. He then went back to the car to bring in the money box and one of Evie's bags. Junior locked the room door, placed the box and bag on the floor, pulled off Evie's shoes, then pulled a thin sheet over her and Theo.

Sitting on the other side of the bed, he pulled off his shoes before lying down on top of the sheets. *I'll just close my eyes for a bit*, he told himself.

Eve

Eve felt for Theo. Well, she subconsciously searched for the hand or foot that kept hitting her. "Stop kicking me," she growled. About thirty seconds passed before she sprung up and peered around the room.

Beside her, Theo lay on his back flailing like an inexperienced swimmer. His smile was wide as he babbled spit and unrecognizable words. She took hold of his tiny fist and playfully gave it a shake. Theo's smile grew, his arms and feet kicked vigorously while his spittle turned into small bubbles.

"You're in a good mood," Eve smiled. She continued to wave his hand. "You waking me up because you're hungry?"

"I fed him."

Eve almost jumped out of her skin. She spun her head around to see Junior sitting on the floor in the corner, his eyes fixed on her. He looked comfortable like he'd been there for a while.

"What time is it?"

Junior raised his arm and noted the time on his watch. "Almost 4 p.m." He pushed to his feet. The motion opened the unbuttoned shirt he wore, exposing his muscled chest.

Eve turned away. She shook her head to shake the image free.

"Get cleaned up," Junior gruffly insisted. He crossed the distance between them in two strides; he lifted Theo, then sat on the bed. "We have to get back on the road."

She had questions. *Was he taking her home? Did he know where to take her? How long would it take?*

Eve scooted off the bed. She saw one of her bags so she snatched it up on her way to the bathroom. Before she closed and locked the door, she glanced over her shoulder at Junior.

Theo was standing on Junior's thighs, or more like Theo was pushing up and down on his own wobbly limbs.

Eve fought the smile that almost escaped. Not because she didn't want to smile. She fought it because when she reached home, wherever home was, she would never see Junior again. He may never hold, play with, or see his brother again.

JUNIOR

The way Evie looked at him right before she entered the bathroom was still on Junior's mind hours later as he drove. Neither of them talked much over the hours of driving. Her faith in him, to go with whatever he decided without asking a hundred questions always humbled him.

Junior did some research on where he was taking her. He was going to Maryland, where her family lived but he wasn't going to the same city. He was going to a county known as Columbia, which was founded by a man who wanted to eliminate racial, religious, and class segregation.

He wasn't sure if he would take her to Columbia at first. The county became an option ever since Junior overheard some patrons discussing it at the diner he went to when he went to Anniston in search of his mother. No, not until after he caught Cefus attacking her did he decide. The need to protect her, to be available to protect her, was overwhelming because he had feelings for her. Feelings he constantly fought.

To Junior, there was no other choice. He could not just hand Eve over to strangers. He needed to keep her safe. So he circled Columbia on the map before leaving, and that's where they were heading. Not to her family.

Because I want to keep her. Because I am no better than my sick father.

251

Junior bit back his sense of guilt, blinking several times to focus his watery eyes. He didn't get much sleep last night. What little he did get didn't amount to much.

He knew that they weren't followed. Cefus wasn't stupid enough to call the law other than Gifford and his goons, and they wouldn't have much power this far away. Even so, Junior was unable to relax.

"You're getting good at that," Junior said as he glanced at Eve. She was changing Theo's diaper again.

"This is nothing once you've done it a few times." She pulled Theo's t-shirt down and fixed his socks that were sliding down his heels. "We are going to have to find a garbage can soon. I don't want these diapers stinking us out." Eve placed the balled up dirty diaper in a paper bag where two more soiled ones sat. "You look tired." Her tone was subtle, worried without accusation.

"I'll be fine," Junior said but rolled down the window a bit more. He was more worried than tired. They were close now, and he needed to tell her some of what was going to happen next or she would get suspicious.

She will eventually hate me. He knew she would. He was just another jailer in the end. *No better than Cefus.*

"Look, I didn't get to learn much about your family." *Lie.* "I was busy looking for my mom, a place for Sadie," he choked out his sister's name. "I don't know where they are, other than they live in Maryland, and that was years ago." *Lie.* Junior cleared his throat. "So we need to hold up, find a place until I can find them…for you." *All lies.*

He glanced over at her to gauge her response.

Several worries filtered through Eve's mind after Junior's explanation. Some were of her same fears, but more amplified because *this* was really happening. She was really going home.

"What if they don't like me? Or blame me for..."

Junior shook his head vigorously. "I won't leave you if they aren't nice, safe." He glanced over at her...his gray eyes fixed with determination. "I will check them out first, after I find them; make sure they are good people."

Eve nodded. She had no clear memories of her family, and though the hazy ones she did retain showed no malice, she remained wary. If she learned nothing from Cefus, it was that it's better to be cautious.

Though, was she better off in Junior's care? In many ways, she was more frightened of Junior than she would ever be of Cefus.

Junior brought things out of Eve. The way in which he regarded her, made her aware of herself, aware of the woman she was. He made her feel beautiful, needed, wanted.

He made her want to be his and that terrified her.

SIXTEEN

JUNIOR

He carefully watched as the older woman smiled at Evie and Theo but shot him a curious glance over her shoulder. It was clear that Mrs. Shoemaker didn't trust him as far as she could throw him, and she didn't look like a body builder. He was sure it was because of the bruises on Eve's neck and cheek.

"So," Mrs. Shoemaker gave the door her shoulder and pushed, "it'll be just the three of you?"

Junior placed his hand on the small of Evie's back and gave her a little nudge inside the townhouse. She wasn't doing too well with the attention she was getting from the people they encountered since arriving in Maryland two days before. The amount of people in the city of Columbia made Branson's one stop sign town seem like small potatoes.

"Uh…yes," Junior answered as he took in the room. It was spacious enough, but to him the floor plan was odd. As soon as you entered the attached two-story home, there was enough room to fully open the front door but the stairs were placed directly in front of you. To the right, you were basically standing in the kitchen. A small entryway led the way to the living room that was about the size of the kitchen, minus the stairs, appliances, and cabinets.

"If you choose to sub-lease the place, the furniture is yours to use. If you rather bring in your own, I can get it out of here," Mrs. Shoemaker called from the kitchen which was just a few steps away. "I can show you the upstairs," she said as she made for the stairs.

Junior held his hands out for Theo as Eve walked by. "You go on up. Theo and I will hang out here..." he playfully spun in a circle, enjoying the giggle that came from Theo, "...in the kitchen." She offered Junior a guarded but excited look, and he gave her a smile in return. Junior blew raspberries on Theo's neck. "The kitchen is our most favorite spot, isn't it, little guy."

He wanted this place, needed it if he were, to be honest. The time it took to rent most places was too long for him to wait. This was a sub-lease; a quick, no paperwork deal. Mrs. Shoemaker's son was in the service and had to rent his place out for at least a year. Plus, the ad said it was partially furnished, and it was in an area where shopping was within walking distance.

They needed to be able to get what they needed without a car because he needed to get rid of the wagon and hitch.

Junior continued to softly talk to Theo as he listened to the conversation upstairs. He was sure the old woman would find a moment to question Eve about the bruises, from the concerned, watchful way she kept eyeing them. He was depending on it. Mrs. Shoemaker needed to know that he wasn't the abuser she thought he was. Once her concerns were squashed, they may get the rental.

He listened, and when he heard hushed whispers, he was certain that Mrs. Shoemaker was asking. He would have liked to hear what was being said, but he knew Evie wouldn't lie. She may not offer the entire truth, but she wouldn't lie on him. With that to go on alone, Junior blew more raspberries on Theo's neck as the babe grabbed at his hair.

Theo babbled something resembling a battle cry as he pulled himself close and tried to gum out Junior's right eye. "Thanks for the extra shower," Junior groaned. He moved Theo to one arm then wiped the babe's saliva off with a bib he pulled from his pocket.

"Let me take him," Eve said as she rushed down the last few stairs.

Junior took in Mrs. Shoemaker as she descended. Her worried expression seemed to have dulled a bit. That was good. "Mrs. Shoemaker, I must be honest. Me and my family," Junior motioned to Eve and the babe, "we are just coming out of a very difficult situation. We had to pick up and leave without much of a plan. They're all I have and I must, I *need* to provide for them. We need a place to start."

The woman rolled her hands together and frowned as she glanced at Eve and Theo. It was during her contemplative inspection that Junior felt Eve's small, soft hand slide into his. The move took him by surprise. He wanted to grab Eve up in his arms and kiss the hell out of her if he thought she would allow it. Instead, he linked his fingers with hers and presented a unified front. He saw the exact moment Mrs. Shoemaker had made her decision.

"Well, we can start with a trial run. How about that," she suggested with a shaky smile.

Junior extended his hand. "Thank you. That would be great."

Mrs. Shoemaker sighed then looked around the kitchen before meeting his gaze again. She offered her hand, and they shook on it. "So, I suppose you can move in as soon as you have the first month's rent, plus a hundred-dollar fee for possible damage." She squinted as she added the last part.

Junior suspected that the damage fee wasn't one of Mrs. Shoemaker's son's requirements to sublease the apartment so much as it was hers, but he didn't have a problem with her terms.

"Today then," he smiled, "is cash alright?"

He wasn't sure what earned him the glowing smile from his new landlord. Maybe it was his winning smile or the fact that he offered cash, but it was a done deal.

Junior had one less worry. *...and a hundred more to go.*

Eve

It didn't take long to get settled into the new townhouse. They didn't have much. The furniture that was left behind was nice and appreciated, but Eve couldn't help worrying about damaging it in some way. That would be bad.

"You can sit on the sofa, Evie," Junior told her for the third time that night. Since moving in four days ago, Junior's reminders that the furniture was for them to use was becoming a mantra of sorts. One she regularly ignored.

Eve felt comfortable on the carpeted floor for now. Besides...the floor was Theo's favorite place these days. They were actually enjoying floor time right now.

"Junior, I was thinking, maybe you need to sleep in the bed tonight. You start work tomorrow." She pulled Theo's foot to her lips and managed to blow on a few of his toes before he jerked out of her grasp. She giggled as she spoke, "I can sleep on the couch."

When Junior didn't respond; Eve looked over to where he sat.

The living room had a large L shaped sofa that was off white with large pink roses and stems decorating the entire thing. It was a three-by-one-by-two set up that also had a few matching cushions. The sofa wasn't something she would choose with a small child in the home, but the owner kept it clean, and she wasn't in any rush to soil it.

There was a wooden coffee table placed in front of the L-shaped sofa that Junior was making use of it. He had papers, and piles of money spread out over the entire surface. Junior was so busy with what he was doing that he even ate his dinner there.

"No," he mumbled without looking up, "you sleep in the bed. I'm fine down here." Junior sniffed then sneezed.

"God bless you."

"*Humph....*"

What is he so occupied with?

"Can I help?" Eve really wanted to help. For the past four days, Junior did everything. He let her tag along, but he may as well have left her home. She figured she should be grateful he didn't; she would have died of boredom. Plus, he let her take the lead at the market. But, he didn't speak to her much. Since arriving, Junior said little to nothing at all about finding her family. Which again, she was sort of grateful.

"*Hmmm?*" Junior started placing the money that was spread out in front of him inside different envelopes then he put the envelopes inside the small lockbox he bought at a hardware store yesterday.

"What are you doing, anyway?" Eve peered at him over her shoulder.

For the first time that day, Junior gave her his full attention. "This is your money. I found it with the photos and things I gave you. I haven't used any, hope we won't need to before everything is settled," he lowered his head and rubbed his eyes, "when I leave."

Eve tried to ignore the panic that simmered in her belly but turned away from him in case she wasn't able to keep her expression from showing it.

"I've added half of what I've saved to it. The other half we'll use to live off until I start getting paid." Junior placed the last of the papers on the table in the lockbox. "All our important papers are in here too." When she looked back at him, she was unable to read the look on his face. Then he slid one of two keys across the table toward her.

"Okay," Eve nodded but made no move to pick up the key. She turned back to Theo. He was rubbing his eyes and face in the way babies did when they were sleepy. His daytime naps were already decreasing, and he was sleeping at least six straight hours through the night.

Eve pushed to her feet then lifted Theo in her arms. He squirmed playfully, but she held tight and even rewarded his defiance with a kiss to his cheek. She walked around the table and lowered Theo for Junior to kiss. "Say goodnight to…"

"Daddy," Junior finished when she stumbled over the label. The look he gave her was one of disappointment.

They went over it a million times for the past few months and still, Eve couldn't get it right. There were so many things that caused her pause. She knew that they were just playing a role, but the way Junior made her feel; classifying him as Theo's father and her, his mother, Eve wasn't certain that the invisible lines of their roles would hold.

Junior leaned in to kiss Theo but quickly turned his head and sneezed into his upper arm.

"Are you feeling okay?" Eve frowned as she pulled Theo away. "You look—"

"I'm fine," Junior waved her worries away with his hand. "Just allergies; probably the fresh paint."

"Alright then." Eve frowned as she backed away. No kissing Theo now. "Well, goodnight."

JUNIOR

Done with all the important stuff, Junior placed the lockbox on the top of the coat closet, a few feet away from the table he sat at. He glanced over his shoulder at the key Eve left on the table and shook his head. She didn't even give it or the money a second look when he told her it was her parents'.

In fact, Eve never talked about her parents'. Or maybe it was that she didn't want to discuss them with him. Now that they were out of Branson, she had no one to talk to. He hoped that she would eventually talk to him. That they would become friends instead of just being friendly with one another. But Eve apparently didn't see him as a friend yet. She may never see him as a friend.

It didn't matter. He would break his back to provide Eve with all she needed and do his best to give her all she wanted. Even if it wasn't him, she wanted.

He saw the way men watched her when they were out running errands. Junior knew that they would take notice; Eve was a beautiful young woman. A few even approached her the few times she stepped away from him. One particularly stout man even dared to talk her up while she was standing beside him.

As if I didn't exist.

Soon enough, Eve would entertain the idea of a relationship. He wasn't the one she wanted; that had Junior gritting his teeth to the point of pain. He growled his frustrations as he placed some items over the lockbox to give it cover.

Junior sneezed again as he closed the closet door. He used his sleeve as a barrier then sniffed. He was definitely getting sick. Ignoring it seemed like the best and only way to deal with it, so Junior went to the kitchen, opened the cabinet under the sink, and grabbed the two shopping bags he placed there. He had work to do.

*H*e *didn't.*

Eve glared at the front door in disbelief. She glared at it for over seven minutes but still didn't believe what she saw.

He wouldn't.

But he did. Junior changed the locks. The new lock looked similar to the one that was on the front door of the old farmhouse and it was solely made to keep people inside.

"I can't believe he did this to us." Eve looked over at Theo.

Theo gave her a giggle before chomping down on his plastic key-ring. His gray eyes sparkled with such happiness that some of the anger she felt melted away.

"Don't take his side." Eve rolled her eyes but refused to pout. She was livid, but there was little she could do about it right now. Rather, there was little she was prepared to do. Like calling out for help. However, when Junior returned, she planned to give him a piece of her mind.

"I didn't plan on leaving today anyway." In all honesty, she had nowhere to go and no-one to go with.

Still…

Eve walked over to the double window and raised the blinds. It was early out so the heat of the day wasn't a problem yet. It looked like it would be a beautiful day. She wasn't going out today, but she could still get some fresh air. Eve unlocked and raised the window. The nice summer morning breeze washed over her, putting a smile on her face.

Eve's contentment didn't last long before she was frightened nearly out of her skin. Something touched her foot, but she was a too scared to look down to see what critter was locked inside with her and Theo. It took the force of will to look down and when she finally did, Eve was surprised by who she saw. It took her a moment to soak in that it was Theo who sat by her feet, playing with her shoestring.

"How did you get over her? Did you crawl?"

Excited but unsure, Eve lifted Theo in her arms, walked a few feet from where she stood, and lowered him back on the floor. Then she backed up a few steps. "Come here, Theo…come to me."

Theo sat on the hard kitchen floor, playing with his toes as if he didn't have a care in the world, then as if he remembered something he forgot, he looked up. He smiled, his gray eyes sparkling in the way they did when he was happy, then he rocked forward. His chubby arms bowed then braced his upper body, and he crawled to her.

"Yea!" Eve sang as she swooped him up in her arm. Theo giggled and babbled as she spun him in a circle and kissed his chubby face. "Sadie is going to…"

The words rushed out before she could even think. They were like an instant ice shower over her joy. Everything, all her troubles, came back at that moment.

Sadie is gone. She and Junior were playing the role of mother and father. There was no doubt that Cefus didn't like being bested. He was angry and would be hell bent on finding them.

"Good morning!"

Before Eve could get completely lost in her despair, a high pitched, extremely excited voice broke through to her. There was a woman standing directly outside of her window. Confused by…well, by the woman's presence, Eve slowly walked over to the window. She placed Theo down on the floor, and he quickly grabbed the window ledge to balance himself as he peered at the woman.

"Hi?"

Even though the woman was standing directly in front of the window and smiling at *her*, Eve was still unsure if the woman was speaking to her.

"I'm Toya. Well, my name is actually Latoya, like Latoya Jackson—Michael Jackson's sister—but everybody calls me Toya. I'm your neighbor." Toya cocked her thumb to the left. "You just moved in," she noticed Theo then and waved to him, "with your baby, right."

Eve looked at the woman. Toya was definitely older than her but not by much. She had light brown skin, her hair was cut short and cute, and she wore the brightest top Eve ever saw.

Toya looked Eve over. "You're not from around here, are you?" Toya shrugged then bent over and started to baby-talk with Theo, but stopped when she was eye level with him. "God, look at his eyes. They're so pretty," she gasped.

Eve never encountered someone so oddly dramatic.

"He's so cute. How old is he?" Toya asked as she looked up at Eve.

"His name is Theo, and he'll be seven months soon."

When Toya smiled at her and turned her attention back to Theo, Eve decided that she could use the distraction—a girl wrapped in fluorescent colors and tight pants—to take her mind off being locked in.

"I'm Eve."

"So…you live with your piece." Toya tilted her head as she lifted her brows.

Eve kneeled so that they were face to face. Theo laughed as he smacked his hand at Toya's, which she moved to different spots for him to follow. "I don't think I understand the question."

Laughing, Toya gave her a sly grin. After a few seconds of them staring at one another, Toya sighed. "You really aren't from around here, are you?" With that, Toya stood and walked away.

Totally at a loss, Eve stayed crouched in front of her window wondering what just happened. The sound of Toya's high-pitched voice announced her return before Eve saw the glam girl herself, placing a stool in front of the window that faced her and Theo.

"I've decided. We are gonna be good friends. That means I need to help you get use to city folk because I'm sensing corn fields and hayrides from you. So…I will be your guide to this fun and exciting journey of the land of the living. By your clothing…, I'm also sensing you're kinda old at heart, but we will fix that too. First…pull up a chair and tell me what it's like living with a guy—"

"Toya," a female called out. The woman's voice suggested that she was older in age, and her use of Toya's name sounded like a warning. The same kind of verbal warning Eve's mother often used when Eve said something her mother didn't care for.

"Mema, please, this is for educational purposes. Get with the times, old lady." Toya waved her hand. "Don't worry about her, that's just my grandmother tripping. So…"

Frowning, Eve answered as honestly as she could, "It's alright…I suppose."

"Is he the love of your life?" Toya waited with an excited gleam in her eyes.

"I've known him all my life…really, and I've never been around other guys."

"We can fix that too. I know a ton of guys." Toya smiled wide and winked.

"Toya!" This time, the woman sounded frustrated.

"Fine!" Toya said loudly, but then whispered to Eve, "But only if you want to."

Eve couldn't help laughing. She liked Toya—like Latoya Jackson, Michael Jackson's sister. Now all she had to do was find out who this Michael Jackson person was.

JUNIOR

Junior's head felt as if it was about to explode. The headache he nursed for the past couple of days seemed to have gotten worse rather than going away as he hoped. He had headaches before, even ones as intense as the current one, but by living in a small town, he didn't have to filter as much noise and light as he did now.

In Branson, there was the slow, steady silence of wide open spaces. *Not the case now.*

Everything was different in Maryland. He couldn't find a decent radio station or any of his favorite food brands. Plus, things weren't going the way he planned either. He hated the job he found just a day after arriving. Being hired on the spot at a mechanic shop a few miles from where they were staying was convenient, but Junior knew after just one day that he couldn't work there longer than he had to.

His boss, who was also the owner, was lazy and knew little about vehicles, but boasted he knew all there was to know. One of the mechanics' price gouged almost every customer he had, and the receptionist kept finding ways to touch Junior even though he wore a cheap wedding band he got from a pawn shop.

I won't be there long. Junior laughed at the thought. If he did what he had to do, he would be behind bars in a few short weeks.

Instead of dwelling on the inevitable, he tried to focus on the bright lights of the crowded road and the dimly lit street signs he followed. He made three wrong turns already trying to get "home".

He came to a stop at a particularly bright stop light. His eyes watered so he closed them briefly and gave them a rub. When he opened them, Junior looked in his rearview mirror and noticed a police car was stopped behind him. He cursed under his breath and tried to stay calm but couldn't help shifting in his seat a few times. When the light turned green, he moved the wagon forward. The officer rode behind him for a few hundred feet before turning on the sirens. Junior's heart dropped into his stomach.

He didn't get enough time. He needed to tell Evie things. He wanted to hold and play with Theo more.

"Shit," he hissed as he raised his head to look at the roof of the wagon. He couldn't run, but being caught like this…before he had time to check out Eve's uncle. It wasn't ideal.

Junior sighed as he looked for a spot to pull the wagon over.

He couldn't lie to himself…and at this point, he refused to. He pretty much knew Eve's uncle was just as decent as Pearl. He went through Pearl's things and read enough correspondence and saw many pictures of the families to think differently.

Junior held his breath as he pulled the wagon over and closed his eyes after putting the vehicle in park. It took a few seconds for him to realize that the scream of the siren was fading. Junior's eyes popped open, and he scanned the area. The police vehicle drove by him.

Relieved, Junior exhaled. After settling his nerves, it took him another few minutes to get back into busy traffic. He was still on edge as he pulled in front of the door to the rental he and Eve were sharing.

Junior rubbed his aching head.

His forehead was warm to the touch. Yet, he wouldn't claim it; he wasn't sick. He had no time to be sick.

Shaking, or trying to shake whatever ailment that was creeping up on him, Junior got out of the wagon. He noticed that there was a stool sitting in front of the window and the memory of Sadie washed over him like a tsunami.

Sadie would have liked this place, this city. Wait…why is there a stool in front of the window.

A stool sat in front of the *opened* window. Junior walked up the walk so fast that he lost and had to recover his balance twice. He fumbled with the door for what seemed like forever before he was able to push it open.

"Evie," he hardly heard his own voice over the buzzing in his head. Junior used the key to lock the door behind him. A wave of dizziness hit him hard, but he braced himself on the door to keep from falling. His legs buckled anyway, and he felt himself sliding to the floor. The scent of fresh paint filled his nose. "Evie," he whispered again as he sank.

Eve

When the door opened, Eve bit her lip to control her anger. She was so upset with Junior. However, more than that, Eve hated to admit to herself that she was hurt by his actions. *How could he,* that was what she continuously asked herself throughout the day.

How could he treat us like his property?

"Evie," Junior whispered.

Eve didn't move from the very top stair when she heard Junior enter. She had the perfect view of the front door that was positioned directly in front of the stairs. She ignored the butterflies in her stomach that always seemed to flutter when she heard Junior say her name.

Eve narrowed her eyes and watched as he tried to lock the door with the key. Seeing him with that *KEY* gave her a reason to swat away those pesky winged nuisances that seemed to collect in her stomach.

And why does he have to call me Evie, anyway?

"My name is Evelyn, Eve for short." When Junior leaned his head and half his body on the door, Eve stood. She rushed down the stairs just as he started sliding.

Eve managed to reach him just before he hit the floor. "My God, you're burning up." She slid under his arm, grunting as she used her strength to push him to his feet. "You're going to have to help me, Junior," she urged as she helped him to the steps. "Steps, you need to step up."

She was surprised he was able to help her as much as he did, based on how hot he was. The heat coming from his warm body was hot enough to make her uncomfortable from the contact. His shirt was virtually soaked through with sweat.

The two wobbled a few times and Eve made use of the banister to keep them from falling, but they eventually made it up all the stairs. Eve supported Junior's heavy frame as they moved slowly to her room. She laid him on the bed; well she actually dropped him onto the bed. She removed his boots then his socks, throwing them to the floor haphazardly.

Pushing her long, wavy hair out of her face, she stood over him. He didn't look comfortable at all. *He weighs a ton*, she thought as she pulled and pushed his dead weight this way and that, in an attempt to get him situated.

Satisfied with the end results, Eve got off of the bed and looked down at Junior again. She needed to undress him. Moving slowly, she extended her hand nervously toward his belt buckle but pulled her hand back.

"Oh come on Evelyn," she said, biting her lip. *You can do this.*

She reached for his belt again, but Junior spoke or sighed, whichever the case, Eve jumped back. She tripped over one of his boots but managed to stay on her feet. "Ugggg," she groaned. She straightened then stomped to the bed's edge. She used both of her hands to unbuckle his belt then she unbuttoned his jeans. She unzipped the zipper and was about to move to the bottom of the bed to work his jeans off when she froze.

Junior's t-shirt was jostled and raised. With his jeans unbuttoned and opened, his body was on display. Parts of him she only saw during brief moments were now visible for her to examine. Like...the ripples of raised and toned stomach muscles.

"Oh," she covered her mouth. A fair sprinkle of hair led from his navel to...

So, that's what a happy trail looks like.

"Wow," Eve sighed as she leaned in to get a better look. She bravely brushed her hands over the area, but his heated skin caused her to immediately pull away.

His skin was scorching hot. With new determination, Eve went to the end of the bed, took hold of the ends of his jeans, and shimmied them off. It took more time than she expected it to, but she did it. When his jeans were off, she went to remove his shirt. The shirt was bunched in her hands, just under his neck when Junior attempted to clumsily help by raising his arms up some.

She threw the shirt to the floor, promising herself to pick it up later. She made an effort not to ogle his body as she lifted his head onto one of her pillows. Eve was about to cover him when she was startled by his beautiful gray eyes that were peering up at her. Frightened, she was jumping away when Junior grabbed her arm. She was amazed at the strength of his hold in the condition he was in.

"Don't," he began but stopped to swallow, "don't leave me."

Eve couldn't respond. It wasn't because of his tight hold on her arm or the sudden fear his movement caused. She was stunned silent by the depths of feeling she saw in his pleading gaze. A heartbeat later, his eyes fluttered shut, and his hot hand fell from her arm.

SEVENTEEN

JULY
Eve

For two-and-a-half-days, Junior was out of it, and that worried Eve to the point of panic. Several times she talked herself out of getting him medical help. She was constantly barraged with thoughts of her mother's last weeks and how she wanted to get her help. Just like Junior, her mother forbids it.

Whenever he was somewhat lucid, he continuously said the same things. 'Don't leave me' and 'Don't need anyone but us'. Eve knew that she shouldn't place his request over of his health. Nevertheless, Junior had a plan, and she wanted to give him the opportunity to see it through.

But at what cost?

She just hoped that whatever his illness, that it wasn't something serious.

"You ready?"

Even though Eve knew to expect Toya, she still jumped out of her skin when she heard her voice through the kitchen window. She wondered if she would always be so on edge.

"Yes," Eve answered. She lifted Theo from his favorite new spot, in front of the window, grabbed Junior's keys and her baby bag. She reached for the doorknob and pulled the door open. Eve found the old knobs for the front and back doors, switched them, and threw the new ones out.

That'll teach him.

"You sure you don't want Mema to watch him? She's raised a baseball team, and she's got big boobs. Babies like big boobs," Toya suggested. She sat on the hood of a red car.

Eve did a double take because she was pretty sure that Toya was wearing a bra. Granted, it was like no bra she ever saw before, with colorful stones fashioned in swirl patterns, but Eve was sure it was a bra. At least Toya wore a sheer white shirt over it.

"Nice right," Toya grinned and nodded as she pointed to her top. "Stole it from my aunt. She won't miss it; she has a shitload of them." She pushed off the car, walked the few feet to reach Eve, then took Theo from her.

Theo's hands went straight for the dangling earrings Toya wore. Eve shook her head and locked her door then followed Toya to the red car. It was sleek and a good deal smaller than the wagon, but she liked it. She liked it a lot.

"This is Manny, my cousin. He's going to drive us." Toya introduced as she pointed to the guy in the driver's seat

"Hello," Eve said shyly as she wiggled her fingers in his direction.

When the guy didn't respond, Toya let out an exaggerated sigh.

Eve tilted her head down to get a look at the man who was going to be driving her to the store. Only she couldn't get a good look because his head was down as he peered at a tiny box mechanism in his hand.

"Manny," Toya stuck her hand through the open window and hit his shoulder.

"What girl?" Clearly annoyed, Manny gave Toya a hard look that softened immediately when his eyes fell on Eve.

The way his eyes bore into her, Eve took a step back. She glanced over her shoulder at her door. *Maybe leaving the house without Junior isn't such a great idea*, she thought.

"Stop scaring my friend," Toya scowled. "Besides, she's got a man."

Manny hopped out of the driver's seat and opened the rear car door for Eve. Eve sent Toya a silent question. *Are we safe with him?* She didn't know Toya well, but she got the sense that she was a good person, Mema too. But Manny, though very handsome, just seemed...tough.

He's fine, was the look Toya shot at Eve as she bumped Manny out of the way with her hips. "Get in, Eve," Toya instructed.

Eve reluctantly got in the back seat of the vehicle. She extended her hands for Theo just when Mema, Toya's grams, came rushing over to the vehicle.

"I'll keep an eye on the baby." Mema reached for Theo. She sensed Eve's hesitance and said, "Manny isn't the best of drivers." Mema gave Toya a sharp look then shot a glance at Manny.

Eve couldn't decipher their silent communication, but it made her question if Manny was into bad stuff.

Mema gave Eve the sincerest of looks. "I'll take good care of him, Eve, I promise."

Eve felt that Mema was pleading with her. *Why?* Something, Eve didn't know what encouraged her to nod at Toya to hand Theo over to Mema. The older woman cradled him close as she told him to wave bye-bye. Eve slowly waved back.

"Let's just be on our way or we're never going to get there. We'll be right back, Mema." Toya put one leg inside the car and motioned for Eve to scoot over.

"Nah, you get in the front. I'm not your damn chauffeur," Manny grunted as he got behind the wheel.

"Just drive and stop being a jerk," Toya said as she rolled her eyes.

Still nervous, Eve settled in the seat. She looked up only to find Manny watching her in the rearview mirror. She quickly lowered her head.

"Drive," Toya ordered with feigned annoyance.

Eve forced herself to relax. If she was going to get along in this world, she was going to have to accept that she would garner interest. She knew some men considered her attractive. Her mother tried to keep her covered from Cefus for that reason; though she had a feeling that her appearance meant nothing to him.

Women dealt with attention from men on a regular basis and she could too. Eve dealt with a good deal more and survived. She could surely survive a trip to the store with Manny. Aside from his hardened yet handsome exterior, Toya seemed to have a playful relationship with her cousin. Manny seemed harmless enough. And Junior needed medicine.

JUNIOR

When Junior woke with an all-consuming hunger, he moved to get out of bed, but his body ached something fierce. Every movement he made for the past two days made Junior pray for the day he was back to normal. He promised himself that he would do so many things if he survived this. Like tell Evie how he felt about her, tell her of his true intentions, even take her to her family.

Food was on Junior's mind, but the main thing front and center was Evie. Always Evie.

Junior raised his hand and scrubbed it over his face. His movements were slow because his body still ached. He wanted a shower, food, but first, he needed to see Eve and Theo. Rolling over, he pushed to his feet. Junior braced himself on the bed to stop from falling and instantly regretted getting up. Once the dizziness passed, and that took a few minutes, he slowly moved toward the doorway.

"Evie," Junior called out. He rested his shoulder against the bedroom door frame. He could barely breathe, and the dizziness was threatening to put him flat on his ass. "Evie," Junior said again. He waited for a reply then listened, making an effort not to even breathe so he could hear. Nothing, he heard nothing. No Evie and no Theo.

She's finally left me.

The thought of Evie leaving him was so debilitating that he sunk down to the floor. He felt defeated, but there was no one to blame but himself.

"I shouldn't have locked her in."

She would have left at the first chance anyway.

He wasn't aware of how long he sat on the floor in the doorway. All Junior knew was that he'd give anything, any sum, to see Theo and Evelyn again.

How did I ever expect her to want...

A bustle of sounds from downstairs drifted up to him?

"He likes you."

Who is that and why is she in this house?

Before Junior could actually ask—to speak up—he heard Eve's voice. He was so happy, so damn swept away, that he found the energy to push to his feet. Only, it was then that he realized what the stranger said.

Who likes Evie?

Eve

"He likes you," Toya sang as she walked through the front door with Theo in her arm.

Eve placed the bag on the kitchen table and took Theo from Toya. When they returned, Mema was sitting on the porch playing with Theo and some of the kids in the neighborhood. Eve's face lit up when he smiled and reached for her, but Toya got to him first.

"Well, I love him," Eve cooed as she nuzzled Theo's tiny nose with her own.

Toya chuckled. "Not Theo." She shook her head. "Manny likes you. I've never seen him act like that in front of any girl. Opening doors, carrying bags, not totally occupied with his pager. Girl, he likes you."

"Evie?"

That's Junior calling me.

Eve froze, then she handed Toya a giggly Theo and hurried up the stairs. She saw that Junior was leaning most of his weight on the banister. He wore only his boxers; his straining muscles were on display.

"You're still weak." She ducked under his arm to give him support while she placed her hands around his waist. His body was warm to the touch but not hot so she felt that was an improvement. "Let's get you back in bed."

Junior shook his head. "Bathroom." He moved toward the bathroom that separated her bedroom from Theo's. "I need to shower."

Eve helped him to the bathroom, but Junior sort of pushed her away once he was inside. She knew he didn't like her with him in the bathroom or accepting her help for that matter. *Men,* she rolled her eyes. Just like the men in her books, Junior had pride issues.

"I know you don't want my help but put aside your pride and…."

Junior chuckled. "Not my pride," he gruffly stated as he reached past her and turned on the shower. "But if you'd like to see more of me, you're welcome to stay." He used the toilet back to brace himself.

"Nothing I haven't already seen," Eve mumbled. When Junior raised a brow, her faced burned with embarrassment. She didn't mean for him to hear her. Shrugging, she shoved her shame away and turned the shower off and placed the stopper in the tub. "You're having a bath. You can barely stand."

Junior gave her a stiff nod then pointedly glanced at the door. Eve walked to the door, ignoring Junior. She was closing the bathroom door when Junior asked, "Who's downstairs?"

"Our neighbor," Eve said, then added, "my friend."

She didn't wait around for him to ask more questions. Eve closed the door then went back downstairs. Toya placed Theo in his highchair and gave him a couple of banana cookies.

"He okay?" Toya asked. She was placing some of the items Eve purchased on the counters.

"His temperature seems to be down; he's not as hot to the touch but probably starving, though. I'll make him a sandwich once I get these things put away."

Toya continued pulling items from the bags so Eve started helping. The trip to the store was to get medicine for Junior, but it turned into an entertainment shopping trip as well. Eve was so tired of being bored.

Eve took each step slowly, cradling a barely awake Theo, as she made her way up the stairs. She washed him and put on his jammies in record time. Then she entered his room and gently placed him in his crib. Her little guy was all tuckered out, but Eve was wired.

Junior came downstairs about two hours ago. He stayed upstairs after he bathed, shaved, and dressed while Eve and Toya took care of some things in the living room. Of course, she fed him. Eve made him a sandwich and took it upstairs to him in her bedroom. It was an attempt to keep Junior upstairs longer.

It worked.

She wanted to avoid their 'talk' until Toya was gone. Plus, she got the impression that Junior didn't like the fact that she had someone over. *Well tough tits*, she thought, as she pulled a thin blanket over Theo's tiny body. She wasn't going to be a prisoner anymore.

Not even for Junior.

Eve tip-toed out of the baby's room but stopped in the hallway. "Why would I think that, 'Not even for Junior' as if he mattered?" *Would I allow him to lock me up just to stay with him*? She knew the answer immediately. *No, I wouldn't.* But that question posed another question. Would she stay with Junior if given the opportunity?

"Yes," she breathed.

She would, and she wanted to.

Eve grew accustomed to their life at the farm during Cefus' absence. She was even aware that she grew fond of Junior. Eve even accepted that she was unable to keep her lustful thoughts of him at bay. It was a minor hiccup she willingly endured to keep Junior in her life.

So, they had a lot to discuss.

Eve descended the stairs just as slowly as she climbed them. Junior was sitting on the sofa. He had the new VCR remote she bought in his hand and was staring unblinkingly at the television. He didn't say anything about her purchases which saved her from explaining her choices.

"I thought you left me... When I woke and realized you and Theo wasn't here," he looked at her, the determination on his gorgeous face was set, "I thought you left me."

Eve was speechless. The pained expression on Junior's face was so visible, so potent that she actually felt it. He stood and started toward her. Junior's presence was so large, so overpowering that Eve felt tiny as he approached. She couldn't move, even though she wasn't sure of what he planned to do.

Was he angry? Was this the day he showed her that he was his father's son?

Junior was in front of her before Eve could blink. She felt the palm of his hands on her face, and when she did, she helplessly sighed and closed her eyes. The brush of his lips over hers was next. Eve melted into the kiss, and that enabled Junior to take control, tasting and licking her lips frantically. As if he was a starved man and her mouth was his only source of nourishment.

Eve fisted his shirt as he owned her mouth, her next breath. His hands moved down her arms and over her waist. He squeezed her rear with both hands. The action caused Eve to gasp.

Junior pulled away abruptly. "I want you so damn bad, Evie." He stared at her, his gray eyes burning with desire.

Eve wrestled with the all the emotions she felt in that moment. The throbbing ache between her legs was at epic levels. Her body was ablaze under her skin, the sensation bordering on pain. If he wanted her to say something, anything, he was going to be sorely disappointed. Eve could barely take her next breath.

JUNIOR

Eve's silence was unnerving, but Junior didn't regret it. He placed his forehead on hers in an attempt to keep the vanishing link between them. She was so innocent and looked so damn confused. If he did anything to her at this point, he'd be no better than his piece of shit father.

God, he wanted to taste all of her so damn badly.

She's right here for the taking.

She was, and Junior felt the tug of his dark desires pulling him in. Telling him that he should take what he wanted, but he wouldn't. The fact that Junior even considered such a horrible thing made him sick. He would die before hurting Evie, or any woman like that.

"I'm sorry," he said, lifting his head. His hands were resting on her waist so he let them fall away.

"Wha—," Eve cleared her voice and spoke a little louder but her tone sounded unsure, "What do you want?"

Junior saw a flicker of fear in Evie's eyes before resolve set in. She stood up straighter as if to reinforce the strength she was reaching for. He knew she was still scared. He felt it in her rigid stance.

Ease her mind. Tell her; show her.

Junior tightened his hands around her small waist. "I want to taste you, all of you. I want to start at the top." He kissed her forehead, her cheek, then placed a quick kiss on her lips. He kissed her neck then dragged his tongue over her pulse point. The long sigh that came from her sounded so sweet.

"Your skin is so soft." He slowly moved the thin strap of her sundress off her shoulder. He leaned over, kissed, then licked her there. Then Junior stood to gauge her response but before he could look into her eyes, Eve shuddered, and her head fell to his chest. "Do you like me tasting you, Evie?"

Eve vigorously nodded.

Junior chuckled; delighted that she liked his attention. He cupped her head with one of his hands, threading his fingers through her loose braid. "Would you like me to continue showing you what *I* want?"

"Please," she breathed.

Junior closed his eyes briefly, thanking the heavens above as he backed her up to the wall that separated the kitchen and living room. He wanted to go slow, not freak her out, but his desire for Eve had his sanity hanging on a thread.

He decided to kiss and lick her shoulder and neck as he gathered her dress and slid his hand under it to caress her thigh. Eve shuddered more as he trailed his hand upward to her panty line. He trailed the outer trimming of the fabric, then pulled her leg up over his hip.

Eve allowed this, so he continued. He scraped his nails over the slip of fabric that covered her pussy. This time, Evie softly cried out and fisted his shirt.

"More?" Junior breathed.

"Mmm, yes."

"I want so badly to taste you here." Junior expertly breached her panties and slid a finger around her wetness. She was so wet, so ready and her sighs were growing longer and louder with every touch. Junior gripped her head that he already cradled and gently pulled her away from his chest. He gazed into her hooded, sultry eyes before taking her lips. At the same time, he spread her pussy lips and slid a finger inside her.

Eve tensed but then sighed and nestled down on his finger, showing him that she wanted this just as badly as he did. Or at least she did at this moment. When she started gyrating on his damn finger, he couldn't take any more. He had to taste her.

Junior let go of her head, removed his finger from her pussy, and gripped her ass. He lifted her over his hips and carried her to the sofa. He eased her down on the chaise section and took her mouth as he raised her dress over her waist and ripped her panties off. He heard her grunt but she didn't push him away, so he slid a finger inside her pussy again. Eve broke the kiss as she arched her back and moaned.

Enough! "I *need* to taste you, beautiful. Let me taste you."

"YES!"

He struck fast, like a coiled cobra. Junior pushed her legs up and buried his face in her pussy so fast it took several seconds for his brain to process her deliciousness. He groaned as his cock twitched. He was rock solid since she walked him into the bathroom with that damn summer dress on. When he set eyes on her, how beautiful she looked in the dress, he wanted to both burn and frame that damn thing at the same time.

Now, his face was buried between her thighs, lapping up her sweet cream. Her cries egged him on; his dick throbbed to the point of pain. He sucked her clit into his mouth then let it go with a pop. Evie cried out, digging her nails into his scalp as she pulled his head back to her sweet spot. That broke the damn dam.

He ate her pussy as if he was a thirsty god who just found the last pitcher of Ambrosia. It didn't take long for her to come. Her completion cry was more like a sob, full of passion and surprise. She trembled and cried out as he attempted to suck every drop of her cum up.

Junior wasn't done, or he didn't plan to be done. She started to push his head as she wiggled away from him. He prayed she wasn't finished and that she was like some women who were overly sensitive after an orgasm and couldn't take much licking after.

The sight of Evie lying on the sofa chaise: dress raised and exposing her lovely glistening pussy, her angelic face flushed with spent desire, her hair loose and cascading around her from all her thrashing...she looked like an offering. One he could no longer ignore.

Junior pushed off his sweats and boxers. He pulled a spent Evie to the edge of the chaise so her ass was just tipping off. He gripped his engorged cock and smoothed it over her wet pussy. She moaned, and he continued. The head of his cock found her opening as if it was locked on home.

He looked up to find Eve staring at him. "I want to be inside you so badly it hurts." He couldn't tell if it was fear or excitement in her eyes.

She blinked, and Junior was certain she would wake from the haze of passion and stop him. But she gave him a concerned look. "Does it really hurt?"

"Badly." He wasn't lying. It hurt like hell nursing a hard on that no other woman could sate. Junior didn't go completely celibate when he discovered he wanted Eve. He just refused to bring another woman around her. Yet, none of those women did anything to dull his desire for Eve.

Junior didn't even realize Evie's hand moved until he felt her fingers then palm wrap around his cock. His eyes fluttered closed as he realized that another one of his dreams was playing out in reality.

Eve

"It's going to hurt, isn't it?" Her voice was soft and lacked the trust she wanted to convey. She knew with all she was that Junior would never hurt her intentionally. Eve read enough books to know the mechanics of making love and knew that for some women, sex could be painful. Her mother even spoke to her about sex on occasion and told her that some women felt nothing but pleasure their first time.

Apparently, the books she read liked to embellish the details of the whole experience.

Junior watched her for a moment then pulled her up to a seated position. He was on his knees in front of her so they were face to face. He cupped her cheek, brushing away the unruly strands of hair that broke free of her braid. "It might at first, Evie," he told her honestly, "but I promise to make it feel amazing for you before I finish."

"Alright," she whispered as she tilted into his touch.

Junior took hold of the bunched fabric of her sundress and pulled it up and over her body. She raised her arms for him to pull it over her head. He dropped the dress and began to kiss her. Eve's body ached with need, and it amplified when Junior leaned back and just looked at her. His eyes moved from her face to her breasts and lower, slowly.

Embarrassed, Eve looked down and moved to cover her body with her arms, but Junior stopped her by gently moving her hands to his chest.

"You're the most beautiful creature on this planet, Evie. Don't ever hide from me." He placed a finger under her chin, raising her gaze back to his.

As he eased her back down on the chaise, pushing them up on the sofa more, Eve felt his sinful mouth on one of her breasts. How he knew her body and what it needed was beyond her. She knew Junior lay with women; she wasn't a fool, and she couldn't help wondering if each of them melted under his touch like she did.

Her thoughts were cut short when she felt the head of his penis at her core. *Core*, she giggled inside her head. Core was such a funny word, and she always giggled when she read in her books.

All Eve's misplaced thoughts stopped when she felt Junior begin to push inside her. She made every effort to remain relaxed. She read that it went easier when women relaxed. All thoughts of relaxing died when her body decided to fight her invitation. The pain wasn't sharp like the books said. It was constant and building as he tried to ease inside her. His size was the problem. He didn't even breach the entrance and Eve felt full to the point of tearing, and it stung.

Junior moaned.

That, knowing how much he wanted her, made Eve fight against the pain. She wanted this…Junior. Eve wanted to give him what he desired. Another moan of pleasure came out of him before he thrust forward. Eve's sight wavered as she cried out. Junior's pelvis was flat against her bottom; he was all the way inside her.

He attempted to muffle her scream by kissing her. "I'm so sorry." He kissed her lips then moved to her cheeks.

When Eve was capable of thought, when the pain slowly rescinded, she realized he was kissing her tears away. Junior relaxed his hold on her wrists that he held above her head. Did she hurt him?

"It won't be like this the next time," he whispered in her ear as he continued kissing her face.

Never doing this again, Eve told herself.

She was about to tell him as much when she felt him pulse inside her. *Oooooh*. Her vagina flexed around him in answer. Junior's hold on her wrist tightened as his back rose a bit, then he buried his face in her neck and cursed.

Did she do something wrong?

Junior rose above her, his eyes were dazed steel as they peered down at her. "You feel so amazing. Please tell me I can move now. I need to move."

His need of her, the desperate look on his handsome face; if Evie suffered hell from his breaching her body at this point, she would not be strong enough to deny him. Thank God it felt somewhat…okay.

Her vagina flexed around him again. This time, Junior moved. Slowly out, and at first it felt as if her skin was tearing with his movements. She stilled herself, but the horrid pulling sensation only lasted a second.

"God, Evie." Junior's words trembled with his body as he pushed back inside her.

This time, the friction was unbearable for a whole other reason. Junior pulled her leg up higher on his hip, driving deeper. He soon began a steady, moderate pace as he buried his head in the crook of her neck.

The sensations were almost indescribable as pleasure rippled through her in waves with his every move. Eve pulled her hands free and found Junior's back. His body was coiled tight, his movements controlled.

Her mind was on sensory overload. Junior felt so good, and the nonstop feeling he gave her was mounting and threatened to… "Junior!" she barely recognized her voice. Something burst and it felt magnificent. When her body stiffened from the intense, unfamiliar pleasure, she knew that she was dying, and it was amazing.

Junior lifted his head, slipped his hand to the back of her neck, and held her so that she was looking at him. His eyes…they said so much.

"Waited so long… Can't hold it… Oh God, Evelyn!" His voice still had that astonished wonder to it.

At first, Eve didn't know what the new warmth she felt was, the new pressure, but it heightened everything. She would, *was* dying in Junior's arms, and she was going with a smile on her face while calling out his name.

JUNIOR

This is happening, Junior thought as he poured every drop of his seed into Evelyn. It wasn't a dream or a fantasy. Eve was beneath him. He was inside of her, and nothing in his entire world ever felt so good or so right. He was never letting her go now. Not before and definitely not after having her. She was his. Whether Eve knew it or not, she was his.

EIGHTEEN

Eve

Eve loved the feel of Junior inside her, the strength he covered her in. The sounds he made, the way he was breathing. It was as if he never experienced what he was experiencing with her, with anyone else.

Anyone else...

Junior *had* been with others like this before. Like Terry, and look what happened to them. As much as Eve didn't care for Terry, Junior seemed to have cared for her at one point. Then he no longer cared.

Will he do the same to me?

"You were with me, Evie, and then you sort of blanked out."

Eve closed her eyes to center herself. She was still in Junior's arms. He was still holding her head, and he was still inside her. Lifting her lids, Eve focused on Junior's face. He was clearly concerned.

"I'm here," Eve whispered as she tried to look away.

Only, he wouldn't let go of her head. Junior gave her a little shake that put a halt to her second retreat into herself. The realization that she just slept with Junior, a man who didn't declare anything to her, was embarrassing. Yes, he cared for her and though she knew he didn't see her the way his father saw her mother, Junior didn't love her.

Eve never wanted to be any man's 'piece'. Especially not to a man who knew her weaknesses like Junior did. She wanted to be treasured, loved, and appreciated.

At the farm, Eve convinced herself that she didn't even want a man. That she didn't need love of any sort. Then Cefus left and in his absence, Eve realized that men weren't the problem. Cefus was.

Her father was a gentleman to the end. In fact, every male she encountered, Mabel's husband, Tom Wilson, Ellis the Wilsons' farm hand, the social worker Mr. Hopkins, were all decent men as far as she knew.

If her parents' were alive, they would want a man to court her. She knew little of the world, but vying for a woman's attention couldn't be a foreign concept. Though in most of the books she read lately, couples seemed to come together due to a series of unfortunate situations. Still, Eve wanted to love. She wanted to be loved.

But is Junior even capable?

Though he was nothing like Cefus, Junior could be mentally damaged.

"Evie,"—he gave her head another gentle shake, "don't regret what just happened."

"I don't want to but…"

Eve turned her head and this time, Junior allowed it. She felt him lower himself on her again, felt him bury his head in the crook of her neck. The feather light kisses on her skin caused Eve to shiver. She liked his kisses, the way he touched her; she did love the way he loved her body, but she couldn't allow it to happen again.

Eve placed her hands on his damp chest, loving the feel of his muscles. "I can't be with you like—"

He cut her off as he rose up. "Please, Evelyn, don't do this to me." Junior tried to pull out of her slowly, but Eve dug her heels in the chaise and pushed back. She hissed from the sudden sting of separating from each other but rolled off the sofa to avoid Junior's grasp.

"To you?" Eve searched and quickly found her dress on the floor. She pulled it on while Junior tucked himself away. "Junior, you locked me in here like a prisoner a couple of days ago."

Eve knew that things were different now. Even that she was a novice concerning relationships. That even before sex was a factor, Junior had a hold on her. Junior could own her heart; may own it already. Yet, she wasn't going to allow him or anyone else to regard her as property.

Junior fumbled with his sweats before getting them sorted and pulling them on. "I'm sorry about that, Evie. I didn't want you to leave me." He reached for her, but she managed to dodge him.

Eve held up her hands to stop him from advancing. She didn't feel the tears coming until it was too late. "You locked me up. Just like he... I'm not my mother, Junior." Eve backed away. "What if there was a fire? You may not care about me, but Theo could have..." She let the rest of her words die away, then whispered, "I thought we were different." Eve stormed off, leaving him in the living room.

"Evie," Junior called out.

He said something else, but Eve wasn't listening. She ran up the stairs and into the bathroom. Placing her head on the closed door, she locked it. She knew it wouldn't hold Junior if he really wanted to get in, but it was the only physical barrier she had. Her mental ones weakened when he called out to her, sounding like a wounded animal.

How could she let her guard down? She was supposed to confront him about locking her and Theo inside this house that could have easily become a death trap. What if there *had* been a fire?

It won't happen again. If he thought to jail her again, she was taking Theo and never looking back.

Eve slowly undressed. She turned on the shower and stepped into the bath. Almost instantly, the hot water triggered thoughts of him inside her, moving so masterfully.

New tears mixed with the shower spray.

JUNIOR

Junior picked the remote off the floor and swung around to throw it at the television but stopped before he did. "Fuck!" He sank down on the sofa. How did it go wrong? He had Evie. Had her in the most complete of ways. Then lost her, just like that.

"What the hell just happened?"

I told her that she couldn't leave me. Why can't she see that I don't want to lose her?

"Can't she see that I love her?" He just made love to her. Junior never made love to another. He never lost himself in a woman before tonight.

He never told *anyone* that he loved them, until tonight. How did Eve react? Did she tell him that she loved him too? No, she left him standing there like a damn fool.

Junior let his head fall back onto the couch cushions and stared up at the ceiling. *What do I do know*, he thought?

He breathed in and out slowly. How the hell was he to think straight with the divine scent of Evie's pussy covering his face and the delicious taste of her still in his mouth? His cock jumped, and Junior cursed.

He absently rubbed his aching chest. It wasn't the same pain he felt from losing Pearl and Sadie, but it was a close second. He wanted to go to Evie, to hold her in his arms until she felt for him a tenth of what he felt for her.

Would she see that as caging her in again?

"Fuck," he said, throwing his arm over his eyes. "What do I do, Pearl?"

It was hard to concentrate with her scent and taste threatening to drag him into the depths of insanity if he had to live without her.

Junior thought living under Cefus' rule was Hell. No, Hell was loving a woman who didn't love you back.

Eve

When Eve walked down the stairs with Theo in her arms the next morning; she assumed Junior left for work. As she walked into the kitchen, she could see that he didn't. She wondered if he still had a job. He had gone in just one day before he got sick.

She wasn't going to ask.

Junior was seated on the sofa, and his attention seemed focused on the television. *What is he watching?* On the pretense of getting Theo's squishy toy off of his play blanket, Eve walked into the living room. Junior didn't acknowledge her as she bent to pick up the squishy. She stared right at him, but he didn't so much as glance at her.

The hurt of being ignored was like a spear to the heart. It felt even worse when Theo wiggled to get free so he could go to Junior.

"You missed me, little guy?" Junior cooed as he motioned for her to hand the baby over.

Eve placed Theo on the floor to let him crawl to the idiot, who had the nerve to ignore her. She saw that he opened several of the movies she bought from the store yesterday. Her first time in a superstore went straight to her head. She went a bit purchase crazy, but it seemed Junior didn't care.

Eve turned and quickly left the room. Inside the kitchen, she began breakfast. All while her heart cracked a little more with each passing moment.

After she showered last night, a small part of her hoped that Junior would be in her bedroom, waiting for her. He would tell her that he loved her, that he was scared, confused, and that she was the only woman he would ever love. A dose of reality slapped her when she discovered her bedroom empty. So she crawled under the sheets and cried herself to sleep.

"You're a fool, Evelyn Jones," she whispered, chiding herself. "A right stupid fool." One look at Junior this morning and Eve was rethinking her position on the matter of locking her and Theo inside the house. With what happened last night, she also feared that her traitorous body would never have enough of him.

JUNIOR

Giving Evie her space seemed like the right thing to do. At least that was the theme of the movie he was watching and the theme of every movie he watched throughout the night. Junior was willing to try anything, even taking advice from romance movies.

It took everything in him not to follow her up those stairs last night. It took even more strength to see her in front of him and not touch her just minutes ago. He never should have locked her in.

"What the hell was I thinking, squirt?" he asked Theo. His brother's lack of interest with his question but total fascination with the torn movie packaging was telling. Even Theo thought him an ass. What if there *had* been a fire or an emergency. His stupid insecurities could have gotten his family killed.

I'm more like that bastard than I thought. I have to let them go before I hurt them.

The thought of losing Evie and Theo sent him into a panic. All of a sudden Junior couldn't breathe. His chest ached, and he felt hot and cold at the same time. "Breathe you fucking pansy," he whispered.

Letting Evie go just might kill him. *Better me than them.*

Junior reached for his watch that sat on the coffee table. Theo, who stood between his legs and using the table to stabilize himself, must have decided he wanted the watch too because, at the same time, both of them reached for it.

It took some time, but Junior pried it out of Theo's chunky hands. Theo banged the table and started to cry. "The fittest, squirt." Junior kissed him on the head. "Daddy will buy you your very first…"

Junior shook his head and chuckled. The lines were definitely blurring. No matter how much he wanted it to be true, he wasn't Theo's father and Eve wasn't his wife. Yet, he still felt totally comfortable claiming them. Hell, she didn't even wear a ring. He wanted to remedy that, but last night turned into a nightmare.

This time, when Junior chuckled, it was laced with bitterness and anger. How could she just walk away; after he gave her his heart, laid it out there, all for her to fucking stomp on? The image of her walking away from him last night as he called out that he loved her, flashed in Junior's mind. He fought to force his anger down.

He wasn't mad at Evie. He was angry with himself. He blew it, and he didn't have Pearl around to get advice.

Pearl, Junior sighed. Pearl wanted Evie and Theo with her family. Junior failed Pearl, let Cefus kill her; the least he could do was get Eve to her family. Junior resolved to check out Eve's family as soon as possible. Just to be sure, then he'd let her go. That was the best thing for them all.

A light knock on the door had Eve fumbling with the egg she just cracked over a bowl. Yolk trailed down her palm while shells fell into the pan. "Crap," she said as she tossed the remaining shells in the sink. By the time she washed her hands and grabbed for the towel to dry them, Junior—with Theo in his arms, opened the front door.

"Well…hello," Toya's voice was sultry and all playful.

Eve shut her eyes tight and took a deep breath. Junior probably thought it wasn't wise to get to know anyone because they were sort of on the run or hiding out. She frowned. What were they doing? Hiding out, on the run, what exactly was their status?

"Oh," Toya sighed, "Theo has your eyes. How cute. I'm Toya, Eve's friend."

Eve turned around in time to see Toya reach to take Theo from Junior. Her heart skipped a beat as Junior pinned her with a pointed look over his shoulder. Eventually, he leaned forward and handed Theo over. When Theo was in Toya's hands, Junior stepped aside but kept his eyes on her.

Eve's eyes were locked on Junior's, but she saw Toya take a seat at the kitchen table from out of the corner of her eye.

"I'm Junior," he said as if he were unsure if he wanted to give his real name.

Eve realized he wasn't going to stop staring at her until she looked away. As silly as it sounded, she didn't want him mad or disappointed with her. "Toya lives next door with her grandmother. They've been really nice to me and Theo."

"That's good, Evie." He turned toward the steps and started climbing. "I want you and Theo happy."

293

Once Junior shut the bedroom door, Toya whistled. "Oh hell no, girl; you never said that your man was the hottest white Southern stud in the entire world, with a Rhett Butler accent to boot." Toya leaned over in the chair to look up the stairs as she balanced Theo on her lap. "He's white. You know he's white, right. I thought your baby just had pretty eyes, but his daddy is white!"

Eve tried to respond, but Toya wouldn't stop talking.

"When Mema said there was a white guy over here, we thought it was the movers or something. Or that the landlady's son, whatever his name is, was back. Mema ain't the best snooper, ya know." Toya straightened in the chair. She held Theo up and studied him. "Boy, you're going to be as hot as your dad."

Eve took Theo from Toya and placed him in his highchair as she gave her new friend the side eye. "Yes, I'm aware *my man* is white." She spooned some fluffy eggs on Theo's tray. There was no point in giving him a plate to throw across the room.

"Don't get all hot under the collar, Queen. A fool can see he is yours. Not that it matters, 'cause I'm not a skeez, but he didn't take his eyes off you to even take in my freshness." Toya shrugged. "So, on to pressing business. My cousin is having a house party Friday night. He wants you there."

Eve didn't hear one word Toya said after saying how Junior didn't even look at her. He didn't, did he? *He stared at me the entire time.*

"Hey," Toya said, waving her hand. "You hear me? Manny's parties are always on. He has a pretty nice crib, and he always hires a DJ."

JUNIOR

Junior went straight to the bathroom. He cleaned up quickly and was back downstairs before Evie was done preparing breakfast.

"Are you hungry?" Eve didn't look at him when she spoke.

"No," was all Junior said. He was hungry, but he didn't want food from a woman who was pissed at him. He stood awkwardly at the base of the stairs, watching her back as she cleaned. "I have to run out for a spell," he told her. Eve said nothing else and looked as though she was purposely keeping busy so she didn't have to talk to him.

Junior nodded to Evie's friend before leaving out. He walked to the corner convenience store and used the payphone to call his boss at the garage. Junior explained that he was sick but was able to return to work. Apparently, he still had a job.

On his way back to the house, Junior thought of ways to fix things between Evie and him. When he walked through the door, Evie was sitting at the table talking with her friend about a party. The hairs on the back of Junior's neck stood up.

Eve had never really been around a lot of people. She never experienced parties or dating. She was sheltered, a captive. Even if she declared her love last night, how could he be sure she knew what it was and meant it? She had no experience with men.

What if she went to this party and met someone she liked?

As much as it hurt him to admit, keeping Evie to himself was another way of holding her hostage. He had to give Evie her freedom, but that didn't mean that he would give up on them.

"Am I invited to this party," Junior asked as he leaned on the banister. He flashed Toya a smile and wasn't surprised when she sat up straighter in the chair and smiled back.

"Of course, you are." Toya beamed then she frowned. Toya whispered something about flirting; she cursed, then looked over at Evie. "The both of you are invited."

"What say you, Evie," Junior asked as he approached her slowly. He placed his hand on her waist and squeezed as he leaned into her. He whispered in her ear, "Don't get angry; I'm only kissing you for show. We'll be out of each other's hair soon enough." Then he placed a short soft kiss on her lips. "How about a party?"

When he leaned away from Eve and looked into her eyes, he relished that she actually swooned. *Good, I affect her.* He offered Eve a genuine smile before turning and kissing Theo's dirty face. "Daddy will see you after work. Take care of mommy for me."

Inside the wagon, Junior dropped his façade. He was losing his family, and there wasn't a damn thing he could do to stop it. *Space,* he thought, as he started the engine and drove to the garage. Damn space.

Eve

Her surprise was probably written all over Eve's face. Junior just angered her more with that little stunt. *For show?* She could kick him and his 'for show'. That would serve him right.

The nerve of that jerk putting his…his…

Eve sighed as she thought of his warm, perfect lips on hers.

…and he flashed the 'panty dropper smile' at Toya?

Toya giggled. "You look like you wanted to either jump his bones or knee him in the balls." Eve narrowed her eyes as she looked at Toya. "Alright," Toya held up her hands, "I'll be over after my classes." Toya pushed away from the table and left without looking back.

Eve sat down and ate her breakfast then cleaned the kitchen. Junior wanted to party and told her that they would be out of each other's hair soon. One minute, he wanted her locked away. The next, he couldn't be done with her fast enough.

"And I gave myself to that jerk," she yelled. Theo yelled out with a grin in answer.

Eve sighed. She gave herself to Junior because she loved him. Yes, if she weren't so consumed with his touch, she would have liked to have been married first, but Junior would always be her first.

Would she be his last?

She could admit now that she was hooked on Junior since she was tasked with caring for him after his injuries. He told her that she was just a kid then, and that bothered her. So much so that Eve began to look at him in a different light.

After all, we've been through; he thinks we can just go our separate ways.

Eve could hear her mother's disembodied voice in her head, telling her not to give up. *No, I won't give up.* Eve had some things to do before Friday's party. If Junior thought he was going to flash his 'panty dropper smile' all over the county, she was going to show him what's what.

"As soon as I figure out what, what is?"

It was Wednesday, so there were a few things she needed to do and just a couple of days to figure it out.

NIGHTEEN

BRANSON COUNTY
CEFUS

"Hold your fucking horses," Cefus yelled as he stomped to his front door. If it was that damn Tom Wilson again, bitching about him shooting at those flea bag dogs, he was going to beat the hell out of him.

"Keep your fuckin' inbreed mutts..." he yelled as he pulled the door open harder than he planned. Cefus stumbled back but caught and righted himself. "A suit," he sneered. A well-dressed, well-groomed white man with slicked back black hair stood on his porch. "I don't want what you're sellin'."

Cefus started to close the door, but an expensive shoe stopped him. He looked at the shoe then his gaze slowly climbed to the man's brown eyes. With a chuckle, Cefus opened the door wider and stood his full height. If the bastard wanted a challenge, he was about to get his ass handed to him.

The man backed up and held up his hands, eyeing the scar on the side of Cefus' head. Junior's parting gift was still puckered from the stitches he got.

"I don't want any trouble." He reached into his pocket and pulled out a slip of paper. "My name is Charles Gains, I'm a private investigator. I'm here this fine Wednesday afternoon looking for a family who disappeared about eight years ago."

The paper was a photo, and the man held it up for Cefus to look at. Cefus peered at the photo, focusing on Pearl. He shook his head then stared directly in Gain's eyes. "Never see them kind of niggers around here." He was still peeved that the bitch died on him. He thought of so many things to do to her while he rotted in that jail.

It was fine, though, he thought, *Ol' Evie will have to do.* As soon as he found the bitch and that fucking traitor son of his.

The mongrel, he had no use for and would dispose of before he dragged the other two back. Cefus already fitted the basement with two chains. The chains were far enough apart for Junior to see him fucking…what Junior said, 'was his', but not long enough for him to help her.

Sweet torture.

The image alone brought a smile to Cefus' face, but he fought it back as he stared at the man. Gain's eyes narrowed. *Ol' city boy don't like the word nigger, eh.*

"Yeah well," Gains continued, "A birth certificate was issued to a Jason and Evelyn Shaw. On the document, Evelyn's parents' are listed as Harland and Pearl Jones of Baltimore, Maryland." Gains tapped the photo. "These fine folk pictured here are Harland and Pearl Jones, along with their only child, Evelyn…Shaw."

Cefus' expression was bored, to say the least. He hated suits. Nigger-loving suits he hated more. "Look, Mr. Gains, I haven't seen no fancy NIGGERS round here."

"Your son, Jason Shaw, is he around?"

Cefus spit, just missing the man's fancy shoes. "That nigger-lover is no son of mine. He and his whore are long gone from these parts. And before you ask about the mutt…they took it with 'em." He slammed the door so hard it rocked the entire house.

He had to grip the frame of his door to prevent himself from yelling out in anger. That damn piece of shit son of his once again fucked up his plans. Cefus stomped to the kitchen. The smell of rotted food and garbage burned his nose, but he easily dismissed it. He slid the empty Styrofoam containers and carryout cups around the table until he found the postcard he stole from the Wilsons' postage box.

He originally thought it was from a relative of theirs, but when he put the rest of their mail back, something urged him to keep this one piece. There was nothing written on it other than a return address. On the front of the postcard was a picture of the best looking apple pie Cefus ever saw. It seemed totally unimportant when he swiped it. Now, as he read the address, he realized he must have kept the damn thing for a reason.

Cefus stuffed the postcard in his back pocket. He was going on a road trip.

BRANSON COUNTY
TWO WEEKS LATER

"Digger," Tom Wilson yelled from the border of his property. "Digger!" He jumped over the wooden fence that separated the Shaw land from his. He used his hand to shade his eyes from the sun. "You're gonna get yourself killed messing in Shaw's yard."

"You get him?" Mabel called from behind her husband. She sounded worried. Ever since Eve and Junior left, things were very tense with Cefus and them. His horrible behavior grew tenfold. Even still, most everyone expressed their happiness that those two young people took their baby and left Cefus here to rot.

"Not yet," Tom called out. He put his fingers in his mouth and gave a loud whistle. Thirty or so seconds passed and nothing. Tom took several more steps onto the neighboring property.

"Tom, don't you dare go any further. That monster will soon as shoot you too."

Tom shooed his wife off with a wave of his hand as he focused on the expanse of the downtrodden farm. He said to whoever would listen, time and time again, that the Shaw farm was good land gone to waste.

Mabel sighed from close behind him. Tom was just about to turn around and read her the riot act because no way should she have followed him on Shaw land, but Digger caught his attention. He squinted and leaned forward as the dog sprinted toward them.

"What you got there, boy?"

Mabel moved around him, pushing Tom's protective arm out of the way. She squatted to Digger's level. When the dog reached her, Mabel titled her head, confused at what her dog held in his jaw as Tom focused on the find.

"Mabel—" Tom yanked her to her feet and stared into her eyes. He knew he looked panicked, sounded so too, it was just, he was. "Go call the police department, not here...in Anniston." He watched Mabel run off before he started to fight Digger for his prize. "Tell 'em we found a human skull on the Shaw property," he yelled.

BALTIMORE, MARYLAND

JUNIOR

No man regretted a decision more than Junior did. He stared at Eve from his spot beside the wagon as she handed Theo over to their neighbor, a woman she called Mema. When Eve turned around, the full scope of his stupidity was on display for him and every man who set eyes on her tonight. He bit his lip in an effort to not say something else he would regret.

As Eve glided—yes, glided—to the car on high heels, Junior cursed the store who made the skin tight black ankle length dress she wore. The curve-hugging contraption was going to be the death of him in one way or the other.

Toya assured him that the damnable thing was what fashionable women wore, yet it didn't look like any overalls he ever saw before. The front or what was known as the bib didn't exist on this rendition. Instead, the 'bib' actually stopped just above her navel. The shoulder straps were thin, there were no buckles, and the white slip of fabric that looked like a tightly wrapped bandaged that covered her breast couldn't be an actual garment that was sold in stores.

He hustled to open the passenger door as Evie stepped off the curb. Junior closed his eyes as her new perfume, some light, clean exotic scent, wafted around him. Her long hair was tied up with a few loose tendrils cascading down her virtually naked back.

"She looks hot, doesn't she," Toya said as she sauntered up to the wagon. Junior shut the passenger door after Eve was situated, then opened the back door for Toya. She was riding with them to the party.

"Hmm," was all Junior could say. If he said anymore, rude words might just slip out. He glanced at their front door as he walked around the front of the wagon. Would she think him an ass if he asked her to change?

Junior studied her as he sat behind the steering wheel of the wagon. She looked a bit nervous. It was her first party and being nervous was understandable. Evie was also glowing. She looked amazing; even though he was uncomfortable with others seeing parts of her he wanted to keep to himself.

He wouldn't ask her to change.

"So Toya," Junior sighed, "which way?"

With Toya's direction they were pulling up to the house where the party was within a few minutes. It was actually walking distance from their place. Toya insisted that he let them out at the door before finding a parking space. He obliged, but he didn't like being away from Evie.

Parking space, space, space, he chanted as he watched Evie disappear in his rearview. He found a parking space a half block away. He was actually thankful for the short walk back. It gave him a moment to calm himself.

As Junior approached the house, he realized that it was more crowded than any party he'd ever been to. People covered the lawn, around the sides of the house, and from where he was, he saw that the backyard was bustling too. To Junior that meant trouble; lots of people equaled lots of egos which equaled tons of trouble.

He needed to find Eve and stick close enough to watch her but far enough so she could have fun.

Eve

Dancing was a blast. Eve remembered dancing when she was young and happy. She remembered playing around with her mother as they spun and swayed from one room to the other in their house.

This dancing was altogether different. It was seductive. No matter how fast or slow the music played or the actual movements, as long as she was grinding. Toya showed her the easy to mimic movements, solo and with a partner. All you had to do was move your hips with the music. It was harder to move to the tune with a partner, but she enjoyed it all the same.

Oh, and the music. That was the best, most exciting part. Fast songs, slow songs…rap, rock, reggae. There were so many options and the DJ, the one 'spinning' the records, was *choice*—another word to add to her growing vocabulary. At least that's what Toya said. Eve agreed.

The only downside to the party was the heat. Toya mentioned that it was as hot as a sauna. Eve didn't exactly know what that was, but if the temperature was equal to the inside of the house, she didn't want to know.

Eve pushed the hand of the guy she was dancing with, away for the third time. She decided that she had to add another downside to the list.

"What's your number?" the guy she danced with asked for a second time.

"I don't have a phone," she told him, again. He twisted one side of his mouth. It was the same kind of look Toya did when she thought someone was lying. So, this guy thought she was lying. "I'm going to find my friend," Eve told the guy. She was tired of his persistence, and she didn't like being called a liar, not even indirectly.

Eve turned around and saw Junior standing against the wall, by the stairs. He was always within view. At first, Eve liked that he could see all the attention she was getting. Then she started having so much fun she forgot about being mad at him and just focused on enjoying the new experience.

Eve lifted her hand and waved at him. Junior smiled one of his genuine smiles then nodded.

"Those two skeezers still in orbit around your man?" Toya asked as she grabbed Eve by the arm, leading her toward the rear of the house.

The girls in question were camped out beside Junior for a while, but Eve didn't mind. Junior didn't say or do anything remotely jealous since they arrived. Except, he did look murderous whenever one of her dance partners tried to get touchy, but she'd instantly put a stop to it, and Junior relaxed.

"They're fine," Eve said. She barely avoided bumping into a couple dancing. "Where are we going?" she asked, making an effort to stay on her feet.

"Thirsty?" Toya asked, stopping in the kitchen. She got on her tiptoes and looked over Eve's head, smiled, then turned around to get them an ice cold soda.

Eve turned and looked over her shoulder but couldn't figure what Toya was looking for. She turned back to Toya and took the cola her friend offered. Eve twisted the top off and swallowed almost half the bottle. She absolutely needed that.

She lowered the bottle from her lips and was about to ask Toya what she was looking for, but her question died when she noticed her friend's odd behavior. Toya's lips were lifted into a knowing smile, and her eyes sparkled with mischief.

What is she up to, Eve thought? Just as Eve parted her lips to ask, she felt hands on her hips, and someone's front pressed against her back.

Eve stiffened.

"Having fun?" His voice was so smooth, so husky, and so unique from everyone here that Eve couldn't help melting into Junior. His big hand slid around her waist and flattened on her belly. He pulled her back, pressing her against his...

"Oh!"

"This is what watching you move does to me." Junior spun her around and placed both his hands on the sides of her face. "I *want* to take you home and worship every inch of your body."

Eve couldn't believe Junior said what he said to her...here and now. His clear gray eyes darkened with determination, and they burned with desire for her. He didn't wait for an answer. He just held her head steady and lowered his lips to hers.

JUNIOR

He couldn't take it any longer. He let her have her fun. He even enjoyed watching her as she danced, laughed, and met new people. There were a couple times that he wanted to break someone's hand but overall, Junior enjoyed seeing Evie having a good time.

But, that was the problem. Watching her dance with other men didn't affect him the way he thought it would. Yeah, he was a tad pissed at first, a tad envious, but when he saw the joy on her face, the amazement, he couldn't help smiling at her. As he continued to watch guy after guy ask Eve to dance, he began to feel something he never felt in his entire life.

Pride.

Evelyn was beautiful, inside and out. She was intelligent and innocent even though she was raised in the same shithole he was raised in. She came out of it sweet; the care she gave him and Theo, the way she so easily stepped in and took responsibility.

Junior realized while watching her tonight that Eve was his. He could no more let her go than he could stop breathing. Evie was his to love, to treasure, to protect, and he would do whatever it took to convince her of that truth.

When Toya looked his way then pulled Evie out of sight, Junior followed. He figured it was some sort of thing cooked up by one or both of them when he saw Toya looking to see if he followed. He laughed at that. It was soon evident that it was Toya pulling both their strings. When Evie turned around, looking for what had Toya's attention, all doe-eyed, he knew she wasn't in on Toya's plan.

He couldn't resist sliding up behind an unaware Eve; wrapping his arm around her while she drank cola. The way she stiffened when she felt him behind her was comforting. She should never allow another man to touch her so intimately. The way she relaxed into him when he spoke, his accent being all the identification she needed; that was humbling.

Junior knew Evie trusted him. He needed her to love him, and he wasn't above seducing her as a gateway to her heart. So, he kissed her right then and there.

Junior kissed her so thoroughly that Evie seemed a bit dizzy. He supported her until she was stable then said, "When you're ready, I'll take you home."

"What, oh no you don't."

Junior heard the screechy voice but didn't realize the owner of it was talking to him until someone tried to yank him away from Evie. He pulled his arm free and backed away from the girl who dared to touch him, making sure Eve was behind him. Junior stared down at one of the two girls who talked him up while he watched Evie dance. Both were pretty, but neither held a candle to Eve.

"How you gonna kiss her?" the taller of the two asked.

Her name was Charlotte or Cassie, and he thought she mentioned something about modeling or was it stripping? He glanced over C's attire, big blonde hair, shiny skintight pants, and a half-jacket that covered a shimmery bra. Her eye makeup was so thick he could barely see her green eyes.

Definitely a stripper or filly out to breed. Junior chuckled.

"Did you just laugh at us?" the other asked. She was the cuter of the two.

Jessie was her name. Junior remembered that because the Wilsons' had a cow named Jessie. This girl attire he considered modest compared to her friend, and her hair covered her shimmery bra shirt.

Junior chuckled again.

Jessie narrowed her eyes. "You did not walk away from us for her," she pointed at Evie, but in a flash her hands reached around him and she grabbed for Eve's hair.

"Oh, bitch," Toya moved forward.

But Junior took hold of Jessie's arm before she got hold of Evie. "Don't ever think to hurt what's mine." He tossed Jessie's arm away. She stumbled back.

"Jessie," a husky voice called from the crowd.

"Oh shit," Toya said, "Skeezers always travel with muscle."

"Damn right, whore," C smiled wide. She cut her eyes at Eve then looked at him. "Choose me, and my brother won't kick your ass."

Junior raised a brow as he glanced at her then the parting crowd to size up this brother of hers. C's brother broke through the crowd looking as swollen as the Hulk. Junior sighed then said, "Toya, keep them away from my wife."

"Junior, don't hurt anyone." Eve tried to reach for him, but he saw that Toya kept hold of her.

"Wife;" Chrissy snorted, "your wife is about to see you get your ass whooped."

From somewhere behind him, Junior heard Toya say, "Wife, bitch, and we'll see." Then she did something Junior didn't expect. Toya yelled at the top of her lungs for Manny.

Junior doubted he would get any help from Toya's cousin. From the moment Junior walked through the door, Manny had one eye on him and the other on Evie. It was clear the host was smitten, and Toya said as much a few days ago.

Great, Junior rolled his shoulder when he saw that C's brother had two tagalongs. Not as muscled as 'Brother' but gym bums too. The three guys stopped a few feet away, in what seemed to be a quickly-crafted fighting ring.

"Problem, Carla?" brother asked.

Carla, Junior chuckled for the third time. For the life of him, he seriously wasn't sure why he found the situation so damn funny. Not funny ha-ha, but the kind of funny that grates on your nerves.

Maybe it was the juiced-up trio in front of him or the twisted Barbie dolls who summoned them. Or maybe it was the fact that he was this close to having the woman he loved seeing him as a normal guy, but these assholes seemed determined to see the Shaw in him.

These guys were amped; Junior knew the look. He was a card-carrying member of the same club. Once a member of the 'don't give a fuck club' always a member, so he knew that there was going to be no talking 'Brother' down.

Carla pointed to him. "He pushed Jessie and was about to hit me."

"You fucked with my sister, bitch," Brother sneered.

Junior rolled his shoulders again and was about to lay the big bastard out first so he could focus on the other two, but Manny walked into the ring.

"#1. Got beef, y'all take that shit outside." Manny directed his next words at Brother. "Chris, motherfucker, you of all people know not to pull this shit in my crib." Brother/Chris looked away, shuffling from one foot to the other. "#2. This is my guest,"—he pointed to Junior, "so shit's gonna be fair or you deal with me." Manny eyed Chris and his friends again.

Manny turned to look at Junior. "We can work something out," he said, looking over at Evie, "And I'll disappear this shit right here."

Junior saw the forest for the trees now. Manny was the big man here, so he saw an opportunity to make a play for

Eve. "Nope," Junior said with a grin to Manny, as he motioned for Chris to head outside. "I got this."

"Alright, Farmer Ted, your funeral." Manny lead the way to the backyard.

Junior took Evie's hand and walked with her to the backyard. The crowd already made another ring of people.

"They must fight a lot," Evie whispered. She looked around at all the excited people.

"Idiots," Toya said as she joined them. She looked at Junior then to Eve and frowned. "You're not even the least bit worried?"

Eve

Eve ignored Toya and pulled at Junior's shirt. She started unbuttoning it. "Promise you won't hurt him, Junior."

Junior nodded, but that wasn't good enough. She saw him fight; heard stories at the Wilsons' because the women were a bit worried that he was abusive like Cefus. Mr. Wilson once told her that Junior was a good guy, but he was capable of dark things. That a kid growing under a man like Cefus had demons on his back, and that Junior fought like a man possessed.

She assured them all that Junior would never hurt her, Sadie, or Theo. They took her word for it and never brought it up again.

Eve stopped unbuttoning his shirt and took his face in her hands because he kept his eyes pinned on the Chris guy. When his eyes met hers, she saw a spark she hadn't seen in weeks. She rubbed his cheek, and as if her touch was calming, a new fire took hold of him.

Junior pulled her hands from his face and covered them with his. "I won't hurt him…much—" Several people nearby laughed. "—if you stop being mad at me. I messed up; I won't do it again."

Someone in the crowd yelled out that Junior was a crazy white boy. Another said they were going to stick by the phone to call 911 for him. Eve knew that fighting was dangerous, but she knew that spark too.

She sighed, "Alright."

"Y'all on something…right?" Toya said as she helped Junior take off his shirt. "Good Lord," she gasped.

The noise around them picked up. The comments varied, but they were about Junior and speculation about how he got so scarred. He didn't seem fazed by the talk so Eve dismissed it as well.

With another roll of his neck, Junior gave Evie a quick kiss. "Stay clear. Don't want you getting hurt; I'd have to kill someone." He winked and gave her his 'panty dropper' grin.

Eve smiled, but her smile faded when she saw the spark ignite in Junior's eyes again. He paced a small area while the other guy handed his stuff to his friends. When Chris, the big guy, turned around his gaze swept over Junior. Chris seemed to second guess the course he was on, but his friends rallied around him.

For a moment there, Eve thought he would change his mind.

Manny yelled out, "Let's do this." The crowd roared to new levels of excitement.

They definitely did this fight thing here before, Eve thought.

JUNIOR

Cocky and sure, Chris rushed forward. Junior let him come to him. Like so many, Chris threw the first punch, aiming for his face. *Amateur*. Junior did nothing to block it. In fact, he lowered his head, offering his opponent his skull and braced for impact. The hit was solid.

Chris cursed as he stumbled back, shaking out his hand.

Junior tilted his head, offered Chris a smile, and asked, "We done?"

"Fuck that fake ass cowboy up, Chris," someone yelled from behind Chris. Then a chant began.

Junior shook his head when he saw Chris shake his hand out and advance again. "I gave you an out." Junior ignored the crowd. He wasn't the home team and even if he was, he would still ignore the noise. Paying attention to the crowd was the fastest way to your downfall. Distractions were a bitch.

Junior relaxed. His fists loose, his first two knuckles of each fist ready to take the lead, his wrist tilted downward. He lowered his chin, tightened his fist right before he threw a one-two punch, his arms level with his shoulders. Junior hit home but didn't let up. Chris had no time to defend his body after the blows to his face, opening up for Junior to connect solidly with a blow to his chest and side.

Chris dropped to the grass, fighting for each breath.

Junior backed away to give his opponent space as the crowd roared. He couldn't help glancing over his shoulder to check on Eve. She and Toya were far enough back to ensure she was safe. He was happy that she not only listened but was smart enough to wait for him to come to her because, by the look of it, Chris' friends weren't too happy with his loss.

The friends approached, and Junior readied himself.

"Think before you leap, fellas," Manny said. "Rocky here is my guest and," Manny looked to Toya and Eve, "a family friend. Remember and share that."

Junior had a feeling that what Manny said was law in this circle. He watched as Chris' friends and Jessie gathered him up and walked toward the side of the house.

"You cool now," Manny said to Junior as he slowly walked back to his house, leaving Junior standing in the circle alone. A small group followed Manny inside. It didn't take long for the crowd to congratulate him with calls and back slaps.

Typical, he thought.

"Don't trip over them," Toya said, as she jogged up to Junior. She was staring at Chris and his friends too, then she turned on Junior and playfully boxed at his body. "You're really into this fighting shit. I thought for sure your ass was grass."

Junior didn't respond. He just pulled on his shirt while making his way to Eve, who still stood a safe distance from the commotion. Junior noticed that a girl he saw with Jessie and her friend earlier saying something to Eve.

"So, you box?" Toya kept up pace.

"Nope," Junior said. When he reached Eve the girl was walking away. He took Eve's hand. "What was that about?"

Eve gave him a tight smile. "Nothing important."

He wasn't going to push even though he knew whatever was said affected Eve. "Ready to go?"

TWENTY

Eve

They didn't speak on the ride home from the party. Toya probably sensed something was off because she just requested a radio station then sat in the backseat as quiet as a church mouse for the short ride. Eve collected Theo from Mema and thanked her. Her little guy didn't even stir when Junior took his chunky butt from her and took him upstairs to his room.

Eve didn't follow after them. She was feeling some kind of way from her encounter with the girl who approached her at the party. The girl didn't know her, didn't know Junior, but for some reason, her words affected Eve. She went over to the kitchen sink and ran some water into a cup. She took a long drink.

"What's bothering you?"

Again, Junior snuck up behind her. His lips were so close that if she moved, they would be on the back of her neck. She shivered from the thought and again, she relaxed into him. "Nothing," she lied.

He placed his hands on the counter, caging her in and pressed up against her. "I don't want you thinking about something else while I'm making love to you." Another shiver racked her body. "Tell me." He kissed her neck.

Eve sighed, and in her love drunk stupor, she said, "She said that I shouldn't get too comfortable because once you're done, that…" Eve turned around to face him. "That when you are done fucking my hole until it's wide and no longer usable, that you're going to leave me for one of your own. That I am just a white man's toy, just like her white ass was just a black man's toy."

Junior's eyes seemed to darken with every word she relayed. When she was finished quoting the girl's words, she wondered if his eyes were ever light gray. *Had to be the shadows of the room*, she thought, as they stared at one another.

Without saying a word, Junior turned around and walked away from her. She couldn't see from the kitchen but heard a lot of shuffling and some things moving around. He was in the closet. When he returned, he carried something in his hand. Stopping in front of her, Junior held up a small felt box. She wasn't foolish enough to think it was an engagement ring, but she was curious.

"Most of my time in school was spent getting into trouble or football. By the time I got to Branson High, fighting wasn't much of a challenge and I focused only on football and…" he swallowed, "…and thinking about you, Evie."

Eve frowned. She didn't understand what he was saying.

"Thanks to your mom, I wasn't a complete tool, and I graduated and earned my high school diploma." Junior opened the box. Inside was a gold ring, with a wolf inside a red and blue crest. "I never opened this, never gave it to a steady chick like my friends did. Saw no reason to because there was only one girl I wanted to have it, but living the way we did… It seemed like we had no future. But, with you and Theo, I want one. I want you for forever, Evie; I want us so badly that…"

"I can't image letting anyone else touch me the way you do." Her voice was low and thick with emotion. "And I never, ever want to find out." Eve expected the kiss, but when Junior took her mouth, she was shocked by the intensity and the emotion he put into it. She wrapped her arms around his neck and tried to hold on.

Junior smoothed his hands over her ass as he pulled her dress up. When he broke the heated kiss, both of them were out of breath. "No panties?" he moaned.

"Toya says they leave lines," Eve panted.

"I like Toya." He lifted Eve up on his hips then worked his belt open and pushed his jeans down. She kissed his jaw and neck as she anxiously awaited his next move. He moved his finger over her still swollen vagina. She hissed when he slipped his finger into her moist folds, working around her natural lubricant.

Eve yelped as Junior hoisted her up a little more and when he pushed his penis into her, she couldn't help it; she cried out his name.

Growling, Junior turned them, pressed her against the kitchen wall, and took her hard. "I'll never let you go," he grunted. "Never!"

JUNIOR

He was supposed to go to work, but Junior didn't want to leave. He sat on the floor with his forearm resting on his knee, his chin perched on the back of his hand. Right in front of him, Eve lay on her bed. The bed she welcomed him in.

Junior still couldn't believe she wanted him.

He made love to her most of the night. He took his time learning her body's every curve, every beautiful blemish on her skin, tasted every inch of her. By inspecting her, he discovered one thing. Evie was far more beautiful than he originally thought. She was so much more than he deserved.

The longer he watched Evie as she slept, the more he knew it was true.

Junior turned his hand over and looked at his class ring resting in the palm of his hand. It wasn't an engagement ring, but he would get her a real one. That meant he needed to get to work, so he placed the ring on the nightstand and got to his feet. He placed a kiss on Eve's forehead then left the room.

Inside Theo's room, Junior found his son still asleep. He smiled but didn't disturb anything. Junior quietly left the room and was outside and in the wagon within five minutes. The sooner he got to work, the sooner he returned to his family.

CEFUS

Cefus tapped on his steering wheel as he listened to the radio. When the gas pump dinged, he pushed open his car door, replaced the gas spout, capped the gas tank, then got back inside his truck. The sound of his running engine hummed when he turned the ignition over, thanks to Junior. At least the worthless fuck was good for something.

Cefus pulled out of the gas station and into traffic. According to the map, he would be in Columbia, Maryland just in time for dinner.

"Are you even listening to me?"

Eve rolled the ball to Theo, her mind in sync with the repetitive motion, her brain elsewhere. She was on cloud nine since waking hours ago. Last night seemed like a dream. She knew the only way to know that it wasn't was for her to see Junior and gauge his response to her.

"Eve," Toya tapped her shoulder, "girl, where are you today?" Eve looked up at her friend. "Ah, I see, you got some last night."

"What are you talking about," Eve asked, hoping she sounded nonchalant. "What were you saying?"

"Nope, uh un, you're not switching the subject now. You weren't paying attention so that topic is dead. I like the topic of hot country boy riding black beauty better."

"I'm not sharing details of intimate things with you, Toya." Distracted, Eve missed the ball Theo rolled to her. She lay flat on her stomach and reach for it under the dusty refrigerator. Once she got hold of the ball, she got to her feet to rinse it.

"It was good, wasn't it?"

Eve dried it and sat it on the counter. She needed to start dinner and give Theo a snack. Reading her mind, because Eve could be set to a clock, Toya lifted Theo from the floor and used a wet wipe to clean his hands.

"Not sharing, Toya," Eve smiled as she peeled a banana. She mashed half and placed it in front of Theo then offered the other half to Toya. Toya broke off a piece.

With a mouthful of banana, Toya begged, "But give me something. Please!"

Eve knew that she was beaming. She was the luckiest woman in the world, and she honestly couldn't help it. To be in love and to be loved back was the most amazing thing ever, and it was hard to contain the effects.

"Last night was amazing," she sang. "He's always amazing."

"I'm so jealous," Toya pouted.

Laughing, Eve said, "With all those guys you see." She swept her gaze around the kitchen for Theo's bib. "Could you keep an eye on the big guy while I run up and get him a bib?"

"Sure thing."

Eve jogged up the stairs and into Theo's room. She heard a knock on the door as she sifted through the drawer for a clean bib but assumed it was Mema. Eve made a mental note that she would have to go to the laundry center real soon, maybe tomorrow.

Bouncing to the stairs, she hummed a song she recently heard on one of the movies she watched. Halfway down, dirt-crusted boots came into view. Eve slowed but continued to descend. Her chest tightened as she made out the edge of a familiar shirt. She washed that shirt enough times to know it.

Rushing down the rest of the way, Eve sucked in a gasp. Sitting at the kitchen table with Theo on his lap was Cefus. Toya sat across from him with a smile on her face, unaware of the danger they were all in.

"Hello, pet," Cefus smiled up at her.

Eve didn't respond. She wasn't sure if she was even capable. Her fear for Theo was so strong that she wasn't even sure how long her legs would keep her up. Fighting her fear, Eve walked to Cefus and reached for Theo.

"Oh no," Cefus grinned as he pulled out a gun then placed it on the table with the barrel pointed at Toya.

Toya froze but managed to shakily mumble out, "What the hell is going on."

"Please," Eve begged.

"Zip your whore mouth," Cefus said to Toya, then focused on Eve. "Where's Judas?"

BRANSON, ALABAMA

"We're here on outskirts of the property of Cefus Shaw, where at least two human bodies were discovered during the past few days. We haven't been able to get an official statement from authorities, but what this reporter has heard is that this land is being considered a crime scene." The reporter motioned over his shoulder at the several vehicles including a county coroner's vehicle.

He then reached for a woman who stood nearby. "Patty, what do you know about the people who live here?"

"Well Fuller," she smiled wide as she spoke into the microphone, "that there is Cefus' house. We are good friends, Cefus and me. He lives there with his son who recently married and had a baby with a black girl." She whispered 'black girl'. "But she's very pretty." She said that louder. "Well, anyway, his daughter just died."

"The baby?" the reporter, Bob Fuller, asked.

"No," Patty laughed, "Cefus' daughter. Sadie was her name. Sad too 'cause she was one of them special types; pretty that one was, though. It's a shame really." Patty shook her head.

"Indeed, it is," Bob Fuller agreed. "Authorities are looking for Cefus Shaw and his son, Jason Shaw for questioning. I'll keep you all posted as this story develops, back to you, Michael."

JUNIOR

Thoughts of Evie filled Junior's head throughout the entire day. The feelings he felt were the happiest he ever experienced in his life, and he liked it; though those feelings didn't make his day go any faster. So when quitting time came, he was the first one to clock out and head home.

As he drove, he thought of the next step in their lives. He planned to marry Evie. Really marry her. If she wanted a big wedding, he'd work hard, the hardest, to give her that. They needed a bigger place, and he needed a better job. He was strong and didn't mind hard work, so maybe construction or shipyard work would do.

He wanted Evie to go to school. She was so smart and would probably love learning in a positive setting. For Theo,

Junior planned to make his son's life better than his and Evie's. Their son was going to be raised by two parents who loved him and would never hurt him. They had each other...

Would they?

Eve wanted to meet her family. *What if they don't want her with me? What if they see me as the bad guy?* The thought instantly soured Junior's mood as he pulled into his usual parking spot in front of the townhouse.

Junior slammed the wagon door, but the door bounced back. He really needed to fix that. While closing the door slowly, thoughts plummeted into his head. He had nothing to offer Evie except a few thousand dollars, most were money her parents' left behind. Would he want his daughter marrying a guy with nothing?

Hell no!

Pearl wouldn't want that for Evie either.

By the time he pushed his key into the door, his happy day was transformed into the worst fucking day ever.

As Junior stepped inside, he noticed that Eve was standing by the stove with her back to him. Even though his thoughts blasted a cold bucket of water over his fanciful dreams, seeing her still brought a smile to his face.

The fear in her eyes when she turned her head to regard him made Junior move inside faster. "What's—"

"Shut the door."

Every muscle in Junior tensed at the sound of his father's coarse tone.

"The door," Cefus said again, waving a gun at the door.

Junior looked at Eve as he closed the door. She backed up against the far wall that separated the living room from the kitchen. She looked unharmed but terrified.

Eve looked down to her right and Junior's gaze traveled with hers. He was so focused on Eve when he opened the front door that he didn't notice Toya on the floor against the wall with Theo on her lap.

Theo smiled, babbled, and reached for him, but Junior turned to face Cefus, who sat across from the girls at the kitchen table, his gun trained on Toya and Theo. Junior took a step toward his family.

"Move and I'll fill them with holes." Cefus was looking at the girls, but side glanced at Junior and raised his brow as a challenge.

Junior relaxed back on his heels but gave Eve a pointed look. He hoped she understood. "What do you want?" Junior asked.

As soon as Cefus turned his attention on him, Junior struck. He pushed the kitchen table with all his strength, digging his boots into the floor for purchase. Cefus whipped the gun around; a shot rang out at the same time the wooden table slammed into Cefus' midsection. Cefus grunted from the impact; Toya screamed, and a cry came from Theo.

"Run!" Junior yelled as he struggled to keep Cefus pinned to the wall. He saw movement out of the corner of his eye. All he could hope for was that Toya and Theo didn't get hit. "Get out," Junior yelled to Eve.

"Not leaving you," she called out. She whipped around and grabbed something.

Cefus grunted but gave up trying to push the table off him. He aimed the gun instead. Junior kept pressure on the table but tried to bend to avoid the shot that would surely hit him. Another shot echoed through the house at the same time a loud thud sounded.

The opposing pressure let up, and Junior slowly stood. Cefus was slumped over in the chair. The gun hung loosely from his fingers. Junior immediately took the gun, pushed it in the back of his jeans, then went to Eve.

She was shaking violently, her eyes wide with alarm. "Are you hit," Junior asked. He took hold of her face, using his hands to go over her scalp then her arms. He twisted her around, not aware of how rough he was being. When he searched her back then looked over her legs he closed his eyes and sighed.

He glanced at the cast iron pan that was at her feet. She must have hit Cefus with it. He grabbed her upper arm and dragged her out of the opened front door. He quickly walked to the neighbors and slammed his fist on the door several times.

"Are you alright," Toya asked through the cracked door.

Junior pushed inside, his gaze seeking out his son. Theo was in Mema's arms, who was huddled in a corner. Junior ran to them, grabbing Theo from her. He heard Mema say that she called the police, but he couldn't focus as he and Eve searched Theo's body for injury.

Junior sighed with relief when he didn't find any as he hugged his son tight to his chest. His heart beat a mile a minute. "God," he said, kissing the babe on the forehead as he continued to wail. He pulled Eve into his arms and held them both for a moment.

"Stay here," Junior ordered as he kissed Eve on the head.

"No," Evelyn begged. She was crying, and it both pained Junior and gave him a sense of pride. She held it together till now. "The police will handle him."

"No," was all Junior said as he pushed her aside. He slammed the door as he exited.

Outside, people were cautiously gathering, and he knew the police were on their way. Junior went inside, took hold of Cefus, who was still unconscious, and carried him over his shoulder to the wagon. He grabbed his keys and opened the wagon. He wasn't careful as he tossed Cefus inside the hatch trunk. The old bastard didn't even stir.

"I told you to stay inside," he said when Eve ran to him.

Her wet eyes pleaded with him as she wrapped her arms around him. "Please, just wait for the police."

Struggling for patience, Junior took her face in his hands again. He knew that she was small, but right then his hands seemed so much larger than her delicate face. Junior gazed down at her. "You made me feel alive, Evie, loved me. For the first time in my life I had love. You gave that to me."

"Please," she begged.

"I love you, Evelyn." Junior kissed her. He wished he could make her understand what loving her meant to him. What having her in that Hellhole with him meant.

Junior set Evie aside and slid inside the wagon. The sound of sirens coming was getting closer. He blocked out Eve's cries and screams as he pulled off. In the rearview, he saw Toya grab hold of her before she could run after the wagon.

Junior focused on the road. It hurt like hell driving away from her, away from Theo, but he had to end this.

Eve

This wasn't happening. None of it was real. The drive her and her parents set out for a new start in the South, her life at the Shaw Farm, her parents' death, Junior… It was all a horrible nightmare.

No way could life hurt this badly.

"Miss," the police officer said.

The young officer stood in front of Eve, and she couldn't help thinking how sharply dressed he looked in his uniform. It was like that lately, her mind wondering, random things pushing through the sadness.

"Miss," the officer said again.

This time, Eve felt a hand squeeze her thigh. She looked down at the strong, masculine hand that belonged to the man sitting beside her. Maybe it was there the whole time; she wasn't sure. She looked up at the officer.

"Mr. Shaw is refusing your visit request," the officer told her. He rubbed his neck when Eve didn't say anything but stare at him. The officer gave her a sympathetic nod before moving away from her.

Eve fought the tears that threatened to fall but couldn't stop her foot from tapping the polished floor or her fingers from rubbing over the class ring she wore on a chain around her neck. She blinked several times as she rubbed it.

"Why is he doing this to me," she whispered, "to us?"

"He must have his reasons, sweetheart."

Eve turned to her uncle. His concerned expression pushed her over the edge, sparking the fat tears that fell from her eyes. Her uncle wrapped his arms around her and gave her a tight hug. Eve cried in his arms for Lord knows how long before her uncle pulled her to her feet.

"We'll come back soon," he promised.

Soon. Eve held in the maniacal laughter she felt bubbling in her. Four months, that's how much time had passed since she last saw Junior. He kissed her and drove off with Cefus in the trunk. He never returned to her, for Theo, and now he refused to see her.

Why?

Eve allowed her uncle to walk her toward the exit. As she moved through the double doors, a man nicely dressed with the same gunmetal-gray eyes as Junior, looked at her as he passed. For some odd reason, Eve found herself waving to the handsome man. He offered her a slight smile then dipped his head as he continued on inside.

TWENTY-ONE

JUNIOR

The officer outside the cell told Junior to put his hands through the rectangle opening. Junior did as the officer said. He waited as a pair of metal cuffs were placed around his wrist. He eyed the guard with the gun, 'The Asshole', as the other officer who placed the cuffs on his hands slid the cell door open.

When he stepped out of the cell, another pair of cuffs was placed around his ankles.

Rather than letting 'The Asshole' push him or blacken his other eye, Junior moved in the direction of the room the officers took him to at least twice a week for questioning. He shuffled down the hall, ignoring everything going on around him. When he stopped in front of the interview room, one of the officers pulled open the door so Junior shuffled inside.

The man sitting at the table wasn't someone he saw before. The guy was clean. Not like he showered clean, but clean cut. He was dressed smoothly; like someone you saw on one of those nighttime soap operas on television. His blond hair was cut perfectly; the edge lines were exact. He smelled of money, and the way he sat in the chair said he was relaxed in this setting, but he only looked as if he were in his twenties; with limited experienced but Junior suspected he was older.

'The Asshole' didn't like that he stopped just inside of the doorway to look at the stranger, so he gave Junior a hard push. Junior stumbled forward, the chains clanged as his cuffed hands slammed down hard on the table, but he kept his mouth shut. Prisoners complained prisoners paid; that was the way of it.

The stranger turned his attention on the officer as Junior slid into his seat. "Officer," he said, "I'll be representing Mr. Shaw from this point on, in all his legal matters. I would be cautious with your attention and your hands if I were you."

Junior watched in shock as the officer in question shrank out of the room. The other officer chuckled as he followed. Junior turned his attention back to the stranger who sat across from him. They stared at one another for at least a minute before Junior spoke, which again was odd. Junior spoke to no one since being brought in.

"I can't afford you, and I didn't request you." It was the truth.

The man didn't say anything for a few moments, then he said, "You can't, but we'll discuss payment later. As for who requested me,"—he slid a folded letter across the table.

Junior picked up the letter. He looked up at the man again before unfolding and reading it.

Mr. Langley,

There is a young man in a Branson, Alabama prison who needs your particular skills. He is a Shaw, but he didn't inherit the venom most of your ancestors seem to have. J trust you will offer your assistance, or J will be forced to get more involved.

-Oz, the Grand and Dominant

Furrowing his brows, Junior leaned back in the chair and chuckled. "Is this a joke? I don't know anyone named Oz."

"I assure you that "Oz" is not a joke. He and our family have a history of sorts. The fact that he overlooked that history and took a liking to you is," the lawyer tilted his head, "interesting. So, as the letter states, we are related, and that's a good thing because you get the family discount."

Junior raised both brows then looked to the door. Were the authorities playing a game to get a confession? He wouldn't confess to things he didn't do, but he wasn't talking to the police or the state-appointed counsel they continued to push at him either.

"It's in the eyes." The lawyer motioned to his own eyes.

Junior straightened up and really looked at the stranger. At no point did Junior make that connection when he saw the man but now… "Cefus never spoke of family like you."

"Well," the lawyer said plainly, "Cefus wouldn't. My name is Kenneth Langley. I'm your…let's just say, uncle. We'll discuss the connection at a later time. I don't make it a habit to keep up with the Shaw side. We've been estranged for a very long time you see. I can admit that when I received the letter telling me that one of you was a good and decent Shaw, well I had to help. In order to do that, you will have to talk to me."

"There were two of us," Junior corrected.

"Of course," Langley agreed. "Sadie seemed like someone I would have enjoyed knowing." Junior nodded just as someone knocked on the door. Langley ignored it. "I have one question; did you kill any of the people buried under the tree on your property?"

"No."

"Alright."

Junior watched Langley stand then walk to the door. He almost thought that the knock was something he imagined, but when Langley tapped the glass, an officer opened the door.

"Alright then, I'll have you out of here in a couple weeks." He motioned for Junior to stand.

"That's it," Junior asked, "you aren't going to ask me more. You're just going to believe me?"

Langley waved him up again. "I have an ear for truthful words, and I did a bit of homework before arriving. Now, I have work to do if I am going to be true to my word."

Junior took a moment to inhale the fresh scent of freedom as he walked out of the jail with his lawyer beside him. He was impressed. It only took a few days for Langley to get him released and all charges dropped. Langley tried to explain it to him, saying that two of the bodies were determined to have been buried under the old tree when he was a young boy.

From character witnesses and police records, it was clear that Cefus was responsible for the two.

Unfortunately, the coroner was unable to determine how Pearl died, but they did note the abuse of her body. With Eve, the Wilsons', the social workers, and his coach as a character witness, Langley convinced the state that he was as much a victim in the situation, and it would be in their best interest to drop all charges against him.

"So," Langley turned to Junior, "what are your plans?"

Junior looked at Langley then down at the pavement. A few people walking by caught Junior's attention for a moment, but he looked back at Langley. "I honestly don't know. Until today, I thought my life would be behind bars once I got Evie and Theo to safety."

"Well, you're a free man now, and I know that a beautiful young lady and an adorable little boy would love to see you."

"I can't." Junior slid his hands in his jean pockets as he avoided Langley's gaze. He wouldn't admit to a virtual stranger that he wasn't good enough for the woman he loved. Besides, someone like Langley would see it anyway, especially since he met Eve.

"Maybe you need some time to think." Langley patted him on the back. "Ever been to California?"

Within the hour, Junior was on a plane to California with Langley. It took that long for Langley to convince Junior that he didn't need to shadow Eve. She and Theo were with her family, and they were very capable of caring for her for a few weeks. She and Theo left the townhouse because reporters were becoming a nuisance, trying to get her story.

Junior was told that all this time Eve's uncle was looking for her and her parents. He even hired a Private Investigator. When they filed Theo's birth certificate, that was the first lead in years. The investigator visited Cefus just days before Cefus drove to Maryland.

"Would you like something to drink, Mr. Shaw?"

Junior closed his eyes and tried not to shiver. He hated that name. When he opened his eyes, the stewardess, who stood over him and Langley, was watching him. "Water please," he said. He took the bottle she handed him but just placed it between his legs.

"If we need anything else, Jill, we'll see to it ourselves." Langley glanced at the woman then back to his paperwork. Junior watched the stewardess put the things on her tray away then go through a doorway. "First time on a plane," Langley said.

Junior chuckled, "Yes, but this isn't a plane. It's a private jet…and it's nice."

"Thank you." Langley took a sip of his drink. "Since we are alone, would you like to tell me what happened to Cefus?"

Junior's reaction was instant, and at that moment, he wished he played more poker with the guys. His palms started to sweat, and he felt warm all over. "No," was all he said.

Langley nodded. "Then shall we deal with other matters. The farm is yours. It was your mother's farm left to her by her parents'. She left it to you."

Only a few weeks passed since Junior discovered that his mother was the third body under the old tree. She was one of Cefus' first victims. Though the coroner would have eventually figured out who the bones belonged to, it was a letter from Sheriff Gifford that helped them with the initial conclusion.

Before Anniston officers got to his home, Gifford hung himself. In his suicide letter, he told of the hold Cefus had on him and brought a few more crimes to light. Gifford liked young boys, and Cefus found out about it. The information kept him in check, and he was willing to do anything to keep it quiet.

Cindy Shaw was murdered and buried under the old tree was one. The reason for her death was another blow to Junior's sanity.

It was Langley who told Junior what was in the letter the day before his release. "Apparently, Cefus had been molesting Sadie for years before your mother found out. Her attempt to take you and your sister and leave Cefus ensured her death. Your mother loved you and Sadie," Langley told Junior before leaving him to deal with the information in the interview room of the jail. They offered to exhume Sadie and perform an autopsy, but Junior refused to allow it. Sadie was finally at peace, and there was no point in digging up dead issues.

"Burn it, sell it, I don't care." Junior sighed, then closed his eyes. Living on the farm was hell, and he didn't plan on returning. There wasn't any reason to. The Jones' bodies were given to their family and buried while Junior was in jail. His mother was placed beside Sadie in Branson's county cemetery.

"Consider it done."

Eve

"**E**ve! Hey girl, wait up."

Eve pivoted around to see Toya was running toward her from the Cogan Math and Science building. She waited until Toya caught up with her before continuing on.

"Did you pass?" Toya held up her hand, her fingers crossed.

Eve sighed for dramatic effect as she reached inside her shoulder bag. She pulled out her test scores and held the sheet up for Toya to see. She watched as Toya's eyes read over the document; her friend's expression turning from worry to confusion to all out happiness.

"You did it!" Toya hugged Eve and began jumping up and down.

Even though Eve wasn't in a celebratory mood, Toya's excitement made her grin from ear to ear.

Toya stopped jumping and held her at arm's length. "When will you start? Are you coming here? We are going to have a blast." Toya spun around and began to pace. "Parties, we can get an apartment,"—Toya spun and regarded her, "of course you and Theo will get the bigger room."

Eve frowned.

"What?" Toya asked.

"Nothing," Eve answered as she stuffed her General Education Diploma in her bag. She made her way to the parking lot where she parked her aunt's car.

"I didn't mean anything by it, honest." Toya's footfalls echoed off the pavement as she ran to catch up with Eve.

"I know. I'm just tired. Studying to get my license and my diploma has drained me." Eve continued on when Toya stopped.

"Oh okay," Toya said. "Hey, call me later. I want to hang out this weekend."

Eve gave her friend a wave then maneuvered around the parking lot. She found the blue sedan, got inside, checked her mirrors and behind, then pulled off. She wanted to get back home as soon as possible because her aunt left for work in about two hours.

Her uncle, Ben, and Aunt Felicia, were amazing since the day they came for her and Theo, two days after Cefus attacked them. That was about five months ago. They treated her and Theo as if they knew them well. They were helping her get her life together so she could give Theo a proper start. They even accepted her feelings for Junior, even though he didn't feel the same.

The man she loved was released from prison almost two weeks ago. Junior called the day he got out and every other day since, but when they spoke he avoided any talk about coming for her and Theo. Their conversations never lasted long.

He missed the holidays and Theo's birthday, and though they never really celebrated such things, she wanted to now. Eve lied to Toya. She wasn't tired. Eve was frustrated, and she didn't know what to do.

JASON

The library door Jason that just closed behind him was pushed opened, but he didn't turn around. Instead, he started toward Langley. He wanted to talk; wanted to for a couple of days now but had to work himself up to it.

If I don't make eye contact, maybe she will go away.

"Jason," Kayla whined from behind him, "you said that you would play chess with me later. It's later."

Jason tried not to sigh when he turned around. In front of him, Kayla Harper stood, poised and perfectly straight. She was a beauty with brown skin, chocolate eyes, the mannerisms of an adult but the body of a twelve-year-old girl. Though she wasn't related to Langley by blood, the preteen referred to Langley as her uncle as well, and this kinda made Jason her cousin.

Jason figured Langley was adopted because everyone he called family was black. It was also apparent that Langley and his family were very wealthy and knew important people all over the world. In just two weeks, Jason traveled to two states, met a Senator, and hung out at an Indian reservation.

"Kayla," Langley interrupted, "I believe Ingrid stocked the pantry with your favorite cookies this afternoon."

"Did she get my cocoa too?" Kayla asked with unrestrained enthusiasm.

"You have to go and see, dear." Langley closed the book he was reading and looked up. He winked at Jason as Kayla ran from the room, closing the door behind her. "I apologize, Kayla likes winning, but the competition is usually stiff around here."

"So she likes beating me to the point of embarrassment because you all beat her," Jason laughed.

"It would seem so." Langley smiled then asked, "Is something on your mind, Jason?"

Jason took a seat on the sofa that faced Langley. He tilted his head then scratched at his ear as he thought about how to start. Then he figured he may as well start with a question. "Is it true that whatever I tell you is confidential?"

"What you tell me, Jason, I will never retell."

Jason nodded. It was a few days ago that he requested that Langley call him by his legal name. He never was a Jr., but the nickname stuck all those years.

"Alright," Jason said as he looked around at the door, swallowed, then scratched his ear again. "I need to tell you what happened to Cefus."

FIVE MONTHS AGO

Junior kept glancing in the rearview mirror as he drove. He wasn't sure where he was driving or which direction he took. All he knew was that he wanted to get Cefus as far away from Evie and Theo as he could. It wasn't until he passed familiar landscape did he realize where he was headed.

335

He glimpsed in the mirror again, and there was still no movement from Cefus. Junior weaved through traffic with his destination in mind. Soon the number of motorists thinned the more he drove until his was one of the only cars on the road. Pulling off on a dirt road, almost hidden due to the lack of daylight, Junior picked up speed.

The dirt road split in three directions, but he took the center. Junior parked the wagon and got out of the car. He aimlessly looked around the new housing development, trying to figure out what he needed. Several of the homes were almost completed. Having worked on a construction crew for a summer, he knew that some of the workers sometimes left their gear on site.

Junior frantically searched the area for the things he needed. He grabbed an X-Acto knife and some electrical wiring then ran back to the car. Cefus was still out when he returned. Junior cut a few long pieces of wiring off the roll then pushed Cefus over on his stomach and tied his hands tight behind his back.

The jostling brought Cefus to. His laughter was weak but chilling. "You think you're gonna be done with me? That you can be done with me, and that will be it," Cefus slurred.

Junior ignored Cefus as he pulled him out of the car. Cefus fell to the ground, seemingly weakened from the blow Evie inflicted. Junior pulled Cefus to his feet and pushed him forward.

Cefus tilted his bleeding head then dropped to his knees. "That little bitch is gonna pay."

"You'll never see Evie again," Junior promised as he hoisted Cefus' limp body over his shoulder and carried him the rest of the way. Junior, not so gently, dropped Cefus on the cold dirt ground near a backhoe. He grabbed a pick ax that was lying nearby and climbed into the foundation pit of a soon-to-be foundation of a home and started digging.

"That black bitch hurt me real bad, boy. You get your ass over here and take me to a doctor."

Junior kept digging. He pushed himself to keep digging. "It's just you and me, boy; family is all there is," his father moaned. "It's just us, is all."

Junior winced as tears fell from his eyes, but he kept digging. Eventually, Cefus just started mumbling nonsense.

Junior dug for about an hour and a half. Eventually, he removed his shirt just to keep cool. Still, he continued to dig and ignored his father. It wasn't until Cefus said Sadie's name that he paused.

"Fucking family," Cefus moaned. "The stupid bitch would be here if she didn't deny me what was rightfully mine."

Junior dropped the pickax and climbed out of the hole. He stood over Cefus, who pushed himself over so that he was looking up at the sky. "What did you say?" Junior demand as he grabbed Cefus up by his shirt.

"Fuck you!" Cefus smiled as he tried to spit in Junior's face. The wad of saliva failed to launch and ended up trailing down Cefus' chin.

Junior stared into Cefus' eyes for several beats. Those eyes looked like his but in them was nothing but hate. Cefus started laughing again. Any doubts Junior had died at that moment. He hated Cefus more than he ever did.

A smile was all he gave Cefus as a response.

"There's that inner killer, that Shaw spirit," Cefus chided.

Junior offered another smile then he threw Cefus into the foundation. Cefus grunted then cursed. Junior jumped in and rolled Cefus into the hole he dug, making sure he was face down. Cefus cursed him, made threats, even found a bit of his waned strength… but it made no difference as Junior shoveled dirt on top of him.

Once Cefus' body was fully covered, Junior packed the dirt tight with the shovel then continued to fill the hole. He repeated the fill, pack, fill process until the hole was completely filled and the original foundation look undisturbed and ready for cement.

PRESENT

When Jason finished talking, he waited and waited. During the entire tale, he was unable to look at Langley. But now he looked up. What he saw wasn't what he expected. In Langley's familiar gaze, Jason saw understanding instead of fear, acceptance instead of judgment, compassion instead of coldness.

"Do you remember the location?" Langley asked. Jason nodded. "Is this the reason why you haven't gone to Evelyn and your son?"

Jason understood that Langley knew he wasn't Theo's biological father. His eyes must have spoken his nonverbal fears.

"Calm; you and Evelyn are Theo's parents', and I've made it so no one will ever question that," Langley assured him. Jason sighed and nodded again. "Answer my question, Jason. Is this why you're here and not with your family?"

"Evie deserves better than me. She's...she is everything. She can become whatever she wants. Evie is smart, beautiful; she deserves the best."

Langley leaned forward in his chair and did something Jason hadn't seen him do in the two weeks they'd been together. Langley smiled. "My world is somewhat different from yours, Jason. Aside from the wealth you see, my associates, and I are...let's just say we have a primal nature. But in both our worlds, there is one thing that remains the same and that's love. You have taken care of this woman; made sure she had, protected her, and killed for her. Do you think another man would love Evelyn or Theo more than you do?

"There are cycles you must go through in life, Jason. Accept that, then mold yourself into the man you want to be. You are my family, so money will no longer be an issue for you from now on. Accept that you are the best man for them because you are, and set some goals to reach for. What I can promise you, if you stay away too long you *will* lose her."

"About what I've done," Jason asked.

"I'll handle that. Now," Langley stood and clapped his hands together, "shall I ready the jet?"

TWENTY-TWO

Eve

The sound of voices carried up to the room Eve shared with Theo. She kept her eyes closed and refused to move. It was too cold to get up.

"Up," Theo said, patting her face.

Eve groaned then said, "Guess we should get up, big guy." She tickled Theo's side.

"Op," he giggled as he tried to push her hand away.

"No, you stop," Eve sang.

Theo was taller, walking, and speaking. His light brown silken hair was curly, his skin almond colored, and his eyes were the color of a Shaw. He was smart and gooey sweet.

"Up, up," Theo demanded as he climbed on her and pushed up and down several times.

"Yes, up," Eve agreed. However, she didn't want to get up. It was cold, and the last thing she wanted to do was crawl out of bed.

She focused on the muffled voices downstairs. By the sound of it, there were at least three people downstairs. Eve wondered who would come by so early. The holidays were over, and her uncle and aunt's adult children were long gone, back to their homes with their children. They didn't live close so they mostly visited on the weekends and today was Wednesday.

School was back in session, and everyone was back to work. Eve went to the community college yesterday to pick up her GED results. This morning she was going to check out a daycare for Theo so she could start school herself.

So up it is. Eve shivered as she thought about getting out of bed, so she just threw off the blankets and darted to the closet. She pulled open the walk-in closet door and quickly found some socks to put on.

"Daadaa, dada." Theo's excited voice carried in the small space.

"Soon, big boy, dada will be with us soon." She said it so many times that she said it subconsciously this time. She pulled a long sleeve sweater over her head. She purchased it last week with money Jason sent.

Every week, he sent her money since his release. Where he got the money, she wasn't sure, but she could set her watch to the check's arrival. He also started signing his letters and the checks Jason Shaw, so she figured she would use it from now on.

"Dadadada." This time, Theo's voice was so close, almost as if he were...

Theo could walk, but he was scared of sliding off the bed so Eve spun around. Her body swayed as dizziness tried to claim her.

"Evie?"

Jason! She heard the question in his voice. She could see the fear of being rejected in his eyes. He left her alone and was scared that she would hold it against him. *Silly man*, she thought as she rushed forward to touch him. He was here. He was really here.

Eve cried as she covered his face with kisses. Things got a bit awkward because Theo tried to cover Jason with kisses as well, and Jason was busy trying to do the same to them.

"I'm sorry for—" he started.

"Don't," she whispered as she held his face in her hands. "Don't. You're here now."

"I have to say this, Evie." He swallowed as his own tears fell. "There's nothing that I want more than to be what you deserve, Evie, but I'm damaged. But I'm also selfish, and I refuse to live in this world without you and Theo." He gazed into her eyes as he rubbed her cheek. Theo, not understanding the moment, wiggled and patted Junior's face as he spoke. "If you want me, I'll spend our lives making you happy."

All she could do was nod her response for several seconds, then she said, "I want you. I love you so much."

Jason smiled wide then kissed her. It wasn't the best kiss he ever gave her but she would remember it always.

EPILOGUE

Theodore

The first floor of the house was empty as Theo walked through it. He continued through the house to the back door, opening the screen and walking outside to the yard. He saw his mother first. She was sitting on the bench his father made for her a few years ago for Christmas.

"Hey, Mom," Theo said as he dropped his bat, ball, and mitt then sat beside her. "Whatcha doing?"

"Reading," she smiled as she touched his hand. "What are you doing?"

Theo twisted his feet in the dirt nervously but felt his mother squeeze his hand. "I," he started then stopped, "I wanted to ask you something."

"Alright." She closed her book and turned to face him. "What's on your mind?"

Theo swallowed hard but sat up straighter. "Do you think I'll be like Cefus?"

As soon as the question left his mouth, he regretted it. His mother's eyes grew distant, and her demeanor seemed to change almost instantly.

"I'm sorry, Mom. Just forget it." He tried to stand, but his mother took hold of his baseball jersey and made him stay put.

"Never be afraid to ask me anything, Theo. Your father and I decided a long time ago that we would tell you the circumstances of your birth and last year when you turned fifteen; we felt you were mature enough to know."

"I am mature enough," Theo tried to convince her.

Theo remembered that day as if it were yesterday. A week after his birthday his parents' waited until his sisters were asleep to sit him down. They started by telling him how much they loved him then they dropped a bomb. He wasn't their son; he was their brother. They explained the nightmare that they suffered at the hands of his biological father at the Shaw farm, who his birth mother was, and how much she loved and sacrificed for him to be born.

Of course, he asked a lot of questions and was surprised when they answered them all. But since then, Theo kept his worries to himself. He was afraid that he might have the same darkness in him that Cefus did.

"No, Theo," his mother took his hand in hers, "you are nothing like Cefus."

The sound of the side gate to their yard opened and in walked his father who carried his sister, six-year-old Cindy Mae, who was cradled in his arms. Sadie Pearl, who was nine, was hanging off of their father's back. They were all laughing as they slowly approached.

"Theo," Cindy called when she saw him. She wiggled free and ran to him. Cindy jumped on his lap, kicking her legs out while resting her head on his chest. "Daddy said that we can go to the office with him tomorrow."

"Me too," Sadie said as she slid to the ground and skipped over to Theo. She took his hand and swung it side to side. "Are you going with us?" She smiled happily. "Or are you going with Mom." She frowned.

"And what's wrong with going with Mom?" Jason Jones asked as he pulled Evelyn Jones up off the bench and kissed her.

"Ooooooh," Cindy cooed. "You love Momma."

"I love you too," their father said as he held their mother close. He nipped Cindy's nose. "So, what's wrong with Mom's job, for take your child to work day."

"She's a teacher, Dad. We go to school every day," Sadie whined.

"Come on, girls," Eve said with a little laughter in her tone as she stood, "let's go have a snack while Daddy talks to Theo."

"You're in trouble," Sadie teased. She and Eve walked away hand and hand.

Cindy wrapped her arms around Theo's neck. "You can have my dessert if Mom takes yours, Theo."

"I'm not in trouble, Pinkie," he smiled then kissed her on the cheek. "Now you better catch up, or Sadie will eat your dessert before you get there."

Theo laughed as his sister ran for the house, her pink bow slipping from her hair as her pigtails bounced from side to side.

Jason chuckled as he took a seat beside Theo. "Having some issues, sport?"

"Do you worry I'll be like Cefus?" *There was no point in beating around the bush*, Theo thought. He watched his father carefully, to see if he flinched or looked uncomfortable in any way.

With confidence in his tone and love in his eyes, Jason looked at Theo and said, "You are your own man, Theodore. Evie and I raised you with love and security. You also have your mother's gentle heart, son. Aside from that, Pearl was the kindest, most amazing woman I ever knew. She protected and loved you as you grew inside her. That kind of love is

345

inside you." He patted Theo's chest. "You forgot, I'm Cefus' son too. Am I like him?"

"No, Dad," Theo sighed with relief. He hadn't thought of it that way. "What happened to Cefus?"

"You know," Jason stood, "to be honest, I bet he's face down somewhere in some ditch." He pulled Theo to his feet. "Forget ol' man Shaw. That's why I took your mother's last name. So we didn't have to speak him up in any way. We talk of Pearl, Harland, Cindy, and Sadie all the time, but we won't bring Cefus into this house, okay?"

"Okay, Dad," Theo agreed. "Thank you."

"I love you, Theo, never forget that," his father said. "Last one inside has to do the dishes tonight." His father took off running for the house.

"No fair," Theo took off after him. His father's limp was barely noticeable today.

Theo fell asleep that night with a smile on his face. He dreamed of a large tree and underneath it was four people smiling at him. A beautiful woman he knew was Pearl, and her handsome husband Harland, who had her tucked into his side. Beside them was a beautiful woman who he figured was Cindy and beneath her, sitting in the grass playing with a butterfly, was Sadie.

Of course, when Theo woke, he would rationalize the dream as a subconscious, implanted memory because of his talk with his father the day before. But right now, in his dream, he felt connected to the loved ones he would never truly know but knew watched over him.

CHAINS REFORGED BY LOVE

About The Author

Shea is a woman in love with the idea of love so it's no wonder she writes Romance Novels. The East Coast native is a romantic to her core and reads and watches anything with a love story. She especially likes binging on the Hallmark Channel around Christmas time.

She enjoys meeting people and chatting, collecting Barbie dolls, toys, and is addicted to The Sims games. Shea also loves music and has mentioned that she writes better when she has movie scores playing as white noise in the background.

This new and exciting author writes Adult Romance in the sub-genres of Contemporary, New Adult, Paranormal, Sci-Fi, and Erotica. Come…Taste A Sample.

Connect with Shea Swain

Website: www.Sheaswainwrites.com

Shea Swain

ABSOLVE

A Short Romantic Drama
Available Now

Nisa Dithers was left broken when her younger brother was involved in a tragic accident. Affected by the tragedy more than she cares to admit, her life became an echo of what she'd planned it to be. Her dismal existence is interrupted when a man she doesn't even know, steals a kiss.

Trent has done everything in his power to right the wrongs he's done in his life, but he'll never atone in his eyes. Yet, just a moment in Nisa's presence had him dismissing his failures. Stealing a kiss was just the beginning. For the first time in a long time, Trent was looking forward to tomorrow.

Absolve is a short story of living with the pain of loss and accepting the beauty of forgiveness.

Excerpt

Her

Nisandra Dithers couldn't help smiling at her family and friends seated around the long table at Stackers, a nice family restaurant where she once waitressed. She and her former coworkers had joined together four regular tables to accommodate everyone in her party. Fondly looking at them, she found herself thinking that they were a nice group, the kind of customers Nisa would enjoy serving if she were waiting tables tonight.

"Well, I for one don't like the idea of her going to a college so far away."

"We all know you're old Fritz; you don't need to open your mouth with nonsense to prove it." Aunt Helena teased him as she winked at Nisa from a few seats away.

Chained to the Devil's Son

Nisa looked over at her mother, who sat just to the left of her. She knew it was going to be hard for the both of them when she left for college in the fall. They were so close; tied at the hip everyone always said. Nisa didn't think she'd ever gone a full day without seeing her mom's beautiful smile. That same smile comforted her now as her mother gave her hand a gentle squeeze under the table.

"Nisa will be just fine, Fritz. We've raised a very smart young lady," her father, Eric, said from his seat to her right.

Nisa had to squeeze her eyes shut and take a deep breath before she started to tear up again. Her family was amazing. All of them were, even her great-uncle Fritz, who was definitely stuck in the seventies with his hair styled in an afro; and wearing an old leather ankle length coat and a Dashiki. Uncle Fritz was a bit of an acquired taste and still called her white girl from time to time, even though he swears to the one drop rule.

She opened her eyes, watching and waiting for his next comment. He was a bit rough around the edges and during his visits he managed to offend everyone before driving the half day's distance back to his home. She often wondered why he drove so far just to bicker with his family.

"Well, its cause she's a Dithers," Fritz said, as he looked at Nisa.

Nisa smiled but held her breath. There was no telling what Uncle Fritz would say next.

"It's a good thing we're built strong. Can't say much about her other half though," Fritz said, in a matter-of-fact tone as he forked some pie into his mouth.

And...*there it goes*, she thought. She looked around the table, but no one gave Uncle Fritz's comments a second thought. Even Spencer, who usually loved to verbally spar with her Uncle, said nothing. It seemed that everyone had decided to overlook Fritz's nonsense today.

"Are you crying again?" A set of hands appeared from behind her and arms wrapped around her shoulders.

"No, I'm not crying again Derek." Nisa rubbed her little brother's arm as he rocked them. "I'm just happy, that's all."

"I'd be happy if I was leaving too. You'll get to stay up all night and eat what you want," Derek pouted.

Nisa laughed and so did everyone within earshot at the table. She patted Derek on the arm before he moved away asked for their father's keys. "Where do you two think you're going?" Nisa questioned as she watched Derek and her cousin Walter move away from the table.

Walter sighed. "Geez Nisa, we're done dessert. Derek's just gonna show me the game you bought him."

Her cousin Walter was a pain in the butt as cousins went and he often told her that she was a nosey fun-dimmer but he and Derek were as thick as thieves. Her mother's sister, Aunt Helena and her husband, lived around the corner from them so that meant Walter, their son, was around all day and most nights.

Living away from home is going to be awesome, she thought with a smile.

"We're nine years old," Walter whined.

"Yeah," Derek frowned, "we're not babies."

"Let them go," one of her relatives at the table called out.

Nisa wasn't sure who had spoken, out of the dozen or so relatives but she gave the boys a slight nod. She watched the boys jogged through the isle and past their waitress toward the entrance.

"How we doing?" Their waitress, a girl Nisa just met on her last day a week ago, asked.

"We're about done," Nisa's father replied.

Nisa watched the waitress as she smiled then turned to get their check. Staring at the girl was a way for Nisa to avoid Spencer, her boyfriend, who was watching and waiting. She hadn't given him an answer yet and he would be fishing for one as soon as he got her alone. Her only defense was avoidance, for as long as she could manage. So, she turned to her mother to discuss…anything.

A good fifteen minutes later, Spencer had managed to corral Nisa as her entire party gathered near the doors to leave. "Did you think about it?" he asked, as he pulled her closer and kissed her on the cheek.

Nisa appreciated his discretion in front of her family because a full kiss with them around, especially when she was about to deliver bad news, would be a bit awkward. She placed her hand lightly on Spencer's chest and was about to tell him her answer when all hell broke loose.

It was the sound of the screeching tires that Nisa heard first. The abrasive tone raised above all the other sounds around her. The echo of their ending celebration, the low hum of the music, the laughter and cheer that spilled out of the restaurant, it all faded under that horrifying screech.

The crash seemed to shake the entire building. Though Nisa couldn't see it, the sound was unmistakable. Her family and friends were gathered in the restaurant's all glass windowed enclosed lobby, blocking any view of what happened. Everyone was focused on what was most likely a nasty accident by the sound of it.

Nisa instinctively whirled around, searching for her little brother. He was her responsibility, hers to care for. *Derek.* "Derek," she whispered, as she pushed through the unmoving crowd. Someone screamed. Another scream filled the night and it sounded like her aunt.

"Derek," Nisa called out.

Where is he? He hadn't returned with Walter after going to the car. That was over ten minutes ago. Nisa continued to push through her family and out onto the paved walk. *Surely he was back by now.*

Outside, her view was hindered but she saw part of a black sports car flipped over, partially on top of another car.

A red sedan that looked… The crushed sedan looked like her parent's car.

Did Derek and Walter move away in time? Were they sitting inside the crushed sedan?

"Derek," Nisa screamed out this time. "Oh God…" Hands, Nisa felt hands pulling at her. They were preventing her from getting Derek. He lay still on the ground. He'd fallen, that's all.

Why would they stop her from going to him?

"He needs me. Derek, get up. Derek?"

Lascivious

Come…Taste a Sample on
Available Now

Reece was hot as Hell. A good guy with the right amount of bad boy mixed in. Yes. But to Lilly, Reece was just Reece. To see him as anything else was silly. That was until the day Reece had carried her to her room, lost his balance, and his fingers had slipped into her panties. For Lilly, it had awakened her dormant desires. She wanted more.

When Lilly was left in his care Reece had no intentions of breaking her trust. For Reece, the slipup had changed everything. Lilly had already been skating on the edge of his self-control, wearing little to nothing around the house. One little touch and Reece couldn't release unless he conjured an image of Lilly naked and beneath him. How in the hell was he going to resist little Lilly when he wanted inside her so badly?

EXCERPT

Lilly Miles barreled down the hallway at full speed, slowing only when she turned the corner that led to the kitchen. The ripped V-neck of her loose fitting half shirt hung low in the front, exposing one perfect mound of her firm breasts.

"Don't press play yet," she called, as she grabbed the popcorn from the breakfast bar and the chilled bottle of water next to it. Her run became a fast walk when she entered the living room. She set the large metal bowl and bottled water on the table in front of the sofa, then flopped down next to Reece. He sighed but scooted over, giving her ample room on the sofa to sit comfortably. "I'm sorry," she winced, "Brenda saw Heath with Cindy Middleton and she wanted to tell me."

"I don't like that boy, Lilly. He's probably dating that chick," Reece said, as he pushed play on the remote.

Lilly ignored the space he offered her and sat Indian style so close to him that her long smooth leg rubbed up against his knee. "Heath and I aren't exclusive Reece. He can date who he wants. If you give him a chance," she started, scooting back on the sofa, "I'll promise to never be late for movie night again."

Reece settled back on the sofa and tried to give his full attention to the movie. But he was in a foul mood and it wasn't about that little punk Heath, although the little bastard did grind his fucking gears.

His problem was Lilly. She was an eighteen-year-old fucking wet dream walking and she didn't have a damn clue. If she did, she wouldn't be parading around the house in those barely-there gym shorts. Shorts like those should be outlawed. If he had practiced law instead of becoming a cop, then those damn shorts would be the first on his list of things to rally against. The way they rode up her toned, tan thighs was going to be the death of him.

Reece had asked her a hundred times to wear clothing more suitable around the house but, as usual, Lilly ignored him. If her parents hadn't passed away when she was just thirteen years old maybe she would know better than to prance around like this.

He glanced over at his ward. Her long dark hair was pulled into a loose knot at the top of her head. Several shorter strands fell from the mass, making it look sort of messy yet sexy. Her youthful skin was surprisingly clear and soft, as if puberty had no adverse effects on her. Those hazel eyes were a gift from her mother and so were her extra-long dark lashes, full pouty lips, and her shapely body. Reece had never seen her breasts uncovered but he was certain that they were perfect.

"Fuck", he thought, as he took her in. Just before he looked away, Lilly luscious lips spread into an innocent smile. God, her smile was going to be his undoing. Reece threw his head back and silently prayed, asking God to forgive his thoughts. What the hell was wrong with him? In his defense, he'd never imagined having Lilly under him but looking at her and cataloguing her attributes was dangerously close to the act.

Reece reached forward and grabbed a handful of popcorn out of their shared bowl on the table. He munched as he tried to focus on the movie and shut down his thoughts about Lilly. He made a mental note to talk with her about her clothing again.

After the movie was over, Reece stretched his legs and tried to raise his arms above his head but Lilly's head and upper body were resting on his side. She had fallen asleep. So much for movie night, he thought, as he slowly slid from under her and stood without waking her.

For a few seconds, Reece just watched her. Lilly was so beautiful and the way she was laid out on the couch made her so tempting. His eyes moved over her lovely face, her lips, and down her neck. He tensed when he saw that her shirt had fallen open.

Reece had full view of one of Lilly's perfectly round— what looked to be a B cup—breasts. Her dark nipple looked firm and the image of sucking it into his mouth flashed in his mind. He tried to shake the thought from his head.

Oh shit! Reece almost came undone when he looked away from her breasts to find her trimmed pubic hair and the smooth pink lips of her sprawled out pussy staring up at him. The shorts she wore were loose around her thighs and with no panties on, Lilly's sweetness was fully exposed. She was still sitting Indian style but her upper body had fallen over when he had moved, causing the striking scene before him.

Shit, shit, shit…his cock was as hard as granite. "Shit," he whispered. He was hard because Lilly's perfect little pink pussy was winking at him. Reece turned away and paced the length of the sofa a few times. He couldn't stop the thoughts that ran through his head. His cock flexed when the image of him on his knees licking her cunt dry, popped into his head. *Fuck*! Reece backed away nervously. His breathing grew ragged as he rubbed his wet palms over his thighs. This was stupid. "Just pick her up and put her in her bed like usual", he told himself, but didn't move.

"Move asshole," he whispered to himself, after turning around to see her pussy glistening in the light of the television. Reece sucked in his bottom lip and bit down hard enough to taste his own blood. God, he wanted to taste her. "You're fucking sick," he whispered. "Fucking sick," he said again. *Move!* The sooner she was in her bed; the sooner he could get those damn images out of his head.

Reece bent over and place one arm under Lilly's upper back and other under her legs then lifted her up in his arms. He couldn't resist rubbing his cheek over her head but once he realized what he was doing he stopped.

Walking down the hall as fast as he could, Reece pushed open her bedroom door and hurried to her bed. The grey and white room didn't scream eighteen-year-old teenager. It kind of whispered it. There were no posters of shirtless actors or music stars. No brightly colored patterns or art work tacked on the walls. Clean lines, framed art, and a neatly arranged closet greeted him as he entered.

Reece gently started to place Lilly on the bed, he froze when Lilly shifted in his arms. When he attempted to lay her down, she rolled and he fumbled to catch her legs as her lower body hit the bed. That's when he felt it. Warm moisture covered his two fingers that had slipped between her thighs. Reece kept his hand and fingers perfectly still as he lowered Lilly's upper body onto the bed.

He kept his hand in place as he slowly dropped to his knees. Reece looked at his fingers that were inside the folds of Lilly's slick hot pussy. He didn't want to remove them. He wanted to play, taste, and suck on her core until she screamed with delight.

Reese shook his head. *It's not right.*

Yet when he attempted to pull his fingers free, Lilly moved. Reece stilled again, determined not to wake her. No way was he going to get caught with his hand in the cookie jar. Another shift caused his fingers to slide over her little nub and she moaned. Reece's cock throbbed and jerked so hard that he felt it was going to burst.

She moved her hips again and more of her wetness coated his fingers. Reece wasn't sure what made him do it but he slid his fingers slowly around the outside of her slit, crossing over her clit twice. His actions didn't wake her but he couldn't keep silent. Reece moaned softly and his cock jerked several more times as he played with her pussy. His hips involuntarily rocked forward. When he realized what he was doing, he abruptly pulled his fingers free.

Damn.

Reece pulled the sheet that sat at the foot of the bed over her with his clean hand then hurried to his room. He closed his bedroom door and went straight to his bathroom. He hurried to the second door to his bathroom that led into the hallway and locked it. Reece went to the sink and turned on the hot water to wash his hands. He reached for the soap but stopped before he pressed the pump.

It dawned on Reece that he wasn't breathing so he took a deep breath. He closed the toilet seat and sat down then scrubbed his hand over his face but froze again. *Fuck…*it was the hand that had been in Lilly's sweet pussy. He could smell her innocence on them and she smelled so good he almost came in his shorts.

He moved his fingers under his nose and took a deep sniff. Her pussy smelled so good that his cock jumped repeatedly like a bird pecking at corn. Without thinking about what he was doing, Reece placed the two fingers on the tip of his tongue.

He moaned as he pulled his aching cock free of his shorts. While he kept his coated fingers on the tip of his tongue he let his hardness go long enough to pump some lotion that sat on the bathroom sink into his palm.

He smoothed the lotion over his aching cock and started pumping up and down. A guttural rumble rose from his chest and came out as a heady moan when he allowed his lips to close over his fragrant fingers. Reece pumped his hardness with more vigor. Lilly's taste was blinding and his head spun as he savored it. Moaning over his fingers again, he savored her alluring smell that was under his nose and in his mouth…and he loved it.

Reece growled and pumped faster. Her taste was almost gone from his fingers so he started to lick them greedily, wanting—needing more. He wished his face was buried between her thighs and that he was licking her sweet twat. He strained, panted. He was close, so close…. *God, I'm so damn close*! His head fell back and he growled as he squirted stream after stream of cum into the air. His hand continued to pump until he was drained completely.

Chained to the Devil's Son

INVIDIOUS Betrayal

A Para-Sci Romance by: Shea Swain
Available Now

When Aria Cole turned eighteen, she wanted nothing more than to trade childish balloons and sugary confetti cake for Dirty Martinis and dancing all night. Determined to shed her Perfect Princess image and surround herself with guys who didn't know she was the daughter of an overly protective small town Sheriff, Aria decided a fun-filled night in the big city was the answer. Being assaulted and marked for death was not what Aria had envisioned.

At twenty-one, former child prodigy Ian Howl finally agreed to work for his uncle at Howl Industries. Independently wealthy, he needed a change from his idle playboy lifestyle and wanted a challenge. To celebrate his new position, a lavish party was thrown in his honor. However, Ian's version of fun didn't include being drugged and mixed up in a murder plot.

A chance meeting had brought Aria and Ian together but what they endured that evening linked them forever. Ian wanted answers and revenge. Aria wanted to forget that awful night. But forgetting is not an option when you know too much.

Hunted and terrified, Aria must rely on and trust a stranger with her life. Haunted by guilt, Ian's primary concern was Aria's safety and if he had to unleash hell to achieve it, then so be it. Neither of them could have anticipated the events that brought them together but once their mutual passion and power is realized…many lives are forever changed.

Prologue

April 8th, 2012

Ian Howl cradled the delicate, unconscious, girl in his arms as he swiftly made his way through the maze of a mansion to get to the garage. Her head rested on his chest and his arms supported her back and legs as he held her close. The swell of her feminine curves against his body felt all too consuming; the warmth of her skin was like a sweet yet biting burn. Tapping down on his ill-placed desires, Ian forced himself to focus on the present: their escape.

He ignored the hulking guard that sat in the security room who called to him as he rushed by. Turning a corner, Ian glanced over his shoulder to see if he was being followed. He hoped for a confrontation-free getaway, but the odds were against them.

Gently, he lowered the arm that cradled the girl's legs so that they slowly slide down his body until he balanced her on the balls of her feet. Holding her close to his chest, he placed his thumb to the security scanner on the wall. He vaguely thought of her bare feet touching the cold floor, but it was something he couldn't help right now. He needed to get her out of there and a chill was the least of his worries.

Three heartbeats later, the door that lead to the massive garage swung open with an air-locked *swoosh* that brought his hope soaring to new heights. They were almost free.

Ian noticed his car was blocked in, so he grabbed a random set of car keys from the wall hook and pressed the door unlock button. The headlights of a beautiful Porsche flashed, but the vehicle was in the rear of the garage and several cars surrounded it. The third set of keys he tried unlocked a luxury sedan that wasn't blocked in and was close to the garage doors. Ian had eased the girl into the passenger seat of the sedan and was securing the seatbelt around her when he felt a heavy hand on his shoulder.

"Where do you think you're taking that car, kid?"

Ian turned his head around to see Brad... Or was it Brent? He didn't remember the guard's name, but Ian knew the guy was built like a defensive tackle. Striking first would surprise Brad/ Brent. So he grabbed the hand on his shoulder and pulled the guard into his elbow, targeting his large, beefy face. The guard stepped back, holding his gushing nose. Ian spun around; he thrust the base of his palm upward into the man's shocked, bloody, face causing him to stumble back again then fall to the floor. The guard didn't get back up.

"Please," the girl whispered.

Ian whipped his head around to see that she was still unconscious and strapped in the car. Rushing to the driver's side of the commandeered vehicle, he hopped inside and started the engine. The automatic doors to the parking garage opened when the car tripped the underground sensor and they barreled down the path toward the front gate of the property. Luckily there were still party guests inside because usually those sensors only allowed vehicles with an installed security plate placed under the hood to pass through without human intervention.

Again, the underground sensor allowed the vehicle to pass through. The large main gates had opened, but they were not in the clear yet.

Ian didn't floor the gas pedal until he was clear of his uncle's property. He wasn't being followed, but he continued to check the rearview mirror, knowing their absence would soon be reported.

The girl moaned, pulling his gaze from the road.

Her long dark brown hair was matted to her head, practically covering her delicate face, so he brushed some of it away. Bruises covered her body but her dry lips, puffy red eyes, and the darkening hand prints on her throat were the most obvious. She was in bad shape, and Ian feared that the thin sheet wasn't enough to keep her naked body warm.

"Help me," she moaned.

"I'm taking you to a hospital," Ian told her. He fought the bile that rose from his stomach. Disgust and shame assailed him, but right now he couldn't think of his role in what had happened to her. He had to get her medical help, but he didn't know Howard County, Maryland, all that well. The only time he even came to this part of Maryland was when he visited his uncle.

Ian brushed the back of his hand over her bruised cheek and was about to place it back on the steering wheel when her eyes popped open, jarring him a little.

She didn't move right away. She just looked at him with a hollowed gaze as if her mind had to reboot. Then those chestnut-brown orbs changed from confused to feral in a flash. Before he could react, she was screaming, "No hospital! No cops!" over and over as she kicked at him and pushed at the passenger door with her hands. Ian grabbed at her feet, but his hand slipped and she nailed him hard on the side of his head with her foot.

"All right, no hospitals!" Ian yelled her as he slammed his foot on the brake, causing the car to skid along the nearly empty road. The force of the sudden stop propelled her forward and the side of her head collided with the dashboard. Her body went limp.

"Shit!" he yelled as he slammed his hands on the steering wheel. Ian pulled the car off to the side of the road, took his cell phone out, and dialed his father's cell. The phone rang several times, then the voicemail picked up. He listened to his father's commanding voice, but he disconnected before the taped greeting ended.

"Damn it, Dad, this is important!"

Ian glanced up at the rearview mirror, peering out into the quiet darkness, lost in thought. The weight of his cell phone in his hand made him find his focus again. He turned the phone over in his hand twice before shutting off the power. Ian stared at the cell phone in his hand for a long moment as he unconsciously rubbed at a spot under his armpit.

"They will be looking for me, us."

He glanced at the girl then felt under his arm again. As long as she was with him, they would find her.

Shea Swain